Enigma Books

Also published by Enigma Books

Non-Fiction

Hitler's Table Talk: 1941–1944
In Stalin's Secret Service
Hitler and Mussolini: The Secret Meetings
The Jews in Fascist Italy: A History
The Man Behind the Rosenbergs
Roosevelt and Hopkins: An Intimate History
Secret Affairs: FDR, Cordell Hull, and Sumner Welles
Hitler and His Generals: Military Conferences 1942–1945
Stalin and the Jews: The Red Book
Fighting the Nazis: French Intelligence and Counterintelligence
A Death in Washington: Walter G. Krivitsky and the Stalin Terror
The Battle of the Casbah: Terrorism and Counterterrorism in Algeria 1955–1957
Hitler's Second Book: The Unpublished Sequel to *Mein Kampf*
At Napoleon's Side in Russia: The Classic Eyewitness Account
The Atlantic Wall: Hitler's Defenses for D-Day
France and the Nazi Threat: The Collapse of French Diplomacy 1932–1939
Mussolini: The Secrets of His Death
Mortal Crimes: Soviet Penetration of the Manhattan Project
Top Nazi: Karl Wolff—The Man Between Hitler and Himmler
Empire on the Adriatic: Mussolini's Conquest of Yugoslavia
The Origins of the War of 1914 (3-volume set)
Hitler's Foreign Policy, 1933–1939—The Road to World War II
The Origins of Fascist Ideology 1918–1925
Max Corvo: OSS Italy 1942–1945
Hitler's Contract: The Secret History of the Italian Edition of *Mein Kampf*
Secret Intelligence and the Holocaust
Balkan Inferno: Betrayal, War, and Intervention, 1990–2005
Calculated Risk
The Murder of Maxim Gorky
The Kravchenko Case: One Man's War On Stalin
Hitler's Gift to France
The Nazi Party, 1919–1945: A Complete History
Encyclopedia of Cold War Espionage, Spies, and Secret Operations
The Cicero Spy Affair
The First Iraq War
Becoming Winston Churchill
Hitler's Intelligence Chief
Salazar: A Political Biography
Nazi Palestine
Lenin and His Comrades

American Police—The Blue Parade 1845–1945: A History
The Decision to Drop the Atomic Bomb

Mysteries

Operation Neptune
Paris Weekend
NOC
Code Name: Kalistrat
Pax Romana
The De Valera Deception

Michael McMenamin
&
Patrick McMenamin

The Parsifal Pursuit

A Winston Churchill Thriller

Enigma Books

Published in the Unirted States by
Enigma Books
New York

First English Edition

Printed in the United States of America

ISBN 978-1-936274-23-9
e-book ISBN 978-1-936274-24-6

Library of Congress Cataloguing in Publication Data Available

To Carol and Becca, the loves of our lives.
And, with love and affection, to our 92-year-old patriarch
John McMenamin, our father and grandfather respectively.

Publisher's Note

Some may question casting Winston Churchill as a key character in a series of historical thrillers set during 1929-1939, his "Wilderness Years" when he was out of power, out of favor and a lone voice warning against the rising danger posed by Adolf Hitler and Nazi Germany. They shouldn't. Saving Western Civilization in 1940 when England stood alone as a beacon of liberty in a sea of tyranny tends to overshadow Churchill's earlier accomplishments.

Churchill is, in many ways, a perfect historical figure around which to craft a period thriller. Winston was an adventure-seeking young man, a fencing champion in prep school, a championship polo player in the Army and a seaplane pilot in the early, peril-filled days of flight in 1910. In between, he was a much-decorated war hero in bloody battles on the Afghan-Indian border, in the Sudan, and in South Africa where his commanding officer nominated him for the Victoria Cross, Britain's highest military honor, and where he escaped from a prisoner of war camp and made his way to freedom over hundreds of miles of enemy territory. In World War I, while other politicians, safely abed, sent millions of young men to their death, Winston was with his troops in the trenches of the bloody Ypres salient daily risking death himself.

More importantly for this new series, Churchill maintained a private intelligence network in Britain and Europe during the 1930s which often left him better informed than his own government. The writing team of the critically acclaimed Churchill biographer Michael McMenamin and his journalist son Patrick McMenamin use this fact as a catalyst for their stories. With Churchill at the center spinning his own web, he lures into many adventures his fictional Scottish goddaughter, the beautiful Hearst photojournalist Mattie McGary and the American law professor Bourke Cockran, Jr., a former U.S. Army counter-intelligence agent. Winston, a romantic at heart, brings the two young people together. Romance blooms but it is not a match made in heaven. Both characters are strong-willed individuals and their Celtic tempers frequently clash. Cockran is the fictional son of Churchill's real life mentor Bourke Cockran, a prominent turn-of-the –century New York lawyer, statesman, orator and presidential adviser whose life is chronicled in *Becoming Winston Churchill, the Untold Story of Young Winston and His American Mentor* by Michael McMenamin and Curt Zoller (Enigma Books, 2009).

The first three novels take place during 1929-1932 before Hitler's ill-fated, but entirely legal, appointment as the German Chancellor. In *The DeValera Deception,* Winston, Mattie and Bourke tangle with the IRA and a real-life, pre-Hitler, Russo-German conspiracy to dismember Poland. In doing so, they discover a plot in the US to assemble arms for an IRA *coup d'etat* in the new Irish Free State and Cockran seeks revenge for his wife's murder by the IRA in the 1922 Irish civil war. In *The Parsifal Pursuit* [Enigma Books, Spring, 2011], Winston sends Mattie on a grail quest in the company of a handsome villain intent on her seduction, a journey shadowed by the Nazis who want the ancient Christian artifact for Hitler. Also at Winston's behest, Cockran travels to Germany to represent a beautiful blonde heiress who is the victim of a Nazi fund-raising tactic—extortion of her business by a protection racket worthy of Al Capone. In *The Gemini Agenda* [Enigma Books, Fall 2011], Winston and his private intelligence network put Mattie and Bourke on the trail of a plot by Nazi scientists to kidnap and conduct lethal eugenic experiments on American twins. Shockingly, they learn the conspiracy is funded by Wall Street financiers and elements of US Army Intelligence who hope to unlock the secret to creating a master race. I hope you have as much fun reading these stories as I did.

A new Winston-Mattie-Bourke trilogy set in 1933–1934 is in the making so stay tuned…

Robert Miller
Publisher
Enigma Books

"Live dangerously; take things as they come; dread naught; all will be well."

Winston S. Churchill
The Daily Mail
28 December 1931

Prologue

England and Austria

1914

I have frequently been astonished since I have been in this House to hear with what composure and how glibly Members, and even Ministers, talk of a European war. I will not expatiate on the horrors of war, but there has been a great change which the House should not omit to notice... Democracy is more vindictive than cabinets. The wars of peoples will be more terrible than those of kings.

Winston S. Churchill, 13 May 1901

"The Fleet Will Be Ready"

WINSTON Churchill was late. Again. It was a lamentable habit which he had tried many times to cure but there was always so much to do. The Prime Minister would have to wait. He rose from his desk, walked to his office door, and caught the attention of his private secretary.

"Pray telephone the Prime Minister and tell him I will be not punctual for our 4 p.m. meeting. Half past four will be closer to the mark. Explain I've only now received an urgent naval intelligence report which requires my immediate attention. There's a good lad."

Churchill returned to his desk and opened the red dispatch box which had been sitting there since early morning, taking out a single sheet of heavy bond paper, dense with crisp black type—a report from naval intelligence at the British Embassy in Berlin. Churchill read it with care. He looked up, re-lit his cigar, then read it a second time. Slowly.

When he was done, Churchill walked over to the window and stared out into an overcast sky. Rain soon would come. So would war. He shook his head. *Von Moltke.* Who would have thought the Chief of the German General Staff would be the one to betray the Kaiser? Every generation had its Judas and von Moltke had no way to know his warning to Austrian Emperor Franz Josef would also make its way to English ears and eyes. But there it was in black and white. The Kaiser was determined to acquire what even Napoleon had not.

He knew others thought differently of him but Churchill neither wanted nor welcomed a war. He had warned against it for fourteen years, but old men didn't know war like he did. Now, it was all beyond his control. War was coming and he could do nothing to stop it. Just as he could do nothing to stop the Kaiser's latest scheme. That would be up to a forewarned Franz Josef. Churchill could do only what was within his power. When war came, he vowed to himself, the British fleet would bloody well be ready.

The 39-year-old First Lord of the British Admiralty jammed on his hat and picked up his walking stick. The Prime Minister must be told. At once. The clock on his office wall clicked once more. 4:35 p.m. Winston Churchill was late. Again.

"The Holy Brotherhood"

Castle Lanz
The Austrian Alps
March, 1914

MAJOR Josef Lanz was no stranger to violence. A shade over six feet, he was taller than the average man under his command in the elite unit of ten Austrian Army mountain troops standing patiently behind him on their wooden skis, semi-automatic carbines slung over their shoulders, awaiting his order. He pushed the hood of his white parka back and his dark hair and sunburned face stood out against the blinding white of the snow. A pale scar ran diagonally across his left cheek, a souvenir of more youthful days and happier times. He took off his snow goggles and looked at his army-issue wrist watch below which was a discrete Celtic sun cross tattoo in deep red with a small circle over the center of the cross.

Lanz turned to the man beside him, his second in command, Captain Hans Weber, who had the same tattoo on his wrist. "The snow is letting up. Have the men camp here for the night. Tell them we will ski out at first light. Post no sentries. You and I will ascend to the castle but only after the men are asleep. The threat to the *heilege* lance, is real. And it comes from our German friends, not the Black Hand."

Captain Weber's eyes narrowed at Lanz's words. "I understand, Major. No sentries."

Weber knelt, unstrapped his skis and walked back to the men standing on their skis in silence looking like medieval monks in white-hooded mountain parkas.

AT the base of the castle, which had been in the Lanz family for generations dating back to the Crusades, the Austrian major approached a small wooden door. Freshly varnished, a brass lock of modern design was flush with the wood. It had taken both men nearly thirty minutes to make the trek up. They were carrying identical oblong parcels approximately six feet long, each wrapped tightly in oiled, waterproof canvas. As they placed their packages down in the snow, Weber expressed his surprise at the modern door and lock.

Lanz caught his glance. "Ever since our Order was reborn, I have come here each summer with a single craftsman; each time a different man; each time blindfolded, content to ride in comfort on one of the small Haflinger pack horses bringing supplies and fuel. I knew this day would come where we would once more need to protect our sacred relics from the barbarian hordes, whether they be our German brothers to the north or the savage Slavs in the east."

Lanz reached inside the pocket of his parka, fished out a key, inserted it into the brass lock and turned the key to the right. The polished door slid silently open on oiled hinges. The two men were standing in a small dark antechamber, the fading afternoon sunlight from the open door their only illumination. Lanz produced an electric torch from his field pack and directed it toward the far corner where stone steps led upward.

"I'll hold the light and you engage the metal lever on the left. That will start the generator. Then we dine on warm food and sleep in comfort. 0300 will come soon enough."

"Yes, Major," Weber said, as he walked over and pushed the lever upward. He was rewarded with three incandescent globes of light springing to life and illuminating the stairway.

"To our duties first," Lanz said. "Take the second replica upstairs to the Great Hall. The hidden space beside the fireplace. Make an entry in your notebook as to its location."

"Where are you going, Major?"

Lanz smiled. "My apologies but you know better than to ask. Both of our notebooks will be delivered to the Archduke himself. But even he will not be able to learn the true location of Castle Lanz from reading them, let alone where within its grounds the holy relic is hidden. That is my secret alone. Rest assured, my old friend, it will be a fitting location."

NIGHT had long since fallen as the two men approached the five tents in silence. The snow-covered mountains were pale against a stark canopy of stars, a few embers in the campfire still glowed amidst the dormant ashes surrounding them. Nearby, stacked neatly against one another in a circle, a group of 7.92 mm Mannlicher M98/40 assault rifles stood ready. Lanz counted them. There were ten. He turned to Weber and unslung his weapon, a Bergmann MP 18/1 submachine gun, and watched while Weber did the same. Lanz crossed himself and turned to Weber, who also made the sign of the cross, then pulled the bolt back on his 9 mm weapon.

"Ready," Weber said.

Lanz did not like what came next. That was why two days ago, in the small village of Dolloch, he had rousted the parish priest at dawn from beneath his eiderdown comforter and made him hear his men's confessions. "Wake the men, Hans. Our Savior waits for them with open arms for their sacrifice in safeguarding the secret of the Spear."

Weber brought a whistle to his lips and gave three short blasts, the shrill sound echoing in the thin mountain air. One by one, the flaps on the five tents opened and the men mechanically stumbled out and arranged themselves in an orderly line, still wearing the white parkas in which they had slept. Without warning, Lanz opened fire and Weber did the same. The men's bodies danced like marionettes on a string, as the 9 mm rounds ripped into their chests and bellies, blowing out their backs with great gouts of blood. In twenty seconds, all the men had collapsed, their white parkas now stained red, their bodies twitching, a few still alive and moaning.

They stopped, smoke still rising from the perforated barrels of their Bergmanns as they slung the weapons over their shoulders. They each withdrew from their holsters an M 1903 model Mannlicher locked-breach automatic pistol and walked over to the bodies. Going down the row methodically, a *coup de grace* was delivered to the temple or forehead of each man, whichever was more convenient, until they discovered, to their dismay, only nine bodies.

"Find the missing man," Lanz ordered. "There can be no witnesses."

Moments later, a short burst of automatic weapons fire broke the silence and a frightened solider who had been answering a call of nature stumbled forward. The youngest unit member, Corporal Merz, was clutching his bleeding belly with both hands, as Weber prodded him with the Bergmann's snout and then forced him to his knees.

"Excellent, Hans," Lanz said. "This is all for the best. Corporal Merz, you have fulfilled your duty to our Lord and you shall stand guard over our sacred trust for eternity." Lanz turned and walked over to an oblong canvas knapsack while Weber took a handful of the Corporal's hair and jerked his head back, exposing the neck.

Lanz approached, carrying a sword and scabbard. He slowly pulled out a three foot long broadsword honed to razor sharpness on either side. Gripping it with two-hands, he stood on the wounded soldier's left as Weber held his head up, Merz's eyes closed, his consciousness fading.

"Prepare him." Lanz ordered. "You are about to meet your Savior, Corporal".

Weber slapped the man's face sharply and his eyes slowly opened as Lanz swung the edge of the sword in a wide arc, hitting Merz's neck barely an inch below his upraised chin and cleanly severing his head from his body, limbs twitching and blood spurting high in the air from the stump of his neck to stain the snow beneath, before it fell lifelessly to the ground.

Weber held the head high in the air for Lanz to inspect. Its eyes were wide in terror and Lanz nodded his approval, as the eyes closed. "You're a good man, Merz" Lanz said and the eyes opened to focus on him, blinked a few times as if in recognition and closed for the last time.

"Place the Corporal's head on a spike above the castle gate", Lanz said. "It will serve as a warning to any curious mountain folk that Castle Lanz remains under the protection of the Holy Brotherhood."

The two men mounted the head on a spike above the main gate beside a large white flag with a blood red Celtic sun cross in its center.

Then, they struck all of the tents and, in two trips, carried them and the men's rifles up to the castle, leaving them in the antechamber just inside the door. Strapping on their skis, they glided silently down to the carnage below. They paused by the stiffening bodies of their men, a light dusting of snow already beginning to obscure the blood on the men's parkas. Lanz and Weber each crossed himself again.

"Does this mean war?" Weber asked but Lanz did not reply, his eyes fixed on the ten bodies whose souls had been sent to their Creator. " Josef?" he asked, using Lanz's Christian name for the first time.

"I am afraid so. The Archduke agrees with me. Serbia is becoming intolerable. The Slavs must be taught a lesson. Don't worry, my friend, it will be a short campaign."

"I wish we could give them a proper Christian burial."

"I share your sentiments, but the ground is frozen. By spring, the wolves in these mountains will have made away with our men and left no trace. It will be as if they were never here," Lanz said as he looked back at the castle. "But what we have left here must never be disturbed nor discovered. You and I are the only ones who know. Anyone else who learns or even guesses about this location will forfeit his life. The secret of the Holy Spear must be preserved at all costs. "

Part I

Germany

5 November – 6 November 1923

People who knew him in Vienna [in 1911] could not understand the contradiction between his well-mannered appearance, his educated speech and self-assured bearing on the one hand, and the starveling existence that he led on the other, and judged him as haughty and pretentious. He was neither. He just did not fit into a bourgeois order.... In the midst of a corrupt City, my friend surrounded himself with a wall of unshakeable principles which enabled him to build an inner freedom in spite of all the temptations around him.

August Kubizek,
Young Hitler—The Story of our Friendship

1.

Interviewing Hitler

Café Heck
Munich
Monday, 5 November 1923

ADOLF Hitler was as nervous as a schoolboy on his first date. His hand actually shook as he poured tea for 23 year old Mattie McGary from a delicate Dresden china teapot, politely passing a heaped plate of cream-filled pastries to her before taking two for himself.

The interview had gone well. Mattie's editor at London's *Daily Mirror* would be pleased. Hitler had been surprisingly open and candid, just as he had been in their first interview earlier in the year. She had all she needed for a good story and Hitler seemed to really like her. Once they finished the interview in his office at party headquarters, it was Hitler who suggested she join him for afternoon tea at the nearby smoke-filled Café Heck.

Inside the dark-timbered coffee shop, she studied Hitler's face once again. His skin was a pasty white and his limp hair brown, but his eyes were a piercing blue, the color of a cloudless summer afternoon in the highlands of her native Scotland. Mattie could tell, by how often during the interview he had fixed her with a direct gaze, that he expected his eyes to captivate her. She had played along and it had worked. Men could be so stupid.

She was ready to take the chance. Her father had told her the Celtic and Christian legends of the Holy Grail and how a spear played a prominent role in both. She was a Christian but not a devout one like her father. After he stepped down from Parliament, he had devoted the rest of his life to a study of the Grail legends culminating in his last book *World History In the Light Of the Holy Grail.* He never lived to see it in print. After his sudden death on a twisting mountain road, she arranged with the University of Edinburgh to have it published in 1921.

Mattie adored her father. He was the one who always understood her. He might not always have approved of everything she did but he always encouraged her dream to be a journalist, something her mother never understood. But her father, bless his memory, never tried. He knew all about dreams and fairy tales and happy endings. Happy endings weren't always there, but the ones that were started with a dream.

Mattie had to ask. She owed it to her father. Her source in Vienna had shown her a battered, leather-bound nineteenth century edition of Wolfram von Eschenbach's *Parsifal* covered on almost every page with handwritten notes. She had copied the more startling notes into her own edition of *Parsifal* on the corresponding pages, translated them into English, and then had them checked by a German scholar at Cambridge. Whoever made those notes in his own handwriting believed that Parsifal was an historic character; that the Lance of the Roman centurion, Gaius Cassius, which pierced the side of Christ, was indeed possessed with magical powers, a talisman treasured by kings and conquerors over the centuries; and that it was actually on display at the Hofburg Museum in Vienna. The name she saw on the inside cover of the book was in penciled block letters, "Adolf Hitler, Vienna, 1911".

Mattie started cautiously. "*Herr* Hitler, have you been to the Hofburg Museum?"

"Of course, *Fraulein,*" Hitler replied, his voice hoarse from relentless public speaking. "When I lived in Vienna before the war, I spent many hours there when I was not painting. I made my living that way. Painting. I painted every day. Five, six paintings a week. It was hard work, barely enough to keep the wolf from the door. So when I rested, I roamed through the Hofburg."

"Do you know the Lance of Longinus?"

Hitler's eyes narrowed and then relaxed. "I do, indeed."

"Is it true you believe in its mystical powers as the Spear of Destiny?"

Hitler's eyes flashed with anger but he quickly smiled and the moment vanished. *"Fraulein* McGary," he said, shaking his head. "I was born and raised a Catholic. I could scarcely be unaware of the legend associated with the Longinus Spear. That whoever claims it and solves its secret holds the destiny of the world in his hands, for good or evil. I assure you I have long since outgrown the superstitions of my childhood. By the time I came to Vienna and first saw the Spear, I was no longer a child."

Mattie bored in. "Excuse me, *Herr* Hitler, but I have seen a copy of *Parsifal* with your name inside the front cover and the following passage handwritten in the margins on page 96:

I knew with immediacy that this was an important moment in my life when I first saw the Spear. And I could not divine why an outwardly Christian symbol should make such an impression upon me. I felt as though I myself had held it in my hands before in some earlier century of history – that I myself had once claimed it as my talisman of power, held the destiny of the world in my hands. Yet how could this be possible? What sort of madness was this that was invading my mind and creating such turmoil in my breast?

She read him the passage and his pale complexion turned red after she finished, but with anger or embarrassment, Mattie could not tell until Hitler spoke. Anger. It was definitely anger.

"Lies! All lies! I have enemies, *Fraulein*, many enemies. They would like nothing better than to make me out the fool. But their days are numbered. I can assure you of that."

Mattie played her trump card. "I have a photostat of the page on which that passage appears. Here," she said, sliding the page across the table, "isn't that your handwriting?"

Hitler picked up the page and looked at it carefully. "A crude forgery, *Fraulein*."

Hitler's eyes locked on hers and he lowered his voice. "No German journalist would dare publish such ridiculous accusations. They would be taught a lesson they wouldn't forget. Don't make the mistake of assuming, because you are a woman and a visitor in our country, that you are immune from the consequences of your conduct."

2.

Champagne or Me?

Munich
Tuesday, 6 November 1923

MATTIE was worried. Back at her hotel one day later, watching the late afternoon sunset from her room's balcony, she was still kicking herself. Hitler was right. She wasn't immune. Something big was about to happen, and she knew it— the signs were everywhere. But she had no way of knowing exactly what or when. No Nazi would give her the time of day now.

The word had spread fast and it was worse than Mattie imagined. She had good sources within the National Socialist Workers Party whom she had worked hard to develop. Günter, a young post-graduate in the Nazis' Economic Section, cancelled their dinner date for last night, barely two hours after she had left Hitler at the Café Heck. Today, Dietrich, a reporter for the *Volkischer Beobachter*, the Nazis' daily newspaper in Munich had cancelled lunch. Three other telephone calls to various midlevel functionaries she had charmed were still unanswered.

Damn! She had pulled strings to get this assignment; to prove to her bosses that a woman could be just as good a foreign correspondent as a man. They had been skeptical. Politics and coups were more complicated, they told her, than battlefields. Even though the *Daily Mirror* employed more women reporters than other Fleet Street papers, it was only because it had started out as a women's paper, a mistake its owners soon rectified. She shook her head. That damn Spear and the Holy Grail! It wasn't a rookie mistake but she knew how it would look back in London. She was too young, they would say, and even though some women now had the vote, it didn't mean they were up to a man's job. Mattie had run out of options. And sources. This story could make her career and now there was only one source left.

The man wasn't even a Nazi, for goodness sake. But he was close to Hitler, or at least he claimed to be. His mother was an American and he had gone to school there. Harvard, no less. He had been trying to seduce Mattie ever since they had been introduced two months before at the opera. *Tristan and Isolde.* Mattie had been tempted. He was tall, good-looking, well-read and, by evening's end, the life of any party he attended, playing the piano well into the wee hours. There were two drawbacks to allowing him to succeed. First, he was a sometime source and Mattie tried to avoid romantic entanglements like that. More importantly, he was married and that bothered her, having met his beautiful wife on several social occasions.

Mattie was neither a prude nor a virgin. In the years after the war, she had several brief affairs, typically on assignment, but "no strings" was her rule. A married man would seem to fit that rule but she had declined numerous such invitations. It just didn't seem right. But this story was too important. She wasn't going to give any male higher-up the satisfaction of saying that she wasn't up to covering something as big as the revolution in Bavaria she knew was coming.

There were no guarantees it would work and if it didn't, she would be out of luck. But rules were made to be broken, even those she set for herself. Mattie left the balcony and began taking off her clothes as she walked to the bathroom and turned on the spigot. Naked, she looked at her body in the mirror and smiled. Ernst "Putzi" Hanfstaengl was about to get lucky.

After her bath, she placed an order with room service for champagne and caviar and then she called him. The maid answered the telephone and Mattie asked for Putzi.

"Hanfstaengl here," he said in a deep baritone, speaking English with only the trace of a Bavarian accent.

"Ernst, this is Mattie McGary," she said, holding the telephone receiver in her left hand and toweling dry her short red hair with the other. "I wanted to thank you personally for arranging my interview with *Herr* Hitler yesterday. Have you heard about it?"

There was a knock on the door. Telling Hanfstaengl to wait a moment, Mattie put the phone down. Slipping on a green silk robe, she walked to the door, opened it and stood aside as a white-coated waiter entered and set up her room service order. She handed the waiter an English pound note and went back to the phone, ignoring the waiter's profuse expressions of gratitude. "No?... Well, why don't you come over to my room then. I have some champagne chilling and I'll tell you all about it."

Mattie turned and smiled at the waiter who made an elaborate show of opening the champagne, pulling the silver dome off the caviar over ice, and then backing away from her, bowing as he left as if she were royalty. She smiled again. Tipping in a foreign currency which wasn't losing its value on an hourly basis often produced that effect.

Hanfstaengl called up fifteen minutes later and Mattie heard the buzzer to her room a few minutes after that. Mattie paused and looked again at the floor-length mirror. Golden red hair, green eyes and a figure full of curves. She picked up the bottle of champagne and two flutes and walked towards the door, briefly looking back over her shoulder at her reflection in the mirror.

Nice ass, McGary, she thought, as she opened the door, wearing nothing but a smile, to greet Adolf Hitler's foreign press secretary. "How nice to see you, Putzi. Please come in."

Hanfstaengl was broad-shouldered, six feet four inches tall and in his mid-thirties, with dark brown hair slicked back. Mattie smiled as she saw his eyes grow wide in recognition of what was about to happen next. Satisfied at the effect her breasts had produced, Mattie turned and walked back across the room to the low table in front of a dark brown leather sofa and slowly bent over from the waist to place the flutes and champagne down. You are such a shameless hussy, she thought, as she poured their drinks. But ambition trumped her scruples. Women had enough obstacles to overcome as it was. A little harmless slap and tickle with Putzi wasn't going to get in the way of this story. Besides, it wouldn't become a habit. She looked back over her shoulder. "Where would you like to start? With champagne? Or me?"

Part II

America

25 May – 26 May 1931

I have studied with great interest the laws of several American states concerning prevention of reproduction by people whose progeny would, in all probability, be of no value or be injurious to the racial stock. I'm sure that occasionally mistakes occur as a result. But the possibility of excess and error is still no proof of the incorrectness of these laws.

Adolf Hitler, 1931
(Otto Wagener, *Memoirs of a Confidant*)

3.

Churchill's Cable

Court of Appeals
New York City
Monday, 25 May 1931

BOURKE Cockran Jr. was tense. Churchill's cable that morning
was part of it, but he was always this way before a battle, even a
bloodless one like today in the Court of Appeals.

He hated this part. The waiting. Ten more minutes. In the trenches,
it wasn't the night raids he hated so much as the damned waiting. His
CO would inform him of the raid hours in advance. That left nothing to
do but sit there with his feet in water, stare at a wall of mud and let the
sporadic thumps of artillery give him an idea of the fate that awaited him
in No Man's Land.

Today he had only the sharp clicks of the bailiff's shoes echoing off
the high ceiling of the court room to accompany his thoughts as he
waited to face the three-man firing squad of the New York state
appellate bench. His odds of success were better in the trenches. Still, at
least the courtroom was dry and warm. His feet weren't in water and
there was no wall of mud.

He checked his watch: Five minutes to go. Oral argument started at
1:30 p.m. precisely.

Cockran heard the door to the court room open. He turned his
head and stole a glance at the benches behind the bar where members of
the public were seated, disappointed when he saw that Mattie McGary
still had not arrived. She had promised to come. But that had been

before their row the night before. He checked his watch again, out of habit, knowing he had at least five more minutes left before the judges arrived

Ordinarily, Cockran liked the intellectual challenge of appellate oral arguments. But not today. Not a case like this. He was too emotionally involved, having taken up the fight against sterilization laws after his father, U.S. Congressman W. Bourke Cockran, Sr., had passed away in 1923. He had lost Judy Dill's trial five days ago. The State of New York had declared her an imbecile and ordered that she be sterilized within the week. He had filed an emergency appeal. Cockran had taken Judy's case and others like it as a tribute to his father's memory. It was a matter of principle, individual rights. Governments had no business deciding who could and who could not reproduce. He learned that from his father.

But after today's argument, it would all be over, for better or worse, and he could concentrate on repairing relations with Mattie. They had the rest of the week together before they were to sail to England on the *Europa* this Sunday. They had plenty of time.

Cockran took another glance behind him. Still no sign of Mattie. He checked his watch again. The judges were late. Judges could do that. They were judges.

After landing in England, it would be a working holiday for Mattie who had a week of interviews scheduled in Berlin. For Cockran, it was a real holiday, first week in Kent at Chartwell, the country estate of their mutual friend, Winston Churchill. After that, Cockran's young son Patrick would accompany Churchill on his research tour through the battlefields of Germany and Austria, where his famous ancestor the first Duke of Marlborough had first brought glory to the Churchill name. Meanwhile, Mattie would join him for two weeks in Venice in their own *palazetto* he had leased off the Grand Canal where Cockran hoped to find a diamond ring for her as well as the courage to propose marriage.

Churchill's cable was a sudden dark cloud in the otherwise sunny sky before him after the Dill case. The cable was ambiguous. Typical Winston. U.S. COMPANY IN TROUBLE IN GERMANY. STOP. SITUATION URGENT. STOP. YOUR CUP OF TEA. STOP. TRAVEL REQUIRED. STOP. DETAILS TO ARRIVE BY

COURIER. STOP. *Your cup of tea.* He often suspected that "his cup of tea" tended to be whatever Winston wanted it to be. Winston was shameless that way. But his friends loved him nonetheless. Whatever Churchill had in mind, however, would have to wait a month. Two weeks with Mattie in Venice took precedence. As did revising the proofs of the biography of his father. Judy Dill's trial had put him off schedule and his editor Simon Mason in Oxford was becoming more nervous by the day.

Simon notwithstanding, Churchill had a strong hold on Cockran and always would. He had known Winston since he was six years old and the then 26 year old soldier, war hero and newly-elected Member of Parliament had sat with him for hours on the floor of his father's study and patiently arranged and rearranged miniature die-cast metal soldiers and cannons with him, complete with running commentary and sound effects. Winston had done the same with Cockran's own son, Patrick, nearly two years ago and promised to do so again at Chartwell..

Churchill was, in a word, charming, as well as sentimental, loyal to a fault but also ruthless in using his friends to accomplish his goals of the moment. Still, how could Cockran say no to a man to whom his own father had been a mentor? To a man who had once said to Cockran, "Your father was a great man, Bourke. He had the biggest and most original mind I have ever met. I feel I owe the best things in my career to him. He taught me to use every note of the human voice like an organ. I learned from him how to hold thousands in thrall."

Well, so long as he could finalize his father's biography and then spend two weeks in Venice with Mattie, the short answer was Cockran couldn't say no. Not without having the ghost of his father nagging his conscience, the very same ghost that had brought him here today to defend Judy Dill's right to keep the state from making her reproductive decisions for her.

Cockran only hoped he could manage to match half of his father's eloquence during the forthcoming argument. He also hoped none of the judges would quote Oliver Wendell Holmes, that ancient ninety year old walking advertisement for a mandatory Supreme Court retirement age. He hated it when that happened. And it happened a lot in sterilization cases.

A door opened off to one side of the bench and the bailiff stood up. Cockran rose immediately at the bailiff's "All rise", unconsciously buttoning his pin-striped suit coat over his vest while the three judges entered the courtroom. Cockran stood erect, unsmiling and alert.

Cockran was a big man with his father's broad shoulders and large head, softened by his mother's hazel eyes. Several inches over six feet tall, he almost looked the judges in their eyes despite their elevated positions on the bench. A reporter had once described his father's face as being hewn rather than chiseled but Cockran's mother had done much to soften that effect in their son. Cockran's own face was more finely drawn, chiseled rather than hewn, topped by light brown hair where his father's had been dark. But he was unmistakably his father's son.

If the judges looked expectantly at him—and they did—it was not because of his face or hair. They were waiting to hear his voice, his father's voice, the silver tongue, the golden throat and the Irish baritone of Bourke Cockran's son, the son of the greatest orator of his generation as everyone had said only eight years ago at his father's funeral mass.

If any of the judges had heard his father speak, however, they were about to be disappointed with the son. The Cockran voice was there, deep and resonant. But untrained. And undisciplined. For Cockran's temper sometimes made words into weapons and adversaries into enemies, something his even-keeled father had never done. But Cockran's father, a nineteen-century gentleman and statesman, had never fired a weapon in combat nor taken a human life. The same could not be said of his son.

WESLEY Waterman III was an important man. He did not like to be kept waiting. That was the problem with trans-Atlantic telephone calls. You could never tell when problems would arise and cause a delay. Like the call he had been expecting at 12:45 p.m. He looked up at the clock on the mantel above the fireplace in his office. 1:00 p.m. Only 30 minutes left. The Chairman and President of International Calculating Equipment, or "I.C.E." as it was known around the world, had to leave for the Court of Appeals on Madison Square in 15 minutes and he didn't want to miss either that or this long-scheduled telephone call. He glared at the phone as if he could will it to ring.

Which, at that precise moment, it did and he picked up the receiver, his voice booming out "Waterman here."

There was a click on the other end. *"Ja?"*

"Has our competitor accepted our offer?" Waterman asked.

"Nein," said the man on the other end of the line. "The Englishman continues to insist his German interests are not for sale," the man said in a heavy German accent.

"Not to anyone, or simply not to I.C.E.?" Waterman asked, pronouncing each letter of his company's acronym.

"Not to anyone," the German answered. "Though he has not said so, it is my belief that the Englishman is especially hostile to I.C.E."

"And well he should be," Waterman said. He leaned forward in his chair. "Here is what I need you to do, Reinhard. First, hire some people to talk to his solicitors in Britain. Have them deliver the message that it is not in their best interest to represent Sir Archibald Hampton."

"Intimidate them?"

"Use your imagination," Waterman said. "Hire away his German lawyers as well. Make him another offer and change none of the terms. Tell this Englishman that he should be grateful because there will be no more offers. After that, we'll deal with his estate or his heirs."

"There has been one new development," the German said, "which we learned from our tap on his telephone. *Herr* Himmler informed me of it only this morning."

"And?"

"He's hired a new American lawyer. From New York."

"Here in New York City?"

"Ja," the German said. "How should we handle him?"

"Don't worry," Waterman said. "Give me his name."

"Cockran. Bourke Cockran."

Waterman laughed. "I know him. He'll fold under a little pressure. Academic types usually do. I'll take care of him. You take care of those English and German lawyers."

"Ja, Herr Waterman. I will see to it."

"Good," he replied. "Please extend my thanks to *Herr* Himmler on the thoroughness of his intelligence sources. Tell him I look forward to our meeting next week and to showing him our latest machines. Once in use, they will make preserving racial purity that much easier."

Waterman, in fact, had never seen Cockran in action as a lawyer. That would come later today. But he knew the man's father and had heard him speak. A golden voice but nothing more. A Tammany Hall hack. An Irishman with the gift of the gab. Let that self-righteous English peer try to hire Cockran. What did he care? If Cockran were like most lawyers he knew, there would be no problem. Toss him a bone or two and he would sit up on his hind legs and beg for more. And if not, Wesley Waterman had other and more permanent means at his disposal as well. Sons of hollow Irish political hacks were one thing. Irish mob bosses like Owney Madden with hired muscle for sale were something else entirely. One way or another, Cockran was not going to become Sir Archie Hampton's lawyer.

4.

The Chief

HEARST'S phone call put a spanner in her plans. Before it, Mattie McGary was looking forward to an ocean crossing followed by a fortnight on holiday in Venice with her lover, that big beautiful Irish bastard Bourke Cockran. A few hours later back at Cockran's country home "The Cedars", the voyage was abandoned and she was packing her bags with an adrenalin rush fueled by landing an exclusive interview with a leading European statesman and the prospect of an exciting new adventure which would have made her father proud. The Venice holiday had been relegated to a pleasant interlude between two more big steps up the ladder in her rising career. But she would phrase that differently when she gave her man the bad news.

Mattie and her boss William Randolph Hearst, known to his staff as "The Chief", had been walking in the garden of the old Belmont Mansion on Sands Point—Hearst's new Ivanhoe castle of a home on Long Island's Gold Coast—when he reached inside his tan Harris tweed sport coat and pulled out a long brown envelope and handed it to Mattie.

"What's this?" she asked.

"A one-way ticket on the *Graf Zeppelin* which leaves tomorrow morning from Lakehurst, New Jersey for its home base in Friedrichschafen. The day after you land, you have an appointment in

Berchtesgaden with the leader of Germany's second-largest political party.

"Adolf Hitler?"

"Yes. I understand you interviewed him twice prior to his Beer Hall *putsch* in 1923."

"Not many people know that, Chief. Where did you hear about it?"

"From Hitler himself. Through Ted Hudson, my chief resident correspondent in Europe. He's been negotiating with Hitler to sign an exclusive contract to write for my newspapers but so far unsuccessfully. Mussolini writes for me. So does Churchill. I want Hitler too."

"But why me?" Mattie asked.

"Hitler refuses to negotiate further with Hudson. He demands twice what we pay Mussolini and Churchill and he says he will only consider a lesser amount if we send you as a representative, the one he refers to as 'that beautiful and talented young Englishwoman.'"

"I'm not *English*," Mattie said as if it were an insult. "I'm a Scot."

"A distinction which is lost on Hitler." Hearst put his hand on Mattie's back and gently directed her out of the garden and towards the beach. "Hitler is important to me, Mattie. He may well become Germany's leader just as I am certain Winston will one day lead England. I want him to write for my papers and you're the person he wants to see. Please do this for me."

Hearst was a gentleman. He wouldn't think of ordering Mattie to go. She knew that. But she also knew that Hearst never took no for an answer. He paid well, far more than his competitors, and all he demanded in return was absolute loyalty and total obedience to his every request, which he was always careful to couch in the most polite and reasonable way.

Mattie adored Hearst because he was the first man she had ever worked for who didn't look on her as a woman journalist. He was a top-flight journalist himself and didn't care whether you wore a skirt or a pair of trousers, as long as you got him the story he wanted. It also didn't matter to him that Mattie wore trousers more often than a skirt on the job.

She was William Randolph Hearst's number one photojournalist and went all over the world, covering riots, wars and insurrections in pursuit of exposés on Hearst's and her own *bete noire*: The international arms dealers who had helped foment the Great War and from which they had reaped obscene profits. They were still there and she was going to find them, drag them from their hiding places and hold them up to the sunlight. It was an endless adventure. It often put her in peril but she didn't mind. As her father's friend—her godfather Winston Churchill—had written, "there is nothing more exhilarating in life than being shot at without result."

In fact, it was Winston who gave her the idea of becoming a journalist. Her father's library contained all of Winston's books. As a teenage girl, she found the political ones boring but she devoured the adventures. Subduing rebels in North-West India; riding in the last British cavalry charge in the Sudan; and, best of all, escaping from a Boer prisoner of war camp in South Africa. He had been a soldier and a war correspondent at the same time. Once she learned the *Morning Post* had paid Winston £250 a month in South Africa, she was hooked. That's what she wanted to do and that's what she did. Her mother was aghast, as were all her relatives. Except for Winston who encouraged her and her own father who supported her. And that was all she needed.

Deciding between an ocean voyage with the man she loved and an interview with a politician she didn't like was not difficult. After all, the last time they met, Hitler had threatened her. She hadn't published the *Parsifal* segments of her Hitler interview but not because of *Herr* Hitler's threats. The greater events of the Beer Hall *putsch* were a much bigger story and didn't leave space for the superstitious scribblings of a younger Hitler. She hadn't liked the Nazis then and she felt no differently now. True, Hitler was a far bigger figure today as leader of the second-largest party in Germany but Mattie wasn't tempted by that. When she was younger, she might have been but she was older and more experienced now. Besides, she hadn't been in love then and right now an Atlantic crossing with Cockran was a lot more appealing than once more meeting that pasty-faced man with his striking blue eyes and surprisingly bad breath.

Mattie was still torn, in a sense, between two men she loved, each in his own way, and having to disappoint one or the other—Cockran or

Hearst. She decided to press the Chief on the need to meet so quickly with Hitler.

"Why must I leave tomorrow?" she asked. "Bourke and I will be sailing on the *Europa* this Sunday. Once we arrive, I can fly to Germany."

Hearst frowned. "We don't have the luxury of time, my dear. Scripps-Howard is sitting on Hitler's doorstep like a vulture waiting to swoop in if we fail. I'll be damned if I'm going to let Roy Howard best me again. It was bad enough when he bought out Pulitzer's New York papers. This is most important to me, Mattie. Please say you'll go."

Mattie sighed. She was licked and Cockran had lost. Hearst was disarmingly direct. He was incapable of dissembling. When he said "please" and asked twice, it really *was* that important to him and she knew she couldn't turn him down.

"Okay, Chief, I'm your girl," she said and gave him a hug and a kiss.

"Wait a moment," Hearst said as Mattie turned to depart. "There's more."

"More?" Mattie said, turning back, raising her eyebrows at Hearst.

"Yes, my dear. I had a long telephone call from Churchill this morning and he presented an interesting proposition. It may cost £10,000 but, if you agree, I'm inclined to accept."

"Winston?" Mattie said, frowning, looking at her watch. "Will this take long, Chief? I've got to leave for court. I promised Cockran I'd be there to watch his oral argument in the state court of appeals. It's a big case for him. Those damn eugenics zealots are trying to sterilize another young girl. What has my dear godfather proposed this time?"

5.

Science and the State

COCKRAN gripped the podium. "May it please the court, this case is about—"

"We know what the case is about, Counselor," the presiding judge said. "We've read your briefs. All seventy-five pages. The Supreme Court disagrees with you. Twenty-seven states already have sterilization laws on the books. Don't you agree *Buck v. Bell* controls here?"

"No. Absolutely not," Cockran said, his voice firm. He knew what came next. Someone would quote Justice Holmes' opinion in the *Carrie Buck* case holding compulsory sterilization laws constitutional as if that justified a denial of due process in this case. Cockran intended to strike first and attack the weak record on which eight old men in black robes had destroyed, in the name of the state, the child-bearing ability of a normal, healthy young woman.

"With all due respect, the Supreme Court ruled on an incomplete record and poorly-defended case. The short-comings of the defense in that case should have no bearing on the lower court's denial of due process in this case because—"

"On the contrary," the presiding judge said and cut him off with a dismissive wave of his hand. Cockran forced himself to take a deep breath and keep his Irish temper in check. So much for striking first. He could do nothing but wait.

No Man's Land was better. There, you could shoot people.

"The appellant in that case, Carrie Buck, was an imbecile, like her mother before her," the presiding judge said as he reached for his reading glasses. "She gave birth to yet another imbecile. Mr. Justice Oliver Wendell Holmes explained exactly why she was a public menace:

> *We have seen more than once that the public welfare may call upon the best citizens for their lives. It would be strange if it could not call upon those who already sap the strength of the State for these lesser sacrifices, often not felt to be such by those concerned, in order to prevent our being swamped with incompetence. It is better for all the world if, instead of waiting to execute degenerate offspring for crime, or to let them starve for their imbecility, society can prevent those who are manifestly unfit from continuing their kind. Three generations of imbeciles are enough.*

"Hear, hear," croaked the bald judge beside him. The one young judge remained silent.

There it was. Rarely a sterilization case went by without someone repeating that ignorant passage from an aging jurist long past his prime. Cockran especially despised the comparison of sterilization laws to drafting men to fight and die overseas in Europe. *Men shouldn't be forced to do that either, you damned fools*, he thought. *Didn't the 13th Amendment abolish slavery?*

The presiding judge continued. "Mandatory sterilization can only be illegal when performed against the will of the patient. Who then is to consent or decide for the appellant whether it is best for her to have this operation? She cannot determine the matter for herself because she has a congenital mental defect. Tell us, Mr. Cockran, how could an imbecile like Carrie Buck make a decision for herself?"

Cockran stayed with his strategy. Hit the facts. "Like all the other decisions she made every day of her life before the state threatened to take away her reproductive ability. The central fact that Justice Holmes ignored about Carrie Buck is that she was no imbecile. Carrie performed well in school. Her teachers said that her schoolwork was 'very good.' Carrie Buck was declared an imbecile based on the hearsay accusations of another family who had motive to do so and a doctor from the institution that sought to sterilize her. Yet Justice Holmes accepted this classification at face value, and ignored overwhelming evidence to the contrary."

"Counselor," said the young judge in a soft voice. "It is my understanding that Miss Buck was considered a social deviant and that was the reason for her classification as an imbecile." The other judges watched their younger colleague, though it was difficult to read them. They didn't appear happy, that much was clear. "It seems this is also the case with your client, Miss Dill. If so, is there some reason this girl does not deserve to be so classified?"

"Yes, your honor. There is no record evidence or scientific basis to warrant doing so. The State of New York considers Judy Dill to be a 'social deviant' only because she was seduced by a wealthy boy who told her he loved her. Now she is pregnant out of wedlock with his child. His family, not surprisingly, calls her a prostitute and a social deviant and demands she be classified as such, just like Carrie Buck. But like Carrie Buck, she has a job and supports herself. Human beings make choices in their lives, irrespective of their ancestry. Everyone makes bad decisions. Even Supreme Court justices are not immune to moments of human fallacy especially as they age, yet we do not insist on their sterilization for feeble-mindedness."

Cockran was met with silence, but the young judge actually smiled. Cockran suppressed a smile in response, and decided to push the envelope even more. Now it was time to attack the sheer arrogance of the law itself. "Laws become lawless when they do not know where to stop, and only the courts may send the sort of message that stops them. There are men in Europe and here as well who call themselves scientists and claim that persons of Jewish or Gypsy ancestry have higher rates of birth defects and deformities. If you cannot see fit to stop the madness of this law, what is to prevent the State from passing a law that requires the sterilization of entire races of people deemed inferior?"

Cockran saw immediately that this was a bad ploy. At least one of the older judges actually thought this *was* a good idea, judging by his expression, but Cockran pressed on, "This is a country that values liberty at the price of all other values. It is the primary value. No value is well-earned that sacrifices liberty. If there be intellectuals who wish to treat human beings as horses, let them do it in Europe where the power and authority of the state are valued above the rights of individuals. We must never allow that to happen here. America was forged in the flame of individual liberty, a flame we must forever keep burning bright."

Cockran tried not to think about the possibility of an adverse decision as he walked back to counsel's table, sat down and gathered his papers. He didn't like to lose. Ever. But he had done his best and soon it would be out of his hands. The judges followed their inquisition of him by lobbing softballs at the government's lawyer—they even finished his sentences for him in a few instances. They gave Cockran his five minutes of rebuttal, but they no longer responded with questions. It was like talking to a man late for a train—he might nod his head as you spoke, but he didn't hear a word you said. Still, he had hopes that the younger judge might rule in his favor. A dissenting opinion wouldn't help Judy Dill, but it would do more than the courts had done so far to stem the tide of eugenics which, with forced sterilization laws, had produced nearly 50,000 victims.

But as he turned to leave the court room, Cockran was no longer thinking about what he couldn't control. Instead, he had turned his mind to Mattie, still hoping she was one of the late arrivals to the argument. To his disappointment, she wasn't among the spectators gathering to leave. Cockran was making his way through the crowd when a voice stopped him.

"I must congratulate you, Mr. Cockran." It was a deep strong voice which came from behind him. Cockran turned around and instead of the man he expected to see, he saw a stunning blonde goddess, tall with fair skin, deep blue eyes and curves to turn the head of any man.

"Excuse me?" Cockran said to the goddess.

"Congratulations," the voice said again and Cockran realized the voice belonged to a big, broad-chested man standing next to the goddess. In his late forties, his thinning brown hair was carefully barbered and his bullying six foot four frame stretched the seams of his Brooks Brothers suit. He looked like the sort of man who had played football for Yale or Harvard at one point in his life. And Cockran knew him.

"You gave an eloquent and stirring argument," the man said, looking down at Cockran, "but I'm afraid the court is against you. You're going to lose."

"It's not over yet," Cockran said. "We've met before, haven't we?"

"Yes, once or twice," he said. "Wesley Waterman, President of International Calculating Equipment." He stuck out a big hand. Cockran shook it. "I'm also president of the American Eugenics Society."

"I see." Cockran said but couldn't keep his eyes off the stunning woman in front of him.

Waterman noticed and frowned. "I'm sorry, Mr. Cockran, have you met my wife Ingrid?"

Cockran was surprised that he was gesturing to the goddess. Ingrid extended her hand, "No, we've not. It's a pleasure, Mr. Cockran."

"Please, call me Bourke," he said taking her hand briefly, noting for the first time that she was wearing a tailored gray flannel dress.

"I'm Ingrid," she said and smiled. It was a beautiful smile.

"She was born in Connecticut," Waterman said, "but pure third generation Swedish ancestry. Remarkable. She represents all that the science of eugenics is trying to promote."

Ingrid's face had remained impassive while Waterman recited her genetic credentials. "I admired your argument today," she said. "Truly." She smiled again. It was still beautiful.

"Yes, your devotion to protecting the unfit is admirable," Waterman said quickly, "but it is misplaced. And futile. The law and the courts stand against you."

Cockran turned back to Waterman. "Even if there were any science supporting eugenics, it still wouldn't make sterilization right. Or moral."

"Oh, but we do have science on our side," Waterman said. "Darwin has clearly demonstrated the law of evolution which favors the strong over the weak."

"Darwin identified a law of nature," Cockran said calmly. "Not a law of man. He never argued that nature required help in the form of a state-sponsored war against the weak."

"Ah, but nature takes care of animals because they lack one basic human frailty." Waterman paused, then smiled. "Compassion, Mr.

Cockran. Animals lack compassion. We care so much about our fellow man that we keep alive the moron whom nature intended to starve. That moron passes on his seed—or worse, violates a virtuous woman. In the long run, it threatens the very quality of our human race. Why, take my wife Ingrid, for instance..."

I'd like to, Cockran thought, as Waterman launched into a description of his wife's Nordic features. He looked over to Ingrid who rolled her eyes. Cockran knew little about Ingrid but he knew there was gossip about Waterman's first wife. He had put her in a sanitarium and been named the guardian of her person and her inherited millions right before he divorced her.

"Just look at her cheek bones," Waterman was saying. "Exquisitely sculpted..."

Ingrid leaned closer to Cockran. "As you can imagine, my husband is also an active member of the ABA," she said, her voice low and pleasant.

Cockran frowned at the *non sequitur.* "No, I wasn't aware your husband was a lawyer."

Ingrid Waterman laughed. It was a clear, unaffected laugh, as pleasant and melodious as church bells on a clear, cold Sunday morning. "Not the bar association, Mr. Cockran, the American *Breeders* Association. And I don't mean livestock."

"Oh, I see," Cockran said, uncertain as to where she was taking their conversation.

"Yes, Wesley has high hopes I'll take the blue ribbon this summer at the annual convention of the ABA. The 'Fecund Females—Nordic Extraction' classification. Who knows? Maybe I'll even take 'Best in Show'," she said with perfect deadpan sincerity.

Cockran played along. "I wish you good luck. You certainly look like a 'Best in Show'."

Waterman frowned, narrowing his eyes at the fun the two of them were making of him but his wife ignored him and upped the ante. "You're very kind, but blue ribbons do more for Wesley than for me. I've often suggested that a public mating of the 'Best in Show' virile male and fecund female —all in the interests of science, of course— would be a more tangible award."

Cockran stifled a laugh and rewarded her with a broad smile as Waterman spoke in a tight voice. "You shouldn't poke fun, my dear, at such a serious subject as improving the genetic qualities of the human race."

He turned back to Cockran. "Her lack of gravity aside, she has all the physical qualities of a superior human being, with a superior intellect to match—the kind of human beings you only find in Nordic, Aryan stock. Every moron, every whore, every criminal, every misfit we allow to breed is a threat to the future of mankind. Purifying humanity will take time but we have no choice. Remember, Rome wasn't built in a day."

Waterman turned to his wife. "Come, Ingrid. I must return to the office. I still have much work to do before our charity affair this evening."

"I may pass on that, Wesley. My genetic superiority notwithstanding, I am feeling a bit under the weather."

"As you wish, my dear," Waterman said and looked at Cockran. "Mr. Cockran, I congratulate you once again. I hope someday you come to see things my way. Good day."

"Good day," Cockran said. "Oh, and one more thing Mr. Waterman?"

"What's that?

"Aryans didn't build Rome. They burned it to the ground."

6.

The Spear of Destiny

*The Belmont Mansion
Sands Point, Long Island
Monday, 25 May 1931*

MATTIE listened to Hearst as they walked up from the beach. "Winston told me it involved an expedition to locate something called 'the Spear of Destiny.' He said you would know what he was talking about. Seems it may be missing from a museum in Vienna and Winston is raising capital to mount an expedition to retrieve it. Said you would understand."

Mattie's pulse quickened. She understood perfectly. It meant everything to her late father, Winston's closest political friend in Parliament back in 1904 after Churchill bolted the Conservative party and joined her father's Liberals. The Spear of Destiny missing? Mattie knew she'd never make it to court now. But what could a girl do? It was her father's life-long obsession, after all. "Tell me more," Mattie said.

"Not much more to tell. Some professor-type has Winston convinced that the Spear in the museum is a fake and the real one is hidden somewhere in the Alps," Hearst said.

"The Alps? Where?"

"In Austria. That's where the expedition comes in. They aren't sure exactly where so it may take some time to locate it. They figure a proper expedition may cost upwards of £20,000. Winston says he's persuaded an industrialist friend of his, Sir Archibald Hampton, to put up half the cost. For the other half, we would have exclusive worldwide rights on the photos and the story," Hearst said as he looked down at her. "Do you think we should? Is it that big a story?"

"If it's true, Chief, it really is," Mattie answered and gave him the short course on the history of the Spear she had learned from her father. Constantine, Charlemagne, Frederick the Great. Bloodthirsty believers all who held the Spear before them as they waged war without quarter.

"So, this means you would be interested in covering the story yourself?"

Mattie hesitated. Of course she was interested. How could she not be? She looked at her watch. Cockran was only minutes away from his oral argument and she was going to miss it. Worse, later today, she would have to tell him they wouldn't be sailing together to Europe as planned.

But Venice? No, she couldn't blow that off too, especially not after their fight last night. They both had been looking forward to Venice. Still, things like this were her father's lifelong obsession and now his daughter was being offered the real-life equivalent of a grail quest. Could she really pass it up? She sighed. Yes, she could. She loved her father and missed him still. But she had chosen Cockran. He was the man in her life now and she loved him. He came first. She had compromised on Hitler to please Hearst. She would not compromise on Venice.

"How soon would the expedition have to begin? After Hitler, I've got some interviews in Berlin with international arms dealers. Then it's two weeks in Venice with Bourke."

"Fine with me. Take your time. Just bring me back a good story with lots of photographs."

Well, that was easy, Mattie thought as Hearst escorted her to Cockran's big Packard town car and bade her farewell. Cockran's chauffeur Jimmy opened the door for her and, as Mattie sank back in the tufted leather upholstery, she realized she was one happy girl. Her father had once told her that happiness was a simple and uncomplicated matter requiring only three things. Someone to love. Something interesting to do. And something to look forward to. Mattie smiled. She had all three. The someone she loved would be disappointed but she knew exactly how to make it up to Cockran later.

7.

A Problem with the Kaiser

KURT von Sturm liked the Oak Bar at the Plaza. The dark wood, the smoky atmosphere. In fact, Sturm liked America. It was only his second visit and it was a different America than the one which had captivated him during the summer of 1929. This America was still prosperous, of course, but there were unemployed men living in shacks in Central Park who had not been there previously. It was such a large country, however, that he found it difficult to believe that the economic bad times would last as long here as they had in Germany.

Sturm's eyes carefully roamed the room after he had taken a corner table, looking for enemies where there should have been none. And there weren't. But old habits were hard to break and Sturm had no intention of starting now.

Assassins lived longer that way.

Sturm glanced up as the waiter brought him a crystal tumbler of Bell's 12 year old scotch. Prohibition was on its last legs yet a drink in New York had never been hard to come by. He drank sparingly but his mission in America was complete so he raised his glass in a silent toast before he spoke in German to his companion, "I return to Germany tomorrow on the *Graf*. How did you fare on your recent visit to Holland?"

Anton Dressler, a white-haired Swiss banker in his late 60s, short in stature but with a trim body and a long patrician face, frowned and drained the last of his cognac. "Not so well, my young friend. But I do not wish to discuss so sensitive a subject here. Walk with me to my apartment. We'll discuss it on the way." Dressler leaned in close and whispered "We have a problem with the Kaiser."

Dressler spoke softly as the two men left the Plaza, declined the offer of a taxi and began walking north on Fifth Avenue. He was also the Chairman of the Geneva Institute for Scientific and Industrial Progress—known informally as the Geneva Group—and his code name was "Zurich". It was in that capacity and not as a banker that he now spoke. "I had not mentioned this to Geneva's directors because I thought I had a ready solution," Dressler began, "but it seems I was mistaken. The Kaiser, it appears, is a superstitious man. He has persuaded the Crown Prince to reject our plan to place him on the German throne after our assassination of President Hindenburg unless he is given an ancient artifact he calls the Spear of Destiny, the spear which the Roman centurion Longinus reportedly used to pierce the side of Christ on the cross."

"It seems the Spear has been possessed at one time or another by all of the great German emperors, including Barbarossa and Frederick the Great. I had not thought it a problem to deliver the so-called sacred talisman to the Kaiser because I had already arranged with the director of the Hofburg Museum in Vienna, where this Spear is on display, to loan it to a Berlin Museum as part of a special exhibition of historic Germanic artifacts."

Sturm, who served as the Geneva Group's executive director, was surprised. "Really? Aren't the Austrians especially prickly about their German neighbors on matters like this?"

Dressler linked his arm with the taller man's and patted him with a kid-skin gloved hand. "It is the way of the world, Kurt. A generous contribution to the museum's acquisition fund and an equally generous deposit in the museum director's account in my bank in Zurich."

"So what is the problem?"

"The Kaiser no longer believes the Spear at the Hofburg is the true Spear once possessed by his illustrious ancestors. He thinks it's a fake."

Sturm sighed inwardly. The current German Chancellor, Heinrich Brüning, was a disaster. He could not muster a majority in the Reichstag and was running the government by presidential decree, driving Germany deeper into depression by raising taxes and contracting the money supply. But the aging President Hindenburg refused to replace Brüning. In despair, German patriots, including the German member of the Geneva Group code-named Berlin, had asked the Geneva Group for help in implementing their solution—elevating the current number two man at the Ministry of Defense, General Kurt von Schleicher, to the chancellorship, where he would immediately institute a massive public works program and a dramatic rearmament of Germany. The Germans assured the men of Geneva that all German industrialists and bankers would support von Schleicher as chancellor. Unfortunately, President Hindenburg refused to go along, whether out of snobbery or senility was difficult to determine.

Sturm believed it was a blend of both. Von Schleicher had been only a captain during the Great War, rising to the rank of major. He was not well known to the German people, but the Geneva Group believed he would be when the truth was told about the role he played in rearming Germany. Despite the restrictions of the Versailles treaty, Germany had continued during the 1920s to develop advanced weapons pursuant to a secret military treaty with the Soviet Union. Deep within the Ural Mountains, German engineers designed and tested artillery, airplanes, tanks, poison gas, as well as an entire range of rifles, light and heavy machine guns and lightweight machine pistols. As a consequence of the treaty, the German Army was limited to 100,000 men, an army of sergeants, it was called. But it was an army which could quickly be armed with the most modern weapons in Europe. The prototypes were there. All that was needed was to flip a switch on the electric power and let loose the waiting factories.

The weapons project in Russia was set in motion by the German General Staff in the days after the Great War. It was supervised by a highly secret task force called *Sondergruppe R*. The commander of *Sondergruppe R*, the man who had implemented the plan of the German General Staff, was Kurt von Schleicher. So, when Hindenburg had flat out rejected the industrialists' requests that von Schleicher be made chancellor, they turned to the men of Geneva for a solution. A permanent solution. Hindenburg was to be assassinated and replaced as head of state by someone more amenable to the wishes of the German industrialists—a return of the Kaiser or, rather, his son, the Crown Prince, as a constitutional monarch for Germany. A unifying symbol for the German people. Sturm's job, as usual, was to implement the frequently violent wishes of the men of Geneva, something at which, over the years, he had become quite skilled.

"The old man believes the Spear is a fake? What does he want now? For us to magically find the true Spear?"

"In a manner of speaking, yes," Dressler replied, handing Sturm a manila envelope. "This contains the German translation of a monograph recently published in England by an archeology professor claiming that the Hofburg Spear is a fake and that the real Spear was hidden somewhere in the Austrian Alps before the war."

Sturm carefully folded the envelope in half and placed it inside his suit coat. "I'll read the monograph later. Am I correct that my former monarch and his eldest son now want us to go off on a wild goose chase in the Alps based on an obscure article by an English archeologist?"

"It's more than that. The Kaiser and his son firmly believe that Germany would have prevailed in the Great War if it had possessed the Spear. German intelligence apparently reported to the Kaiser before the war that the Emperor Franz Josef personally vetoed an exhibit of the Spear and other artifacts in Berlin. He feared the Kaiser would never return them, which the Kaiser indicates was correct. That is why he believes the Englishman's story. Hiding the Spear, he says, is something Franz Josef would think to do. More importantly, the Englishman has been to Doorn at the Kaiser's invitation. They were quite taken with his story and his credentials."

Sturm shrugged his shoulders in resignation. "He's a senile old fool but I understand. What do you wish me to do?"

"I told the Kaiser and the Crown Prince that you would interview the Englishman and determine for yourself his reliability. If you are persuaded that his conclusions are accurate, I want you to enlist his help in finding the Spear. Travel to Doorn yourself and meet with the Kaiser and the Crown Prince. They claim that they have further information, intelligence they received after the war, which may assist you in the search for the Spear."

"Very well, I will do as you ask, *Herr* Dressler. But a return of the royal family is not what Germany needs. I wish the men of Geneva could understand that."

Sturm knew the men of Geneva had another reason for replacing Hindenburg with the Crown Prince and Brüning with von Schleicher. Fear. They feared another European war. They wanted the profits that came from German rearmament, but another general European conflict was not in their best interest. Many smaller wars among lesser peoples in South America, Asia, the Balkans and the Middle East were more to their liking. Once his role as the man responsible for Germany's weapons development became known, the men of Geneva hoped von Schleicher would become as popular as the one man in the world they feared the most. Adolf Hitler.

While some in the Geneva Group had dismissed Hitler as nothing more than a rabble rouser, others had read his autobiography, *Mein Kampf*. They knew that, like von Schleicher, Hitler would rearm Germany. But von Schleicher was a cautious and conservative man. Hitler was not. Hitler was a radical, a revolutionary even. He could very well start a general European war. And now Hitler was the leader of the second-largest party and the second most popular man in Germany. Democracy had failed. A strong man was the only antidote to Hitler's popularity.

"It's nothing more than a means to an end, Kurt. With the economy getting worse, Germany needs a strong leader, one who will be unafraid to openly rebuild Germany's arms industry. Von Schleicher is that leader and the Crown Prince a unifying symbol for your countrymen."

The two men reached the apartment building on Fifth Avenue where Dressler's bank maintained a permanent residence for visiting bank officers. The uniformed doorman held the door open for Dressler as he shook hands with Sturm. "I am sorry you could not join us for dinner."

Sturm smiled. "I regret it also, *Herr* Dressler but I am dining tonight with an exceptionally beautiful young woman I met a few days ago at a reception given by the Swedish Consul General. And, most conveniently, her husband will not be home this evening."

Now it was Dressler's turn to smile. "Enjoy yourself, my friend. I will see you soon in Geneva. Godspeed. Find the Kaiser his Spear."

8.

Wild Bill Donovan

New York City
Monday, 25 May 1931

MATTIE McGary, clad only in a long green silk robe, sat in an armchair by a roaring fire, making notes for her interview with Hitler. She was impatient for Cockran to arrive. He would be home any minute now and she didn't intend to let him make it past the comforter she had spread in front of the fireplace. She heard his key in the lock and turned off the lamp beside her. This left the room illuminated only by fire as, earlier, she had closed the drapes to shut out the light of the pale afternoon sun.

Mattie greeted Cockran and gave him a long, warm kiss, molding her body to his.

"Hello, beautiful. I missed you today," Cockran said, a boyish grin on his face.

"Hello yourself, big man," Mattie said. "I missed you too. The Chief called. He has a new home in Sands Point. I had to go see him. It was business. I'm sorry I wasn't there."

"You didn't miss much."

"It was bad?"

Cockran face darkened in anger. "It wasn't good. I tried out what we discussed. The real facts about Carrie Buck, but…."

"It didn't work?"

"No , damn it!" Cockran said and slammed his briefcase down on a hall table. "The bastards didn't care. They just didn't care. Or at least two of them sure didn't. What the hell is this country coming to when the government plays God and decides who can and can't bear children? It's just so goddamned wrong!" he said in a loud, angry voice.

Mattie pulled back and took Cockran's face in both hands. He could get this way when something mattered to him and stay in a bad mood for hours. Mostly, she just kept out of his way when his temper got the best of him and it wasn't directed at her. But if she did that, her plans for the evening would go unfulfilled. It was time to tame the savage beast.

"Darling, you gave it your best shot. No one could have done more," she said. "Most men wouldn't have tried. I'm proud of you. Have a martini. You deserve it."

"Make it a double," Cockran replied as he followed her into the room. "Did I forget to pay the electric bill this month?" he asked, pointing to the fire as if he had just noticed it.

"No, I only thought it would be cozy to have drinks by the fire before we dressed for the Orphans' charity ball." Mattie replied, vigorously pumping the cocktail shaker up and down, then side to side.

"And the comforter in front of the fire?" he asked as she bent over to pour his martini.

"Floor burns," she replied.

Cockran looked puzzled. Apparently she had to spell it out for him. "It prevents them."

Cockran smiled and took a sip of his martini before he took off his coat and loosened his tie. He hesitated a moment. "Uh, where are Paddy and his grandma?"

"A walk in the park followed by dinner at the Palm Court. They won't be back before seven." She opened the robe, slipped it off her shoulders and arms and let it fall to the floor, pooling around her ankles. "So what are you waiting for, sailor?"

As Mattie lay back, Cockran sank to his knees, hovering above her, stripping off his shirt. She could see the thick curls of brown hair covering his chest as he unfastened his trousers. She closed her eyes and felt his tongue trailing a path from her breasts to her belly and below until the familiar stubble of his five o'clock shadow was brushing the inside of her thighs. His tongue soon reached its goal and her body was engulfed by wave after wave of sensation, rolling from her hips along her spine and through her neck until she reached her first orgasm. When they finally finished, Cockran was sprawled on top of her, his hands beneath her breasts. She sighed. The trial was over at last and her man was back. This was lots more fun than fighting.

It would be two years this summer since she first seduced Cockran. It was Winston, of course, who brought them together that summer in 1929, having persuaded each of them to help him track down and destroy a huge IRA arms shipment. With that danger behind them, Cockran had tried to end things between them but, to his considerable surprise, she had refused to let him do it. Apparently, no woman he dumped in the past had ever done that.

Besides, Mattie didn't believe him. He had been so transparent, saying the memory of his late wife would always come between them. It sounded rehearsed and he admitted later he had used that line before to ease his way out of relationships that were becoming too serious. No way, buster. She had ghosts in her past too. Mattie had only known Cockran two weeks by then but she thought he was someone she could fall in love with and she could tell the same was true for him. It might not work out, she knew, because he had a young son Patrick and she was used to living alone and doing whatever she damn well pleased. But she wanted to see how it would play out so she told him no. She wasn't going to leave unless he looked her in the eye and swore he had no feelings for her. Cockran wasn't a good liar and didn't try. Soon after, she discovered she *was* falling in love with him and he with her. They still had their share of arguments—like last night—but who didn't? They made each other laugh and, to her delight, his son Paddy became her biggest fan. He read all her articles and loved to hear stories of her adventures.

"**WOULD** you like a drink?" Cockran asked as they entered the ballroom. It was the first thing he'd said to Mattie since they'd left his Fifth Avenue townhouse in a taxi.

"Yes," Mattie said. "Johnny Walker and water would be nice."

Cockran was behaving badly and he knew it. After making love, Mattie had told him about Hearst and an expedition he was financing to find some ancient Christian artifact that meant a lot to her father. That was fine with Cockran. He knew how close Mattie had been with her father, the same as he was with his. Suitably softened up—and set up—she had hit him with the bombshell. She was leaving tomorrow on an airship for Germany.

Cockran knew he should count his blessings. He was lucky. Most men thought themselves fortunate to find one woman in their life to love. Cockran had found two. It didn't seem likely when he lost his first wife, Nora, the mother of their ten year old son Patrick, in the Irish Civil War nine years ago. Nothing had seemed very likely to him back then, a barren future without the love of his life, his young son the only consolation and a constant reminder of what he had lost. Cockran didn't think he could ever bear again the impossible pain he felt when he lost Nora. Over the years, he began to see female friends but he never hinted at a future together; and sooner or later, the women would drift away in search of more commitment than he could give them.

But two years ago, Mattie had changed everything. She helped him let go of the guilt he'd felt over Nora's death and, against his earlier resolve, Cockran had fallen in love. Mattie was irrepressible and irresistible. Going on two years now, it was Cockran's longest relationship since Nora's death. Unlike the other women he had dated, Mattie didn't seem to mind that he never talked to her of a more permanent future for them. They simply enjoyed the present and each other for they both knew from tragedies of their own how fragile life could be.

She wasn't perfect. Who was? She had a flaw, possibly a fatal one. Mattie was impulsive. Aggressively so. He had quickly discovered that. All he had to do was take a look at the photo spread from her latest assignment, see the young corpses slumped against their guns, and gauge how close she had come to being killed herself. Her only excuse was to quote one of her photographer mentors, Alfred Eisenstadt, who told her if her photographs weren't good enough, she wasn't close enough. To hell with Eisenstadt! He just didn't want to see her hurt. If Mattie wanted to cover stories half way around the globe, fine—but let them be natural disasters, or politics. Just not every god-damned war or insurrection that the 1930s, thus far, seemed to supply in ample abundance. And above all, she didn't have to get that damn close!

"Is that demon rum I see?" someone said to his left. Cockran turned to see the large frame of Wesley Waterman. He held a glass of orange juice. "Nursing the wounds of defeat?"

Cockran didn't reply, handed the second drink to Mattie and introduced her to Waterman.

"Well, Mr. Cockran, as you trial lawyers say, 'sometimes you win; sometimes the client loses.' It won't be the end of your world when your client loses," Waterman said.

Cockran let his anger flash. "Tell that to Judy Dill. It's her rights and her body you and your government thugs will be violating."

"I meant that sincerely, Mr. Cockran. Not to tease or taunt," he said in a softer voice. "You did the best you could with a bad case and a worse client."

"Is this the livestock breeder you mentioned this afternoon?" Mattie asked and he could see she was trying to distract his anger.

"No. Humans, dear," Cockran said. "Humans."

"Can you breed humans?" she asked in an innocent tone.

"Mr. Waterman and the so-called scientists he funds think we can."

"And should," Waterman finished. "It's the only way to improve the human race."

"Speaking of improving the human race," Cockran said. "How's your lovely wife?" Cockran looked at Mattie and said, "We met this afternoon. She's a blonde knockout."

Waterman pursed his lips. "Ingrid is not feeling well. I decided she should stay home."

"Sorry to hear that," Cockran said. "I think she and Mattie would have a lot in common."

"I'm sure she's a lovely gal," Mattie said. "But if you'll excuse me, I see a few girlfriends of my own I must say 'hello' to." Mattie turned and weaved through the crowd, her gown sliding wonderfully with her hips which Cockran thought Waterman watched for far too long.

Finally, Waterman turned and calmly placed a strong hand on Cockran's shoulder. "Mr. Cockran," he said in an amiable tone. "You're a fine lawyer. Perhaps I.C.E. could send you some legal work. I see no cause for us to be hostile. We might even become friends."

"Thanks but I've got more than enough on my plate. As for friends, I don't think so. The members of the Harvard Club may find you a congenial fellow but you and others who believe in the pseudo-science of eugenics turn my stomach."

Cockran glanced at his shoulder, his muscles tensing beneath Waterman's grip until, finally, he let go. "I see. Have a good evening then, Mr. Cockran." Cockran nodded and watched Waterman go. Cockran knew he had been rude but why the hell had Waterman offered to send him I.C.E. legal work?

Cockran wandered through the crowd, keeping an eye on Mattie. She laughed with friends, talked to the women she knew, flirted harmlessly with their husbands or escorts. She did a fine job pretending to have a good time

"What the hell," said a familiar voice behind him. "What's with the long face? I thought this was a charity function, not a wake."

Cockran turned around to see the ruddy face and large, compact body of his old wartime CO, William "Wild Bill" Donovan, Medal of Honor recipient and head of the law firm where Cockran occasionally received an assignment, usually in international law. His brown hair was streaked with gray but the eyes were still as clear a blue as when they first met. He didn't like to be called "Wild Bill" so, to Cockran, he was simply Bill or, on formal occasions, "Colonel". A great friend. An even better lawyer. Five for five in the Supreme Court and he wasn't yet 50.

"Too many Republicans like you here for it to be a wake," Cockran said.

Donovan grinned. "And a damn shame that it's not. If it were an Irish wake, fella might be able to enjoy himself."

Cockran laughed.

"So, how'd oral argument go today?" Donovan asked.

Cockran answered by downing half his scotch.

"That bad, huh?"

"Two of them wouldn't recognize due process if it bit them in the ass."

"What about the other one?"

"At least he had an open mind. Maybe he'll write a dissent."

"You think he can pull one of the other judges to his side?"

"No, Bill." Cockran said, taking another sip. "They're going to screw her over."

They talked for a while. Donovan rarely missed social functions like this while Cockran usually did. But Cockran had met Mattie at a similar cocktail party the year before and that was when Donovan had made him a job offer. Cockran had a good set-up with Bill and was officially listed as "Of Counsel" to Donovan & Raichle, specializing in international law—the same subject he taught at Columbia's law school. The work had been good. Never more than he wanted and it sometimes put him in the courtroom, which kept his skills sharp and allowed him to offer his students both a real life as well as an academic view.

Donovan traveled frequently and was almost never in the office at the same time as Cockran so he decided to take advantage of the opportunity to talk to his boss one on one. "Was there a package at the firm from Churchill this morning?"

"From Winston?" Donovan said. "I'm not sure. There were four large files delivered to our offices this afternoon. It was addressed to you but it wasn't from Churchill."

"That's probably it," Cockran said. He told Donovan about Churchill's cable

"Yeah, the files are probably from Winston. Don't worry," Donovan said. "I'll review the file first thing in the morning. See me at 8:30. I'll tell you what I think."

"Make it closer to 10:30." Cockran said, scanning the crowd again, looking for Mattie.

"I don't mean to pry," Donovan said gently, "Are things okay with you and Mattie?"

Cockran turned back to Donovan. "Why? Is it obvious?"

"To me? Of course. I'm a trial lawyer," he said. "Your body language betrays you."

"Things are fine," Cockran started to say. He was about to continue when Mattie snuck up behind him and touched his elbow.

"Bourke," she said. "Do you mind taking me home? I have more packing to do."

"No," he said. "That's fine."

"Hi Bill," Mattie said with a smile. "Sorry I'm checking out so early."

"Not at all, my dear," Donovan said. "Ruth will be happy for an excuse to leave."

Mattie and Cockran said their goodbyes to the people they knew and slipped out from the party. It was still early, the sky a dark shade of blue, when they hailed a taxi on Rector Street. Cockran was quiet for much of the ride home, mildly annoyed that Donovan had been able to read him that well. He was a trial lawyer too and ought to hide his feelings better.

"Bourke, I really am sorry," Mattie said. "You know how the Chief is. You worked for him once. No one says 'no' to the Chief; you just don't do that."

Cockran nodded. "I know."

"We still have Venice."

"Unless the Chief calls again."

"That's not fair," she said.

"Sure it is. He might."

"Of course, he *might*. 'Might' is a pretty big word, Cockran. Lots of things *might* happen—it's not fair to pin that on me." Cockran sensed her growing impatience but he couldn't help himself.

"It's more than just 'might,' Mattie, it's probable and you know it."

"So what? It's my job!" she said, her voice rising as she threw up her hands.

"I know," he said. "I don't mean you shouldn't do your job…"

"That's what it sounds like," she said, interrupting.

"It's your career, not mine."

"Damn right, it is!"

"It's only that …" he stopped himself. She was right. He wasn't being entirely rational. Her new assignment for Hearst that kept her from joining him on the *Europa* wasn't the issue. What really bothered him were the assignments she *did* have control over. That's what he didn't understand. What did she have? A death wish? "What happens after Venice?"

"What do you mean?"

"After Venice. After your expedition in the Alps. Then, you'll rush off to some slaughterhouse like Bolivia or India—where men are busy killing each other and they might not make an exception for pretty redheads."

"Jesus, Cockran," she said. "What's that have to do with the Hitler contract negotiations? Or my expedition in the Alps. I thought those were the sort of safe things you *wanted* me to do."

"You're right. They are. Just don't pretend that you're *choosing* jobs like this contract negotiation," he said. "Left to your own devices, you choose places like Bolivia and India where you risk your life, month in and month out. You know that Paddy thinks of you like his mother."

"*Don't bring Paddy into this!*" Mattie said, her voice almost a shout. "I am *not* his mother! No matter how he feels about me, or how I feel about him. You leave him out of this!"

"I can't leave him out," Cockran shot back. Now, he was really angry too. "He loves you, I love you and you'll soon be throwing yourself into another *war*! Two of them, to be precise!"

"I'm a big girl, Cockran," she said. "I can take care of myself."

"No, you can't," he said, resignation in his voice. "It's *war*. No one can take care of themselves in a war. No more than you can flip a coin and make it turn up heads."

Mattie said nothing and Cockran continued. "When are you going to stop chasing the merchants of death? Trying to avenge the loss of your fiancé Eric and your brothers? When are you finally going to start living your own life?"

Cockran watched as Mattie's face registered what he said, the shock setting in, her eyes beginning to water. Then she shook her head and looked down, taking a deep breath, before looking at him again.

"I love you so much, Bourke, I really do," she said in a tired voice, "but I've heard all this before. I *am* living my own life. It's the one I've chosen, just like I've chosen to be with you. I know you love me but it seems like you're always questioning my career and the risks I take. It's getting old. It's probably a good thing we're not going to sail on the *Europa* together."

This wasn't turning out the way he intended, Cockran thought, as she continued. "Maybe we need to take a break from being together.

Step back and assess what we both really want and need. I may not be the kind of girl you need and I want a man who spends more time in my corner and less at my throat."

"That's not fair," Cockran replied. "I only meant to…."

"Let's not talk about this any more tonight. But think about what I've said."

They both fell into silence and stayed that way the rest of the ride home. He'd done more than enough damage. Especially with Mattie leaving in the morning. The possibility of ending things between them, as she had suggested, was new and not what he had in mind. Not at all.

9.

Dinner Can Wait

New York City
Monday, 25 May 1931

KURT von Sturm was as human as the next man and appreciated the company of attractive women. In his line of work, which required frequent travel, sustaining a relationship with a woman was difficult. So, whenever he traveled and it did not otherwise interfere with his responsibilities, he enjoyed having female companionship. Tonight looked to be one of those promising nights.

While Sturm was partial to beautiful women, he preferred that they have brains as well so that he was not bored in those intervals before and after he took them to bed. Over the years, he had learned that the best places to find his kind of woman—bright, beautiful and willing—were not Berlin nightclubs or high-end New York speakeasies, but rather at diplomatic receptions. Sturm had always been able, dressed in a dinner jacket, to meet women on those occasions who appeared on the surface to meet his three criteria. After that, he would ask them their husbands' occupations and have them discreetly point out their spouses to him. Single women never made it onto Sturm's list. The potential of too many strings was much too high. Sturm then would circulate through the reception and introduce himself to each of the husbands of his prey. He would then take the potential cuckold's measure and assess his chances with the other man's wife. If the husband were much older than the wife, his chances increased. The same was true if he were pompous or simply too full of himself for no apparent reason. He realized some people might find his methods to be unromantic and a trifle cold-blooded, but Sturm found them to be both practical and successful.

The evening before, Sturm had chosen the American's wife. The Frenchman's wife had been too aggressive, the wives of the Italian and the Swedish Consuls not as attractive. Besides, he knew the American woman's husband would be spending tonight at his club after attending some function downtown and would be sailing the next morning on an extended European business trip. Sturm had all of tonight before he returned to Germany on the *Graf Zeppelin* tomorrow. Making love in a woman's home was far more romantic than in a sterile hotel suite.

Sturm was deep inside Central Park by this point and he could see the lights of the apartment towers on Central Park West where she lived. He could have taken a taxi from the Plaza at the southeast corner of the park, but Sturm was a punctual man and never arrived late or early. With twenty minutes to spare, he decided he could use the exercise and cut across the park. Uncharacteristically, he allowed his mind to drift in anticipation of what delights lay ahead.

There were three of them, predators moving quickly, two hitting him high and the third grabbing his legs. The three men were unshaven and dressed in rough clothes. They had obviously practiced this maneuver before, because they all hit at the same time, knocking him off his feet. One of the three reeked of alcohol, and Sturm saw a knife in his hand.

Sturm reached out and grabbed the man's free hand and pulled him forward, a move that surprised his adversary. Before he could react and bring his knife to bear, Sturm had freed a razor sharp assault knife of his own from the strap on his leg beneath his trousers and plunged its serrated edge directly into the man's kidney from behind. The man's cry of pain was choked off as his system went into shock and he rolled silently off Sturm, his body convulsing as the blood pumped out. Sturm jerked the knife free and swung it in a wide arc, severing the tendons of the second man's left ankle. The man cried out in pain and went down.

The third man began to flee. Sturm reached inside his suit coat pocket and pulled from its shoulder holster a Luger T-08 semi-automatic pistol, its short barrel extended by a sound suppresser. He took careful aim and fired one 7.65 mm Parabellum bullet which made a small hole in the back and then blew out the front of the third man's head. Sturm preferred the smaller cartridge to the heavier 9 mm which provided greater power but slower muzzle velocity precisely for the effect it produced once inside its target.

Sturm turned back and looked down at the terrified man below him, clutching his bleeding ankle, his eyes wild with fear. Sturm shook his head in regret. It was the same in New York as in Berlin. Men who were out of work, men who were hungry, men who would do desperate things. While Sturm would probably be on his way to Europe before the police mounted an investigation, a man in his particular profession could take no chances. He could leave no witnesses.

Sturm fired once more, a small round hole appearing between the second man's eyes. He pressed the Luger back into its shoulder holster, wiped his knife clean on the pant leg of the first man's trousers, before returning it to the strap on his leg. He brushed the dirt from the back of his gray flannel jacket and trousers, smoothed back his blond hair and continued his journey through the park.

FIFTEEN minutes later, Sturm was inside the lobby of the Majestic Apartments at 115 Central Park West. Five minutes after that, he entered the penthouse suite in the Majestic's northern tower, the door opened by his hostess for the evening who wore a long, flowing, cream-colored silk gown with a modest neck, cut daringly low in the back. A pale pink sash around her hips was tied in a small bow at the back whose subtle movement drew his attention to her attractive backside as she walked towards a two-story high window with a spectacular view of Central Park below.

"Would you like some champagne? I've given the servants the night off."

Sturm joined her at the window and, with a flute of champagne in his left hand, he lightly moved his fingers along the entire length of her bare back. "I'm so pleased you were free tonight," Sturm said.

"As am I," she replied. "The headache that caused me to beg off accompanying my husband to that dreadful charity affair has miraculously disappeared."

Sturm raised his flute in a toast. "To your headache."

She smiled and they clinked glasses. She turned back to the park and Sturm followed her gaze onto the dark patchwork of trees below. "Tell me, do you seduce many married women?"

"Only the beautiful ones. And never before in New York."

"You told me last night that this is only the third time that you have been in the city."

"But only the first time I've met such a beautiful woman."

She laughed. It was a delightful laugh. "Don't try that line with me. I saw three other gorgeous women throwing themselves at you last night. Especially that French diplomat's wife. She couldn't keep her hands off you. So why me? I am certainly less experienced at this."

Sturm smiled. He liked Americans. So open. So direct. Emboldened, he replied in kind, "Three reasons. You were the most beautiful of the four. You were the only blonde. And your husband was easily the most boring of the four husbands."

The woman laughed and choked on her sip of champagne. "Oh, my god! Excuse me," she apologized as Sturm handed her his handkerchief. Still laughing, she continued "Not the most romantic way to start our evening but you are so right. My husband is a businessman and that's all he talks about. He's also a very tall man and something of a bully, quick to use his fists. Other men are afraid to make a pass at me because of his reputation. So why are you different?"

"Perhaps your husband's reputation is over-rated," Sturm said. "Or it could be that I am leaving America on an airship for Germany tomorrow morning."

She laughed again. "Well, then, let's not waste any more time. Dinner can wait."

"Being with you could never be a waste of time," Sturm replied, "before or after dinner," as he took off his suit coat in a practiced maneuver which took his shoulder holster and weapon with it, and draped it carefully over the back of a chair, the weapon hidden from view. He stood behind her, one hand caressing her neck. Putting the flute down, he gently turned her face to him and kissed her, a kiss she eagerly returned.

The room's only illumination came from the fireplace and a few candles placed at various locations around the room. An excellent dancer, Sturm was also a skilled and demanding lover. On the dance floor as in bed, his partners followed his lead. She offered no complaint as he picked her up and carried her into the master bedroom. She was still breathing heavily while he placed her down upon the covers and slowly removed her silk gown, inch by inch. Beneath she was naked save for a filmy pair of step-ins. He paused to admire her breathtaking body, inwardly shaking his head. How could her husband pass up an evening alone with such a woman?

Sturm slipped her undergarment down over her hips, parted her legs and moved his face between them. She gasped when one and then two fingers moved inside her, her passion growing as his fingers moved faster. "No, don't stop" she said when his fingers left but she said no more when his tongue replaced them and she grabbed his head tightly. Moments later, he felt her body convulse. As he knelt up between her legs, removed his shirt and unbuckled the belt on his trousers, he knew the best was yet to come. Her husband really was a fool.

Later, she laughed softly as they lay there, like spoons, Sturm behind her caressing her breasts.

"What's funny?" he asked.

"How close I came to turning you down last night at the reception."

"And you find humor in that?"

"No. But I know the French girl slightly from talking to her at other functions. I'll bet she has no idea how much she missed. She's quite indiscreet after several drinks, and I know her husband and her many lovers never did for her what you just did for me." She laughed again. "Hell, my husband never has either. He's never done to me what you did at the beginning. And he's had plenty of mistresses to help him practice. Thank you. You win the blue ribbon."

"You're welcome," Sturm said. "It was my pleasure."

She laughed softly. "Don't kid yourself. The pleasure was not yours alone. Can you stay for breakfast as well as dinner? My husband is spending the night at his club downtown."

Sturm smiled. A few minutes later, dressed in one of her husband's monogrammed robes, Sturm watched her hips sway seductively beneath her own silk robe as she walked into the dining room where they drank more champagne and ate lobster and caviar by candlelight. She had no idea how much more he had in store for her the next morning.

STURM rose early and perked coffee. The night before, they had made love again throughout the apartment—in front of the fireplace, up against the great room wall, on top of her husband's desk. This morning, the dining room table proved irresistible as the coffee grew cold.

"Oh, my," she said breathlessly, propping herself up with her arms on the starched damask of the dining room table, her breasts glistening with perspiration as he stood between her long legs which were still wrapped tightly around his waist. "That was some encore. My husband's business trip will keep him in Europe the rest of the month. Are you quite certain you cannot extend your stay in America?"

Sturm smiled and reluctantly turned down her tempting invitation. For Kurt von Sturm, duty always preceded pleasure. Ingrid Waterman was a marvelous woman and an exceptionally passionate one as well, but he had a zeppelin to catch.

10.

The Hunt Begins

COCKRAN noticed Mattie was still stiff when they arrived at the airfield in Lakehurst. Neither had spoken to the other since their fight in the taxi the night before except to discuss their respective travel details which would reunite them in Venice. Two arguments in two days was *not* how he wanted to part with the woman he loved. But this was not their first fight nor, he suspected, would it be the last. It was probably how most Celts—Scots or Irish—procreated. Fights followed by fierce lovemaking. But that hadn't happened last night. He wished it had but both were too stubborn for their own good and making up typically took at least 24 hours, time they no longer had.

Cockran escorted Mattie out onto the tarmac to the wooden steps leading up to the passenger cabin of the *Graf Zeppelin*, its size and beauty still a wonder to him nearly two years after he had first seen the globe-trotting airship in Los Angeles. They briefly kissed and told each other, "I love you," but he knew they both were still upset. "See you in Venice," Mattie said, with a weak smile. Someone who didn't know them would not think they were lovers.

"It's a date," he said but he was not happy. How had they gone in just two days from his hoping to buy her an engagement ring in Venice to her saying perhaps they were not right for each other? Maybe two weeks apart would give her time to think. Maybe what he said would start to sink in. He hoped so. He loved her dearly but she had covered far too many wars and taken far too many risks in her work for Hearst. She was wrong to claim he was trying to control her life. He was just trying to keep her safe. And alive. Why couldn't she see that? Cockran walked back through the departure lounge. He glanced over to a coffee and tea stand, where two uniformed members of the *Graf Zeppelin*'s crew stood beside the armrests of a couple of chairs. They were talking with a striking figure in a well-tailored three-piece suit. A face from the past. Cockran recognized him though he couldn't place where. He was tall, his blond hair neatly combed, and a scar on his right temple. A handsome guy but not the kind of face you'd mistake for somebody else.

THE breeze ruffled Kurt von Sturm's fair, straw colored hair as he thrilled once more at the sight of the giant silver airship, the largest in the world, floating patiently at its mooring mast, its surface gleaming in the bright morning sunlight. These giant airships had once been his life and the two members of the *Graf Zeppelin*'s crew to whom he was talking had flown under his command during the war.

"It is an honor, *Käpitanleutenant*, to have you flying with us again."

Sturm gave a short bow. "No, Fritz, it is you who honor me. I am merely a passenger."

"Your time will come again, *Käpitanleutenant*. The *Graf* is only the beginning of a new era in travel. We are building more airships and one of them should be yours."

"You are very kind. Have you seen to the passenger arrangements I've requested?"

A broad smile crossed Fritz Esser's face. "Indeed, I have, *Käpitanleutenant*. The passenger manifest is full but I have arranged a single cabin for her side by side with yours."

"And the dining salon?"

"Yes. A table for two by a window. Only you and the *fraulein*. She is very beautiful."

Now it was Sturm's turn to smile. "Yes, she is."

"Have a pleasant voyage, sir."

"Thank you, Fritz. Because of your good work, I believe I will."

Sturm marveled at his good fortune as he walked through the double doors of the passenger reception area out toward the great dirigible. First, a successful mission in America. Then last night and this morning spent seducing yet another man's beautiful wife. Now, a glorious airship voyage. And, most extraordinarily, three days and two nights alone in the sky with another beautiful woman as his companion, someone he had coveted from afar more than once. His time with the delightful Ingrid had been but an overture. This woman would be a symphony. He wondered if she would remember him. He didn't think so. Other men had been monopolizing her attention on those occasions. Munich in 1923 on the eve of the Beer Hall *putsch* and then again in California two years ago. Sturm had envied her companion on the latter occasion because of the obvious tender feelings she had for him. But now the field was all his. The hunt was about to begin, his prey unsuspecting. Perfect.

Sturm had a highly developed sense on matters like this and he had not failed to notice the tension between the woman and her escort. A tension that was not there two years before. A vulnerability to exploit. And more than enough time to do so. Due to the nature of his profession, married women were his preferred prey but he was more than prepared to make an exception if the reward would be bedding a woman so brave and so beautiful. It had been nearly two years since last he saw her but time had only enhanced her beauty. He had never forgotten her. While she was with the same companion then as now, she was not wearing a wedding band or even an engagement ring. He wondered why. Details. A man like Kurt von Sturm always noticed details. He lived for the chase and the reward awaiting him at the end of the hunt. He had *never* lost once a woman was in his sights. And now, at long last, Mattie McGary was squarely in his sights.

Part III

Germany, America, and England

26 May – 1 June 1931

Never forget we are a knightly Order, from which one cannot withdraw, to which one is recruited by blood and within which one remains with body and soul so long as one lives on this earth.

Heinrich Himmler
[Peter Padfield, *Himmler, Reichsfuhrer, SS*]

11.

A Knightly Order

REINHARD Tristan Hoch paused, his violin tucked beneath his chin, the bow hovering above it, and glanced to his left. Twelve more minutes and it still wasn't right. What would his father have said? *If you don't practice at least four hours a day, you will never be a musician. You cannot expect to get it right if you only spend ninety minutes.*

Hoch drew his lips into a determined, thin line. *Yes, I can,* he thought, *and I will,* as he began again. The strains of Bach's second Brandenburg concerto soon filled the small room and flowed from two open windows. Between the windows was a full-length mirror, the polished wood of its frame gleaming in the afternoon sun which streamed into the room.

Precisely twelve minutes later, a perspiring Hoch lifted his chin from the violin and bowed elaborately from the waist, his image reflected in the mirror. At last. Perfect. Like in everything else he set out to do. Student. Naval cadet. Naval communications officer. Husband. Father. Musician. Intelligence Director for the SS. How wrong his father had been.

Reinhard Hoch religiously played the violin for ninety minutes every day save Sunday, his wife and small son banished from their apartment until he finished. He stood, violin in his left hand, bow in his right, and looked at the mirror in the bedroom of his apartment, only a five-minute walk from the Brown House, the headquarters in Munich of the National Socialist Workers Party. Even clad in black trousers, it was clear his hips were still too wide. They were, he believed, the only flaw marring his otherwise classic Nordic features and physique. Still, Hoch had no trouble luring attractive women to his bed, before or after his marriage. Blond hair, icy blue eyes. A trim six feet tall. A long, narrow face dominated by a prominent beak of a nose which he considered aquiline and his enemies, of which there were no shortage, whispered was proof that Semitic genes once had polluted his family's Nordic gene pool. He drew his lips into a thin line and was pleased at the effect it had. When he relaxed them, however, they were still thick and fleshy. It was not exactly another flaw, but one he could control when the occasion demanded it.

Hoch knew his hips could not be controlled so easily, only camouflaged, which is why, after he had joined the SS earlier that year, he always dressed in black. From head to toe, he enthusiastically embraced the SS trend away from SA khaki. A foreshadowing, perhaps, that the SS one day would be independent of the SA's motley crew of thugs, bullies and faggots. He believed that black had a slimming effect, drawing attention away from what his enemies called his "womanly and un-Germanic" hips. He knew that Karl Wolff was the one who had first said that. He had built up quite a dossier on Wolff and one day he would use it. Even Heinrich Himmler wouldn't be able to protect his adjutant forever.

Reinhard Tristan Hoch smiled, making his lips thin as he did so. Being head of intelligence for the SS had its advantages. He hoped he would be the one to wield the sword when Wolff was stretched out on the sacred altar at Wewelsburg Castle, his neck the target.

Hoch put on his black tunic with silver piping and buttoned it. He turned around and looked back over his shoulder at his reflection and approved of what he saw. Yes, the tunic masked his flawed hips. A good Berlin tailor could work wonders, even one like that Jew Jacoby. He rubbed the toe of his knee-high black calfskin leather boot against the back of his pant leg to remove a small smudge, as he placed his black peaked hat on his head and pulled the bill down well in front, centering the hat as he did so.

It was time for his weekly meeting with the leader of the SS, the former gentleman farmer who used to raise chickens and now held Hoch's future in his hands. Heinrich Himmler.

HUGE red swastika flags hung from staffs across the entire façade of the Brown House. Hoch walked up the steps and paused as two black-uniformed SS men opened the great bronze doors, nearly fifteen feet high. Inside the lobby, Hoch was surrounded by marble. The far wall contained a tablet on which were recorded the names of the thirteen SA men who lost their lives in the 1923 *putsch*. As Hoch ascended the grand staircase to Himmler's office, the rich wood paneling, marble floors and heavy silk draperies reflected the Party's wealth and silently mocked its name as a workers' party, let alone a socialist one.

At Himmler's office, Hoch was greeted coldly by Himmler's adjutant, Kurt Wolff. He smiled as he looked down at the slim, fair haired man seated at a rich mahogany desk and thought of the cold steel of a sword slicing through the base of his neck.

"Hoch is here," Wolff said into the phone in a flat tone. Wolff looked up with a bored expression on his face. "You may go in now."

Himmler's office was large, with high ceilings. One wall of the room contained a large tapestry while the wall opposite had several gilt-framed paintings, none of which Hoch recognized. On the wall behind the desk of the Reichsfuhrer SS was an assorted collections of swords, shields and a coat of arms. The desk was easily twice as large as the one manned by Wolff. In the middle of the desk sat a faded red velvet cushion on top of which rested a seven foot-long ancient looking leather case which extended over the edge of both sides of the cushion. It was nearly as long as the desk itself. The case contained an ancient battle spear.

Hoch approached the desk, but the SS chief ignored him, continuing to write on the pad in front of him. Three minutes passed before Himmler looked up and blinked at his visitor through thick pince-nez glasses. His hair was shaved at the sides and back of his head, leaving a dark round island of hair on top. But no amount of barbering could disguise the fact that Himmler's face was a wide oval, more Slavic than Nordic.

"Proceed," Himmler said and, for the next fifteen minutes, Hoch delivered a report on the success of his two-man business extortion squads during the past week; the number of visits; the revenues received; and new sources targeted.

"Excellent," Himmler said when Hoch had finished. "You have done your usual thorough job, Reinhard, for which I congratulate you. Any problems to report?"

"Only one. Sir Archibald Hampton has missed the first two monthly payments which he promised to make after his down payment secured his daughter's release."

Himmler frowned. "Two? That is unfortunate. Never forget, Reinhard. The SS is a knightly order. Sir Archibald's knighthood makes him our brother. But he leaves us no choice. A man who does not keep his word has lost all honor, the most precious thing a man may possess, and so his life is forfeit. Make the necessary arrangements. The privilege of wielding the sword shall be yours."

Hoch put his feet together and made a short formal bow. "Thank you. I am honored."

Himmler gestured dismissively with his hand as if it were not that important and then pointed his finger at the wall behind his desk. "Do you know whose coat of arms that is?"

Hoch didn't.

"Henry I. The Bird Catcher. The first of the great Saxon kings. He was the warrior king who turned back the Magyars from the east. These are the actual swords and shields which he used in battle. They have tasted the blood of his enemies."

Hoch nodded, wondering where all this was leading.

"The tapestry, the paintings. All the artifacts in this room are genuine, with one exception," Himmler said, as he glanced at the spear in the cracked leather case on his desk.

Hoch nodded again, still wondering.

"Some information has recently come to my attention which will permit me, with your help, to complete my collection." Himmler smiled again. "The legal owner of the *heilege* lance will be our Fuhrer, but I shall be the one to hold it in trust."

Himmler rose and walked around from behind his desk. Hoch rose also and waited expectantly. He still didn't know what was going on. "Walk with me," Himmler said, as he left the room and started down the hallway. "I want you to select twenty of your best men, arm and equip them well. Be prepared to depart in less than a fortnight. Tell them their names will live forever when the future history of Germania is written. Not many are afforded during their lifetimes the opportunity for a Grail quest. Fewer still receive the high honor of being chosen to lead the quest. Parsifal was one. Now you. Think of it. The Spear of Destiny. Finding it will make you a legend also, Reinhard. I wish it were me."

"Thank you. I am honored once more," Hoch said but he still had no idea what made Himmler so excited. He resolved to find out. Parsifal? Wasn't that one of Wagner's operas?

"**I DON'T** give a damn about the extortion payments," Wesley Waterman shouted over the telephone at Reinhard Hoch.

Hoch was seated at his small desk in his small office in the Brown House, one tenth the size of Himmler's. The big man's voice on the telephone softened. "I appreciate your gesture, Reinhard, in offering me a share of the ransom Hampton paid for his daughter. I don't want money. I want Hampton's company. I'm paying you well to accomplish that."

"For which I am most grateful, *Herr* Waterman."

Waterman ignored him. "If everything you tell me is correct, his daughter ought to be easier to do business with."

"Actually, she is his stepdaughter. She is a true Aryan and, despite the unpleasant circumstances, I enjoyed our time together. I think you will find you can do business with her."

"Perhaps. I had forgotten that Hampton is not her father. No matter. Her mother was not of good stock. One of Miss Hampton's maternal grandparents was a Jew."

Hoch was surprised. "Are you certain? The Hampton woman has blonde hair, blue eyes and no discernable Jewish features." He made a mental note to have it checked out by the genealogy branch of the SS.

"Quite," Waterman replied. "Harmony Hampton is unquestionably a Jewess. You Germans are such novices when it comes to the science of eugenics. All the important and serious work is being done in America. You have so much to learn from us. We have been sterilizing criminals and mental defectives in the United States since 1907, nearly twenty-five years now. By my count, 49,653 of them. Germany has yet to forcibly sterilize a single person."

"With your help, *Herr* Waterman, that will change in Germany once we come to power,"

"Perhaps," Waterman said, "perhaps not. You Germans may not be as ruthless or efficient at weeding out the weak as we are. I hope you prove me wrong."

Hoch lowered his voice, feigning servility. "I hope so also, *Herr* Waterman."

"Tell me the next steps," Waterman ordered.

"I've sent two of my best men to England. They will escort Sir Archibald back to Germany. Then, we will gather the Knights together and, after a brief ceremony, Sir Archibald will pay the ultimate penalty for betraying his word to a Knight of the SS."

Waterman's voice boomed. "Good. Keep me informed. If you can do this for me, there may be hope for Germany after all."

12.

Protection Money

GOOD Morning, Mr. Cockran!"
Cockran was met by the warm greeting and a hint of surprise
in the receptionist's voice as he stepped off the elevator on the 59th
floor of the Chrysler Building and into the wood-paneled lobby of
Donovan & Raichle. When you worked part-time, people always seemed
surprised to see you. Cockran returned the greeting and headed down
the hall towards his office.

He especially liked the building. When Donovan offered him a
position as "Of Counsel" to the firm—able to accept, reject, even
propose any cases he liked—he'd used the location to help sell it. "I've
got a lease on office space in that new tower Van Alen and Chrysler are
building," he'd said. "They say it'll be the tallest in the world." But a
rival architect was trying to beat Van Alen downtown at 40 Wall Street.
The competition had been exciting—each architect changing plans in
mid-construction in a bid to top the other by inches. It finally ended
when Van Alen secretly constructed a 150 foot steel needle to place
atop the Chrysler Building at the last moment. So, before construction
of John Raskob's Empire State Building was completed in early 1931,
Donovan had been right. They did work in the world's tallest building.

Cockran reached his desk and found a thick folder waiting for him.
He rounded the desk and saw the name of one of the largest New York
law firms on the side and the title "National Business Machines—

Manufacturing Plants/Germany". Then he noticed the sheet of paper lying on top. It was the decision in *Dill v. State of New York*. He picked it up. A *per curiam* decision. No written opinion. The bastards didn't have the guts to tell her why she was being sterilized.

Cockran sat down heavily in his chair and stared at the decision. His bad mood from his fight with Mattie had just gotten worse. He noticed it was a 2-1 vote. The younger judge had dissented, though he didn't write an opinion either. *Coward*, he thought. Cockran balled his hand into a fist until the knuckles turned white. He wanted to hit something. No, he reconsidered, he wanted to hit *someone*, preferably one of those judges. What bothered Cockran the most was that he was powerless to do more. It was the role of a judiciary to stop the state from abusing its power. When it opted not to exercise that role, there was nothing a lawyer could do. That's the way a constitutional democracy was supposed to work. Judges could err, and there was nothing you could do about it. But it was just so wrong, so *goddamned wrong*.

"Bourke?"

Cockran blinked and looked up at Bill Donovan. He hadn't realized how long he had been staring at the decision. "Hi, Bill."

Donovan stood before Cockran's desk, watching him. "I'm sorry," he said.

Cockran nodded, then reached for the decision to put it aside. It was something they were both getting used to. Since joining Donovan's New York firm, Cockran had defended three young women faced with compulsory sterilization and now he'd lost all three cases.

"Have a chance to look at the folder from Churchill?" Donovan asked.

"No," Cockran said. "I just got in."

"It's about time. Office hours start at nine." Donovan said. "We're lawyers, not bankers."

"You knew I had to see Mattie off on the *Graf Zeppelin*." Cockran said, briefly annoyed even though he knew Donovan was only trying to take his mind off Judy Dill.

"I know but in the meantime, half the world's moved on without you." Donovan took the file off Cockran's desk and dumped himself in the chair opposite as he unfastened the strap and lifted the flap on the file folder. He glanced at a few smaller files, then seized upon one. "Here," he said, tossing the file onto Cockran's desk. "This is the skinny on Sir Archibald Hampton."

"This him?" Cockran asked, lifting from the file a portrait photo of a handsome man with silver hair, a strong jaw and a trim mustache.

Donovan nodded. "He's Chairman of the Board and owns a controlling interest in National Business Machines inherited from his American wife. NBM has two plants in Germany. Both are in Munich."

"Business machines?"

"Computing machines. Tabulating. Recording. It's a big industry and growing. Businesses need to keep track of everything. Governments too. NBM is a big player. Not as big as I.C.E. or NCR but big enough."

"So, NBM was doing well?"

"*Was* being the operative word, yes. Their German plants have taken considerable lumps as of late. Emphasis on the lumps, but I'll get to that." Donovan guided Cockran through the folder, explaining that the company was selling a new technology. "Only I.C.E. has anything to compare. Most companies were afraid to invest the kind of money it takes to change an operation. NBM's main clientele were businesses big enough to invest in the equipment, especially new businesses—the kind of companies that had prospered all over Germany with the flood of American investment money after the German economy stabilized in 1925."

"And that dried up after the crash," Cockran said.

"Exactly. After '29, investment money from America slowed to a trickle—and competition in that shrinking market has been brutal."

"I take it this is where the 'trouble' comes in."

"You're smarter than you look, Kid," Donovan said. Cockran grinned, his mood improving. They had met when Cockran was twenty. To Donovan, he would always be a kid.

Donovan flipped through the folder again. "Trouble started small at first—broken treads on the assembly line. Nuts and bolts suddenly go missing, that sort of thing. Takes you just as long to find the problem as it does to fix it. Then the saboteurs upped the ante—began threatening workers and their families. The main Munich plant has had to replace three different foremen in the last three months."

Donovan found another photo and held it up for Cockran to see. The man in the photo had an eye swollen shut and five stitches on a busted cheekbone. "This guy was the factory's night shift foreman since the plant opened in '25. He quit the next day."

Donovan put the picture away. "His replacement lasted two weeks. Had his skull cracked, knocked him into a coma for the next week and a half. And that's nothing compared to what they did to their last night shift foreman."

"What'd they do to him?"

"Ran his hand through some machinery, crushed most of the bones in his right hand."

"And what about the authorities?" Cockran asked. "Have they been any help?"

Donovan laughed. "I'm afraid they have other priorities."

Cockran frowned. "I don't understand. Why wouldn't they be concerned?"

Donovan tossed another file onto his desk. "Take a peek at this one."

Cockran glanced at the label. "Politics?"

"Right." Donovan said. "Political violence in Germany is rampant. Most all political parties have their own shock troops, especially Communists and National Socialists. You've heard Hitler's National Socialists became the second largest party in Germany last fall?"

"Nazis?" Cockran said. "Mattie covered them in the early 20s. Interviewed their leader Hitler before his failed Munich coup. A *Reichswehr* veteran. Enlisted man. Supposedly a great speaker. She's interviewing him again next week. She doesn't like Nazis but she rarely talks about what happened in Munich. Even last summer when they scored a huge upset and became Germany's second largest party, she seemed uncomfortable talking about them."

"There's good reason not to like them," Donovan said. "Nazis promise something for everybody and pander to anti-Semites by blaming the rest on Jews. That's not unusual in Europe, France especially. But the Nazis also have the most highly organized paramilitary forces in the country." Donovan explained, "They regularly use it against Jews and communists but they target businessmen as well.

It's like the rackets here. Protection money. Pay or your business gets hurt. Owney Madden, Dutch Schultz and Al Capone would be right at home. It's how the Nazis make a lot of their money. NBM's German lawyers say the SS is behind it."

"The SS?" Cockran said.

"Hitler's Praetorian guard," Donovan said. He rifled through the folder one more time, talking as he went. "Just last month, the SS pulled off a vicious little operation, even for them. Instead of hitting the Brit's factories or his workers, they went straight for the boss."

"Sir Archibald?"

"His stepdaughter, Harmony. The Nazis kidnapped her." Donovan found what he was looking for and held out another portrait photo. Cockran took it and saw a beautiful young woman, with shoulder length blonde hair, a pert nose and big, round blue eyes.

"Pretty and smart to boot." Donovan said. "Studied at Somerville College in Oxford. She's an instructor there now in art history. She's also a painter herself. Not bad, either, from the looks of it. She's had several local exhibitions and even one in London. A sculptor as well. No exhibits as yet but her nudes are said to be, ah, exceptionally realistic. She went to Berlin to visit her father on the 1:37 train. Never made it off the train. The Nazis snatched her and no one saw anything. Sir Archibald had to cough up plenty to get her back."

Cockran's eyes lingered on the photo as he placed it on his desk. "She's safe now?"

Donovan nodded. "Yes. Apparently unharmed. Look, I hope you take the case," he said. "Germans don't give a damn about Brits, but they do care about Americans especially if they're throwing around the weight of our government. I'll contact the State Department and set up a visit with the American Ambassador and our Consul General in Munich."

As Donovan talked, Cockran's eyes lingered again on the photo of Harmony Hampton, his thoughts drifting to his wife Nora and Ireland in 1922. Violence can come for anyone at any time. Nora had been defenseless when it came for her and he had not been there to keep her safe . Looking at the photo, he felt an urge to keep Harmony safe in a way he hadn't been able to keep other women in his life safe from harm.

Maybe he could help the girl's father. Lord knew he hadn't helped Nora or Judy Dill. Besides, this was Winston asking.

"Well, Bourke?" Donovan asked. "What do you think?"

Cockran looked up. "I'll review the file and let you know. I'm inclined to take it."

"Good lad," Donovan said. "Our usual arrangement on the fee?"

Cockran nodded his agreement.

IT had been dark for several hours by the time Cockran decided to call it a night. He'd spent the entire day poring over the documents in the folder. He placed a note to Donovan on the folder telling him he'd be back in the morning but that he was still inclined to take the case.

His steps echoed throughout the lobby of the Chrysler building as he glanced up at the murals of automobiles and factory workers that covered every inch of the high, vaulted ceilings. The street outside appeared almost deserted. Unusual for 42nd Street. He nodded good-night to the security guard as he put on his brown fedora, making his way through the large doors of steel and glass. Once outside, he saw a few automobiles, but no taxis. He had given his chauffeur Jimmy the night off. He crossed the street and turned west towards Grand Central, hoping for a taxi on Park Avenue. As he walked, he angled his head up to look at the glistening spire of the Chrysler building, something he always did on the way home from his office. It looked like a sparkling flute of champagne in the sky. Who gives a damn if the Empire State Building's taller, Cockran thought. It wasn't beautiful. His building was.

The sky was clear which meant good flying weather tomorrow. He'd promised Paddy a ride after school the next day in his new PCA 2 Pitcairn-Cierva autogiro which he had purchased the previous fall, ostensibly to fly him to weekend sports car races. In truth, he just loved to fly almost as much as racing his Auburn boat-tailed speedster. The PCA 2's passenger compartment held two and Patrick was bringing his best friend Michael Darrow and they were the envy of their classmates as a consequence.

Suddenly, he sensed movement in his periphery, off to the left. He brought his eyes down—just in time to see a short, stocky man with a soft cap pulled low over his forehead rushing toward him. Cockran turned to face him—but another pair of hands grabbed him instead from his right side. He felt the pressure of a pistol against his ribs, while the stocky man quickly added a second pistol to his left rib cage.

"Trouble finding a taxi?" the stocky man asked, his Irish accent clear.

Cockran's face flushed at his inattention as he sized up the situation. He could see now that they were young, barely in their twenties. When they began pushing Cockran towards a long black Oldsmobile, he kept his temper in check and rejected making a move now. That could wait. It was something other than a mugging and Cockran wanted to know who had sent them and why. He took additional comfort in the fact he had his .45 caliber service automatic in a shoulder holster, something he had done regularly once unemployment soared in the wake of the crash in '29. Hard times make for hard people but only fools walked the streets unarmed at night.

Cockran told himself to remain calm as they pushed him into the motorcar. He had to be patient but he knew his temper could change that balance like the flash of a light bulb. He took a deep breath. Once inside, the stocky kid took the lead. "We'd be liking a few words with you, is all, Mr. Cockran. National Business Machines is not a good client for your health. I think you'll be wanting to reconsider your decision to take this case."

Cockran smiled in surprise. How the hell did they know that when he hadn't even told NBM he would take on the case? Yet here was a dumb mick trying to change his mind with a gun. That didn't work with Cockran. *There's only one way to deal with men who talk with guns — speak their own language.* His old friend Michael Collins taught him that. One of his "Rules". Mick. The Big Fella. The man who freed Ireland from the British in 1921, now dead nearly nine years. Cockran intended to follow that rule when the time was right and that wasn't far away. Still, he'd like to know who'd hired these two bozos.

"You think this is funny?" the stocky man said. Cockran hadn't realized he was still smiling. "You won't think it's so funny when Billy cracks your knee cap. Maybe he even pays a wee visit to your son and makes him a cripple just like his Da."

Cockran stopped smiling. His captor mistook the smile's absence for fear. "There's a smart boyo," the man said. He waved his pistol in Cockran's face and looked over to Billy. "Now, wasn't I telling ya lawyers were smart fellas?"

Cockran felt blood rushing to his face again. He saw Billy had put his gun away, apparently thinking one was enough to cow Cockran. Threaten his son? Fuck patience!

The stocky kid leaned towards the driver, facing forward. "Pull over at the next block,"

Cockran swung his left elbow at the stocky man's temple—only the man had turned back to say something. It was the wrong moment and Cockran's elbow plowed into the man's nose instead, which made a sudden popping sound, followed by a startled cry. The man reached for his face with both hands, his gun dropping to the floor. The quiet one froze for a moment, startled by the sickening noise. By the time he made a move to grab him, Cockran had freed his service .45 from its holster and raised it to meet the boy's forehead. He brought his free hand around to seize the boy's right hand and stop it from going to his gun.

"Don't even think about it, Billy," Cockran said. "You'll live longer."

The quiet one stayed quiet, but Cockran could hear the stocky man moaning as the pain quickly registered. Cockran had to move fast. He had meant to knock the stocky man unconscious but the awkward blow left his hand feeling slightly numb. Cockran let go of Billy's hand and reached inside the boy's coat for his holstered .38 pistol. It felt soft in his half-numbed hand. He gripped it as best he could and shoved the barrel into the stocky man's stomach.

The driver was next. "Pull the car to the curb right now or I'll kill them both." Cockran said in a cold voice. "Keep your hands on the wheel or you'll die too." He felt the car pulling to one side. The stocky man was still moaning and clasping his nose with both hands.

The motor car came to a stop against the curb and Cockran kept his .45 close enough to the quiet one's forehead to keep the boy honest. "Get out," Cockran said. "Facing me." The boy did as he was told, fumbling behind him for the door and backing out. Once he was out, Cockran let himself glance at the driver—both hands were on the wheel, as told—then at the stocky man. His hands covered his face and they were stained with blood from his shattered nose. The man seemed oblivious to the gun Cockran had stuffed in his belly, so Cockran pulled it back. He pushed himself out the door using his numbed left hand to steady himself.

Cockran finally got a good look at the quiet one once he was out of the car. He was big. Real big. How did I miss that? Cockran thought. Good thing he drew the .45, when he did. Otherwise, it would have taken more than a little effort to cut him down to size.

"Tell whoever sent you that no one threatens me—or my family," Cockran said and paused, "unless they want to deal with Bobby Sullivan." The quiet one's face grew pale. "You ever hear of Bobby Sullivan?" Cockran asked

He nodded. "Yes, sir."

"If anything ever happens to my son, if he so much as trips and skins a knee, I'll tell Bobby it was you two who did it. Got it?"

His eyes grew wide. He gulped. "Yes… yes sir, Mr. Cockran," the boy said, his voice now an octave higher.

"Get out of here."

The boy got in the car and shut the door behind him. Cockran watched the car drive away, down Park Avenue. When it was five blocks away, Cockran relaxed, shoved the extra pistol into his jacket pocket, and then holstered his .45. As the adrenaline faded, his left elbow began to throb quietly, and he rubbed it. *Smooth, Cockran*, he thought. *Real smooth.* He was more out of practice than he had thought. His old instructors at MID would have chewed his ass over tonight's performance. Still, one thing was clear now that he had decided to take Hampton's case.

It was time to call Bobby Sullivan.

13.

Dinner in the Clouds

On Board the Graf Zeppelin
Tuesday, 26 May 1931

MATTIE looked down out the window of her small cabin, hoping she had caught Cockran's eye when she waved as the airship rose silently into the sky, faces below fading into   dots. She sat on the cushioned surface which later that day would convert to her sleeping berth.

Mattie had wanted to cry when she said goodbye to Cockran because they hadn't made up from their two arguments. But she didn't. Mattie rarely let anyone see her cry, not even Cockran. She had decided that early on, in her first job at the *Daily Mirror*. She knew men considered it a sign of weakness. But her father taught her to never consider herself the weaker sex. Girls could be as tough as boys. Now, alone in her cabin, she did cry, sobbing softly at the thought their arguments had not ended in the usual way—one of them making the other laugh. This wasn't what she had wanted. She wished she could take back almost everything she had said, especially about Patrick. She might not be able to openly admit it, but there were times when she wished she were his mother. Times when she longed to be part of a family again.

Cockran really cared. She knew that and she was impressed he had so much insight into her. That he knew how much her work was connected to her family. Making her father proud; avenging her brothers and her late fiance Eric. But the way he had presented it last night was new. It made her feel like he was asking her to choose between him and her memory of them. He couldn't expect her to choose between her past and her present. They were both part of who she was. Besides, he had a past too, his late wife Nora who would always be the love of his life. Mattie knew that and she loved him all the more for it. She would never make him choose.

Being in love was more trouble than she imagined. She had been in love only once before, but that was a lifetime ago. She'd been so young, only eighteen, and Eric had been but three years older. They had been engaged that summer and he died that fall at Ypres in the last days of that bloody war. She couldn't bring herself to call it the Great War. It was a brutal, meaningless war as far as she was concerned. A war which took both her brothers, her fiancé and her mother a year later during the world-wide flu epidemic. Only her father had survived the war and then he too was gone, killed by a hit and run motorcar as he hiked on a twisting road near their Highlands retreat across from the Isle of Skye. She was left alone, as if abandoned by a vengeful God in whom she found it increasingly hard to believe, at least not in the way her father had.

Mattie closed her eyes and took a deep breath. She had work to do. She emptied the overstuffed manila envelope Hearst had given her the day before and began to read.

Two hours later Mattie had worked her way through the Hearst clippings up to August, 1930, less than a year ago. The National Socialists were still obscure then. Only twelve seats in the Reichstag. But they were prosperous and spent as much money as the ruling Social Democrats, the Communists, or the various right-wing nationalist parties. And they did so more effectively. As one left-wing journalist noted, "None of the party election machines works with one-tenth of the wit and resourcefulness that are employed by the advertising and P.R. departments of dozens of factories, stores and fashion designers. Except, that is, the National Socialist Workers Party, whose P.R. department is the equal of any commercial concern and displays Hitler in a variety of heroic poses under the campaign slogan, 'Hitler Over Germany'."

Mattie was surprised to note, in reading several of Hitler's speeches during the 1930 campaign, that, in contrast to 1923, Hitler never attacked the Jews and never appealed to any narrow special interests, whether it be farmers, factory workers, Catholics, Protestants, white-collar workers, or the upper class. Rather, Hitler rose above all that, calling on them as Germans to create a new society where their country was more important than their individual interests. It was in many respects a positive message. The vicious gutter-level attacks on the Jews, of which there were plenty, came from lesser functionaries like Goebbels, Hess, and Heinrich Himmler who spoke to the party faithful while Hitler took the high road with everyone else.

The Nazis even chartered a private aircraft for Hitler so that he gave as many as four to five speeches a day throughout the country, giving truth to the "Hitler Over Germany" slogan as he flew from one cheering crowd to another. It paid off, because on election day, the Nazis jumped from twelve seats in the Reichstag to one hundred and seven, making them the second largest party in Germany. Now Mattie understood. There had been over two million unemployed workers in Germany in late 1930. In her experience watching *coups d'état* in many countries, unprincipled politicians were the ones who usually benefited from a bad economy.

It had been that way for Germany in 1923, she knew, only it had been runaway inflation deliberately fostered by the government rather than the high unemployment of today. All the Nazis had then, she thought, was armed force, not the power of the ballot box. Today they had both, an inflammable and unnatural combination for an opposition party in a democracy.

Munich
Wednesday, 7 November 1923

"I DON'T understand," Mattie said once the music stopped. "Explain it to me again, Ernst. What does a nice Harvard boy like you see in Hitler? I've only met him twice. I grant you my German isn't as good as I would like, but he seems to me just another beer hall agitator."

"Please, call me Putzi," a perspiring Ernst Hanfstaengl said as he stood up from the bench of the grand piano on which he had just finished one of Beethoven's piano sonatas, and bowed stiffly from the waist at the polite applause from his guests.

The room was filled with attractive women in evening gowns and men in tuxedos. White-coated servants circulated, serving drinks and hors d'oeuvres. Hanfstaengl was one of the more distinguished men there, Mattie thought, in white tie and high winged collar. Mattie could tell he was using his height advantage to steal a glance down the low-cut front of her backless silver gown which offered a vivid contrast to her golden red hair and green eyes.

Mattie smiled. Men. It's not as if he hadn't seen her breasts before. The night before actually as, astride his thick waist, she had played her last card. It came up trumps when a spent Putzi had promised to keep her close to the action on the eve of what might well be a *coup d`état* for Bavaria and a big breakout story for her. A brief romp with Putzi was a small price to pay.

"Let me put it in terms of your own country," Putzi said, removing a cigarette from a silver case. "I've read Scottish history. William Wallace was a commoner, not a nobleman. Yet he inspired the Scots to rise up and throw off their English oppressors. Personal courage. An ability to inspire others with his words. I see the same things in Adolf Hitler."

Mattie stood up and smoothed the front of her gown. "That's interesting," she said, "because Herr Hitler doesn't think of himself as a leader."

Hanfstaengl picked up the champagne flute he had placed on top of the piano and took a sip. "I'm quite sure you're mistaken. Why do you say that?"

Mattie smiled. "I have good sources."

A frown flashed across Hanfstaengl's face. "As a journalist, Mattie, you must realize," he said stiffly, "that all great men have their enemies. You can't believe everything you're told."

"Relax, Putzi. My source is reliable. Hitler himself told me he was not a leader nor did he aspire to be one. A drummer is what he believes his role to be. He compared himself to John the Baptist, preparing people for the arrival of a great leader who would avenge the honor of Germany and its betrayal by the November criminals."

Hanfstaengl laughed nervously, taking a shaky drag on his cigarette. "You got me again. You and your little jokes. When did Hitler tell you that?"

Mattie laughed. "Don't worry. It wasn't during my interview the other day. The drummer comment was from my first interview last winter. Why do you ask?"

Hanfstaengl leaned in toward Mattie and lowered his voice. "It is true he once saw himself that way. But no longer. Will you still be in Munich tomorrow?"

"Of course."

"Come to the *Burgerbraukeller*. Eight p.m. You'll be my guest. I'll make sure you have a ringside seat. Tell no one," Hanfstaengl said conspiratorially and placed his index finger by his nose and his sweaty left hand on her bare back, drawing her close and whispering.

"You're very kind, Ernst. Thank you." After last night, she'd bloody well better get a ringside seat.

"Please, call me Putzi. When will I see you again? Later tonight in your room?"

They were still beside the piano and Mattie stiffened as Putzi's hand slowly snaked down her back and below her waist, fondling her bottom through the gossamer-thin silk of her gown.

"Tempting, but not tonight. I'm on deadline. Besides, isn't that your beautiful wife over there wondering what your hand is doing right now? I'll take a rain check." Mattie said as she reached behind her and deftly removed his wandering hand from her bum. A rain check, Mattie thought, that will never be redeemed. She had concluded that last night would be enough to keep her on the Nazi press chief's good side during the next few days.

She smiled to herself when she saw the stunning Mrs. Hanfstaengl leave the room on the arm of a strikingly handsome blond-haired man, unnoticed by her husband. Putzi should spend more time tending the home fires, she thought, as she watched the attractive couple slowly ascend the stairs, the man's arm around the woman's waist, her head resting casually on his shoulder.

On Board the Graf Zeppelin
Tuesday, 26 May 1931

THERE was a tap on her cabin door. Mattie opened it to find a white-coated steward in black trousers who bowed and told her that dinner was served. Mattie hesitated. She was still dressed in her customary travel outfit of a silk blouse and tan wool trousers. She thought briefly of changing to a dress and decided it was too much trouble.

The steward escorted her to her table in a corner of the grand salon adjacent to a window which afforded a magnificent view of the Atlantic Ocean only three hundred feet below. The room was twenty-five by twenty-five feet, with four tables set for dinner, three tables seating six and one seating two. Each table had a view out of the slanting windows on either side. All the tables were full except the one to which the steward took Mattie.

"May I introduce your tablemate for the journey, *Fraulein? Herr* Kurt von Sturm."

Mattie was disappointed. She would have preferred to dine alone. She was still feeling melancholy about Cockran and the last thing she wanted to do was make polite dinner conversation. At least he was easy on the eyes, she thought, as the tall, blond-haired man seated at the table rose to greet her, his deep blue eyes locked onto hers. He was an inch or two over six feet with an athletic body, his pale hair brushed neatly to the side. But for the two-inch scar on his right temple, he would have been almost too handsome. "*Herr* von Sturm, may I introduce *Fraulein* Martha McGary?"

"Pleased to meet you," he said, offering his hand. It was warm and firm.

"My pleasure as well, *Herr* von Sturm" Mattie replied, trying her best to smile even though she wasn't up to the real thing. He seemed familiar but she couldn't place him.

Sturm was dressed in a dinner jacket, a small ribbon bar over the breast pocket, a military decoration, blue on either side and white in the middle with a tiny gold cross. She recognized it at once. As they sat down, Mattie had the irreverent thought that, compared to the diminutive Goebbels and the dumpy, round-faced Himmler, Sturm was the Aryan poster boy the Nazis preached about in their propaganda. Mattie looked around the salon and saw that all the other men had dressed for dinner and the other two women had as well. She made a mental note to break out the silver gown for tomorrow evening.

Sturm asked if she would like a drink and then took the liberty of ordering their *aperitifs,* Pol Roger champagne. She was impressed. Winston's favorite.

Sturm smiled. "You may not recall, but we have met before."

"Really? What were the circumstances?" Mattie asked. She was puzzled. How could she possibly have forgotten meeting a handsome guy like Sturm?

"The summer of '29 in America. My employer and I were guests of Mr. Hearst at his home in California on the occasion of the *Graf Zeppelin*'s voyage around the world. We had tea one afternoon with your president, Mr. Hoover, Mr. Churchill from England, Mr. Hearst, Mr. Cromwell, my business colleague, and one other gentleman whose name I don't recall."

"My goodness," Mattie said. "I'm embarrassed. We did meet. I apologize."

Sturm smiled. "Apologies are unnecessary. I don't recall saying a word that afternoon. I believe President Hoover, Mr. Churchill and Mr. Hearst did most of the talking. A beautiful woman like you, however, need say nothing and would still be remembered."

Mattie laughed. The guy was smooth. Ordinarily she would never have forgotten but it was the first time she had met Herbert Hoover. The other man whose name Sturm couldn't recall was Cockran, and their romance had barely been a week old. She smiled. Kurt was handsome, a Norse god even, but he was no Bourke Cockran with that crooked grin and boyish smile. She had been besotted with him back then in those early days and still was now.

"I saw you again at the reception in Los Angeles for the crew of the *Graf Zeppelin.* I noticed your photographs that morning in the *Herald-Examiner* of the Long Beach warehouse explosion. They were quite spectacular. Breathtaking. But to take such exceptional photographs must have placed you in great danger. I had wanted to congratulate you at the time, but let me do so now. We were only briefly introduced, but I had never before met someone so brave and so beautiful and also so talented."

Mattie rolled her eyes. That was laying it on thick but no girl ever gets tired of being told she's beautiful. "Thank you. A wise man once told me 'If your photos aren't good enough, you're not close enough.' But tell me *Herr* von Sturm, what is it that you do for a living?"

"Please, *Fraulein*, call me Kurt."

"I'm Mattie," she said and then he smiled. She liked men who thought her beautiful. He was certainly taking her mind off Cockran and, right now, that was good.

"I'm the executive assistant to the president of a large German steel company."

A steward approached. "Our first course, *Herr Käpitanleutenant*, is vichyssoise."

"*Herr Käpitanleutenant?*" Mattie asked. "I thought you were a businessman."

"Hans served with me in the war."

Mattie paused for a moment before she spoke. She knew men usually didn't talk about what they did in the war, especially if they had been in combat and a genuine hero like this man. But with all she had lost in the war, she felt like a fellow survivor. Still, she prodded gently. "I should have known. I noticed the military ribbon on your dinner jacket. What is it?" Mattie asked, knowing full well what it was.

Sturm smiled. " Others were equally deserving."

"But it *is* the Blue Max, isn't it? Imperial Germany's highest honor? Like our Victoria Cross and America's Medal of Honor?"

Sturm stiffened. "I am not familiar with other countries' military decorations."

"What service were you in?"

"I flew naval airships."

"Like the ones that bombed London and Paris?"

Sturm didn't reply right away and Mattie regretted putting him on the spot. When he finally spoke, it was slowly, almost reluctantly. "I flew on three airships which conducted bombing runs to your homeland. The last one I commanded myself. Hans served with me on all three ships. He can attest that we never dropped bombs in populated areas. We did so only on military or industrial targets. Even if it meant coming home with full bomb racks."

"Forgive me. I should know better than to ask questions about the war. No one who was there likes to talk about it. I am sorry I asked the question."

"Don't be sorry. We were on different sides and it was a natural question. I am proud of my service and I have no apologies to make. But I know that airships as grand as this are not well suited as instruments of war and never were. Do you remember what Hugo Eckener said at the luncheon ceremony honoring the crew of the *Graf Zeppelin*? I had heard Hugo speak like this many times and I know it by heart: 'Due to its light construction and the vulnerability inherent in its large size, the *Graf Zeppelin* can thrive and exist only in an atmosphere of unclouded peace. It is like one of those opalescent butterflies, which fascinate as they flutter in the summer sunshine, but seek a sheltered corner whenever a storm blows up. Often, when people greet it so enthusiastically as it appears in the heavens, I have felt as if they believed they were seeing in it a sign and symbol of the universal dream of lasting peace among peoples.'"

Mattie smiled. "I remember that. It was very moving. Certainly airships filled with hydrogen are no weapons of war. How did you come to serve on airships?"

"My father."

Mattie was puzzled. "Your father sent you off to fly airships? How did that happen?"

"I asked; my mother said no; and eventually my father brought her around. After that it was easy."

"Your father must have had a lot of influence to get you into such an elite outfit."

"In a manner of speaking, I suppose he did," Sturm replied, pausing while the fish course was served, Dover sole, and a chilled bottle of Moselle uncorked by the steward.

Mattie nodded but said nothing, a technique she had picked up from Cockran. An old lawyer's trick. Silence. Many people are uncomfortable with silence in a conversation and after awhile will fill it, often saying more than they intended. It worked with Sturm. He focused his eyes over Mattie's left shoulder as if he were staring out to sea and finally turned back.

"My father was Peter Strasser," he finally said.

"I'm sorry, the name is not familiar," Mattie said.

"My father was head of the Imperial German Naval Airship Service. He was Germany's most decorated naval officer. He died in the war."

"A zeppelin crash?"

"Of sorts. We were flying in a group of six of our newest airships, the 'height-climbers' designed to fly above twenty thousand feet to evade British aircraft. My father was in the lead ship and, unfortunately, the British had made advances in their aircraft as well. His zeppelin was shot down. But it never crashed. It burned and disintegrated before it ever reached the ground. They gave him the Blue Max posthumously. It's his ribbon I wear, not mine. Mine is somewhere in a drawer. But my father's ribbon is always with me."

Mattie was horrified. "I'm so sorry," she said reaching out to place her hand over Sturm's. "Please forgive me for raising such a painful subject. I had no idea."

Sturm briefly put his hand warmly over hers. "No apologies are necessary. You had no way of knowing. My father has been with me since I boarded this ship. I can't think of zeppelins, let alone fly in them, without my father's memory at my side."

The steward was back, serving the main course, pork tenderloin medallions, potato pancakes and sauerkraut along with an excellent red Rhone, Chauteauneuf du Pape.

"This meal is delicious," Mattie said. "As good as any on an ocean liner."

STURM was surprised that Mattie had managed to draw him out about his father, let alone the fact that it was his father's ribbon, not his own Blue Max, which was his constant companion. No one else knew that. Until now. He almost never talked about his father , and certainly not about the horrific circumstances of his death which Kurt had witnessed.

The McGary woman was indeed as beautiful as he had remembered, both in Munich and in California. And with brains to match her beauty. Worthy prey indeed. A long silence followed as they ate, giving her the opportunity to recover from her embarrassment over his father's death, Sturm could have predicted her next question.

"Forgive me for asking, but why is your name Sturm, not Strasser?"

Sturm paused. "It's a long story and might bore you. Would you like the short version?"

"I can't imagine you being boring, but sure, let's have the short version."

"Is this off the record? I wouldn't want any of this to appear in Hearst's newspapers."

"Of course. It's off the record. A talk between friends. Nothing more."

Friends already? Sturm thought this was a promising start. He leaned closer to her.

"I'm a wanted man in Germany for crimes I committed over ten years ago. Property was destroyed and men who tried to stop us were killed. Arrest warrants were issued and I am a dangerous fugitive who changed his name to avoid arrest," Sturm said and then leaned back.

Mattie laughed. "You're joking. Now you must give me the long version."

Sturm paused. Mattie was still leaning forward. There was a risk in telling her the full story but it was minimal. No German government in its right mind would dare arrest and try him today. He poured them both another glass of wine and leaned closer.

"It was after the war," Sturm began in a low voice, "and the Allies had awarded to themselves all eighteen of our naval airships as reparations."

Sturm could see it now as he told the story to Mattie. It was the night of 23 June 1919. Only eighteen zeppelins had survived the war, standing silently in their sheds at Nordholz and Wittmundhaven, awaiting delivery to the victorious Allies. Two days earlier, in a daring act of sabotage, the officers of the German High Seas Fleet interned at Scapa Flow in Scotland opened the sea valves of their ships, sinking them all. Sturm persuaded his fellow naval airshipmen to emulate the bravery of their seafaring brothers. They split themselves into two teams of ten men each, Sturm taking the group assigned to Wittmundhaven, only a few kilometers from the North Sea and the barrier islands of the East Friesians.

When the sun rose the next morning over Wittmundhaven, all eight of the great zeppelins had been destroyed in vast explosions, leaving them a twisted mass of blackened duralumin. All the unprepared Allied sentries were dead, their throats cut, something he did not tell Mattie. The scene was duplicated simultaneously at Nordholz. Notwithstanding the Blue Max the military had awarded him for his valor that night and for the whole of his earlier wartime service, a warrant was issued for his arrest by the new Socialist government in Germany several months later. Forewarned, Kurt changed his name from von Strasser to von Sturm and, courtesy of an introduction from Hugo Eckener, went to work for Fritz von Thyssen, the head of Germany's largest steelworks, and also known to Sturm as "Berlin", a key member of the Geneva Group, something else he did not tell Mattie. Germany took care of its heroes, even if its spineless Socialist government did not.

"That's an amazing story," Mattie said. "I'd love to be able to write it someday."

Sturm stiffened at hearing this but Mattie quickly reassured him, putting her hand over his. "But you have my word. It stays with us."

Sturm relaxed and poured the last of the wine into each of their glasses. "But enough serious talk for tonight. What are your plans for tomorrow?"

"Reading, mostly. There's not a lot to do around here other than meals. Perhaps some photographs if we see something interesting."

"I can arrange something interesting for you to photograph. How would you like a tour of the interior of the *Graf Zeppelin*? From stem to stern?"

"Is that possible?"

"The zeppelin commander, Max Pruss, flew with my father. It won't be a problem."

"Swell. I accept. I can't wait."

Sturm and Mattie rose from the table. Mattie reached out a hand to say goodnight which Sturm clasped and brought briefly to his lips.

"Thank you for a delightful evening."

"Thank you as well. I enjoyed myself."

"I assure you, the pleasure was all mine. See you tomorrow morning," Sturm said. And certainly tomorrow evening as well, he thought. Tonight had gone well. The prey unaware, the hunter closing in.

14.

Bobby Sullivan

New York City
Tuesday, 26 May 1931
Evening

MOST people passed Bobby Sullivan on the street and paid him no mind. If they did, they might have assumed that he had once been a prize fighter, taking in a broken nose, curly dark hair, and a wiry athletic build on his nearly six foot frame. Unremarkable and unnoticed except for the coldest blue eyes Cockran had even seen. Most people who saw those eyes would avert their gaze, hoping he wouldn't look at them again.

Cockran sat across from Sullivan and two pints of stout in an Irish speakeasy in Hell's Kitchen. He'd placed his call to Sullivan the moment he reached his townhouse.

"Two men?" Sullivan asked.

"Three, counting the driver," Cockran said.

"Armed?"

"Two were. Not sure about the driver."

"Took a swing at them, did you?" Cockran nodded yes. "Not too smart." Sullivan said and brushed his dark hair away from his forehead, his lecture concluded. "How's your elbow?"

"Better than his nose," Cockran said.

"Threatened your boy?" Sullivan asked as Cockran took a sip and nodded again. "A mistake to make you angry. Better to do it my way. Never get mad. Get even."

Cockran couldn't be sure and would never ask, but he suspected he was Sullivan's only friend in America. Sullivan was new to America, but Cockran had known him, or rather, known of him, since 1920. That was shortly after Cockran arrived in Dublin as Hearst's chief European correspondent and first met Michael Collins. At the time, Collins was a flesh and blood legend, systematically dismantling the British intelligence network in Ireland, one body at a time. The most wanted man in Ireland and the most elusive, with the biggest price on his head.

Bobby Sullivan was Collins' most feared assassin in what Collins called his "squad", popularly dubbed "The Apostles" when their number reached twelve. The British had other names for them. Hit men. A murder gang. For once, the Brits were pretty close to being right.

Recruited at age seventeen, Sullivan had killed ten men before he was nineteen. In those days, Cockran and Sullivan seemingly had little in common. Sullivan the assassin, Cockran the journalist. But Cockran had killed before both during and after the war as an Army MID agent. He had left all that behind by the time he met Sullivan. He had been the peaceful go-between who brought together Michael Collins and his father's old friend Winston Churchill, the new British Colonial Secretary, contacts which eventually led to freedom for the Irish Free State.

Their relationship began in the summer of 1922 when Eamon de Valera and the IRA looked freedom in the face and refused to accept it. In the Irish civil war that followed, Cockran's young wife, Nora, had been one of the first victims, abducted during an IRA bank robbery, then raped and murdered. Something quite similar and horrific had happened to Sullivan's older sister, but she had been permitted to live, only to be abandoned by her husband.

At the time, Cockran and Sullivan didn't know that women close to them had been harmed by the same men. Both had waited a long time for revenge—seven years. Two summers ago, old enemies of Ireland resurfaced with a gun-running operation in America, a prelude to an IRA *coup d'etat* in the young Irish Free State. Bobby Sullivan and quite a few from Collins' old squad had traveled to America and joined forces with Cockran and Winston Churchill to stop the operation. Fortuitously for Cockran and Sullivan, it included the men responsible for the harm done to Sullivan's sister and Cockran's wife. Grimly, they had killed those responsible. It left them friends. Afterwards, Sullivan stayed in America and Cockran had used what remained of his late father's political influence to help Sullivan secure a New York state private investigator's license.

Cockran supposed that Sullivan actually did things from time to time which private dicks did. But that wasn't why the big man had turned pale last night at the mention of Bobby's name. Even the Irish mob boss Owney Madden wanted to keep on Sullivan's good side. Bobby took the occasional free lance assignment from Madden. Not as many as were offered and not as many as Owney would have liked. Bobby Sullivan could be very selective about whom he killed.

"These lads," Sullivan said. "One short? One big?"

Cockran nodded. "You know them?"

"Aye," he said. "Little Colin and Big Billy. T'was me who trained them as bodyguards."

"They weren't guarding anybody."

"Doesn't sound like it," he said and smiled. "Lucky for you they were slow learners."

Cockran laughed. "You know better. Lucky for them I wasn't in a bad mood." He couldn't tell if Bobby was apologizing. But he knew this was as close as it got. "I may need your services. I've got a new client." Sullivan listened while Cockran talked.

"So, what do you think?" Cockran asked after he had finished explaining to Sullivan the sabotage at the two plants owned by Sir Archibald Hampton's company in Germany.

"You'll pay for a first class steamship ticket to Germany?"

"Yep. First thing tomorrow. Paddy and I leave Sunday. I'll wire you there."

"And, after Munich, a side trip to Ireland on the way home?"

Cockran nodded. "You'll have a few days to check things out there before we arrive."

Sullivan shrugged. "Owney won't be happy. He has a couple of jobs lined up for me on the West Coast, but sod him. I've never been to Germany."

"Thanks. I appreciate it," Cockran said. He was pleased. *Diplomacy without a credible threat of force is like Guinness without a creamy head. No one pays attention.* That was one where even Churchill agreed with the Big Fella's rules.

"'Tis nothing. But I have one question."

"Go ahead," Cockran said.

"How long will you keep my hands tied in Germany?"

Cockran shook his head. The two men were a lot alike but their differences ran deep.

"How long, Bourke?"

"When I decide that German law can't protect NBM's factories there."

"Does it look like I went to fucking University?" Sullivan said. "Spell it out."

Cockran grinned. "I think you understand me fine. You just don't like it."

"I don't mind," Sullivan said. " 'Tis your assignment. Only the law never much concerned the Big Fella when he had me hunt down Black and Tans on the streets of Dublin."

"No, you're wrong. Mick had great respect for the law," Cockran said, sipping at his Guinness. "*Irish* law. The Black and Tans were agents of an occupying army that was never there with the consent of the governed. They were legitimate targets."

"Good," Sullivan said. "I hadn't been losing sleep over it, but it's nice to know."

"You know my rules. Never initiate force except in self-defense. That's key. Men have a right to defend themselves and what they own. So do companies and so will we."

Cockran knew that Sullivan never waited for someone to hit him first. If you were a threat to him or anyone under his protection, that was all he needed. And that was where he and Sullivan differed. Cockran's father had been a lawyer and instilled in his son a respect for the rule of law, not men. Cockran agreed with his father. Up to a point. But the rule of law was still administered by men—and when men failed or refused to do so, Cockran could be as cold and ruthless as his blue-eyed friend who sat expectantly in front of him.

Cockran's own philosophy came from both his lawyer father and Michael Collins. Neither man entirely trusted governments. Cockran shared that mistrust. "Governments create nothing," his father always said. "They have nothing to give but what they have first taken away from others." Where his father differed from Collins was what to do when a government took something from you or yours or did not provide the protection it promised. Cockran's father would accept a court's verdict. Collins wouldn't.

"Here is where you and I part company." Cockran said. "The rule of law defends what men own. That includes the NBM factories that Sir Archibald owns in Germany. We use no force, except in self-defense, until it is clear the German government has failed or refuses to defend NBM. Until that point, even if it seems right to you, we do not initiate the use of force."

"And aren't you a regular Marquis of Queensberry? I don't remember you waiting for the courts to make a decision when the Big Fella gave you that list with the three names on it."

Cockran shook his head slowly. Bobby damned well knew that Cockran hadn't been acting as a lawyer during the deadly Irish civil war back in 1922, a war that imperiled the Irish Free State's hard-won liberty. That summer, Bourke Cockran had been an avenging angel ready to kill anyone remotely related to those responsible for his young wife's murder. Collins had used Cockran's rage and grief to recruit him to carry the Irish civil war to America to eliminate the three IRA paymasters in America—their top fund raisers and bankers. Sullivan had been there with Mick Collins in a back room at McDaid's Pub in Dublin and had passed across the scarred table a Webley revolver in a paper sack. Cockran had been the last assassin Collins recruited. The last Apostle. It was a bloody summer. Collins himself was assassinated by the IRA in his home county of Cork. So were the three IRA bankers in America. But the death of Cockran's wife had not been avenged. Not then.

It was a hard memory, one he didn't like to dwell on.

"It's not the same. The IRA bankers weren't breaking the law in America but they were enemies of the Irish Free State in a time of war. I can argue that they were legitimate targets because their purchase of arms would have led to the killing of more innocents in Ireland. The government in America wouldn't stop them. I did." Cockran drained his

Guinness. "But we both know that's not why I did it. I was an assassin, nothing more. You and Mattie are the only ones who know that. I won't be playing a role like that ever again. Once was enough."

Sullivan didn't respond but stared at him with those cold blue eyes. Did he believe Cockran would never do that again? Or was he simply aware that he had touched a raw nerve he shouldn't have? It didn't matter to Cockran. He just had to follow Cockran's rules. "The country we're in makes no difference. So long as its government is just and honest, we let the courts decide and, in the end, we abide by what they say. Due process. But when people place themselves above the law and governments do nothing to stop them, then all bets are off."

Sullivan grinned, never a pretty sight. "We get them first."

"Those are the times when St. Thomas Aquinas says that's OK. I didn't always fully appreciate that but Mattie helped me work it out. And she's not even a Catholic."

"And far better than your sorry Irish arse deserves," Sullivan replied. "Keep me posted."

"What? About Mattie?"

"No. Just tell me when you and St. Thomas decide you're ready to untie my hands in Germany. Based on what you told me about our client and those Nazi thugs, I'd be thanking you if it were sooner rather than later."

15.

Peril in the Clouds

On Board the Graf Zeppelin
Wednesday, 27 May 1931

THE *Graf Zeppelin*'s interior took Mattie's breath away. She had always been fascinated by the complexity of man-made creations and attempted to portray that in her photographs. Factories with their assembly lines, steel mills and molten metal, dams and their huge hydroelectric generators. In her private moments, she admitted to herself, if to no one else, that Margaret Bourke-White had done it first and, truth be told, done it better than Mattie. But Mattie's photographs of industrial scenes were pretty damn good. When she wasn't taking photos to illustrate her stories, photography was an avocation, a way to relax. Well, maybe it was a bit difficult to relax when you're on a catwalk fifty feet above a huge pot of molten metal in the process of being poured. But nothing had prepared her for this.

Mattie stood inside an immense cathedral in the sky, the duralumin girders and bracing wires were like a huge spider web extending the length of the ship. The outer skin of the airship was translucent so that the light glowing in and around the sixteen huge gas cells lining the ship's interior between the girders and wires made her appreciate the immense sense of space. It was like nothing else she had ever seen, nothing else ever built by man. Mattie was walking on a catwalk which ran along the base of the ship, stopping every ten feet or so to take photographs. She was wearing a pair of cotton and canvas slippers that were designed specifically for use on zeppelins to avoid generating any sparks. The zeppelin's catwalk was barely two feet wide and formed the base of an inverted triangle so that the duralumin girders flared out on either side of her, the triangle's top two feet above her head.

Sturm took her the entire length of the ship. She was surprised at how many men were at work wherever she walked, taking photographs as she went. The men were high on the framework, adjusting the tension of wires, tending to the large Maybach engines. She even saw men sewing and splicing fabric as if they were making a sail.

"What are those men doing?" Mattie asked.

"You can't see it because the gas cells block the view, but there's a small tear in the ship's outer canvas fabric. The canvas is coated with a mixture of resins and aluminum flakes which gives it a silvery appearance. These men are stitching together a patch. Once they have it the right size, they'll climb up the vertical ladder closest to the tear. Then, using harnesses and cables, they will lower a rigger over the outer skin of the ship until he reaches the tear. He will slash the torn fabric away and then, like a seamstress, he will sew the patch into place."

"That sounds dangerous."

Sturm smiled. "Very dangerous. Captain Pruss will slow the ship down from our current cruising speed of eighty miles an hour. Trying to work and sew with hurricane force winds in your face would be impossible."

"Can I watch?" Mattie asked. "I mean photograph the men making the repair of the fabric?" Mattie could see Sturm did not believe this was a good idea.

"I don't think so. The procedure is dangerous enough as it is."

"Please. Two minutes. All I need are two minutes."

Sturm hesitated and looked up. "Well…. One minute. You'll stand on the ladder with just your head and shoulders outside. I will be right behind you, my arms around your waist."

"Great. Just great," Mattie said. "That will be more than enough time." Actually, Mattie knew she would have settled for thirty seconds, which would have given her four, maybe even five photos. Now she had twice as much time.

Inside the hull, there was no sensation of movement through the air, but once she saw the riggers start to climb up inside the vertical ladder leading to the top of the ship's hull, she turned to Sturm, "Have we slowed down yet?"

"The captain started slowing the ship down about five minutes ago. By the time the men reach the top, he will be doing less than twenty miles per hour."

"He? I thought all ships were female."

"Not zeppelins. German airships have always been male. Now, look over there," he said, "the riggers have reached the top. The repair should take no more than thirty minutes. If it takes longer, the riggers will have to come back inside because the ship will have lost too much altitude at twenty miles per hour and the captain will not go closer than a hundred feet to the ocean. When the last of the four-man crew has gone out, we will wait ten minutes. Then you and I will go up the ladder, you first, me behind. Remember, the wind will be very strong."

Mattie climbed the ladder which was enclosed in a tube of canvas and stopped at the top.

"Only your head and arms will go through the hatch," Sturm said. "Take one more step and then wait until I am in position."

Mattie felt Sturm's body push against hers as he came up behind her. She felt both his arms circle around her waist, his strong hands pressing firmly on her stomach, close enough for her to smell the wood and citrus fragrance of his aftershave.

"Now," he said, and, as she poked her head out and up into the air, she felt his arms tighten around her waist, just as the wind hit her. While the airship was barely moving, the wind was gusty and the sight was amazing. Three men were standing along the top of the zeppelin, each wearing broad leather belts tethered to a rope anchored between two hatches along the zeppelin's hull, approximately eighty feet apart. The first two men were playing out additional rope to the third man who stood there, his feet braced, carefully lowering a fourth man down over the side of the hull. That rigger was wearing a shoulder harness as well as a broad belt.

Mattie took one more step so that the upper half of her body was through the opening and she could rest her arms on the airship's surface, providing a steady platform for her Leica. She took several shots of the three men directly in her line of sight and then changed lenses for a close-up of the man over the side, now trying to stitch the fabric over the tear.

Mattie felt Kurt's hands loosen their tight grip around her waist. "Mattie!" he shouted, above the wind. "One of the crew has called to me from below. A jammed winch. Stay here until I return. Don't move. Descending on zeppelin ladders can be difficult."

"All right. I've only got a few more shots anyway."

Mattie watched the three men on top of the airship, each holding onto the rope that held the sewing rigger over the side. Even with her telephoto lens, that rigger was almost lost to view. Suddenly, the man closest to her was pulled off his feet, whether from a gust of wind or a tug from the sewing rigger below, she could not tell. Mattie was paralysed, but only for an instant. She could see now what had knocked the rigger off balance. They were beginning to pull the fourth man up from the side. Mattie heard the noise of the engines increase. The ship must be close to a hundred feet to the ocean surface, she thought, and now they're going higher. As the engine noise rose, the fourth rigger came into view. The man in front of her regained his feet and was braced on the top with the other two, hauling the rigger back up the smooth silvery skin.

For a moment, the rigger in front blocked her view, and Mattie climbed up the four steps and onto the top of the zeppelin, recalling Eisenstadt's advice, "If your photos aren't good enough, you aren't close enough." Hooking her right arm under the rope between the two hatches, holding her camera in both hands, she crept forward on her elbows and knees until she was five feet from the hatch. She had a clear field of vision between the first and second riggers and, using the telephoto lens, shot the last four exposures. Her camera was dangling around her neck and she used both her hands to move back along the rope to safety. She was less than two feet from the ladder's hatch when suddenly the rope started moving. Away from her! Too Fast! She screamed as the rope cut into her bare hands. Instinctively, she let go and she started to slide to the left, the silvery skin of the airship affording no purchase. She hooked her right elbow under the rapidly moving rope, the leather of her jacket protecting her arms, and tried to swing her right leg back up. The hatch was that close. If she could hook her boot inside the hatch, she might be able to save herself. But each time she swung her right leg, it slid smoothly and helplessly back over the slippery surface to its original position. Her right arm was tiring. She didn't know how long she could hang on, especially if that damn rope didn't stop moving soon.

Mattie looked to her left. The fourth rigger was only five feet from the other three men. Mattie gave a start when she felt a big hand clasp hard, painfully hard, into her upper right thigh, while another hand grabbed her leather jacket just above her waist and strong arms began to pull her to safety. She turned to see the face of Kurt von Sturm, the wind blowing his hair straight back, his features hard and cold, with no flicker of emotion, a sharp contrast to the fear in the fourth rigger's eyes that she had captured with her camera as his comrades pulled him up.

Back inside the hatch, the top half of Mattie's body was bent over the zeppelin's hull, her feet firmly planted on a ladder rung, Sturm's hand wedged all the way up between her thighs, holding tight in its original grip. "Step down slowly. One leg at a time until both of your feet are on the next rung. Repeat that until you have both hands on the top rung. Then tell me."

Mattie did so, one leg at a time, aware as she moved each leg of exactly where Sturm's hand was located. But the hand in her crotch never relaxed its grip as she continued to lower herself, step by step, rung by rung, until at last her hands rested firmly on the top rung.

"I'm there. Both hands on the top rung."

Instantly, Sturm's hand relaxed and he pulled it back from between her legs. "Don't move. I'm coming up."

Mattie could feel Sturm move up behind her until his feet were on the same rung, and she felt his hips press firmly into her backside, his arms reaching around her to grasp the ladder's rails, as he put his face over her shoulder and up against hers. His skin felt surprisingly warm against the chill of hers. He spoke directly into her ear.

"I'm going to step down to the next rung where I will hold you by the waist, one leg at a time, each of us in unison, until we are at the bottom. Do you understand?"

"Yes." She said with a tremor in her voice.

"Excellent. On my command, right foot. Left foot. Good. Now repeat."

And so it went until they reached the bottom of the canvas encircled shaft and were standing on the comparative safety of the main catwalk. Later, Mattie was surprised not to receive a lecture from Sturm for her foolishness. Instead, he had merely told her that the interiors of zeppelins could be dangerous places for the inexperienced; that he had gone down to help a crew member free a jammed winch which kept the crew at the other hatchway from using their winch to help reel in the other rigger. No one was intended to hold on to the ropes along the ship's spine in the way she had. He shouldn't have left her alone and he was sorry for that. He said all this in a measured, rational voice in which Mattie detected no emotion. At the time, none of this registered. All she wanted to do was return to her cabin. She needed a drink. Maybe two. She had damn well been close enough and she hoped her photographs were good enough.

MATTIE shimmied into the backless silver gown and then pulled each side of the gown's front up over her breasts, the exposure at each side revealing nearly as much as the low-cut front as she tied it around her neck. Not bad, McGary, she thought, to fit into a ten-year-old gown. She was still shaken from her brush with death but the scotch had dulled the worst of it. She was looking forward to dinner. She felt foolish for having taken such a risk today but, with adrenalin still present in her body, it almost felt like old times when the glow from finishing a dangerous assignment lingered with her back in civilization.

Sturm was wearing black tie again and he rose as the steward escorted Mattie to their table. An image of Cockran, who also looked great in black tie, flashed through her mind.

"Your dress and you are both as beautiful as I remembered," he said.

Mattie looked at him with a quizzical expression. "Remembered?"

"I saw you once in that very gown, or one that was remarkably similar."

"I take this gown everywhere. I had it with me when we were in California, but it's only for evenings. I'm quite certain I wasn't wearing it on the two occasions we were together."

"It wasn't in California," Sturm said and looked away out the window at the ocean below before turning back. "It was at a private residence in Munich. The host was giving a recital. 1923. I remember the date because it was a few days before the National Socialists' *putsch*."

"Really? In whose home?"

"Ernst Hanfstaengl."

"Oh, my goodness!" Mattie said. "Two nights before the *putsch*! Why were you there?"

"I was invited by friends. They wanted me to meet Hitler, but he never came."

Mattie raised her eyebrow. "Yet you remember me after all these years?"

Sturm ducked his head. "You were the only foreigner there. The only one with red hair. Combine that with the dress you were wearing," he gestured with his eyes towards Mattie's décolletage. "Most men would remember you. I tried to find a way to be introduced, but our host, *Herr* Hanfstaengl, appeared to have you monopolized. And none of his friends would interrupt him. I thought of introducing myself, but my English then was very poor." Sturm smiled at her. "I suppose you could say I was too unsure of myself."

"Sure you were," Mattie said. "Just like Germans are known for their sense of humor."

Sturm smiled. "Well, I confess I did turn my attention elsewhere once I saw that an introduction to you was unattainable that evening."

"Well, I hope you enjoyed that evening nonetheless."

"Oh, I assure you, I had a very enjoyable evening. Our host's wife was a delightful and most talented woman and, with you to distract him, her husband never noticed our absence."

"Really? So that was you going up the stairs with Putzi's wife?"

Sturm only smiled. "A gentleman never discusses a matter of the heart with others."

After Captain Pruss furnished a victorola and records, Mattie and Kurt started dancing right before their second bottle of champagne. She was happy that he hadn't held the incident on top of the zeppelin against her. Had it been Cockran, she never would have heard the end of it. Sturm was a graceful dancer, sure of himself and light on his feet. Mattie easily followed where he led. A subtle pressure here and a raised arm there left Mattie with the feeling that she possessed the same skill on the dance floor as he did, something she knew was not true.

There were two other women on board, traveling with their husbands and, for a while, there were three couples dancing in the salon, the other passengers having retired to their cabins. Eventually the other two couples retired, and Mattie took a break, sipping champagne poured from the last of their second bottle and looking at the lights of passing freighters below while Sturm changed the record on the victorola. It was a slow song, popular in America the previous summer. Sturm came over and extended his hand to Mattie. "One last dance."

"Seeing as how there are no other partners available, how can I refuse?" Mattie rose and was struck again by the surreal quality of the evening, dancing in the clouds, three hundred feet above the Atlantic Ocean in the arms of a blond Norse god. Airship travel just might have a future after all. She marveled at how Sturm could move so gracefully around the salon, never brushing the four columns approximately six feet apart and forming a square in the center of salon. Mattie followed Sturm's moves effortlessly as he spun her out and brought her back close, his hand warm against her bare lower back. While dancing, her body relaxed into his and she found sheer pleasure in the movement. She was at one with the movement and the moment.

He brought her close and, instead of spinning her out and bringing her back, he bent his head down and placed his lips on hers and, to her surprise, she returned the kiss and molded her body to his while his hands roamed over her bare back. It seemed to Mattie at the time the most natural thing in the world. She didn't know how long the kiss lasted, but it was impossible not to feel Sturm's growing arousal. Time stood still and only the absence of music and the scratching of the needle on the record brought her back to a reality where her body was equally aroused.

Mattie broke off the kiss, softly pushed him back, and his hands slid smoothly away from her. She could feel her face was flushed and the rest of her body as well. "We really should stop now before this goes further." she said with a smile. "What will the servants say?"

"I apologize," Sturm said, stepping back. "I was carried away. The champagne, the music. Your extraordinary beauty...."

Mattie smiled. "No apologies necessary. But I am in love with someone else and shipboard romances are never a good idea."

Safely back in her cabin, Mattie took a deep breath. She had been electrified by another man's kiss and that scared her about as much as dangling outside the zeppelin earlier in the day. She was in love with Bourke Cockran. What the hell had she been thinking? That was the problem. She hadn't been and her body had been primed to betray her.

Maybe Bourke was right. The adrenalin had certainly worn off by now and she felt wretched about what she had done. That was the problem. She had acted first and thought later, the kiss no different than her impulsive move for a better angle to photograph the zeppelin rigger. She tried to pass the kiss off as gratitude for Kurt saving her life but she gave it up. No, face it, she told herself, she had been strongly attracted to that mysterious blond man and that kiss was proof. She hadn't felt that way so quickly about a man since, well, since she first met Cockran. Thank God, she thought, the voyage would soon be over and there would be no more nights dancing with Kurt von Sturm to tempt her.

Mattie took off her dress, threw on her robe, walked to the loo and washed her face. She was lonely. And barely a day apart from Cockran. She wanted to erase all that happened today and tonight but it wasn't going to be easy. Back in her cabin, she didn't need one, but she fixed a drink anyway and sat at the edge of her bed, staring down at the dim lights of a freighter below. She felt worse now than when she boarded the airship. The thing Cockran didn't understand—or maybe he did— was that after her father had died on that lonely mountain road in Scotland, when the last living member of her family had left this earth, something inside her switched off. The part of her that worried about dying; that cared whether she lived or died. All she had left was her career and for that she would risk almost anything. It made her feel alive. The truth was that when she climbed onto the outside of the zeppelin today, she didn't think for a second about her own safety or that she was risking her life. She had left that part of her behind a long time ago.

Bourke was right. She couldn't give up her career but if she cared at all about him and Paddy—and she loved them both so much—she had to stop being so impulsive, so heedless of danger, so indifferent to the possibility of her own death. She just wasn't sure she knew exactly how to switch that part of her back on.

16.

The Crown Prince

Amsterdam
Friday, 29 May 1931

THE roar of the three engines on the *Lufthansa* trimotor was deafening as the large plane powered down through the clouds on its approach to Schiphol, the Amsterdam aerodrome. Kurt von Sturm made a mental note to take the train back to Berlin. The current generation of airships was not designed to compete with airplanes on short flights from one city to another, but the comfort and quiet of an airship on long journeys would never be challenged by these metal-clad monsters which had to stop and refuel every few hours. An airship flight was more like a train where you could have civilized conversations uninterrupted by the roar of engines.

Sturm stared out the window, still bemused by his failure to seduce his prey. And he had been so close, their kiss long and passionate, her body pressed eagerly to his. Perhaps if he had pushed matters, he may have succeeded. But, he thought, the kiss alone had been worth it.

Sturm's only companion on the Lufthansa flight from Munich to Amsterdam was the folder which German Army Intelligence, courtesy of General von Schleicher, had prepared for Sturm regarding the Kaiser and his son, the Crown Prince. Sturm leafed through its contents. The Kaiser had been in exile in Holland for over eleven years, living at his estate in Doorn in the manner he imagined an English country gentleman would do, a way of life entirely fitting for a grandson of England's Queen Victoria. Rumors of a Hohenzollern restoration had been rife in Germany for years but, according to German intelligence, the Kaiser was not actively behind any of their plots. The old man was a patriot, willing to do his duty if his country called as it now was doing, thanks to the Geneva Group.

The Crown Prince was another story entirely. The men of Geneva did not want a short-term figurehead to replace Hindenburg once he had been eliminated. Trading one aging legend for another would not provide a continuing symbol of Germany's unity. That left the Crown Prince who was no prize. The intelligence dossier on him stated that he drank to excess, was a heavy gambler and had personally broken up four marriages with his womanizing. Though he appeared to have, on the surface, an impressive war record, Sturm noted that the Crown Prince himself had never personally been under enemy fire even if he had issued the orders that sent his units into battle. The Crown Prince did not lead from the front but rather from far behind the fire trenches at his headquarters securely in the rear.

Doorn, Holland

STURM had never met the Kaiser in person. They sat in the Kaiser's study in his large rambling home in the Dutch countryside. The atmosphere was gloomy and oppressive. Dark wood paneling, heavy mahogany furniture, and floor to ceiling drapes which allowed little light to enter the room. The Kaiser wore a heavy Scottish tweed suit and his thinning hair was pure white as was his mustache and neatly-trimmed Van Dyke beard. He looked frail but otherwise in good health, his cheeks pink and the rest of his complexion ruddy, reflecting that he spent much time out of doors, tending the formal gardens side-by-side with the gardener.

The complexion of the Crown Prince was equally ruddy but, Sturm surmised, for different reasons, most notably the large crystal tumbler of scotch in his hand, obviously not his first of the day, even though it was barely 3:00 p.m. The Crown Prince wore white flannel trousers and a navy blazer with the Hohenzollern family crest on the breast pocket.

The Kaiser spoke first. "We are pleased that you have agreed to assist us in restoring the *heilege* lance to the House of Hohenzollern. A spear once possessed by our blood relatives, Frederick Barbarossa and Frederick the Great, deserves a more fitting home."

"What my father means," the Crown Prince interrupted, the curled ends of his mustache quivering as he talked, "is that the recent study published in England is but one piece of a larger puzzle which coincides with intelligence received by us, both before and after the war. We don't know by whom, but we know we were betrayed before the war. That is the only explanation for Franz Josef canceling the plans for an exhibition of German historical treasures in Berlin which would have included the Spear of Destiny. His Majesty and I interviewed Professor Campbell and we believe his monograph is accurate. The spear now at the Hofburg is not genuine "

Sturm watched silently as the Crown Prince became more animated. "Professor Campbell told us privately what he had withheld from publication, namely who took the Spear and where it was hidden. Recently, additional intelligence has come to us from agents still loyal to the German crown. A retired officer of the Imperial Austrian Army may have information to help us. Here is his name and address," the Crown Prince said, handing Sturm a folded piece of stationery. "He lives on the outskirts of Alexandria, Egypt where he's been known to boast in nightclubs of the role he played—always a central role—in spiriting the sacred lance from the Hofburg and carrying it to safety at a mysterious castle high in the Austrian Alps."

The aging Kaiser spoke again. "Find this man, *Herr* von Sturm. Find this officer. Make him tell you where the Lance is located. We don't have much time. Hindenburg is old, older than me. My family is prepared to reclaim our heritage once the President is called to his reward in the afterlife. But before that can happen and the Crown Prince can take his rightful place on the Prussian throne, we must have the Spear. Without it, Germany will never regain her greatness. With it, we will. Find us the Spear, *Herr* von Sturm. Find us the Spear."

17.

Negotiating With Hitler

Berchtesgaden, Germany
Friday, 29 May 1931

MATTIE McGary smoothly downshifted her silver BMW roadster as she approached yet another hairpin curve. She negotiated the curve and then pushed the accelerator to the floor once more, the wind ruffling her tousled red hair as she did so. At first, the interview with Hitler had seemed an honor bestowed on her by Hearst, trusting her to negotiate important contracts with Hitler today followed by Mussolini on Monday. Now, however, they were simply chores whose completion would bring her that much closer to commencing her quest to complete her father's life work. Finding the missing Spear of Destiny. She had a sudden pang of guilt. Would she feel the same way in Venice, wanting the fortnight with Cockran to pass quickly? If so, she'd better not let it show. That would not help patch things up between them.

The cloudless sky above her was a deep cerulean blue and the air was crisp and cool. Already, she was beginning to feel better about her last night on the airship. Thank God the music had ended when it did. She knew she had to find a way to begin being more careful, the way she used to before the war, but as she powered into another hairpin turn, tires screeching, she laughed. It wasn't going to be easy. She had been living this way for so long and she liked it. Maybe just letting Bourke know she was aware it was a problem would be enough for awhile.

Hearst had made her agree not to bring up controversial subjects during her interview with Hitler. Securing his signature on the contract took precedence over headlines. Nazi anti-Semitism was one of those *verboten* subjects, so Mattie had decided to make a two-pronged flanking attack. She would begin by asking Hitler's views on the arts, painting and music especially, which would give Hitler the opportunity to blame the Jews for degenerate art and music. Once she had Hitler softened up, she would move in and nail him with an ever-so-sweet question regarding the notorious anti-Semite Henry Ford whose photograph, according to the Hearst clippings she read, occupied a place of honor on Hitler's desk at the Brown House. An autographed photo, for god's sake! *Herr Hitler, what do you most admire about Mr. Ford?*

Mattie repeated the question aloud until her voice was completely neutral, betraying no hint of her own feelings. She turned right onto a smaller winding road, only one car-width wide. A mile up the road, she pulled up in front of a sturdy gate. Two men, both dressed head to toe in black, stood in front of the gate, each holding a submachine gun suspended from a leather strap over his shoulder. She gave them her name and one guard went back to the guardhouse while the second guard kept his submachine gun trained on her.

The man checked and nodded his head affirmatively. "The *fraulein's* name is on the approved list of visitors." Mattie saw the second guard relax slightly, his finger moving away from the trigger, but he otherwise kept the weapon pointed at her while the first guard returned and thoroughly searched her car from the boot to the hood, as well as the undercarriage beneath.

The scene was a distinct contrast, Mattie reflected, to the last time she met Hitler when the two of them had strolled alone together to the Café Heck in mid-afternoon, with no bodyguards anywhere in sight. She wondered how else he had changed from the man she saw in the *Burgerbraukeller* that fateful November night in 1923, three days after her interview.

Munich
Thursday, 8 November 1923

THE *Burgerbraukeller* was heavily timbered, smoke-filled and noisy, the smell of beer and sweat permeating the atmosphere. Mattie was sitting in the balcony with a good view of the speaker's platform erected at one end of the large, high-ceilinged room. She and Helmut Stein, her photographer, were good friends, as well as colleagues, so the wait had been pleasant. They bought two hefty steins of rich *Doppelbock* and waited for the fireworks Putzi had promised.

"I just don't understand," Helmut said, for what may have been the fourth or fifth time. She had lost count. "Why does the press pay so much attention to the National Socialists?"

"I suppose that's what we're here to find out tonight, now isn't it?"

"Tonight? More like every waking moment of the day with you. Why must you cover these people? Why go so far as being friendly with a fat-headed bigot like Göring and even flirt with that pretentious bastard Hanfstaengl?"

"Look," she snapped, "If I don't see them socially, I won't get the story and you won't get your photos. They want to take over. If they try, that means news and I intend to be there. I'd shake hands with the devil if it meant I'd have a front row seat at the Apocalypse."

Helmut responded by taking a large gulp of his *Doppelbock*, a man's way of pouting in Germany. She didn't regret what she'd said; she meant every word of it. Nothing irritated her more than when someone tried to get in the way of her story. Mattie was relieved to have their awkward silence interrupted by the short, heavily-jowled figure of Gustav von Kahr, the Bavarian Minister-President, as he began to speak, reading in a dull monotone.

Kahr was thirty minutes into his speech when it happened. There was a loud clamor at the opposite end of the hall and the crowd's attention was drawn away from the droning Kahr to the steel-helmeted Storm Troopers entering the room, nearly fifty of them, all heavily armed. On the floor below, people were standing on their chairs to see what was happening and, above them, Mattie, Helmut and others rose as well. The Storm Troopers were holding the crowd back and Mattie watched as the familiar figure of Adolf Hitler strode in hatless, holding a pistol at his side, flanked by two armed body guards. Hitler wore a severe black dress suit, his Iron Cross prominently displayed around his neck. It looked to Mattie as if Hitler were shouting something, but no one could hear him above the noise of the crowd. She watched as the two body guards roughly moved two members of the audience out of the way and placed a chair in the middle of the aisle. Hitler stood upon the chair, raised his Browning pistol high above his head, and fired a shot straight up, the noise reverberating through the hall. The crowd grew silent.

"The national revolution has started! There are six hundred armed troops surrounding the building. If anyone resists, I'll have a machine gun put in the gallery!" Hitler shouted, gesturing upward to where Mattie and Helmut sat. With body guards clearing a path, he then strode to the speaker's platform and, at gunpoint, forced President von Kahr to leave with him.

Mattie watched the bulky body of Hermann Göring take von Kahr's place at the podium. "Calm yourselves, everyone," Göring said. "Our action is not directed at the President, the army or the police. Remain in your places. You've got your beer. There's no need to leave," Göring said and took a long swallow from the stein in his hand. The crowd laughed.

Ten minutes later, Hitler was back. He repeated Göring's assurances that their actions that night were not directed at the army or the police. "The only ones who need fear us are the Berlin Jew government and the November criminals of 1918. General Ludendorff must become leader-in-chief of the National German Army. President von Kahr is talking right now with the head of the Bavarian militia and the police. They are struggling hard to reach a decision. May I say to them that you will stand behind them?"

Mattie shivered as the crowd of beer drinkers bellowed their support. Beside her, Helmut looked very pale. Below, Hitler raised his pistol. "I can say this to you. That the German revolution begins tonight or we will all be dead by dawn!" The crowd cheered again.

Thirty minutes later, President von Kahr returned to the stage, accompanied by Seisser, the head of the Bavarian state police, and General von Lossow. Hitler stood off to the side, beaming approval as each man in turn pledged his loyalty to the dawn of a new day in Germany. The crowd once more roared its support with twice the intensity as before.

Haus Wachenfeld
Obersalzburg, Germany
Friday, 29 May 1931

HITLER had the same piercing blue eyes Mattie remembered from 1923. But the nervous mannerisms were no longer there. He was now as smooth and self-assured as any politician Mattie had ever interviewed. Smoother than most, Mattie had to admit when she found he was not so easily outflanked on the subject of Jews as Mattie had planned. When she asked him about art, Hitler was quick to condemn the art of modernists like Chagall and the Jewish influence through their art commentary. He hastened to identify, however, several minor Jewish artists whom he knew personally and whose classical art he admired.

"I am, most of all, a hopeless Romantic, *Fraulein.*" Hitler said. "Rembrandt, Brueghel, Vermeer, Tintoretto, Tiepolo, Titian, Leonardo, Botticelli. And the Dutch, of course, van Dyck and Reubens. But, of the Spanish, I fear, only Goya is worthwhile."

Mattie was out of her league. She had no idea whether any of those artists were Jews. Probably not but it was the same with music. Hitler knew more than she did. He named several Jewish musicians whose work he enjoyed. The closest he came to an anti-Semitic comment was his observation that it was odd the Jews had failed to produce a single great composer, given how many talented musicians there were among the Jews. They were good at copying, Hitler explained, but not at originality.

"What about Mendelssohn?" Mattie asked, hopefully. At least she knew *he* was a Jew.

Hitler made a face. "*Ach*, he proves my point. Mendelssohn is overrated. His music is pleasant enough but too cloying and sentimental. Second-hand. Hardly original. But Edvard Grieg and his score for Ibsen's *Peer Gynt*? True genius. You were here in 1923*, Fraulein, "* Hitler said. "Did you not see the superb stage production in Berlin? My intellectual mentor, Dietrich Eckhardt, was the producer. He and Ibsen were great friends."

Mattie had not and said so. She thought briefly of asking questions about Henry Ford at that point, but Hitler clearly had his anti-Semitic antennae up and, so far, Mattie was no match for him. Much to her surprise, Hitler raised the same subject which had caused him to lose his temper with her years ago.

"Consider Wagner for a moment, *Fraulein*. He is an acquired taste for some but there is no denying his originality. Or his power. In many ways, Wagner foretells the future. *Parsifal* is a good example. When you and I last talked, I had only read the opera. I did not see it performed until 1925, shortly after I was released from prison. But once I saw it, all became clear. The idea of a state built on the principles of a medieval Order, fanciful though it may seem, is one that for years has struck me as thoroughly feasible. I can see the same thing in *Lohengrin*," Hitler continued, "with knights in shining armor called to the service of the Grail and pledged to lance adversaries low with the sword."

Mattie nodded and kept taking notes. Hitler remained silent until Mattie looked up into his blue eyes. It struck her that Hitler had deliberately chosen where to sit, his back to the clerestory window, so that the sunlight streaming down created a halo effect around his head.

"*Parsifal* represents a model of what I want to create in Germany. Within Monsalvat lived a community of knights, united in their religious fervor and their iron determination, ready at any time to shed their blood and also, with a clear conscience, the blood of others. Those knights were prepared to sacrifice their lives in the sure knowledge that they would be born again in the blood of the Holy Grail. I intend to form my religion for Germany on *Parsifal*. The man who sees National Socialism as nothing but a political movement knows hardly the first thing about it. It is more, even, than a religion—it is the collective will of a new race of men."

Hitler paused in his monologue and took a sip of mineral water. He smiled.

"I believed, but I could not say these things when last we talked. It was too soon. The people were not ready to hear the truth. Soon they will be. Soon they will understand. And then the whole world will understand that a new race of men has been reborn in Germany. That is why I reacted so harshly when you raised with me the question of the Hofburg Lance. I regret I misled you. I appreciate your restraint in not running a story about our interview when the annotations you showed me were in fact mine," Hitler said. "I made them at a much earlier age, before the war. They do not represent what I believe today."

Mattie tried to recall what Hitler had written in the margins of that book, but eight years was a long time. Still, she wasn't going to let him know that. Having vowed not to make the same mistake twice, she initially had no intention of broaching the subject of the Spear again. But now, Hitler had opened the door.

"So how do your views today differ from the notes you made in the margins of *Parsifal?*"

Hitler was not to be drawn out. He smiled and gently shook his head from side to side. "*Fraulein*, it is not necessary for the people to know precisely what I believed then or indeed what I believe now. I have many more things to say to the German people but that time has not yet come. For example, we will not, at this point, begin a public discussion of racial issues. That would only cause more divisions among the people. Above all, my goal is to unite our people."

"But still, the Spear is important to you, is it not?"

"Of course it is important, but only as an historical artifact. From the coronation of Charlemagne as the first Holy Roman Emperor, to the fall of the old German Empire a thousand years later, forty five emperors have taken possession of the Spear of Destiny."

Mattie knew this. She was James McGary's daughter. But how much did Hitler know? She kept her tone curious. "Who was the first historical figure to hold the Spear, *Herr* Hitler?"

"Meuritius, the commander of the Theban Legion, held the Spear in 285 A.D. when he was forced to participate in a pagan festival sacrifice intended to renew the legion's belief in their Roman gods. Meuritius was a Christian and declined to do so. He submitted to a ritual decapitation, hoping thereby to spare the rest of the Theban Legion, who had likewise refused to worship the old Roman gods. The Emperor Maximian ignored his sacrifice and ordered every tenth man in the legion decapitated. Still, the Thebans refused to renounce their Christianity and so Maximian massacred the entire legion, decapitating over 6,000 legionnaires, the largest single act of human sacrifice in the history of the ancient world."

"My god, how positively barbaric," Mattie said. She was James McGary's daughter yet she had forgotten about the mass beheadings. "I thought the Romans were civilized."

"History is not always what it seems on the surface, *Fraulein*. Still, there were unintended consequences from making martyrs of the Theban Legion for it led to the rise of Emperor Constantine and the eventual conversion of the Roman Empire to Christianity. Constantine was the first world figure to wield the Spear. Theodosius possessed it when he tamed the Goths in 385. The same for Alaric the Bold, who sacked Rome in 410. Or the Visigoth Theodoric, who turned back Attila the Hun at Troyes in 452."

"My goodness," Mattie said. "I had no idea that all those early leaders had possessed the Spear." Mattie knew this, of course, but, like most men, Hitler clearly thrived on flattery.

"It was only the beginning," Hitler said. "Then came Justinian, who held the Spear aloft when he exiled the Greek scholars from the territories of the old Roman Empire. The Frankish General Karl Martel carried the Spear in his victory over the Arabs at Poitiers in 732. Then it passed to Charlemagne in 800 AD, the first Holy Roman Emperor, who fought forty-seven successful campaigns with the Spear at his side."

"What about the German kings who held the Spear?" Mattie asked.

"Ah, yes," Hitler said. "The Germans, of course, are the most worthy and significant world-historic figures to hold the Spear."

"Of that, I had no doubt," Mattie replied. She had no shame. She knew all this from her father but she still had a business deal to negotiate once Hitler stopped boring her.

"Frederick Barbarossa conquered all of Italy holding the Spear and drove the Pope into exile. But even more magnificent than Barbarossa was his grandson, Frederick II, Frederick the Great. Fluent in six languages, he spoke Arabic with his Muslim soldiers, kept a large harem, and was courageous in battle. He was even well-versed in astrology. He prized the Spear of Destiny above all and once allowed Francis of Assisi to carry it on an errand of mercy."

"You mentioned the Teutonic Knights earlier. Do you ever anticipate their rebirth?"

"You have seen them already, guarding the entrance to my *schloss*. The SS. Their leader is one of the few men in our movement who understands the symbolic significance of the Spear. The SS are the best of the best, chosen according to my model. They are ready at my command to shed their blood in a noble cause as well as to shed the blood of others. In my earlier days, I often used the phrase 'heads will roll' to symbolize the changes I would make once in power. But with my SS, it is much more than a mere slogan."

And with that, Hitler rose, ending the interview. "Come, *Fraulein* McGary. Let's walk outside and discuss the business matters which brought you all the way from America."

"But *Herr* Hitler," Mattie protested, "I have only one more subject I wish to raise. Our American readers would like to hear your views on Henry Ford."

Hitler paused in midstride and turned back to Mattie with a smile. "Henry Ford is a great man. He brought an affordable automobile to the masses. His Model T was a work of true genius. Once I am chancellor, I intend to do the same thing for Germany. In the Germany I will build, even the lowliest worker will be able to afford an automobile."

Mattie tried a few more questions, but Hitler ignored her and walked to the terrace where the view was spectacular. You could see nearly fifty miles in all directions. Four to five mountain peaks and the intervening valleys. Hitler took great pride in showing this to her, naming the peaks and ranges as if he owned them. It was not much different, Mattie thought, from Churchill showing off the Weald of Kent and acting as if it belonged to him as well.

"Tell me, *Fraulein* McGary, why it is that Mr. Hearst pays *Signor* Mussolini and Mr. Churchill $2,000 for each article they write for him, whereas he offers me only $1,500? What have I done," Hitler said, gesturing with his hands, "to warrant such a lack of respect?"

"No disrespect was intended. But *Signor* Mussolini is the head of his government and, at the time Mr. Churchill was engaged, he had only recently stepped down from the number two position in his country's government."

"Stepped down, *Fraulein?* Turned out of power is more like it. Just as will soon happen to the government here in Germany."

Mattie knew she had negotiating room. Hitler was well-informed as to what Mussolini and Churchill were being paid, but he apparently didn't know that both those contracts were up for renegotiation and Hearst intended to increase them to $2,500 each. Hearst had authorized Mattie to do the same if that's what it took to get Hitler signed up. Mattie was determined, however, to bring Hitler in for less. "What amount did you have in mind, *Herr* Hitler?" Mattie asked.

"Twice what you offer. Italy and England are small countries. I received more votes in my last election than Mr. Churchill's party did.'

"I'm sure that's true, *Herr* Hitler, but I couldn't possibly go that high."

"But *Fraulein*, I know there are more people of German descent in America than Italians. My articles will sell Mr. Hearst more papers. Don't forget that there is another American newspaper syndicate eager to sign me to an exclusive contract. I propose $2,750 an article."

No, she wasn't going to forget that. "Their circulation can't match Hearst. I can offer $2,100 an article. More than we pay Churchill and Mussolini."

Hitler frowned. "That's flattering, but Lady Hay Drummond has already offered me more to sign with Scripps-Howard. I'm not at liberty to disclose the amount, but $2,500 per article would carry the day for you. And, of course, you are far more beautiful and charming than Lady Drummond. How did an American acquire an English title anyway?"

By marrying an 80 year old lord who died the first time they made love, Mattie thought, but she kept a poker face and inside she celebrated. She had won. She could afford to be magnanimous. What was it Winston always said? In defeat, defiance. In victory, magnanimity. Yes, that was it. Time to let Hitler save face. "Well..." Mattie began, drawing it out, "the Chief won't like it but if we can sign the papers today, I will ink in $2,400 per article, $400 more than Mussolini or Churchill, and hope that Hearst doesn't take the difference out of my paycheck."

Hitler beamed. "Done, *Fraulein*," he said, extending his hand. "I knew we could do this together. That is why I insisted that you be the one to negotiate. It also gave me the opportunity to make amends for my boorish behavior the last time we met. Will you stay for tea?"

Tea was served on the broad terrace, the mountains still crisp and clear in the distance. As he had the first time they had tea at the Café Heck, Hitler poured and then offered cream-filled pastries to Mattie before snatching two for himself.

Afterwards, he personally escorted her to her BMW and gallantly opened the door for her to get in. When she was seated behind the wheel, he placed both hands on the side of the door and leaned in close. For a moment, Mattie was afraid he was moving in to kiss her on the cheek, but he stopped a foot from her face, close enough for his bad breath to overcome the lingering sweet odor of the pastries. "Let this be our little secret, *Fraulein* McGary. You are the only person, man or woman, to have bested me one-on-one in negotiations." The corners of his mouth turned upwards in a grin. "My enemies must not learn how easily I can be swayed by a pretty face."

"I assure you, *Herr* Hitler, that you drove a hard bargain. But don't worry, your secret is safe with me."

CHURCHILL'S cable was unexpected when Mattie checked for messages upon returning to her hotel. She was feeling proud, having driven more slowly on her way back from meeting with Hitler than she had on her way up the mountain. Hell, at one point, she had even allowed an aggressive Mercedes convertible to pass her on a straightaway even though her BMW could have blown him away. Maybe if she began to act as a cautious person, whatever had switched off inside her would turn back on of its own accord.

A cable from Churchill greeted her return to her hotel. COME TO CHARTWELL SOONEST. STOP. EXPEDITION FINANCES IN JEOPARDY. STOP. TIME IS OF THE ESSENCE.

Churchill. That man knew just the right buttons to push. This would disrupt her plans to see Mussolini on Monday and sign him to a new Hearst contract before heading up to Berlin for her interviews with arms dealers. She would have to call her office in Berlin and have them put Mussolini off until the middle of next week. She knew Churchill was manipulating her. That was what Winston did. She didn't care. It was about her father. About the Spear and the Grail.

As Mattie closed her suitcase, she thought it was funny how life worked. Just today she talked to Hitler about the Spear, the Grail, Monsalvat, Parsifal. Now Churchill had altered her timetable to suit his purposes and tempted her with the same thing. She was helpless to turn him down. Mussolini would just have to wait. Her earlier resolve to be more careful and less impulsive was like a straw in the wind. After a phone call to Winston for more details, she was off to England and Chartwell where, she had learned to her delight, an early arriving Cockran would be waiting for her. On her way to the train station, she passed every motorcar in her path. No one passed her.

18.

Harmony

COCKRAN and his son Patrick arrived at Churchill's country home, twenty-five miles outside London just as the sunset leaked through fissures in the thick English cloud cover. The brutal murder of Sir Archibald Hampton in Germany had come as a shock but Churchill's telephone call had persuaded Cockran to cancel his *Europa* reservations and take the first available liner. Winston assured him that Harmony Hampton, Sir Archibald's step-daughter and only heir, would need sound legal advice every bit as much as her father. The sooner the better.

The chauffeur disappeared with their suitcases as the butler opened the door to greet Cockran and his son. "So good to see you both again at Chartwell, Mr. Cockran."

"Thank you, George. Good to see you," Cockran said.

"How are you today, Master Patrick?" George asked.

"I'm fine, thank you," Paddy replied.

"If you'd come with me, Master Patrick, Mr. Churchill has asked that you be shown directly to his study where he has arranged miniature soldiers just as they were at the Battle of Waterloo. You are free to redeploy them as you wish and Mr. Churchill will join you later."

Paddy's eyes lit up and he turned eagerly to Cockran. "Is it okay, Dad?"

Cockran smiled. Paddy had been disappointed when Cockran wouldn't allow him to bring his own miniature soldiers on the journey, but Cockran knew that Churchill's own vast collection would be ready and waiting for his son. "Of course it's okay. Go ahead."

"If you would be so kind as to wait in the library," George said, "I will inform Mr. Churchill that you have arrived after I see Master Patrick to the study."

Cockran took his hat off and stepped inside while George and Paddy headed toward the stairs. Notwithstanding the threats in America, he knew his son would be safe with Churchill as they traveled through Germany while Cockran and Mattie were in Venice. Even out of office, Winston had two Scotland Yard bodyguards with him whenever he set foot outside England.

Cockran made the familiar turn to his left, heading down the dark hall for the library, when he noticed movement ahead of him. A small, thin frame was gliding gracefully toward him—which meant it wasn't Churchill while the blonde hair meant it wasn't Churchill's wife either. He stopped, watching the young woman approach, angelic in a cream and rose patterned sun dress. As she neared, she stopped as well and observed him.

"Ah, hello," he said, once he saw her clearly. "I'm Bourke Cockran." No reaction. "From America," he added.

"From America, you say?" the young woman said. "I never would have guessed."

"You must be Harmony," he said recognizing the young heiress and academic.

She smiled. She was beautiful. "Yes, I am."

"Please accept my deepest sympathy. I was so sorry to learn of your father's death,"

"Thank you," she said simply, "but he wasn't actually my father. He was my stepfather, though I had come to think of him like a father." Her eyes moistened. "Certainly one who cared a great deal for my safety and...and well being." The tears in her eyes were unmistakable now.

"Are you all right?" Cockran asked.

"Yes," she said but, as she blinked, a tear escaped and rolled over her cheek. "It's just that...that I can't believe he's gone."

"Let's find you some place to sit down," Cockran said, placing a hand on her elbow. Her eyes flashed up at him, startlingly blue through the tears. "The library? A drink perhaps?"

Cockran said nothing more when they reached the library. He helped her to a chintz covered club chair and handed her a handkerchief from his breast pocket before moving over to the sideboard. Confident that it would be well stocked, he found the Beefeaters and fixed her a gin and tonic followed by a Johnnie Walker Red and water for himself..

"Thank you," she said as she took the gin and tonic, her eyes flashing up at him, startlingly blue through her tears.. "I'm doing my best to cut down." She squeezed the slice of lemon on the rim and dropped it into the glass. Then she slipped her finger in her mouth to taste the lemon. "Alcohol is decidedly detrimental to one's health."

"Not if you drink in moderation," Cockran said.

Harmony laughed, a gentle pleasing sound. "You sound just like Mr. Churchill," she said. "'Everything in moderation,' I hear him tell people. I must say, if the way Winston drinks is 'moderation,' then he drinks an awful *lot* in moderation."

Cockran had to laugh. "True," he said. "If there is an amount that defines moderation, Winston is likely near the limit."

Harmony laughed in response. She seemed to be in better spirits now and Cockran had no desire to upset that. But there were still things he needed to know. She wasn't his client, not yet, even though her father had been one, however briefly. "Harmony," he said gently. "Does your father's death mean his controlling interest in NBM has passed on to you?"

"Yes," she said. "Actually, I'm now the sole owner of the family's holding company, Sedgewick & South, which in turn owns most of NBM. Or at least I will be sole owner when I'm 35. Two trustees whom I don't even know control everything until then."

"Have any offers to purchase your share of NBM come to you, recently?"

"Why yes," she said, her tone of voice sounding intrigued. "I received an offer the very next day after..." she trailed off. "I—yes, I showed it to Winston just yesterday. I want to take it and be done with it but he says I should talk to you first."

Cockran wasn't surprised an offer came directly on the heels of something like this. There were vultures everywhere. "But wouldn't you still have to convince your trustees to approve the sale?"

"Yes" Harmony said and smiled. "Will you be my solicitor and help me do that?"

"No," Cockran said. "Not unless the offer accurately reflected the value of Sedgewick & South's interest in NBM before its largest European subsidiary in Germany was beset by sabotage. Which I doubt it does."

"Why?"

"Because your share of NBM is worth far more if the entire company is operating at full strength, free of the terror and extortion activities it is facing in Germany."

Harmony's face clouded over and she sunk deeper into her chair. "That sounds like a lot to accomplish."

"It is, but it's worth doing."

Harmony sighed and took a sip of her drink. "Frankly, I'm not sure it's worth it. I never wanted to own a company. I'm an academic, an artist, and, if I keep working at it, maybe someday a sculptor. I'm at home in my studio and the grassy courtyards of my campus, not a corporate boardroom." They were silent a moment. Harmony returned her blue eyes to Cockran. "I've also been offered a finder's fee."

"How much?"

"£25,000."

Cockran paused and took a sip. "It's a bribe. A large bribe but still a bribe."

"It's £25,000!" she said, "Isn't that a lot of money?"

"Yes but you're being short-sighted. With how I plan to help your two German plants, your interest in NBM could earn you half again as much in less than two years."

She seemed to consider this for a moment, her eyes still on Cockran. She sipped on her drink again. "What did you have in mind?"

Cockran explained his plans to visit the American embassy and consulate, calling on Donovan's contacts to assist them. After that, he would move on to federal and state authorities in Berlin and Munich where, with the support of U.S. diplomats, pressure would be applied to snap the police and prosecutors out of their passivity. With the German government protecting the NBM plants and working to put the SS thugs in jail, Cockran expected life at the plants to return to normal within six months and profits six months later.

"What happens if diplomacy doesn't work?" Harmony asked. "Aren't I still in danger? I was kidnapped once. They could do it again."

"I have a friend from America," Cockran replied. "He's in Germany now checking things out. We'll make sure no harm comes to you. We're both very good at that. Trust me."

"I trust you, Mr. Cockran."

"Please. Call me Bourke."

"Bourke, my boy!" Churchill said as he entered the room, wearing workman's clothes and a light smattering of dirt over the kneecaps. "Wonderful to see you again." They exchanged greetings briefly. "I see you've already met Harmony. Have you discussed any business?"

"A little."

"Good, good. We haven't much time. The sun is going down and you must see how large my goldfish have become since you were last here." He tugged on Bourke's arm and turned to Harmony. "You too, my dear. Harmony has seen my goldfish already, but she adores them. Oh! And go find Patrick. He must see the progress I've made on my wall. A new record. Four hundred bricks in two hours!"

Sunday, 31 May 1931

COCKRAN'S head ached as he rose the next morning. The rest of the evening had been pleasantly sociable; no further business discussed. The four of them—Bourke, Harmony, Winston, and Patrick—had a quiet supper before Harmony and Patrick retired early. Clemmie, Winston had informed him, was still on holiday in America. Which left him alone with Winston and brandy in his study upstairs. Which also left Cockran with the hangover he was currently nursing. He should have known better than to try matching Churchill drink for drink.

Churchill wasn't exactly a father figure even though he was Cockran's senior by 21 years. An older brother, perhaps, or a wise uncle. Which is why, after his third brandy, Cockran had asked Churchill's advice about Mattie, her risk-taking and their quarrel. His father's protégé had not been comforting. Instead, he took Mattie's side. "Live dangerously," he told Cockran. "That's always been my motto. Don't let life pass you by. Take things as they come. That's what your Mattie does. Good for her. You should too. Dread naught, all will be well." Cockran knew not to start an argument with a man he both respected and loved. But what the hell did Churchill know? He had been both reckless *and* lucky in his youth. Dodged many a bullet. Easy for him to say, "live dangerously." But it wasn't his wife who had been raped and killed by the IRA. Would he feel as he did had that happened? Not bloody likely.

After Cockran dressed, he wandered downstairs to the dining room where breakfast was waiting under the soft glow of early morning sunlight.

Harmony was seated alone at a round table, wearing a powder blue cotton dress. "My, you're a late riser," she said.

"It's only nine o'clock. Winston and I kept each other up quite late last night."

"I talked with your son Patrick earlier this morning. He's a charming boy. He was finishing his breakfast just as I sat down. He said he had a battle to fight and charged off up the stairs. But I'd be delighted if you joined me for breakfast."

Cockran did, paying a visit to the sideboard to load up on ham, eggs and a small bowl of porridge. After his hangover had been lifted by food and many cups of tea, they took a walk south through the orchard and into a walled garden built by Churchill's bricklaying skills.

Harmony seemed compelled to talk, so Cockran listened quietly, lending a friendly ear. Her father had died in 1915, but she didn't miss him. He never paid her much attention. She was happy when her mother married Sir Archibald because he had been different—kind, interested, generous. She didn't care as much for the trust he created which would keep her from her inheritance until she was thirty-five, considering it a trifle overbearing as if she were not capable of fending for herself at the age of twenty seven. "But then, dear Archie always thought of me as his own little girl, no matter how quickly I grew up. I mean I served as a nurses' aide during the war when I was barely fifteen, for goodness sakes!"

She was quiet for awhile as they walked down past Churchill's studio and reached the second and smaller of Chartwell's two lakes. Beside it was a large circular swimming pool. She squealed and grasped Cockran's arm. "Look! The swimming pool! Let's take a dip."

"I didn't bring a bathing suit," Cockran replied. "Besides, it's not that warm."

"The pool's water is heated. And there are suits in the changing room of the *loggia*. Mine's already there."

"You go ahead. I'll watch."

Harmony emerged a few moments later wearing a long navy blue terrycloth robe. She let it drop in a single motion, revealing a demure white wool maillot, high in the neck, with a wool belt around her slender waist and a buckle in the middle.

She posed for him and then turned around in a circle.

"What do you think?'

That she was one well-put together young woman was the thought that came immediately to Cockran's mind. The thin white wool was filled out by her small body in a sinuous curve from her breasts down to her hips. Harmony walked away from him and stepped into the pool. She alternated between a side stroke and a back stroke and resumed their conversation while Cockran stood on the side of the pool, halfway between the two ends.

"I received another offer this morning," she said. "It arrived by courier."

Cockran nodded. "I'll take a look at it when we get back," he said.

"The offer for the company is the same but the finder's fee has been doubled."

She turned from her side to her back and stroked back.

"And?" Cockran finally asked.

"And what? You don't think I should accept, do you?"

"No, I don't," he said.

"Why not?" she asked.

"It's premature. You're still not thinking this through," he said.

"But I *want* to accept it," she said. "You're my solicitor. "Aren't you supposed to work in my interest?" She returned to the side stroke.

"I'm am American which means I'm your lawyer, not your solicitor, but I *am* working in your interest," Cockran said.

"Then why don't you help me get what I want? I hired you."

"No," Cockran said evenly. "Your father hired me because he wanted to stop sabotage at the NBM plants in Germany. That's what I aim to do. If you disagree, hire a different lawyer."

Harmony stopped swimming and treaded water in the pool, only her head showing. She looked surprised at Cockran's blunt talk. Too bad, he thought. If she wanted to sell out, fine. She could find lots of lawyers to do that for her. But Cockran intended to do her late stepfather's bidding and restore a sense of order and fair play to NBM's plants in Germany.

Harmony rose out of the pool and it was Cockran's turn to be surprised at what happened next. It was at once apparent that the white maillot had turned transparent as she walked toward him, step by revealing step. She might as well have been wearing nothing.

"Toss me a towel," Harmony said, as she reached out her arms.

Embarrassed to have been staring, Cockran turned away and searched for a towel, finally finding it under the blue robe. He turned back toward her and tossed it to her.

"Here you go. You look cold."

She caught the towel deftly in one hand and began to dry her face and neck and hair. "No, the water was fine. I just need to towel down."

Harmony seemed unconcerned or unaware of her appearance when she turned her back to him and bent over gracefully from the waist to dry her long legs. As she straightened up, Cockran raised his eyes so that when she turned around, it would not be apparent that he had been staring.

Harmony stood up and looked at him. "I know you feel an obligation to my stepfather but, after my kidnapping, it's not a fight I'm willing to take on any longer."

Cockran quickly picked up her robe and helped her into it. She thanked him and wrapped the towel around her neck as they began to walk up to the house, Harmony holding her dress in one hand and undergarments in the other. Suddenly she stopped, staring back at the small lakes. "I just want to end this nightmare,"

She stood there as though she were all alone looking for invisible enemies. She had been through so much . A kidnapping. A ransom. Her stepfather's sudden murder. No wonder she wanted it all to end. Wordlessly, he put an arm around her shoulder to comfort her. Her arms, held close to her damp body, suddenly reached around to embrace him. She seemed so fragile after all that had happened to her. But he couldn't let fear rule her decisions. That wasn't Cockran's way.

"If I sell," she whispered, "I won't have to be scared anymore."

Cockran put his hands on her shoulders and held her at arm's length. "I understand your fear, Harmony," he said, "but these men have to be faced. You cannot tip-toe around them or they will only reach for more. You'll be safe with us in Germany. My friend and I will handle any trouble that may come up."

Fear crossed her face. "You expect me to go with you to Germany?"

"Yes, of course. The German authorities must meet the girl whose factories they aren't protecting and explain directly to her pretty face why they aren't doing their job."

Harmony smiled at the compliment. "How long will we be in Germany?"

"I'm not certain. At least a week."

Harmony paused. "I understand and appreciate what you're doing. And I do want to honor my step-father's memory as well as his legacy to me. After what happened to me the last time, I really don't want to go back to to Germany. But I will. On one condition."

"What's that?"

"You must promise to persuade my trustees to sell the minute you think there's a reasonable offer on the table. Not the top dollar. Just reasonable."

"I promise," Cockran said. "I've always done that. My father once told me never try to squeeze the last nickel out of a deal because you lose more deals that way than you make."

"That's wonderful," Harmony said and promptly hugged him again, her wet hair and damp breasts pressing against his chest. Cockran awkwardly put his hands on her shoulders again, not exactly returning the embrace but not pushing her away either.

19.

An Adventure Awaits

MATTIE McGary was not happy. When she called Churchill after receiving his cable, her heart had leaped when she learned that Cockran had booked an earlier passage and would be at Chartwell when she arrived. So she had spent the last day and a half on trains, not all with first-class compartments, in order to reach Chartwell as soon as possible, only to find Cockran locked in the embrace of another woman. Mattie was standing beside Churchill on the terrace at Chartwell, looking over the grounds where Cockran stood fifty yards below, the woman wearing only a robe, no less, and clutching in one hand her dress and in her other what certainly appeared to be silk unmentionables. What was that all about? And now she was hugging him again!

"Winston, who the hell is that blonde with her arms around my man?"

"That woman, my dear, is why Bourke is here nearly a week early. She is the stepdaughter of Sir Archibald Hampton, who was brutally murdered last week in Germany. Upon my advice, Archie had retained Bourke as his lawyer a few days before he died to help him sort out some problems his plants in Germany were suffering. Harmony is his only heir, and I persuaded her, in order to protect her financial interests, to retain Bourke as well. She was swimming in our pool and I am certain Bourke is simply offering comfort in her time of sorrow. Archie's funeral was only two days ago. I was one of his pallbearers."

"I suppose it's okay." Mattie said. "Were she and her stepfather close?" She watched them resume walking, the woman's loosely knotted robe revealing her transparent swim suit so that anyone could see her breasts on offer beneath. Mattie's eyes narrowed, recognizing a rival.

"Archie was very fond of her. He said she was a headstrong young girl, but he told me he couldn't love her more than if she were his own daughter. With an inheritance from her mother and Archie, young men will be flocking around her like bees to honey. She could use a level-headed chap like Bourke to help her separate the wheat from the chaff."

Mattie nodded. "I suppose so, Winston. If her stepfather meant as much to her as my father did to me, I can sympathize with her grief. So long as she doesn't think Cockran is part of the wheat that gets separated from the chaff."

Churchill chuckled. "Not to worry, my dear, your own beauty will be more than sufficient to keep Bourke focused only on you."

Moments later, Cockran joined them on the terrace. Without his clinging new blonde client. "Well, aren't you a sight for sore eyes?" Cockran said before he took Mattie in his arms and kissed her hello. "What are you doing here? I didn't expect to see you until Venice."

Mattie beamed. It was exactly what she'd hoped for, the kiss perfect as always. She'd missed him. "I heard about your beautiful new client and I came right away to make sure that she's only a client. Does Bill Donovan encourage you to give all your new clients such a cozy hug?"

Cockran laughed. "No, only beautiful blondes. What gives? Why are you here?"

"Same reason as you. Winston tracked me down and lured me here early."

They both laughed. It felt good. Like old times. Not like their parting at Lakehurst.

"What was the bait?" he asked.

"Something about financing for the expedition. But Winston was mysterious."

"How long will you be here?"

"At least tonight," she said, giving his hand a squeeze. I'll know more after I talk with Winston." She looked up at him. "Two nights if we're lucky. How was the voyage?"

Before Cockran could reply, Mattie watched the grieving and now fully clothed blonde client arrive. "Hello, I'm Harmony. Who are you?"

Cockran started to introduce them but Mattie cut him off before he could say a word. "I'm Mattie McGary," she said, flashing a sweet smile. "Bourke's girlfriend."

"Oh. I'm pleased to meet you," Harmony said, extending her hand and sounding slightly disappointed. "Dear Bourke has been such a comfort. I've only known him for two days, but he's the nicest, kindest person I've ever met. But then, if you're his girlfriend, you already know that." Harmony said, placing entirely too much emphasis on "if" for Mattie.

"Yes, I do, don't I?" Mattie replied and gave her another sweet smile.

Mattie felt a hand on her arm. "Excuse me, Mattie. May I have a word please? Before our luncheon?" Churchill asked, drawing her away. They stopped when Churchill had walked her to the other side of the terrace, leaving Cockran and Harmony alone.

"Make it quick, Winston. That client you rustled up for him has her claws a bit too deep in my boyfriend and I don't like it one bit."

"Now, Mattie, a young thing like Harmony can scarcely begin to approach your beauty."

"Don't give me that, Winston. She's drop-dead gorgeous and you know it. She looks like she's not a day over twenty-five." And her breasts are bigger than mine, too, she thought.

"Actually, she's twenty-seven. But what I want is to bring you up to date on the finances of the holy lance expedition. I need advice on how to handle Professor Geoffrey Campbell."

CHURCHILL led Mattie into the dining room, Bourke and Harmony trailing behind. The room was light and airy, with floor to ceiling French doors on three sides, several of them open to the gentle breeze outside. A large round oak table was in the middle of the room around which were six arm chairs upholstered in a cheery pale yellow flowered fabric.

If all went well, Churchill thought, the mosaic soon would be complete and the quest could begin. Geoffrey Campbell, who had arrived that morning, and Churchill's brother Jack rose from their chairs. "I believe you know everyone, Jack," Churchill said as his brother greeted Mattie with a kiss, "and you've met everyone, Prof, except this stunning young woman."

Churchill turned to Mattie. "Martha McGary, Professor Geoffrey Campbell."

"Geoffrey is on sabbatical from the University of Glasgow," Churchill said, by way of introduction. "His specialty is ancient Christian archeology."

Mattie smiled and Churchill watched Campbell's eyes widen. A short man, Campbell was wearing a heavy Scottish tweed jacket, frayed at the sleeves, with patches on the elbows. The stem of a pipe peeked out from the breast pocket of his jacket. His well-worn flannel trousers were unpressed and unruly gray hair was in contrast to his neatly trimmed gray beard.

"McGary? Are you any relation to James McGary?" Campbell asked.

"He was my father."

"It's an honor to meet you, Miss McGary. Your father was a great teacher and an inspiration for my work. Winston told me a journalist would be joining us for lunch, but I had no idea it would be someone as important as James McGary's daughter."

"Thank you," Mattie said, modestly ducking her head. "Please call me Mattie."

"Please, find a seat," Churchill said to the group. "Mattie, you sit by me." He briefly noticed Mattie frown as Harmony quickly moved into the open seat next to Cockran.

While the soup course was served—*vichyssoise*—Churchill's monologue brought the three new guests up to the key point in Campbell's story, his belief the Hofburg Spear was fake.

The entire table paused briefly while the main course of veal cutlets was served and claret was poured. Churchill was not surprised when Mattie spoke first.

"Why do you say it's a fake? What proof do you have?"

"Well, I suppose it is rather harsh to call it a fake," Campbell conceded. "But it most assuredly is not the same spear that was on display before the Great War. It's all very detailed and rather dry, I'm afraid, for anyone except an archeologist, but there can be no question. I've made a meticulous examination of unauthorized photographs of the spear taken in 1912 by your father and compared them with similar surreptitious photographs taken by me only a year ago. The two spears in the photographs are quite similar. In some ways, identical. But they are not the same. I would stake my reputation on it. Indeed, with my monograph, I have."

"But you have further proof. Is that not correct?" Churchill asked.

"Yes, I do. I mentioned it briefly it in my monograph. It's not terribly scientific, but I have an eyewitness. Someone who saw the Spear being removed from the Museum."

"Was the witness reliable?" Mattie asked.

"Oh, quite reliable. He was one of the curators. In fact, he was the only curator who would even talk to me. None of the others would so much as give me the time of day once they heard my theory. They ignored my letters and refused to accept my telephone calls. Rather rude, actually. But not Herman Kluge, a proper Viennese gentlemen. White goatee, *pince-nez*, and an old Kaiser Bill mustache. He wouldn't meet me at the Museum. We met instead at a small coffee house in a seedier section of Vienna. The story he told me had the ring of truth."

Even though they were quite alone and safe from prying eyes, Campbell lowered his voice and leaned forward in his chair, as if dark secrets would soon be revealed. "The curator told me he had been working late at the museum on a snowy night in early 1914 when he heard noises coming from the first floor where there should only have been silence. He crept carefully downstairs and hid on a landing. He was astonished to see fully-armed Austrian Army troops standing guard outside the room where the Lance of Longinus was on display. Kluge was a military buff and recognized their unit insignia and their weapons.

They were elite Austrian Alpine troops carrying Mannlicher assault rifles. The room where the Spear is displayed is two stories' high, with several small balconies along three of the room's four walls. The curator moved carefully back upstairs and quietly opened a door to one of the now darkened balconies. He peered down and swears he actually saw the Spear being removed from its display case and replaced with another. There were only two soldiers in the room, both officers, and while they talked in hushed voices so that Kluge couldn't hear everything, the one thing he caught clearly was something about the Alps, the border and a special military train."

"Go on, Prof, go on," Churchill urged, as he lit a new cigar. "Don't keep us in suspense."

Campbell took a sip of claret and then continued. "The Austrian Alps mostly border Italy so Kluge assumed they were taking the Spear to a mountain stronghold. He told me there are a number of ancient castles there dating from the Crusades and the Middle Ages. They were built to protect trade routes and deter advancing enemies. He was quite angry that a fake was on display at the Hofburg and he had long wanted the deception to be exposed if his position wasn't jeopardized. I promised complete confidentiality if he would give me an opportunity to examine the Spear which is presently in the Hofburg. Kluge agreed. He was a true man of science."

"What did your examination of the Spear show?" Mattie asked in an eager tone.

"Regrettably, I never had the opportunity. As I said, we were in a rough neighborhood and we each went our separate ways. I read about Kluge's death in a newspaper the very next morning. He was robbed and then killed in a particularly gruesome fashion. Severed his head from his body and propped him up against a wall in an alley near the coffee shop, his head placed in his lap. The newspapers suggested it was a ritual killing. The police dismissed that but the killers of Herman Kluge were never apprehended. I left Austria shortly after his death."

"And the true spear?" Mattie asked. "What about the true spear's location?"

"I fear I don't know its precise location," he replied, "but Winston seems to think he does. Or at least what he knows was enough to persuade your employer, Miss McGary, as well as your father, Miss Hampton, to each contribute £10,000 to finance a search for the Spear."

"Hold that thought, Prof," Churchill said as he walked over to a table in the corner of the room. "I have always found that things are never quite as hopeless as they might seem."

A servant appeared, offering brandy to all. The time was right, Churchill thought as he paced the the room, cigar in his left hand, brandy snifter in his right, to play the trump card.

"My part of this story begins when I was at the Admiralty. It was March, 1914. British Naval Intelligence in Vienna had been shown a confidential note sent from Helmuth von Moltke, the Chief of the German General Staff, through intermediaries to Austria's Emperor Franz Josef. The note warned the Emperor of a plot by the Kaiser to take possession of the Spear."

Churchill paused, took his cigar from his mouth and stared at it as if by a stern glance it would relight itself. The cigar stubbornly refused to do so and Churchill at last accepted the lit match proffered by his brother. "I knew German kings had thought the Spear to be a talisman of power. Bloody nonsense, of course, but when I saw that the Kaiser was seeking to possess it, I knew war was inevitable. I warned the Prime Minister, naturally, but there was nothing either of us could do. It was simply one more piece in a vast mosaic which ultimately meant war."

Churchill resumed pacing. "The past is past, however. We must turn our faces to the future. After the war ended, I was Secretary for War and Air and an intelligence report crossed my desk about an Austrian army officer's journal found during a search of the Emperor Franz Josef's private quarters in his palace in Vienna. It was a summary translation only, but the journal spoke of how this officer and his men had hidden a sacred relic in the Austrian Alps before the war.

Churchill looked towards Professor Campbell, who had placed his snifter of brandy down and gripped the armrests of his chair. "I immediately thought of von Moltke's letter to the Emperor, but I had far too many responsibilities to worry about the past. The Bolsheviks were keeping me up all night many times, not to mention the Greeks and the Turks.

"When Professor Campbell kindly forwarded a copy of his monograph, I recalled that officer's journal. As you all know, I have been out of office nearly two years and now I am out of the shadow cabinet as well because I insist on speaking the unpopular truth about India. But I am not without influence among some of our more patriotic civil servants in Naval Intelligence who, like me, look back with fondness on our adventures together during the Great War."

Churchill walked back over to the corner table on which lay, in haphazard fashion, printer's proofs bleeding with Churchill's corrections made by a bold red pencil. He rummaged through the papers and emerged with a small battered leather notebook.

"Ah, here it is. My friends were kind enough to provide an English translation." He crossed the room and gave the notebook and translation to Campbell. "Have a look, Prof. The notebook belonged to a Major Josef Lanz."

"This is all very fascinating, Winston," Cockran said. "Like an adventure story in *The Strand* magazine. But is there some other point to all this?"

Churchill smiled. "Indeed, there is. Please, don't stand on ceremony. Help yourself to more brandy." Churchill picked up his own brandy snifter. "From what I have read, the journal confirms the accuracy of Professor Campbell's monograph. But I also believe there are sufficient clues within the journal itself to actually help us locate this mysterious stronghold."

Campbell looked up from the notebook, his mouth slightly ajar. "Winston, this is magnificent. Kluge was correct. The Spear *was* taken to a mountain stronghold and, if this notebook is correct, there are only three possible locations."

Churchill felt Mattie's hand grip his arm tightly. Yes, all was going to be well, he thought. The bait had been carefully placed; the hook had been set; and now an *après* lunch stroll around the grounds of Chartwell would land the fish.

"Mattie, why don't you and the Prof join me for a brief walk while we explore whether Mr. Hearst might possibly be interested in footing the entire cost of our little expedition."

BEFORE lunch, Mattie had learned that, while Sir Archibald Hampton had been the other backer of the expedition along with Hearst, Hampton's estate was now tied up in court and his funding could no longer be counted on. As they walked, Mattie had assured Winston that W.R. would pick up the entire cost. Churchill had been pleased but she soon learned that her father's old protégé was the problem, not Hearst. It seemed that Campbell had panicked upon learning of Hampton's death. He had gone off and, by a stroke of luck, had found new financial backers who were threatening to upset Churchill's carefully designed plan. She could see from the frown starting to form on Churchill's face that Campbell was in for a rough ride.

"Please repeat that, Professor," Churchill said. "I'm not certain I understand."

"A Swiss foundation has agreed to fund the entire expedition. Twenty thousand pounds. The Geneva Institute for Scientific and Industrial Progress. I leave tomorrow morning by boat train for Paris. Then overnight to Geneva to meet with my sponsors and sign all the necessary papers. I appreciate all you've done, especially the officer's journal, but I'm sure you'll agree a Swiss foundation is much to be preferred to support from an American newspaper empire."

"Pray tell me what assurances you have, what *guarantees* from your new sponsors, that if you find the Spear, it will be placed in the British Museum?" Churchill asked.

"That hasn't been discussed, but naturally I assumed..." Campbell started to say.

Churchill cut him off. "You assumed? Exactly what did you assume?"

Mattie saw Campbell shrink back, like a cornered wildebeest before a lion in the African veldt.

"I assumed that the Swiss would want the Spear placed in one of their own museums."

To Mattie, it sounded like a growl from deep within Churchill's diaphragm before it emerged as a full-throated roar. "That is entirely out of the question. The Spear cannot remain on the European continent. That is the whole point of this exercise. To keep those bloody Germans from possessing a symbol under which they have far too often gone to war."

"I thought the point was to recover the Holy Spear!" Campbell said.

"The point of this exercise concerns the peace of Europe and quite possibly the world. I told you on numerous occasions that I have my own sources of intelligence about Germany. Both in and outside the country. I do not like the news I have received. There has always been talk in Germany of returning the Kaiser or his son, the Crown Prince, to the German throne. What I hear now is far more serious than that."

Churchill paused and pointed his cigar directly at Campbell who took a step back. "Recent reports I have received focus on the Crown Prince as a figurehead, the symbol of national unity for a new and more authoritarian government in Germany. Key conservatives there used to be frightened only of the Communists. Now, they are equally frightened of Adolf Hitler. He's simply too radical for those who like to think they pull the strings of power behind the scenes."

Churchill stared off into the distance, looking east over the weald of Kent. "It is not public knowledge, but I have been told by someone who has spoken to Hitler himself that, like the Kaiser, he has an almost mystical belief in what the Germans call the Spear of Destiny."

Churchill cast a knowing glance at Mattie who knew she was the source of that timely piece of intelligence. "We need to take that symbol away from them, Geoffrey. Take the Spear completely out of Europe and bring it to England. Bring it to this island with the breadth and depth of the English Channel between it and those who would plunge Europe into another war."

Mattie smiled as Churchill played his last card. Who did this mere academic think he was to interfere and dare disrupt the plan Churchill had carefully constructed? Mattie knew he was about to find out just what it meant to disagree with, let alone disappoint, Winston Churchill.

"I will not permit any use of the Austrian officer's journal in this endeavor unless there is a copper-fastened guarantee that the Lance of Longinus will be lodged in the permanent collection of the British Museum. Otherwise, I must insist you return the journal to me."

"But…but, Mr. Churchill, that would be terrible. The journal is crucial to our success. Please be reasonable. This is a sacred Christian relic. In the right hands, the hands of a true believer, it might even possess the healing power which so many have attributed to it. You cannot be so heartless. Please, I beseech you. I met with representatives of the Swiss foundation a few days ago in London and I agreed to their terms. I gave my word as a British gentleman."

Churchill was unmoved. "You may keep your word or you may keep the journal. You may not keep them both unless the Swiss agree to my conditions."

Much as she enjoyed seeing Churchill intimidate the small Scot, Mattie sensed her story and her quest might be slipping away. That was *not* going to happen. Not if Mattie could help it and she thought she could. She watched as Professor Campbell reluctantly handed over to Churchill the journal, the image of a Celtic cross on its worn and faded leather cover.

"Gentlemen. Perhaps a compromise can be arranged," Mattie said. "While Mr. Hearst is willing to fund the entire expedition, he would also agree to share the expense so long as he has exclusive worldwide publication rights. Since you haven't discussed with the Swiss exactly where the Spear will be displayed, why don't you tell them that the Spear must be placed in the permanent collection of the British Museum but you have no objection to its being loaned from time to time to a Swiss museum and put on display for a few months every other year?"

"Well…" Professor Campbell began.

"After all, if we recover the Spear, the two of you will be the ones most responsible. What could be more natural than your wish to see the Lance of Longinus in a permanent collection at the British Museum, which is especially fitting given that Longinus is buried in Britain? Temporary loans of the artifact, even on a regular basis, should be a relatively minor matter." Mattie turned to Churchill. "What do you say, Winston? Would that be satisfactory?"

Churchill removed the cigar from his mouth and pushed out his lower lip. In a pout or in contemplation, Mattie could not tell. After a long moment, Churchill spoke. "Very well. That seems a reasonable compromise. But, Mattie, you must be the one to negotiate the terms with the Swiss, not the Prof here. Will you do it?"

Mattie smiled. "I'll track down the Chief and ring him up this afternoon. I haven't even unpacked my bags so leaving tomorrow morning should pose no problem. Besides," she said with a laugh, "I've just out-negotiated the head of Germany's second largest political party. A Swiss banker will be duck soup."

Churchill beamed as he handed the leather journal back to Professor Campbell, the anger in his voice no longer present in the aftermath of having once more gotten his way. "Never fear, Geoffrey. You are in good hands with Mattie. An adventure awaits. Live dangerously; take things as they come; dread naught."

20.

The Spear Must Be Protected

THE Celtic cross tattoo on the inside of the man's wrist was momentarily visible as he lowered the powerful military field glasses through which he had observed the scene below. Closer inspection would have revealed that the binoculars in question were standard issue to the old Imperial Austrian Army's alpine troops. The man wore a long, dark overcoat, its collar turned up. His close-cropped hair was flecked with gray, a dueling scar prominent on his left cheek. He reached into a side pocket of the long coat and pulled out a battered leather notebook, the Celtic cross imprinted on its cover, and began making notes. The notebook was identical in appearance to the one that had passed between the two men he had observed with the red-haired woman five hundred yards below his elevated vantage point.

The *Ordi Novi Templi* had been reborn in 1905, the ancient sacred vows renewed. As the Prior, he had been celibate since 1915, but it was not of his own choosing. The war had seen to that. Still, it had allowed him to bring to bear on a subject a single-minded focus rare in other men more tempted by the flesh than he. Now, Josef Lanz had a new task and his focus once more would be single-minded. There were other relics over which he and his brothers stood watch, some even more precious than the Spear. But none more important or vital to mankind's future. His great-grandfather had been the one who carried the Spear from Nuremburg to Vienna after the battle of Austerlitz and kept it from the hands of Bonaparte, just as he had kept it safe from the crippled Hohenzollern who had sought the Spear in 1914 to both cure his withered left arm as well as ensure victory in war.

The Spear must be protected. Those who sought it would be deterred. Or they would die.

"**THAT'S** great news, Chief. Thanks. I really appreciate it. You won't be sorry."

Mattie hung up the telephone. Hearst had agreed to fund the entire expedition if that's what it took. How could he say no to his favorite reporter after her coup with Hitler a few days' earlier? Hearst had also acquiesced to Mattie's proposed changes in her itinerary—Geneva tomorrow; Milan to finalize Mussolini's new contract the next day; Berlin for a week of interviews with arms dealers and their agents; and, finally Venice for a fortnight with Cockran. Venice was non-negotiable. She and Cockran had to put their argument in New York behind them and repair the strain in their relationship. With her leaving for Geneva tomorrow, they wouldn't have time now. But, at least they could start the process and finish it in Venice.

Mattie walked downstairs, asked one of the maids if she had seen Mr. Cockran, and was directed outside. She paused at the french doors. Cockran was standing in a far corner, deep in conversation with Harmony Hampton. Mattie paused. It was almost time for cocktails. She decided she would talk to Cockran after dinner. She didn't think interrupting him during a business conversation for a personal matter was a good idea.

"**OF** course, Picasso changed everything." Harmony said as they stood in a corner of the terrace, waiting for dinner. "Modern art has never been the same after Cubism. And while Picasso's paintings display his undeniable talent, I... " She stopped with a guilty smile and took a step closer. "As an art historian, I shouldn't admit this." She craned her neck to whisper the secret in his ear. "But I can't stand to look at them."

Cockran was out of his element and struggled to sound intelligent. "But isn't cubism concerned with emphasizing the, ah, reality of the canvas?" He had no idea what that meant.

"That's what they say but I don't understand why reality is a desirable goal," Harmony said. Cockran was pleased that he hadn't sounded like a complete idiot.

"Reality can be ugly and depraved. Modern art should stand on the shoulders of the Romantic era's giants like Vermeer and Botticelli, even Leonardo. It should aspire to show the best of what men can be."

Cockran was about to reply when Churchill's butler interrupted. "Excuse me, Mr. Cockran, but you have a telephone call. A Mr. Sullivan. He said it was urgent."

"Thank you, George," Cockran said and excused himself to Harmony.

"Cockran here," he said into the receiver.

"The bastards blew up one of your client's factories tonight," Sullivan said.

"What? Which one? How did it happen?" Cockran asked.

"Not the main factory. The smaller one. The one that manufactures the paper punch cards. They'll be out of commission for several months. Curious, though. Two walls blown out but no machinery damaged."

"What's your assessment of the situation?"

"That you better get your sorry Irish arse over here quick or your client will have no plants left for you to beg the Krauts to protect."

Cockran hung up. Sullivan was right. He had to leave first thing tomorrow. There probably wouldn't be time to clear the air with Mattie. That would have to wait until Venice. On the way back to Harmony to resume his ill-informed defense of Picasso and modern art, he was once more interrupted by the butler. Dinner was served.

The evening meal began, as it usually did at Chartwell, with a monologue from Churchill, interspersed with the briefest of comments from his guests sufficient to confirm to their host that he still had their attention and that they understood that immediate freedom for India meant a bloodbath between Hindus and Muslims.

Eventually, as the main course of Cornish game hen was served, Churchill returned to the primary topic from lunch, Professor Campbell's theories about the spear that pierced the side of Christ. Cockran was surprised that Mattie didn't brighten up as she had earlier when they had discussed the professor's discoveries. He understood why it meant so much to her, given her father's lifelong devotion to Grail lore, and he was happy to see her so excited about a project far less dangerous than covering wars in far flung corners of the globe. He wondered if she had managed to talk to Hearst that afternoon.

His question was soon answered as Churchill eagerly told everyone of the latest developments involving possible financing from a Swiss group.

"Do you expect any problems with the Swiss?" Cockran asked.

"None. By the time Mattie is finished negotiating on Mr. Hearst's behalf, the Swiss will be as docile as lambs. The same way she handled *Herr* Hitler," Churchill said with a smile.

"When will you be going to Switzerland, Professor Campbell?" Harmony asked.

"Tomorrow morning, Miss Hampton. Miss McGary and I booked passage this afternoon on the boat train to Paris and the Orient Express to Geneva."

Mattie looked sheepish when Cockran raised his eyebrows in a silent question. *When were you going to tell me?*

"Winston," Harmony said. "You promised to tell me all about the German economy this weekend—something I must know if my lawyer is to succeed in transforming this poor academic into a high-powered business owner."

"A promise I shall keep, my dear," Churchill said.

COCKRAN and Mattie walked up the stairs together, holding hands. Would they go to her room? On the surface, she seemed to be over their argument in New York, a summer storm which passed quickly and left the sun shining again just like before. But Cockran was taking no chances. He wanted to keep the sun shining, warm breezes blowing and Mattie by his side. He wouldn't presume, so he paused at the door to his bedroom. Then he felt a gentle tug at his hand as Mattie pulled him down the corridor toward her room.

"We won't have two nights together like I hoped," she said as they entered her room, "but at least we can make the most of tonight."

Cockran was relieved. She *was* over it. He thought briefly of apologizing and talking it out but quickly rejected the notion. Why spoil her good mood? All he had to do was keep his big mouth shut and make her happy. He could handle that, he thought, stepping up behind Mattie and kissing the back of her neck as he reached around and clasped each of her breasts.

Mattie purred. "Do that again."

Cockran pushed the low front of her dress down, freeing her breasts.

"Not that, silly," she said. "My neck. Kiss it again. But don't stop the other. You *can* do both at the same time, can't you?"

"Once we get these off," Cockran said as he knelt down, unfastened her garter belt, and smoothly slid her silk panties down, "I'll show you three things I can do at the same time."

"Talk is cheap, Cockran," she said as she began to tug at his trousers. This was not the first time they had made love at Chartwell and the beds there made far too much noise on their own. While Cockran attempted to spread the duvet out on the floor, Mattie continued to pull at his clothes until they both collapsed beside the bed, laughing, as he kicked free of his clothes and kissed her again. One thing he adored about Mattie was the sheer variety of their lovemaking. They rarely started the same way twice in a row. Tonight, unlike the last time in New York, she pushed his face from between her legs, rolled him over and, in one easy motion, straddled his waist, her hands pressed down firmly on his chest. Her way of saying she was in charge now. It was fine with Cockran. Mattie stayed on top, quietly riding him with a fierce intensity until he felt her shudder with an orgasm, his own not far behind.

Afterwards, as they lay there together, Mattie still on top, Cockran spoke softly. "I know you're not going into a war zone," he began, "and no one's going to be shooting at you, but take care. I've never skied the Austrian Alps and I know the winter was comparatively mild, but still I worry…"

Mattie chuckled. "Don't worry about me, Cockran. If you promise not to tell anyone, I'll even admit that you might have a point about my taking too many risks. I mean, you're wrong most of the time. Most of the time, I really can't help it. It's simply the nature of my assignments. It's not something I can just give up. Not until we bring the arms merchants under control and expose them to the sunlight."

"For all the good that will do," Cockran said, a resigned tone to his voice.

"Come on, Bourke, be fair. We both agree on this and you know the Chief has important contacts on the Hill. They promised him a Neutrality Act for America if he manages to bring them the goods on the merchants of death and all they do to facilitate death and destruction. It won't solve the problem, but it will be a big start if the richest country in the world is taken out of the international arms trade."

Cockran nodded. "You're right. It's a start," leaving unspoken the rest of the sentence *but it will never be enough because someone else will sell them the weapons.* He wasn't going to begin another argument before they parted the next morning. "But you were saying I might be right some of the time about your risk-taking?" Cockran probed hopefully.

"Sure. Even a broken watch is right twice a day. It happened on the zeppelin, and I was foolish and you were right. I took a wild risk I shouldn't have. And with hindsight, it was unnecessary."

Cockran listened without saying a word as Mattie told him about her excursion through and the danger she encountered on top of the *Graf Zeppelin.* He felt his anger growing as she continued. He knew it had a happy ending because he was holding her in his arms, but happy endings were not always guaranteed. The two of them were living proof of that. Each of them had lost loved ones well before their time. But, Cockran thought with growing bitterness, none of them had died as a consequence of deliberately and recklessly risking their lives. Soldiers in combat took more care for their well-being than Mattie had on the zeppelin.

"It's not going to be easy for me. But you're right that I need to be more careful." Mattie continued, "I've been taking risks for so long, it's almost second nature. I never stop to think if there's a safer way to do my job. But I'm trying Bourke, I really am. I even let another motorcar pass me on the way back from my interview with Hitler."

Cockran bit his tongue. He was *not* going to start a fight. Or, as he reflected later, he certainly hadn't intended to start a fight. It sort of.... just happened.

"Well, aren't you going to say anything?" Mattie said at last as she pushed herself up on her arms and looked down at him.

"What can I say?" Cockran said. "I hope you mean it. But I'll believe it when I see it."

"What do you mean by that?" Mattie demanded. She sat up now, astride him still.

"Look," Cockran said. "Nothing I say ever makes any difference to you when it comes to your own safety. It all goes in one ear and out the other. You twist things so that it looks like I'm criticizing your career when it's just not so. It doesn't matter to you that I love you or that Paddy loves you. What you did on the zeppelin makes that all too clear."

"That's not fair, Bourke. You do matter to me and I'm trying to change. Really."

"Sure. Until the next time you have to choose between a story and your safety."

"That's a helpful attitude. You obviously didn't hear a thing I said about my new insights."

Cockran took a deep breath and let it out slowly. "I'm sorry if you think that, but it's all the help I can offer. After what you did on that airship...," Cockran said, his voice trailing off as he shook his head. "There's nothing to say. And for God's sake, don't give me that 'good enough, close enough' crap from Eisenstadt. I'm up to here with it!"

"Well then, to hell with you, Cockran." Mattie said, her voice rising in anger. "You don't know how hard it is to change habits that I've had for so long. I try to explain how I'm beginning to take your advice to heart and this is what I receive in return? Like I said in New York, I need someone on my side, not at my throat. After I said it, I thought I was wrong. But now I'm not so sure. Maybe we really do need a break from each other. Maybe it's me. Maybe I can't be what you need in a woman. But I do know this. If you're still copping this same attitude when we're together in Venice, I'll have my answer."

Cockran made no reply as Mattie got up and walked to the bed. Words were not going to make this better. At least not the words he had in mind. Why couldn't she get as close as she could for her photos *without* risking her life?

Mattie wrapped the blankets around her and lay on her side facing away from him. Ordinarily, he would have crawled in beside her. Mattie never wore clothes while sleeping and Cockran loved waking up next to her, gently squeezing whatever came first to hand and then going back to sleep. But not tonight. He waited until her deep, even breathing signaled she was asleep and he got up from the floor, put his clothes on and kissed her softly on the cheek, whispering "I love you", before he eased open the door and returned to his room.

21.

The Orient Express

Aboard the Orient Express
Monday, 1 June 1931

THE Orient Express was like an old friend because Hearst's journalists always traveled first class and, for Mattie, it was the only way to travel. She was very much looking forward to her new adventure but she was still playing over in her mind her argument with Cockran last night. Making love had been so sweet and then he had to go and ruin everything by starting the same argument they had in New York a week ago. Couldn't he appreciate that telling him about the zeppelin incident meant she really was trying to change? She shook her head. It could have been worse. At least she had said nothing about her last dance with Kurt.

Mattie knew there had to be give and take in a relationship but she had admitted, albeit grudgingly, that he had a point and that she was going to try to change. Wasn't he supposed to encourage her? Those were the rules, weren't they? Being in love was so confusing.

What made it all so much worse was Cockran's new client. She tried but failed once more to erase the image from her mind. Cockran and Harmony standing at the front entrance of Chartwell, waving goodbye to her and Professor Campbell as the taxi picked them up to take them to the train. That blonde vixen had been latched onto Cockran's arm like a limpet, looking a lot happier than she had the day before, her sorrow for her stepfather blithely put aside.

And why not? She was leaving later that same day with Mattie's man for a cozy little holiday in Germany. Berlin and then Munich. On business. How convenient. Yet when Mattie had suggested meeting them when she came up to Berlin from Milan, Cockran put her off. They would keep in touch but they might not be in Berlin when she arrived.

Mattie looked out the window of her compartment at the rolling French countryside. She was not by nature a jealous woman. But there was something about Harmony that she just didn't like. She had absolutely fawned over Paddy and Mattie could see that the boy had been embarrassed by the attention. Yet Mattie had been so caught up with Winston and Professor Campbell that she had no time to spend with Paddy herself. She knew he idolized her and she could still see the disappointment in his eyes that she hadn't done so.

What bothered her the most was that she had no idea what business was taking the two of them to Germany, only that it involved her stepfather's company. Client confidentiality is what Cockran had said. Like a priest and penitent. She was used to that. Really. A court case was different. Cockran could talk about that more freely because all or most of it was a matter of public record. Not so with Harmony. His business with her was secret. Harmony was free to tell Mattie but Cockran wasn't. He had even encouraged Mattie to talk with Harmony before she left for Geneva. Harmony might benefit, he said, from an older woman's perspective on her problems. Ouch! An "older woman" at thirty-one? Mattie was a journalist, not a nursemaid, and she wasn't going to initiate anything of the sort.

Mattie glanced at her wristwatch. Dinner was being served. Good. She could use a drink right now. If she didn't see Cockran in Berlin, it was no big deal. Within a week, they'd be together in Venice and Harmony could go to hell.

Sitting in the dining car, its burnished mahogany paneling warmly inviting, illuminated by the glow of brass fixtures polished to a mirrorlike finish, Mattie sipped a martini and waited for Campbell to be shown to her table. On an academic's salary, Geoffrey Campbell could not afford a first-class compartment on the Orient Express and was relegated to a second-class carriage with a sleeping berth. By railroad policy, Professor Campbell was not permitted in the first-class dining car either, but Mattie had always believed in tipping well and the five pound note she slipped to the conductor had assured her both a secure location in the conductor's safe for Major Lanz's journal as well as a seat at her table for her father's protégé.

Mattie was looking forward to dinner with Campbell. She never tired of hearing about her father. She and her brothers had basked in the love he felt for them even if his Scottish reserve kept him from telling others how proud he was of his children. For their part, his children never tired of telling others what a great man their father was. Not because he was a Member of Parliament, which the children had never found that impressive because their father told them it wasn't. What they admired most about their father was his ability to spin a great story. The Knights of the Round Table. King Arthur. The Holy Grail. After her two brothers went away to school they learned—and told Mattie— that all the stories their father told them were based on his own articles and books on Celtic and Christian legends about the Holy Grail.

Mattie looked up and smiled as Geoffrey Campbell arrived wearing the same worn tweed jacket she had seen him in the night before. She signaled their waiter to serve the soup course. During dinner, she discovered Campbell had been one of her father's principal assistants on his last book and had edited the final manuscript.

"Did Father really believe the Holy Grail was more than a legend?"

"Aye, that he did. Your father was a Christian gentleman as well as a scholar. He believed that Joseph of Arimathea secured both the Grail and the Lance of Longinus after Christ died. The Grail, he believed, was hidden in the Pyrenees. The Merovingians were its guardians after the Templars were disbanded. He didn't believe their secrets would ever be given up."

"Why did he devote so much research to the Celtic legends of the Cup and the Spear?"

"Your father was a scientist as well as a believer. He could not ignore the reality of Celtic legends so close to Christian ones. But he found no convincing evidence that one legend depended on another. Since your father believed, as do I, that there is only one true God who died for our sins, his conclusion was that the Celtic legends had been divinely inspired so as to better prepare the pagans for their eventual conversion to Christianity, where the Cup and the Spear were much more than legends. They were historic facts."

The waiter cleared away their soup tureens and brought the fish course, Dover sole caught the day before in the English Channel and accompanied by a crisp white Bordeaux.

"When did you first suspect that the Hofburg Lance was a replica?"

"Ten years ago in a graduate seminar taught by your father. Unlike the Shroud of Turin and the pieces of wood purporting to be from the Cross, he believed that the Hofburg Spear was the one ancient relic whose provenance could not be disputed and could actually be traced from one leader to another, starting with the Emperor Constantine. But the photograph he showed us of the Hofburg Spear, which he personally took before the war, did not square with my memory of the Spear when I saw it for myself after the war. It wasn't a big difference and now I know it was not the only difference, but one specific nail was different from the one I saw in Vienna. A nail which had been added during Constantine's reign, a nail from the true Cross. Your father was certain I was mistaken, that my memory was playing tricks on me. But he was a scholar above all so he gave me one of his own photographs to compare the next time I was in Vienna."

Campbell paused and took a sip of Bordeaux. "Even though he disagreed with me, your father sent a letter to a Hofburg curator he knew well, positing my theory and asking him to forward a current photograph of the Lance so that he could compare it with his own photographs. Unfortunately, your father died shortly thereafter and I spent the next two years editing his book. After that, I took a position as a lecturer in archeology at the University of Glasgow, where I still teach today. I was under much pressure from the Master of our College to abandon my Grail studies. I really had no choice. So I put aside my concerns about the Spear. But once the Master retired in the winter of 1930, I caught the first train to Vienna."

Campbell smiled and shrugged his shoulders. "The rest of it you know."

Back in Mattie's compartment after dinner, the porter had made up her bed for the night. Mattie stripped and slid between the sheets.

Moments later, lulled by the familiar clacking of steel wheels on rails, Mattie was fast asleep.

MATTIE woke up and sensed that something was wrong. The train had stopped. She looked at the travel alarm clock ticking away beside her head. 3:48 a.m. She rang for the porter and then quickly rummaged through her suitcase to find her green silk gown, shivering slightly at the cool night air upon her bare skin. There was a knock on the door and Mattie opened it slightly then all the way as she saw the porter's familiar face.

"Edouard, is there a problem?" she asked in French.

"No, *Mademoiselle*," he replied. "We have stopped to take on water and fuel. Our last opportunity before the mountains." Edouard pulled out a large gold-plated stop watch from his pocket of his vest. "We shall be here for another nineteen minutes."

"How long have we been waiting here?"

"For eleven minutes. We always stop at the last station before the Swiss border for thirty minutes precisely."

Mattie thanked him and then padded down the carpeted passageway in her slippers to the W.C. When she returned, the door to her compartment was slightly ajar. She thought she had closed it but she shrugged it off. She pushed the compartment door open and stepped inside. Immediately a large hand clamped strongly over her mouth while an equally strong arm encircled her waist, lifting her bodily off the floor. A closet door opened and a tall man stepped out, a scar on his left cheek the most prominent feature on a hard face with dark brown eyes beneath closely cropped dark hair highlighted with flecks of silver.

"You have nothing to fear, *Fraulein*, so long as you cooperate," the man said in Austrian-accented German. "But if you cry out, I will kill you."

Mattie nodded and her mouth was released. "I don't speak German," Mattie replied.

"I believe you do, *Fraulein* McGary," he said, switching to English. "But as I said, if you cooperate, you have nothing to fear."

"How do you know my name?"

"Your family's name is well-known to any who safeguard our Savior's sacred relics."

"What do you want?"

The man smiled. "I want the journal," he said, pulling a small leather notebook from his pocket and showing it to her. "It looks like this and I believe you have it."

Mattie looked at it. It was a near duplicate of the journal they had received from Churchill, a Celtic cross embossed on its cover.

"I don't have it," Mattie lied. "We left it in England. I only brought the translation."

The man smiled. "Our Order and our holy vows prohibit us from harming innocent women and children. When you accept a man's responsibility, however, as you have chosen to do, you must accept a man's consequences. Hold her, while I search the compartment."

Mattie watched as the man with the scar began to search the compartment, strewing her clothes carelessly around the compartment, ripping open the lining of her suitcase with a stiletto he had pulled from inside his coat.

The man looked at the watch on his wrist and then spoke to Mattie's captor. "Only ten more minutes and the train will leave. We have no more time." He reached into his pocket and pulled the Luger out from the holster where he had placed it during the search. He reached into his jacket's lower left-hand pocket and pulled out a three-inch long sound suppresser and began calmly screwing it into the barrel of the pistol.

"I regret this, *Fraulein* but, as I said, accepting a man's responsibilities leads to a man's consequences."

Mattie froze, her eyes wide. A nod from the man with the scar and the hand over her mouth was pulled back. Mattie's mind was racing. She could tell him the truth, that the journal was in the train conductor's safe, but he might not believe her. The sound suppresser showed he meant business. She quickly weighed her options. There wasn't time for the truth.

"It's in my suitcase. There's a false bottom. I can open it more quickly than you."

The man with the scar finished screwing in the sound suppresser and motioned with his hand once more. Mattie felt the arm around her waist release her.

"We don't have much time. We have no further need for the Britisher. His knowledge of the Spear is too great to let him live. Here is the pass key to the compartment where we left him." he said, handing it to Mattie's captor with his left hand while keeping his silenced automatic trained on Mattie. "If she is telling the truth, she lives. Our Savior would not approve if I failed to keep my word. Her family has endured enough. But if she has lied, she will suffer a man's consequences."

He motioned with the pistol toward Mattie's suitcase and she bent over it, her back to him while her fingers searched for the concealed latch, finding it quickly, her fingers clasping the cold surface of the Walther PPK automatic below. For all her resentment of Cockran's lectures on her safety punctuated by recitations of Michael Collins' rules, there was one of the Big Fella's rules Mattie had always followed: *Never draw a weapon unless you intend to use it. Don't threaten people with guns, shoot them.* Mattie lived by that rule to the letter, and it had saved her life on more than one occasion.

"Here it is," she said as she turned around and fired her weapon, the sharp report of the pistol echoing within the small compartment. Her shot went wide to the left, splintering the mahogany panel behind the man.

The man with the scar had been startled by the noise of the gunshot and his return fire missed the mark also, both his shots muffled by the sound suppresser as they went over Mattie's head, shattering the train compartment's window behind her. Before Mattie could fire again, the man swept past her, clubbing her on the side of the head with his arm and knocking her to the floor of the compartment. The man then deftly opened the exterior door of the carriage compartment by reaching through the now shattered window and darted from the train onto the platform. Mattie regained her feet, looked through the window, the Walther in her hand, but the platform was deserted.

Loud knocks hammered on the compartment's interior door. Mattie stood beside the door, opening it carefully with her left hand and thrust her right hand out, preparing to shoot if it were those men returning. But it was Edouard with a concerned look on his face.

"*Mon dieu*! What has happened, *Mademoiselle*?"

"My companion!" Mattie said breathlessly. "Please check out the second-class carriage. Professor Campbell's berth. I fear the men who attacked me may have attempted to harm him as well."

"Very well."

Edouard returned a few minutes later. "Your friend is unharmed, *Mademoiselle*," he said. "If you will be so kind as to follow me, I have arranged adjoining first-class compartments for both of you in the next carriage. On behalf of the Orient Express, please accept our apologies for this disruption in your travel. I will have someone gather your things and bring them to your new compartment."

Mattie smiled. "Thank you. You are most kind. Would you also arrange for a bottle of scotch whisky and two tumblers? Two *large* tumblers?"

Edouard nodded. "It will be my pleasure, *Mademoiselle*," he said, tipping his cap.

One scotch down and beginning on her second, Mattie finally stopped shaking. "It's been a while since I've been shot at, but it sure looked like he had a journal just like the one we have."

Campbell finished the last of his scotch and poured another as well.

"I miscalculated. It never occurred to me that any of the men who had hidden the Spear were still alive. How could they have known our plans?" he said, shaking his head. "Perhaps you ought to reconsider, Miss McGary. This is far too dangerous for a woman. If I am fortunate enough to meet your father in eternity, I won't be able to face him if I have been responsible for any harm befalling his only daughter."

Mattie bristled. Now was no time to play it safe. If she had been more cautious tonight, she might be dead. "You have absolutely no idea how my father raised his only daughter," Mattie said, draining the last of her scotch and staring directly into Campbell's eyes. "Those bastards can't stop me. And if you want to be able to face my father in eternity, you'd better not try either."

Part IV

Germany, Switzerland, Egypt and Austria

1 June –7 June 1931

[T]he [National Socialists'] road to power was blocked. Only crass errors by the country's rulers could open up a path. And only a blatant disregard by Germany's power elites for safeguarding democracy — in fact, the hope that economic crisis could be used as a vehicle to bring about democracy's demise and replace it by a form of authoritarianism — could induce such errors.

Ian Kershaw
Hitler, 1889-1936: Hubris

22.

The Captains and the Kings

A **SERIES** of long closed motor cars, Mercedes and Daimlers mostly, began to arrive at a large estate in Potsdam on the outskirts of Berlin, near Wansee. It was a clear, crisp evening and the sound of the tires crunching the carefully combed stone in the driveway was louder than the silent purr of the engines. Each motor car contained one passenger. A total of nine vehicles each arriving precisely two minutes apart. The initial arrival was Anton Dressler—Zurich. He was greeted warmly by his host, Fritz von Thyssen, known to the others as Berlin. Zurich watched as each new man was greeted in turn by those who arrived before him. The servants were there to take their outer garments and serve champagne in tall, crystal flutes.

After gathering in the large, octagonal foyer, Berlin directed them into the Great Hall where they continued to converse in small groups. A massive, barrel-vaulted ceiling loomed two stories above them, an interior balcony on all four sides of the room. Paintings and tapestries covered the wood-paneled walls on the first floor while the balcony's walls were lined with floor to ceiling bookcases. Lighting from brass chandeliers cast a warm glow on the figures talking softly below. A fire was blazing in a huge fire place at the end of the room. Lights from sconces on the oak-paneled walls provided the only other illumination in the room. The servants still circulated, carrying more substantial drinks than the champagne offered earlier.

Zurich drained the last of his single malt, placed it on a silver tray held by a hovering servant, and started to move to the large table which dominated the center of the room. He rapped his heavy fountain pen on its mahogany surface to gain the group's attention. The servants withdrew. Social amenities were over. The meeting of the Board of Directors of the Geneva Institute for Scientific and Industrial Progress had begun. There were only three items on the agenda: the restoration of the Kaiser's son to the German throne; the forthcoming war between Bolivia and Paraguay where Geneva was arming both sides; and freedom for the many peoples of India—Muslim and Hindu alike—freedom, that is, to kill each other with the most modern weapons the men of Geneva were all too willing to sell them. That was Geneva's formula and had been for over 30 years. Small conflicts. Little wars. Controllable. Profitable. The ancient hatreds were still intact. Money was still there to be made. The business of the Geneva Group was blood and steel and business was good.

KURT von Sturm rose from his chair at the side of the room after being called upon by Zurich. His voice was neutral as he reported on his recent interview with the Kaiser and the Crown Prince. His voice did not betray his own low opinion of both men. Even the mention of the £20,000 it would cost for an expedition to search for the Spear in largely unpopulated areas of the Austrian Alps did not, by his voice or his body language, betray his skepticism.

Sturm was surprised, therefore, by the discussion which followed his brief recital of the preparation necessary to clear the path for the Kaiser's return—the training of the three-man sniper team to assassinate President Hindenburg. The recital even included the identity of the third man on the team, the "patsy" as the Americans would say, a Communist factory worker at one of Fritz von Thyssen's steel mills who would soon be unemployed and would subsequently serve as a convenient scapegoat when the Reds were blamed for Hindenburg's assassination.

Sturm watched as the newest member, Manhattan, raised his hand and was recognized by Zurich. He unfolded his large frame and rose slowly to his feet. "Thank you, Mr. Chairman. I realize that the group has already decided that there must be someone new to serve as

Chancellor of a new Germany, rearmed and free of the arms restrictions of Versailles. A worthy goal and one I support. But is General Kurt von Schleicher the best man to accomplish this? Does he have what it takes to rally the people to his side?"

Sturm could see the impatience in Zurich's eyes which fluttered slightly as he cut Manhattan off in mid-sentence. "That subject is *not* on tonight's agenda. Von Schleicher was the head of *Sondergruppe R.* He supervised Germany's clandestine military alliance with the Soviet Union for the past twelve years. It is because of von Schleicher that Germany was able to develop in Russia the most modern weapons in Europe. Tanks. Artillery. Planes. More advanced forms of poison gas."

"I understand, Zurich," Manhattan replied in a patient voice. "What I question is whether von Schleicher is anything more than a gray-faced career army bureaucrat who inspires no one, especially when compared to a spellbinding speaker like Hitler. There is a real leader."

Sturm watched Zurich's face slowly turn red while the vein on his left temple became more prominent. Sturm had little respect for Manhattan in more ways than one but the American had a point. Von Schleicher's career depended upon the favor of others more highly placed. Hitler was unique and depended only on intuition and his iron will.

"Lead Germany where? Another world war fought on two fronts? All of this has been discussed and decided previously before you joined us," Zurich snapped. "Hitler is unstable and dangerous. An Austrian rabble rouser, nothing more. Von Schleicher, by contrast, is one of us. The men around this table know him personally, as you do not. He is sound. He agrees with the lessons this group drew from the Great War. He will not risk a general European war, let alone another world war. No one who has read Hitler's book can say the same of him."

Manhattan threw up his large hands in mock surrender. "I defer to your greater wisdom, Zurich. But isn't £20,000 a bit rich? I understand that all monarchs have their little symbols of authority, but couldn't we just buy him another spear instead? A nice shiny new one?"

"That is not for you to decide, Manhattan. We must respect the Kaiser's wishes."

"The old man sounds gaga, Zurich. If it's so important, why doesn't he kick in money?"

Sturm had never seen Zurich so close to losing his temper nor had he ever seen a new member of Geneva take such an assertive stance at only his first meeting. He cleared his throat and rose. Sturm would have to rescue Zurich from the presumptuous American's attack.

"Mr. Chairman, if I may. In a recent conversation with Professor Campbell, the British archeologist who has persuaded the Kaiser that the spear in the Hofburg is a replica, he informed me that an American newspaper publisher has also expressed an interest in funding the expedition. Campbell said that he hoped some arrangement could be worked out between us and the American publisher. I was noncommittal, but if Manhattan's concern is solely about expense, we could partner with the American publisher. Our financial exposure could then be reduced."

Sturm was surprised by the vigorous debate which ensued because, in his experience, dating back some ten years, Zurich's proposals were invariably approved with rarely a dissenting vote. But tonight, the group was not his to control. It wasn't the money, Sturm concluded, no matter what the others said. There were other factors at work. Perhaps it was the members' distaste for doing the bidding and moving at the whim of the former German emperor. In the end, it was Rome who proposed a compromise which secured a bare majority vote over the opposition led by Manhattan. Kurt was authorized to spend £10,000 on the expedition, but no more. The rest would have to come from the Americans.

It was also Rome who raised the last question before the meeting moved on to less controversial topics—war between Bolivia and Paraguay; freedom for India; and the projected profits to follow. "I assume Professor Campbell and his new sponsor are unaware of the Kaiser's interest in the Spear?" Rome asked. "Is that not correct?"

"That is correct," Sturm replied. "Professor Campbell informs me that a new condition of his participation is that the Spear, once located, be placed in The British Museum."

Sturm paused and took a sip of ice water. He smiled. "All of which is quite irrelevant. Once we find the Spear, we will no longer need either the Professor or any American journalists accompanying us. For the inexperienced, mountains can be a dangerous place," he said, drawing an appreciative chuckle from the men of the Geneva Group.

WESLEY Waterman, known to the Geneva Group as "Manhattan", was pleased with his first Geneva meeting. He had used the same tactic many times in the business world where the participants in a meeting were people with whom he had not done business before. Start a disagreement over a minor matter; sit back; and watch how the others react.

Earlier, after Waterman had been furnished the identities of all the members of the Geneva Group, he had been pleased to discover that his company did business in each of the countries from which the members came. He then arranged for his own agents in those countries to prepare detailed dossiers on each member of the Geneva Group. In his estimation, it would take no longer than two years at the most to accomplish his goals.

His eyes circled the room and found the man his dossiers indicated he needed in order to accomplish his first goal—sabotaging the ill-conceived Kaiser plot to assassinate Hindenburg..

"Munich, may I have a private word with you?"

"Certainly, Manhattan. It is unusual for an American to have your insight into German politics. Von Schleicher cannot compare to Hitler. Unfortunately, only a few in the Geneva Group agree with me. There is only so much one person can do."

Waterman smiled. "One man can do a lot more than you think, my friend." This was going to be easy. "Do you know any American journalists here in Berlin?"

"No, I do not."

"No matter," Waterman replied. "I do. When the time is right, I will show you what you can accomplish as only one person. We Americans call it the power of the press."

"I do not understand," Munich said.

"Let me explain. The Kaiser is not the only one who believes in the Spear of Destiny."

Waterman knew Munich was a very wealthy man who owned arms manufacturing works in both Holland and Czechoslovakia which together were second in size only to Krupp. Munich listened as Waterman told the German of his meeting the day before with Heinrich Himmler where he gave the SS Chief more details on the Kaiser assassination plot. He had previously told Himmler by trans-Atlantic telephone of the Kaiser's quest for the Spear of Destiny after Zurich had briefed him in New York. By the time Waterman had finished, Munich's eyes were wide and his head was bobbing in agreement. He was hooked. Just like Himmler.

"*Ja*, I understand. I agree. You need only say the word and I will do what you suggest."

Waterman smiled as he shook Munich's hand. This was not going to be difficult. It would only take a year and a half. With Hitler in power—his second goal—a National Socialist state would be a eugenicist's dream, a shining beacon to all those dedicated to improving the human race and weeding out the weak. One nation with the courage to conduct a unique scientific experiment, impossible to achieve in a democracy, the greatest experiment in all creation—the perfection of the human race. By subtraction as well as addition. And, of course, the profits for I.C.E. would be enormous because a eugenics-based utopia could not exist without calculating machines, thousands of them. Machines to track and categorize every single person within its borders. Doing well by doing good was how Wesley Waterman thought of it.

23.

A Pleasant Surprise

The brass name plate on the shiny black lacquered door was discreet—*The Geneva Institute For Scientific and Industrial Progress.* The door was locked. Professor Campbell pressed the buzzer and a voice echoed from the intercom system set into the side of the doorway. Campbell gave their two names and the voice instructed them to take the elevator inside the door to the third floor. A buzzer sounded and the door unlocked. Mattie opened it and the two of them entered a small anteroom paneled in rich walnut, brass lamps on two walnut tables providing the only illumination. At the end of the room was a small elevator. They walked up to it and Mattie pulled the door of the elevator back, and then the scissored iron gates behind it.

They stepped out on the third floor into a room roughly twice the size of the ground floor antechamber. A very fit young man, no more than twenty-five, sat behind a mahogany desk where a brass lamp provided the only light other than the lamps highlighting miniature paintings on both sides of the walnut paneled room.

Professor Campbell introduced them and explained they had an appointment with *Herr* von Strasser. Von Strasser? Interesting, Mattie thought. Campbell had never told her the name of the Geneva Institute's director. Strasser was a common German name but still, *von* Strasser?

The young man nodded his head and rose from behind the desk. His features which had heretofore been in shadow above the desk lamp, came into view. Close-cropped sandy brown hair. Blue eyes, high cheek bones. Unsmiling. He wore a blue pin-striped suit making him look like a young banker but for his broad chest, narrow waist and large hands. He spoke to them in German, introduced himself as Willi Wirth and apologized for any inconvenience, but made it clear he intended to search them both for weapons, which he did. Thoroughly. First the Professor, and then Mattie who found it unsettling to be patted down, let alone having the young man's fingers plunge inside the waistband of her skirt and circle her waist.

Wirth bowed, apologized again and returned to the desk. He spoke quietly into the phone. "*Herr* von Strasser will see you now," he said, gesturing with his hand toward a door on the left.

A buzzer followed by a click signaled the door had been unlocked. Professor Campbell held the door open for Mattie and they walked into a large office lined with bookshelves, the afternoon sun streaming through two floor-to-ceiling windows on the left, a heavy brass chandelier, all of its lights lit, hanging in the center of the room. The man at the desk had risen upon the door being opened, stepped forward from behind the desk, a greeting on his lips.

"Professor Campbell. I am delighted to…," he said and then stopped in mid-stride.

Mattie stopped at the same time, equally as surprised as Kurt von Sturm to find themselves standing not ten feet from each other. She felt her cheeks flush and hoped she was not blushing as her mind flashed back to the *Graf Zeppelin* and their passionate kiss.

Sturm recovered quickly and, after a pause of only a few seconds, resumed his greeting, "… see you again. And to be accompanied by such a charming and lovely companion. This is a pleasant surprise. How are you, *Fraulein* McGary?" he asked, extending his hand.

Mattie took his hand and shook it. It was still as dry and warm and large as when it had been caressing her bare back. In front of others, they apparently were not on a first name basis.

"I'm fine, *Herr* von Sturm. And you? I trust you have been well?"

"Thank you, yes. But never better than now. Please, come in. Have a seat, both of you," he said, gesturing toward four red leather armchairs placed in a semicircle around a low table.

"I had prepared both coffee and tea," Sturm said, "believing my guests would be American and British. But I think we can dispense with the coffee. Is that satisfactory?"

"Yes, tea would be lovely, thank you," Mattie said.

Mattie was curious as to why Kurt was using his birth name, but this was business and she was not going to bring up anything personal.

Sturm took a sip of tea from the delicate cup, his hands, notwithstanding their large size, looked surprisingly graceful, not at all out of place in such a civilized setting.

"So you two know each other?" Campbell asked.

"Only briefly. Quite by chance we were tablemates on board the *Graf Zeppelin* a week ago. I fear Miss McGary was bored spending so much time talking to a German businessman. But enough pleasantries. Let's discuss what has brought you here to Geneva."

Mattie smiled at Sturm's comments. He was many things but boring was not one of them. She had already rehearsed what she was going to say to a white-haired, balding Swiss banker-type and she decided to treat Sturm the same way. She made her points quickly. Hearst's willingness to fund the entire expedition in exchange for worldwide rights; the requirement that the Spear, if found, be donated to the British Museum; and Churchill's refusal to furnish the Austrian officer's journal if the latter condition were not fulfilled. She mentioned Campbell's concern that he had given his word as a British gentleman to Sturm, but she was certain Sturm would understand and agree.

"I am not a solicitor but I believe oral contracts are as binding as written ones under English common law. Based upon the Professor's assurances, the Institute has already begun making purchases for our excursion into the Austrian Alps. The Institute has ample resources to fund such an expedition and several members of our board of directors are trustees on the boards of several fine Swiss museums who would welcome a gift of the Hofburg lance.

Sturm rose from his chair and walked over to look out the window. "Based on my own research, I believe we can locate the castle containing the Spear without the journal."

Mattie stiffened. She didn't like the direction their discussion was taking. She had read a translation of the journal on the train. While there was no map in the journal, there were signposts and landmarks. Unless the Professor had given a copy of the journal to Sturm....Mattie quickly dismissed that. The only copies were the English translations which British Naval Intelligence made for Churchill. She had one and Churchill kept the other.

"I'm not a lawyer either, *Herr* von Strasser," Mattie began, his last name a signal that she was still all business. "But businessmen need not rely on lawyers to sort out their disagreements. Let's see if we can't find a mutually agreeable solution."   Thereafter, Mattie outlined the compromise—the Spear could be exhibited in Switzerland from time to time under tight conditions of security in exchange for the Institute's funding half the expedition, with Hearst still retaining exclusive world publication rights.

"Four months at a Swiss museum each year?" Sturm asked.

Mattie shook her head. "Three months. Every other year."

Sturm nodded. "Very well. We have agreement," Sturm said and then turned back from the window to face Mattie. "One further stipulation." Mattie's eyes narrowed, but she waited in silence for Sturm to speak. "As I expect to be leading the expedition myself, albeit under Professor Campbell's guidance and direction, I reserve the right to approve all members of the expedition, including any photographers or journalists Mr. Hearst chooses to accompany us."

Mattie was relieved. "Hearst is sending a photographer and a journalist," she said with a smile. "But only one person. Me. It was my idea and I'm seeing it through. If you have a problem with that, then we are not agreed. Plus, I have another condition of my own."

"We're agreed," Sturm said. "Mountains are a dangerous place, even in late spring. I merely wanted assurance that whoever Mr. Hearst assigned to our project would not slow us down or hamper our progress. I am delighted you will be joining us. Your other condition?"

"The expedition cannot begin for at least another three weeks. I am leaving for Italy tonight on business before traveling to Berlin for interviews I have scheduled. That will take a week. After that, I will be in Venice for two weeks on a long-scheduled holiday. If that does not fit with your schedule, then the Hearst organization will go it alone," Mattie said. Two weeks in Venice with the man she loved before the expedition began ought to be a sufficient inoculation against her attraction to Sturm once they were together on their search for the Spear.

"No need for threats," Sturm said pleasantly. "We are still agreed."

STURM waved goodbye as Mattie stepped into a first-class compartment on the train to Milan. She had accepted Sturm's offer to escort her to the train while Professor Campbell had agreed to stay behind in Geneva and help Sturm arrange for the supplies and equipment they would need for a late spring journey deep into the Austrian Alps.

The negotiations had gone better than he had expected and Mattie's presence was a welcome bonus. Of course, he would have to modify his plans. The demise of Professor Campbell was still a given but, with Mattie along, it would have to be a most convincing accident because no similar fate could possibly lay in store for her. Eventually, she would learn that the spear was not going to England but by then, Sturm would have sealed her fate in an entirely different way. The momentary rebuff on the zeppelin was now only a temporary setback. The hunt was still on. The prey was alert to the chase but that simply meant success would be all the sweeter when she surrendered her body to his. And he knew, from long experience as well as their single kiss, that she surely would.

24.

A Return to Germany

COCKRAN made his way from the dining car into the narrow passageway of the overnight rail car, his eyelids growing heavy with sleep. Harmony had retired before him and Cockran had relished the opportunity to be alone with a book and a brandy. Conversation with the engaging Harmony Hampton was interesting, enlightening…and, occasionally, exhausting. She was clearly a bright and well-read young woman who had a talent for turning a conversation to areas she enjoyed and knew a lot about—painting, sculpture, cinema and literature. Except for literature, these were subjects about which he knew little. And, even there, he didn't share her recently acquired taste for Henrik Ibsen.

Arriving at his sleeping compartment, he saw light seeping out from the crack beneath his compartment's door. He stopped and his hand went to the Webley in his shoulder holster. The porter may have turned down his bed but there was no reason for the light to be on.

Cockran pulled the revolver out, thumb resting on the hammer, and quietly stepped forward. The door to his compartment opened inward so he positioned his left shoulder against the door with his left hand resting upon the handle. Webley raised, he twisted the handle, leaned with his shoulder, and flung the door open. He was greeted by a small feminine scream, quickly smothered by a slender hand attached to an equally slender arm of a shapely young body sitting up on his bunk wearing a sheer, pale night gown that revealed much and concealed little.

Her fright quickly turned to laughter. "My, that certainly was a dramatic entrance," she said as she put down the book she had been reading. Ibsen. It figured.

Cockran lowered his gun, turning his attention from the way the gown accentuated the smooth curve of her breasts. "I saw a light on in my room," he said, finding his voice and replacing the Webley in his shoulder holster.

"I didn't want to surprise you in the dark with a woman in your bed," she said with a smile on her lips.

"Why aren't you in your own compartment?"

"I'm sorry", she said, her smile disappearing. "I meant to ask you about this in the dining car but I was embarrassed. I don't think I can manage being alone in my compartment. The last time I was on a train in Germany, I was kidnapped."

"There's no need to be embarrassed. Someone who's been kidnapped has a right to feel frightened." Cockran said as he took a seat by the window. "You should feel free to ask me anything. But I'd prefer that you not surprise me."

"I'm afraid I can sometimes be a little impulsive."

Cockran knew all about impulsive women. He had married one and now he was in love with another. The last time he'd shared a train compartment with an impulsive woman, she'd wrestled him for the top bunk. He lost but Mattie had spent the night with him on the bottom bunk anyway. "Look, your own compartment is on the other side of this wall. If anything happens, I'll be there in seconds."

Harmony shook her head. "I know your Mattie is the adventurous type, the intrepid foreign correspondent, but I'm not that brave. There's no danger at Somerville except drunken underclassmen and squirrels racing across the quad."

"You're right. Mattie's not easily frightened but there are times, for her own safety, when I wish she would be a little less intrepid and a lot more cautious." Cockran said, realizing as he did that he had probably said more than he should have. Harmony sat up straighter at this, revealing more of her nightgown. Cockran looked away. "You really should return to your own compartment."

Harmony reached for the sheet and pulled it up to her neck. "I'm sorry. I didn't mean to make you uncomfortable. I realize how this looks but I don't believe I can fall asleep if I'm alone where the slightest little noise will give me a start," she said. "Please. Just let me sleep here. Don't worry," she said and smiled. "Your virtue is safe with me."

Cockran sat by the window in silence, trying to make up his mind. Anything you did with an attractive woman which you could not explain to your girlfriend was not a good idea. And there was no way he could tell Mattie he had shared a train compartment with a beautiful blonde wearing a sheer nightgown. Still, the girl had been through hell the last time she was in Germany; her step-father had just been killed in Germany; and now her new lawyer had insisted on taking her back to the scene of those two crimes.

"Okay," he said, rising to his feet. It definitely wasn't a good idea but he walked over and pulled down the top bunk. "You can stay where you are. I'll take this bunk after I change in the washroom."

Harmony rose from the bed, keeping the sheets over her chest, and stood on her toes and kissed him softly on the cheek. He could feel her breasts beneath the sheets brushing against his mid-section. "Thank you. Truly. This means a lot."

Cockran took his pajamas from his suitcase and made his way to the washroom. He hoped she wouldn't try to wrestle him for the top bunk when he got back.

Berlin
Wednesday, 3 June 1931

THE air was warm and the morning sun bright as Cockran sat outside with Harmony at a café on the *Kurfürstendamm* waiting for Bobby Sullivan. The night had passed without incident or a wrestling match. But once in Berlin, her anxiety returned and Cockran's suggestion of a two bedroom suite allayed her fears. He checked at the front desk for a message from Mattie and was disappointed to find there was none. He knew she had been in Geneva the day before and had gone to Milan in the evening for her interview with Mussolini this morning. But he had no idea where she was going to be after today except somewhere in

Germany for a week conducting interviews with sources on the arms dealers fomenting trouble in South America and India. When it came to her sources, Mattie could be as secretive as any lawyer.

Harmony finally appeared relaxed for the first time in Germany. She watched the street cars roll by, cradling a wide cup of coffee in her slender fingers as if the street life of Berlin were a familiar shawl she'd worn for years.

"Berlin appears to suit you," Cockran said.

Harmony took a sip of coffee and turned to face him. "Oh, the morning light does wonders for one's confidence. Everyone feels braver in the light of day. And a fortunate few," she said, smiling at him, "appear even more handsome in the light of day as well."

Cockran didn't reply, uncomfortable with the compliment. Harmony placed her cup down and leaned forward. "No word yet from your sweetheart?" Cockran shook his head. "Don't worry," she continued, "you'll hear from her soon. A man like you? No woman would want him to feel neglected."

Cockran looked back to the street and, moments later, was relieved to spot Bobby Sullivan's hatless head of black hair poke out of a streetcar that had stopped across from them. He swiftly topped it with a gray fedora. He was followed by a handsome, thin man with neatly combed sandy hair who put on a brown Homberg. They crossed the street and approached Cockran and Harmony's table.

"Bourke," Sullivan said. "This is Oskar Muller, NBM's lawyer in Germany."

Muller swiftly extended a hand, which Cockran shook. "A pleasure to meet you, *Herr* Cockran," he said in accented English. He turned to his left. "Miss Hampton, I presume?"

Muller took Harmony's hand and bowed over it, expressing sympathies for her loss.

"Oskar has set up meetings with Berlin officials this morning," Sullivan said.

"*Ja,*" Muller said. "They have been most unhelpful thus far. I only hope the presence of an American lawyer and a beautiful young woman can inspire action."

The three of them followed Muller down the busy street of *Kurfürstendamm* towards *Unter den Linden.* "Have you experienced any personal intimidation?" Cockran asked.

"No," Muller said, with a hint of regret. "I haven't done enough to draw their attention. Because of that, I feared that NBM might release me from service." Cockran frowned. He didn't much care for lawyers who were more concerned for themselves than their clients.

They spent the morning with Muller visiting offices belonging to various mid-level functionaries, Muller would translate and everywhere the story was the same: We'd like to help, but our hands are tied. The national government doesn't have the authority, one bureaucrat said, or the resources according to another. Cockran knew it was all a smoke screen. President Hindenburg had placed Germany in a state of emergency during the summer of 1930 where it still was today. If the right people in power had the will, the German government could legally do about whatever it wanted. So far, no one wanted to help stop the sabotage at NBM's plants.

Finally, they were ushered into the office of a relatively high-level official. After he started singing the usual tune, Cockran finally played the American card. "One of our Munich factories is just half a mile from the American Consulate," Cockran said. "Why can't the government investigate credible charges of industrial sabotage? Ask him that."

Muller translated, but the official had an answer ready. "Like he was saying before," Muller said. "Evidence of actual sabotage at the Munich factory is not sufficient to trigger action on the part of the national government. Besides, their resources are limited. Whatever isn't spent on essential services goes for reparations to England and France—"

"And continues straight on to America, where it's recycled, invested and lands right back here in Germany," Cockran said. "Listen, this is an American company. This sabotage is hurting American investors. That hurts Germany. Tell him. Make him understand that."

"I wish I could," Muller said weakly and then proceeded to translate. The official insisted he appreciated how valuable American companies were to Germany prosperity and assured him that the German government was doing everything in its power. But it all rang false to Cockran—whether he said it in English or Muller translated into German

"We're wasting our time," Sullivan whispered to Cockran. "Let's have lunch. If I have to listen to our German lawyer one more minute, I'd better have a beer in my hand or else I'll strangle the little two-faced bastard."

25.

The Adventure Begins

STRIDING across the marble floor of the Hotel *Excelsior Gallia* lobby, Mattie McGary was furious. She had heard rumors—who hadn't?—that Mussolini was a notorious womanizer. But she certainly hadn't expected him to propose a lunch time tryst right there in his office on a desk the size of Delaware and then proceed to try and force her onto her back on said desk. Fortunately for Mussolini, Mattie had left her Walther PPK behind this morning. She didn't think the Chief would have appreciated her shooting the Italian dictator so soon after he had signed a new contract with Hearst. A sharp knee to *Il Duce's* groin had to suffice.

Mattie was handed a message at the front desk along with her key. Mattie opened the envelope. "Urgent. Call me at Zeppelin Company offices in Friedrichschafen—K.S."

Back in her suite, Mattie had the *Excelsior* switchboard place a person-to-person call to Friedrichschafen. Fifteen minutes later, Sturm was on the line.

"Mattie. Thank you for returning my call. Have you had a pleasant stay in Italy?"

"No, Mussolini's a lecherous pig. What's up?"

"Professor Campbell and I travel to Egypt tomorrow aboard the *Graf Zeppelin*. There may be a breakthrough on locating the castle we seek and I thought you might like to join us."

"Why? What's in Egypt?"

"I can't say more now. Please, come to Friedrichschafen. It's only a three hour journey by train from Milan and there are good connections here to Berlin if you decide not to join us."

Mattie agreed and had the concierge secure a compartment on the 3:00 p.m. train to Friedrichschafen while she placed a long-distance call to Cockran's room at the *Kaiserhof* in Berlin to advise him of her change in plans.

But Harmony Hampton answered instead. "No, I'm sorry. Mr. Cockran is not here. Who is calling, please?"

Bitch, Mattie thought. You know damn well who it is. "It's Mattie. What are you doing in Bourke's room?"

"We're in the same suite. There's only one phone but several extensions on the same number. Bourke thought it important for my safety that we share the same suite. He didn't feel I'd be safe alone in my own room." Harmony said, adding in a bright tone, "Don't worry, we share the same bath but we have separate bedrooms. We visited government offices this morning and Bourke sent me back to the hotel after lunch."

"When do you expect him?"

"I don't know. He and Mr. Sullivan said they were going to visit the American embassy but I don't know where else. Bourke said we'd have a late supper together in our suite once he returns." Yes, Harmony said, she'd give Bourke the message that Mattie was arriving the day after tomorrow.

Friedrichschafen
Wednesday, 3 June 1931

KURT von Sturm greeted Mattie in the wood-paneled reception area of the Zeppelin Company and clasped her hand warmly in both of his, holding on far longer, she thought, than necessary. "Something urgent has come up. The Professor and I intend to take advantage of it. He insisted that I advise you in the event you wished to accompany us," Sturm said as he walked back with Mattie to a small conference room where Professor Campbell was waiting for them.

Sturm pulled out a chair for Mattie and offered coffee, which she declined. Kurt explained that he had learned through friends in German Naval Intelligence that Hans Weber, the other Austrian officer mentioned in Major Lanz's journal, was retired and living in a villa in Alexandria. The Lanz journal was not specific enough to narrow the stronghold's location. It could be any one of three remote castles in the Alps. It would take three weeks to visit them all.

"But if we can persuade this Weber fellow," Sturm said, "to help us out, we might be able to find the castle and the Spear in less than a week."

"It certainly makes sense to me, Mattie," Professor Campbell added.

Mattie nodded. "I take your point. But what if he doesn't wish to help?"

Sturm shrugged. "I believe he will. He is a collector of ancient artifacts and Professor Campbell has recently returned from Mesopotamia with items he might wish to purchase."

"Really?"

"No, but greedy men hear what they want to believe."

"What's the rush? Why do we have to go now?" Mattie asked.

"It's fortuitous," Sturm replied. "By ship from France or Italy to Egypt takes several days. There are several passenger seaplane services but they are such noisy machines. I knew the *Graf Zeppelin*, however, had scheduled an excursion down to Alexandria. Once I learned of this Weber's location yesterday, I immediately checked for available cabins and found that three of them were still unspoken for. The Professor and I will share a cabin and you may have the same one you occupied on our trip from America."

Mattie was torn. Given this new development, Alexandria had become the first step in their quest for the Spear. But she had arranged her interviews in Berlin six weeks before. They were key to exposing who was really behind the arms flowing into Bolivia, Paraguay and India. She knew the questions that had to be asked. Could she bear to pass that off to someone else? The choice nagged her during dinner with Sturm and Campbell, but the pull of her father—and the Spear—was too strong. She would go to Egypt. She had to do this. Back in her hotel room after dinner, Mattie had the switchboard place two long-distance phone calls to Berlin. One to Joey Thomas and the second to Cockran. The first call went fine. "Joey? Mattie McGary here. Sorry to be calling so late, but something's come up. I need you to pinch-hit for me for a couple days. Here's the scoop." Whereupon Mattie proceeded to fill him in on the interviews: whom to see; when; and what to ask. She promised to send detailed notes in the mail to him first thing in the morning so he would have them by no later than the day after tomorrow.

"What about Mr. Hudson?" Joey asked.

Ted Hudson was the European bureau chief, based in London. "What about him?"

"Should I clear this with him?"

Hudson was a blond and almost too handsome former MID agent whom she had dated off and on prior to meeting Cockran. In fact, a few years back, they had been occasional lovers but she still wouldn't put it past Ted to steal one of her stories. "No. Include it in your regular report to Ted but make it sound routine. Nothing special."

"You bet, Miss McGary. Thanks again. I won't let you down."

The second call did not go well.

"Bourke, darling, is that you?"

"No, Harmony, it's Mattie."

"Oh…. hello, Mattie. I was about to take a bath. I'm afraid Bourke isn't back yet."

In the background, Mattie could hear the sound of a bath being drawn.

"Look, my plans have definitely changed. I won't be back in Berlin for another two to three days. Tell him I'm flying to Egypt to interview someone. Yes. The same to you. Sorry to have disturbed your bath."

Damn, Mattie thought. It was 11:00 p.m. and Cockran still hadn't returned for that late supper in their suite that Harmony had gushed about. She was not happy that Harmony felt enough at home in Cockran's hotel suite to take a bath—in their shared bathroom, no less—at a time when she expected him back any minute. A gorgeous blonde sharing a bathroom with your boyfriend? And conveniently naked when he arrived? That was a recipe with many possible outcomes, almost all of which were unpleasant. Should she say something to Cockran when next they talked? She wasn't sure about that but she had a sixth sense about Harmony ever since she saw her clinging to Cockran at Chartwell. She didn't trust her alone with Cockran at all, with or without her clothes on.

26.

The Ambasssador

Berlin
Wednesday, 3 June 1931

COCKRAN and Sullivan passed between two U.S. Marines in full uniform and entered the United States Embassy, a few short blocks from the Foreign Ministry. Not needing Muller as a translator for this meeting, they had him escort Harmony back to the *Kaiserhof.* Harmony had promised to obey Cockran's instructions to stay in the hotel suite and lock and bolt all the doors. In turn, he promised that all three of them would have a late supper when they returned. And, by that time, he hoped Mattie would have deigned to share with him her itinerary for the week. If he knew where the hell she was, they could talk by telephone without rancor as it was one of their ground rules that all arguments had to be face to face.

They were taken to the ambassador's office by a young man who showed them into the diplomat's antechamber. A plump secretary ushered them into the office of a balding man with thin wisps of gray hair and wire-rimmed glasses. Gregory Spaulding, the U.S. Ambassador to Germany. He wasn't exactly fat, but his skin didn't cling very tightly to his body—or his chin.

"Gentleman," Spaulding said brightly. "Welcome to Germany!"
They shook hands and sat in the two chairs facing his desk.

"So, you work for Wild Bill Donovan, eh?" the man said.

"Yes," Cockran said.

"Bill and I go way back. How did you meet him?"

"He came to my 10th birthday party. He was Columbia's quarterback and he and my father were good friends. Bill was also my commanding officer in the war."

"Really?" the ambassador said, not offering how he knew Donovan. He looked disappointed by Cockran's apparently stronger association. Inexplicably, Spaulding began to make inane queries about beer halls they'd visited and had they tried the White Mouse cabaret?

Cockran said no, but gave no other response, letting the silence grow.

"Yes. Well…" the ambassador said, awkwardly while Cockran stared at him. Deprive a politician of responses and he usually runs out of fuel for conversation. It was like starving a fire of oxygen. And a political appointee like Spaulding was definitely a politician. Cockran's father had dealt with enough of them at Tammany Hall. "What is it I can do for you gentlemen?"

"That depends," Cockran said. "First tell me all you've done to get more protection for NBM's factories here in Germany."

"Oh, we placed pressure through the usual diplomatic channels, of course, and the German government responded, but our message appears to have lost traction at the regional and local levels. Quite frustrating, actually."

Cockran and Sullivan remained silent. The ambassador looked uncomfortable again. "We've certainly put forth a strong effort on your behalf, gentlemen, let me assure you of that."

Cockran didn't reply. Sullivan let out a long slow breath, his eyes on the ambassador who quickly turned to Cockran. "Listen, this isn't a typical situation. I'm sure you understand."

"Why don't you explain it to us," Cockran said.

"Well, I assume you're well aware that Nazi goons are behind the sabotage,"

"More or less," Cockran said.

"Then you have to understand that the Nazis are packaging this in a relatively legitimate manner and that makes it difficult to prosecute."

"Sabotage is legitimate?" Cockran asked.

"No," the ambassador said. "But to the Nazis, it's fund raising, don't you see?"

They didn't see, so Spaulding tried again.

"Since no one in Germany likes the communists, the Nazis send goons from Hitler's SA, or the SS, to go round to different businesses and ask for what they call 'campaign contributions,' in exchange for which they promise to protect them from communist thugs. They do this all over Germany, especially in Bavaria."

Sullivan spoke up for the first time, "Are there a lot of communists in Bavaria?"

The ambassador smiled. "Not especially, no. Bavaria is a Nazi stronghold now."

"Sounds like a protection racket to me," Sullivan said.

"A what?" the ambassador asked.

"If you want to make money selling protection, sure if it isn't best to sell them protection from yourself," Sullivan said. "Nice work if you can get it."

"Is that the gist of it?" Cockran asked, cocking his head to Sullivan.

"More or less," the ambassador answered. "Though it's a little more nuanced than that."

"Still sounds illegal to me," Cockran said. "Why is this so difficult to prosecute?"

"We suspect the Nazis have infiltrated several levels of local and regional governments. It's clear they have enough friends sitting at the right levels of bureaucracy to slow down any activity they don't like, and to speed up any activity they do. As a result, most local and regional governments just turn a blind eye to their fund-raising practices."

"Why not put pressure on Brüning and the national government?" Cockran asked.

The ambassador's baggy face sagged with fatigue and he removed his glasses to wipe them clean. "How can I explain this to you?" he said to himself. He replaced his glasses. "I suppose you boys know who Al Capone is, right?"

Neither man replied and, after an uncomfortable silence, the Ambassador continued. "The man is the undisputed kingpin of a network of thieves and thugs. Everybody knows it. Certainly the United

States government does. But what can they do about it? Nothing. There's no direct trail to anyone that matters—and even if there were, half the city government and most of the police are on the Capone payroll. He's the unofficial mayor of Chicago."

"Is this going somewhere?" Sullivan asked.

The ambassador nodded. "Just imagine for a moment that Capone wasn't simply the *unofficial* mayor of Chicago. Let's say he actually *were* the mayor—the genuinely elected mayor of Chicago and his mob an actual party. Not just a local party, but one that dominates the entire state of Illinois and recently found itself the second largest party in the country."

"Enough assumptions." Cockran said. "I see where you're going. Tell me why you're not leaning on the German government with the full weight of the U.S. State Department."

"Because you're still thinking like a lawyer," the ambassador said. "If the United States government can't handle a regional crime boss like Capone, what makes you think it can have any impact on a more powerful, semi-legitimized mob in another country?"

When Cockran didn't reply, Spaulding tried a different tack.. "Look, I do understand your client's difficult situation. It's done no good so far but I know officials in Bavaria who might be able to assist you. They don't all have Nazi leanings." He reached for a pen and wrote the names down on a note pad. He tore it off and handed it to Cockran. "One of them is in Berlin for the week. He's at the *Adlon*. I've met him socially and he's agreed to meet you there tonight at 8:00 p.m. He may know the right men for you to meet. Men who can actually help you."

They rose to leave and the ambassador rose with them. "I'm only trying to level with you," he said. "Lawlessness is on the rise in Germany. As lawyers, you gentlemen don't stand much of a chance of stopping them."

Sullivan buttoned his coat, put on his hat, and stared at the Ambassador, unsmiling. "I'm not a lawyer," he said.

27.

By Airship to Egypt

Friedrichschafen
Thursday, 4 June 1931

MATTIE'S mood darkened the next morning when she woke up and made a final attempt, unsuccessfully, to talk with Cockran. What in hell were he and Bobby Sullivan doing out so late the night before and then out so early this morning to hire a motorcar? Worse, why had that bitch Harmony told her that she and Cockran had an early breakfast together and that *now* she was about to change out of her nightgown? *She* should be the only one wearing her nightgown at breakfast with Cockran, not some new blonde client. Later, Mattie met Sturm and Campbell in the lobby. They bundled into a long black Mercedes to take them to the zeppelin hangar and did not notice a small Auto Union sedan which followed them at a discreet distance.

THE scar on the man's left cheek was vivid in the morning sun as he rested his elbows on top of the Auto Union sedan, adjusting the focus on his powerful field glasses. He lowered them once he was satisfied as to the identity of the last three people who had boarded the airship. He returned the field glasses to their case, watching as the great silver ship rose slowly in the air.

Ten minutes later, the man parked his motorcar on the Lake Constance waterfront where a large Junkers W34 seaplane was anchored, its 600 horsepower BMW Hornet engine idling. He walked out the long dock and stepped down into the seaplane's passenger compartment. There were five other passengers, all with close-cropped hair, all wearing dark clothes and all with the same identical Celtic cross tattooed on the inside of their left wrists. The men raised their faces expectantly at Josef Lanz.

"They are on the *Graf.* I hope our brother will not betray us, but the Lord expects us to anticipate what His enemies may do." He paused. "Stefan, you have done well in selecting this seaplane. It will be in Alexandria well before the *Graf.* Are all the weapons securely stored?"

"Yes," the man called Stefan replied. "I supervised it personally."

"Excellent. May the Lord bless our journey," Josef Lanz said as he made the sign of the cross in the air with the first two fingers of his right hand.

On Board the Graf Zeppelin
Thursday, 3 June 1931

THAT evening after dinner on board the *Graf,* Sturm and Campbell repaired with Mattie to her cabin where Sturm spread out several Austrian mountaineering maps on Mattie's berth.

"Here is one possibility," Sturm said, pointing to the first of three maps. "Castles exist for a reason, typically to guard a trade route or an invasion path through the mountains. You would think that most castles would be near international borders, but borders have been altered often in history. Before the last war, South Tyrol belonged to Austria. Now it is Italian. What may have been a border at one time is now deep within Austrian territory. Or outside it. I don't believe Austrian officers would have hidden such a sacred relic so close to their border."

Sturm stopped and placed a second map side by side with the first. "These two spots show great potential. At the mouth of high mountain valleys, impassable in winter, and a point of defense for the other three seasons. Unfortunately, they are hundreds of kilometers apart, each a five day journey from Zell-Am-See. Neither is near an old border so that speaks in their favor."

"And the third castle?" Mattie asked.

"It is the least likely." Sturm said, picking up a third map. "It is the castle nearest to Zell-Am-See. Three or four days away. It is located on a ridge halfway down a valley within the *Grossglockner* range. But it's closer to the old Austrian empire borders than the other two."

While Sturm rolled up the maps, Mattie called for the steward and ordered three snifters of brandy. When the brandy arrived, Mattie and Kurt sat beside each other on the small divan.

Campbell sat on a small light-weight bamboo chair adjacent to the cabin's writing table. "The castles' locations may give us a clue as to who built them. A castle had two purposes, both to protect trade routes and territory, but also to protect the inhabitants within." Campbell paused, brought the brandy snifter to his nose and then to his lips. "A castle high on a valley's ridge, rather than at its mouth, has only one purpose—to protect its inhabitants."

"So?" Mattie asked. "How does that make any difference?"

"Your father would be disappointed to hear you ask that," Campbell began.

Mattie cut him off. "The Templars!" she said. "They built castles as well as fortified monasteries. So the third castle might once have been a Templar-built monastery while the other two could be Templar castles. But didn't they die out in the fourteenth century? Were there Templars in Austria?"

Campbell smiled. "They disappeared but I don't believe they died out. The Templars had a huge cache of gold stored in one of their strongholds in France. The gold was never found. Austria and Switzerland were the two most likely places where the gold was transferred."

Mattie turned to Sturm. "So what is it exactly we expect to find in Alexandria?"

"We have three likely Templar castles. I will be pleased," Sturm said, "if this Weber can help eliminate one or more of the three locations."

"But what if he refuses to help?"

Sturm's smile was cold. "I think not. He would find that to be..." Sturm paused, as if searching for the right English word, "a poor decision."

Mattie chilled. Sturm really *was* a ruthless man. Why was she so attracted by him?

28.

The Factory

IT looked like a prison, missing only a perimeter fence and barbed wire. The largest and most productive NBM plant in Europe was a depressing, two story rectangle of brick and glass.

Sullivan drove their Audi R 19 sports convertible along the access road, fresh from their meetings earlier that day with both the U.S. Consul as well as a few more persons gleaned from the Spaulding-recommended Bavarian official last night at the *Adlon*. On the surface, their Munich meetings had gone better than those in Berlin but that was all—just on the surface. Assurances were one thing and actions another. Cockran didn't like how every Munich official directed their responses to Muller, effectively avoiding eye contact with Cockran and Sullivan..

To Sullivan's credit, he didn't rub it in or quiz Cockran over what St. Thomas Aquinas would do now. They both turned their focus to a better defense for the main NBM plant. The Nazis had to be shown that if they didn't back off, they'd damn well have a fight on their hands. Occasionally, Cockran found it difficult to maintain his focus. Mattie still had left no word. Harmony had frowned in sympathy as he left the front desk this morning, disappointment plain on his face. That Harmony was aware of this bothered him but Mattie's silence was worse. Was this what "taking a break" meant? No contact until she made it to Venice?

Sullivan pulled the roadster into the yard that led to the loading docks on the left and the main entrance to the factory on the right, his eyes scanning the terrain. Cockran did the same. This may have been an ideal spot for a factory, but it was not easy to defend. It sat close to the banks of the Isar River behind it, good for cheap shipment by water but the docks were an easy access point for intruders unless they were patrolled regularly. Neighboring factories sprawled close enough to provide cover for anyone who wanted to approach the NBM factory from its flanks. Only the front of the plant was easily monitored but the building was dominated by large windows making it vulnerable to surveillance from the outside.

Sullivan brought the motorcar to a stop in front of two large, steel doors. A man in work overalls stood with a rifle slung over his shoulder. Cockran helped Harmony out as Muller's luxurious Horch pulled up alongside.

Harmony took in the rough looking guard. "Is he all we have to protect the factory?"

Sullivan tugged on his fedora and winked at Harmony. "Not if we have anything to say about it, lass, and we will."

The guard stood aside when he saw Muller step out of his Horch and let everyone enter. The factory was standard—most of the open space dominated by machinery, with offices above the main floor, off to one side. The guard leaned inside and shouted towards the upstairs level. A tall, scrawny figure looked out of a doorway, saw them, and immediately came rushing down the metal stairway. They had asked for the plant manager, but all they got was a grave looking lad who couldn't have been much over 25. Muller asked where the manager was and got a curt response for his efforts.

"He says he *is* the manager," Muller translated. The young man kept talking. "He's an engineer. Hermann Steinmetz. Senior management quit last week and many in the office did so also. A few remained. They had no choice. They need work. His girlfriend helps run the office."

Steinmetz looked as if he expected you to mock him for his youth. Muller continued asking him questions without prompts from either Cockran or Sullivan, much as he had done a few times during their meetings with Munich officials and it annoyed Cockran. He was about to interrupt Muller when Steinmetz responded to the questions in a burst, waving his hands to emphasize whatever points he was making and forcing Muller to take a step back.

"What are you two talking about?" Cockran asked, irritated.

"He wants to know when NBM will start paying him for his new position."

"We can't help him with that," Cockran said impatiently. "That's not why we're here."

"I know," Muller said. "That's what I've been trying to tell him."

Steinmetz interrupted in English: "Come, come," as he stalked off into the factory. They all followed and gradually picked up the acrid scent of burning oil. They came upon two men working to repair a junction in the assembly line machinery. There was blood on the floor. The boy gestured animatedly at the equipment and Sullivan moved for a closer look.

Muller translated, struggling to keep up. "This...happened early in the morning. The assembly wheel exploded...three men were injured...It appears to have been...tricked?" Muller furrowed his brow, "No, what's the phrase...?"

"Booby-trapped," Sullivan said. "Rigged to explode once the belt started, right?"

"Yes," Muller said.

"Any violence with the security forces last night?" Sullivan asked.

Steinmetz semed to understand and shook his head. "*Nein.*" He kept talking, his agitation growing. Muller translated, "Security didn't see a thing. Says he doesn't know how they pulled it off. He's been keeping a close eye on his workers and doesn't think they were responsible."

Suddenly, Steinmetz brushed back his coat to reveal the butt of a revolver resting in a shoulder holster. He thrust his forefinger in the direction of Muller and kept talking to him. "He...he thinks the security they've hired is useless," Muller translated. "He carries a gun now for his own protection. Some thugs tried to grab him on his way home from the office last week and he held them off with that gun. He fears they'll be better-prepared the next time."

"Come, come!" Steinmetz said and once more stalked off. They followed him into a vacant office that had been converted into a makeshift infirmary—a field hospital of sorts. Three injured men were spread out on desktops. One, the least hurt, was sitting up with a thick bandage around his neck and dried blood staining his shirt-collar and sleeves. The other two had extensive blood-soaked bandages over their faces, chests and arms.

Cockran turned to the boy manager. "Why weren't they taken to hospital?

"Sometimes the ambulance comes when they call for it, but often it does not," Muller translated. "No ambulance came today."

Sullivan spoke quietly to Cockran, "Security is shite, if you'll be asking my opinion."

"You think they're crooked or just clueless?" Cockran asked.

"Doesn't much matter, does it now?" Sullivan said.

"Perhaps we could hire a different firm?" Muller suggested.

"No." Cockran replied. "We need to work with men we can trust. We should be arming the workers. At least the ones with military service, especially any who've seen action. Pay them overtime for the extra work."

"Arm the workers? That's crazy. They'll call us Bolsheviks!" Muller said, obviously appalled. "What about the current security force? Why not just strengthen their numbers?"

"Because they've done enough harm." Sullivan said. "Sack the bastards! The workers can't do worse."

When they turned back to Steinmetz, Harmony asked "Why won't someone get them to hospital? They need medical treatment."

"I'll drive them to hospital, lass," Sullivan said, putting his hat back on his head. "And wouldn't I be needing to retrieve a certain piece of luggage anyway?"

AFTER escorting the wounded men to hospital, Sullivan returned with a suitcase. He placed it on the factory floor and opened the latch, letting the two sides slap down hard on the concrete. There was a stir among the dozen factory workers who stood by watching them. One of them began to smile. A suitcase full of guns could do that to a crowd of men. On one side of the suitcase was what looked like the shattered remnants of a gun: a naked barrel, two handle pieces with grips, and two circular pieces of steel.

"Now, who's the lad knows how to work this beauty?" Sullivan said. Muller translated, but the men remained mute. Sullivan bent down and went to work. His hands moved quickly from one handle to another piece of steel, snapping it together before reaching for another handle and then the barrel. Finally he rose, holding a blue-steeled piece of metal in one hand and one of the steel circles in the other. He took the cylinder and slapped it into place holding the front grip, the barrel pointing down. A Thompson sub-machine gun.

"How about now?" he asked.

One of the Germans raised a hand, then another with a bit more trepidation. Sullivan walked to the first German. "You lad. What's your name?"

"Paul Vorschakker."

"Paul," Sullivan said, handing him the gun. "You just won yourself a Tommy. Congratulations." Paul took the gun firmly and seemed to grow two inches.

Sullivan returned to the other side of the suitcase now, where an assortment of semi-automatic pistols lay. He handed them out to the rest of the group, explaining a few of the intricacies here or there. Then he stepped back, Cockran's cue to address them all.

"Go on. Aren't you the talker?" Sullivan had said. "Just like your da?"

Cockran wasn't half the speaker his father was, but this was one area where he was more experienced—addressing men on the eve of battle. Their job was simple, really. Until further notice, they no longer worked from opening to close—they worked from sun-down to sun-up. One man would be outside each of the four possible entrances to the factory and one man inside. Three men would patrol the vulnerable flanks. The last man, Paul, would wait inside in a central spot with his Thompson, ready to bring down fire wherever it was needed. Sullivan would stop by once every night but he wouldn't say when. They would have to spot him first and raise the alarm. This would keep them sharp. It was easier to stay focused if you knew that *someone* was coming that evening.

"This is dangerous work, gentlemen, don't misunderstand," Cockran said. "It might only last a couple of weeks. It might last a couple of months. But no longer than that. If we can't beat these Nazis back, NBM will be forced to close this factory and you'll all be out of work. You are fighting for your jobs and those of your fellow workers. Make sure you win."

The men listened to Muller's translation solemnly but there was little reaction. They still looked stiff and nervous. He needed something more, a distraction.

Sullivan saw it too and leaned towards Harmony, "Speak up, now, lass," he said quietly.

"What? Me?" Harmony whispered. "What could I possibly say?"

"Doesn't matter what you say," Sullivan replied, "just as long as you say it."

Harmony turned to Cockran, concern in her eyes but he motioned her to go on.

"Are you too blind to recognize when you're being adored by a pack o' lads?" Sullivan said. "They may not fight for a couple of micks like us, but they'll fight for a princess."

Harmony seemed to understand and reluctantly stepped forward. "I... I know that none of you ever asked for this. All you wanted was a job, to provide for you and your families. But if you do this for me, if you protect my factory, you'll have my thanks. *And* your jobs too."

She stepped back toward Cockran and Sullivan, a quizzical expression on her face as Muller translated what she had said. "Do you think that did any good?"

Cockran was proud of her. She had given the men what they needed. "Have a look."

She looked around to see what both Sullivan and Cockran were seeing. The men seemed buoyed somehow—and most of them were looking directly at Harmony with a smile on their lips. She smiled back as if she now understood. "And I promise a kiss and a hug from me for the bravest among you. That is, of course, if your wives and girl friends say it's okay."

The men laughed and cheered when they heard the translation.

"Off you go," Cockran said to them. "Good luck."

29.

A Luncheon in Alexandria

THE *Graf Zeppelin* had earlier flown over Cairo and the pyramids at Giza and now passed low over the curving arc of Alexandria's harbor, barely a hundred feet off the ground. A road ran along the waterfront lined with buildings from one end of the arc to the other.

Professor Campbell described the scene below as if he were a tour guide. "See the two forts guarding the entrance of the harbor? The one on the western tip is Fort Qaytbay and it stands on the site of the ancient Pharos Lighthouse which was built in 279 B.C. and collapsed in the eighth century. It was the marvel of its day, over 400 feet tall. Hydraulic machinery hauled fuel to the top. It had a mirror of polished steel reflecting the sun by day and a fire by night."

The *Graf* passed over the center of the harbor heading south and the Professor continued his travelogue. "Over there are the ruins of the Temple of Serapis and that tall monolith is Pompey's Pillar, over a hundred feet tall. Built in the third century by the Emperor Diocletian. The two sphinxes beside it were built by the Ptolemys."

The big ship turned slowly to the right and headed back to the waterfront and the marine terminal where seaplanes landed and a temporary mooring mast had been erected for the *Graf.*

"We will be staying at the Hotel Cecil," Sturm said as all three of them piled into a yellow taxi which carried them back along the curving waterfront to the European sectors.

"You're certain Weber is expecting us?" Mattie asked as they walked into the hotel's cool lobby. Potted palms were everywhere while polished wooden fans created a gentle breeze over the smooth dark marble floor.

"In a manner of speaking. Weber is a collector of ancient antiquities from the Middle East—Persia and Mesopotamia in particular. He believes he will be meeting with *Herr* von Strasser from Zurich and that Professor Campbell and I represent a wealthy Swiss banker who has financed an expedition into the border area between those two countries and has made an astonishing discovery about which the world knows nothing. Wait here," Sturm told Mattie, pointing to a wicker chair beneath a towering palm, "while I hire a car and telephone Weber."

Moments later Sturm returned with a smile on his face. "No need to check into the hotel. *Herr* Weber has invited us to stay at his villa. It is five miles west of Alexandria on the coast road. Many wealthy expatriates from Europe live there. The locals call it 'Millionaire's Row'."

Sturm summoned a porter to take their bags back outside the hotel entrance where a large cream-colored Packard Phaeton had pulled up, driven by a small, dark-skinned, wiry Egyptian who introduced himself as Anwar. He opened the rear doors for Sturm and Mattie and the front passenger door for Professor Campbell. He placed their luggage in the long automobile's boot and then wheeled the big motorcar around and headed south. He picked up Shari al-Mitwalli, pointing out to them St. Catherine's Cathedral on the right as they approached Shari al-Saba Banat, which they followed until it brought them to the Mahmudiyyah Canal which Professor Campbell explained had been dug in 1820 in order to connect Alexandria to the Nile. The Weber villa was on the canal's west bank within sight of Pompey's Pillar.

The villa itself was a long, sprawling affair, barely visible behind eight-foot-high white-washed walls. They came to an archway blocked by a sturdy iron gate. Anwar leaned on the Packard's horn until two servants emerged from the shade of a nearby guard shack, both of them carrying aged Enfield carbines. Anwar shouted at them and they shouted back in Arabic, a language Mattie did not speak. She caught the word "Strasser", however, and that seemed to do the trick because one of the men leaned his rifle against the shack and swung the wide gate open. Anwar jammed the Packard's accelerator to the floor and the car leaped forward, leaving a cloud of dust and the two guards coughing in its wake.

"Idiots!" Anwar shouted in French as he had done from the beginning, explaining that most Egyptians preferred it as a second language to the English of their occupying power.

The dirt driveway extended for another 150 yards, ending at the front of the villa and a circular drive featuring a marble fountain from whose center rose a five-foot high spray of water.

Their host was waiting for them in the cool shade of the house's entrance. He was a large man in his late forties, with thinning dark brown hair around a large head, a thick neck and three chins which quivered as he walked forward to greet them. Dressed in a flowing white robe trimmed in bright green and yellow, a small fez atop his head completed the picture. Introductions were made and their host led them into the villa through an inner courtyard into a dining room which opened onto elaborate gardens leading down to the canal. Mattie noticed that all the servants were young, attractive Egyptian girls, some barely in their teens.

Lunch was a lavish affair. A cold cream soup made with plums followed by fish caught fresh that day, their host assured them, accompanied by many bottles of chilled white burgundy. Next came lamb, more vegetables and more wine, a red Rhone, with dates and figs as the last course, accompanied by a sweet Riesling.

Mattie had been pacing herself, nursing one glass of wine per course. She noticed Sturm had done the same. The Professor, however, was enjoying himself immensely, two glasses with each course, as he regaled their host with stories of the fictitious expedition he had just conducted in the wilds of the Persian-Mesopotamian border and the treasures he had delivered to his patron in Switzerland. Campbell was obviously a frustrated actor, she thought, as Weber devoured the academic's story as eagerly as he polished off the food and the wine, consuming the better part of a bottle himself for every glass that Mattie finished.

Over the figs and dates, Mattie watched Sturm and the Professor close the deal. Without once hinting that they knew of the Joseph Lanz notebook or Weber's service with the Austrian mountain troops, Weber agreed to use his expertise from his days in the Austrian army to look at their field maps and answer the questions they had about their new expedition. In return, their Swiss patron, who was staying at Shepheard's Hotel in Cairo, would sell Weber any five artifacts he chose from the ten whose photographs Sturm and Campbell would show him tonight.

Sturm's intelligence had assured him that Weber was an indiscriminate collector, an amateur of whom others frequently took advantage. Campbell in turn had assured Sturm that the objects in the ten photographs which he had taken from a collection in a private museum in Geneva, where a friend of Campbell's was the curator, would be unknown to Weber.

Weber poured the last of the Riesling into his glass and raised it in a toast. "To your health, *Monsieurs*, and to you as well, *Mademoiselle*. May we all live well and long."

Weber rose and extended his hands to the young Egyptian girls beside him. "I must retire for my afternoon rest," he said with a leer that signaled it was not the only thing on his mind. "I have instructed my servants to afford my guests every courtesy and to see to their wishes as if they were my own." he said, gesturing expansively toward the other equally young and attractive women hovering nearby.

With that, Weber turned and waddled out of the room. Mattie looked at Sturm. "Swell. So what do we do while he's upstairs playing house with the children?"

Sturm smiled. "Patience, Mattie. Patience. We wait and trust that he will sober up in time for dinner. He has agreed to help us and that is half the battle. In my experience, information extracted under duress is not as valuable as that given willingly."

30.

Cabaret

AFTER a full day of guns and training with the factory workers, Cockran and Sullivan treated Harmony to dinner at a lively cabaret on the outskirts of Munich that Muller had recommended—even though he admitted it was not quite his cup of tea. Muller had begged off, something about attending his uncle's birthday celebration. The cabaret acts themselves were amusing, and there was open dancing between the stage acts. Some of the acts seemed more burlesque than anything else, which Cockran had not anticipated, as creative nudity remained the common theme throughout the evening's performances. Harmony did not appear to be put off or embarrassed by any of the acts, although she appeared withdrawn in between her cheerful and rather particular orders of *Hefeweizen*, "With a thin slice of lemon, no seeds, if you please."

Cockran took a sip of his bock—surprisingly sweet considering its dark color—and leaned forward. "Everything all right?"

Harmony turned to him, "Oh yes, it's fine," she said. "I just keep thinking of those poor men Bobby took to the hospital yesterday."

"They're in good hands." Cockran said.

"I can't help but wonder whether it's all worth it."

"It is."

"One or two factories? Why not just sell? Let those men have a safe job."

"This is about more than your factories. It's about right and wrong."

"Oh, nothing is so black and white as that," she said, irritated. "What about safety? Peace of mind? What's wrong with that?"

"Giving in to extortion will bring you neither safety nor peace of mind."

"I'm just not cut out for this kind of danger," she said, taking a sip of her *hefeweizen* and leaning forward. "And I'd wager you've seen more than enough bloodshed in your life as well. You served in the war, didn't you?"

Her question surprised him. He said nothing but gave her a brief nod of his head.

"I thought so. I was a nurse's aide at the end of the war. I was barely 15 but I'll never forget the faces of those men. Good men, ordinary men, meant to live lives of peace with wives and children, a pint with friends on Saturday and church on Sundays, not a short life filled with blood and mud. You have a beautiful boy back home who needs you. You don't need to fight this battle for me. You don't need to choose violence. Help me sell NBM and we can all safely go home. "

Cockran drank his bock slowly. He *had* seen more than his share of blood and mud in the war but she didn't know the half of it. She knew nothing of his days in MID and the Inquiry during and after the war; or Nora and Ireland and that bloody summer of 1922; or even the equally bloody summer of 1929 when he and Bobby had avenged Nora's death. Violence had a way of seeking him out. "Some men have that choice. I'm not one of them."

Harmony did not answer, but withdrew into herself again as a comedy skit commenced—a short, balding man trying to seduce a buxom blonde. Cockran looked across the table at Sullivan and found cold blue eyes staring back. Cockran returned the stare and saw Sullivan slowly, deliberately rub his chin. They were being watched. It had been nine years since he'd last used these signals, ones they'd been taught by Michael Collins. Cockran brushed back the hair by his ear, a sign which asked where their spectator was located. Sullivan's response was to look to Cockran's left. He acknowledged the signal and reached for his stein of beer.

Cockran's eyes wandered as he drank, resting on nothing specific, but taking in enough to notice a smartly dressed, narrow-faced man with thinning brown hair standing over by the bar, near the entrance. Cockran turned back to the stage just as the skit concluded and the crowd burst into raucous applause at the buxom blonde, now naked to the waist. Sullivan gave Cockran another quick signal—only this one Cockran couldn't quite remember.

Sullivan rose before Cockran could reply and he placed a hand on Harmony's shoulder. "I'll be back in a few, Darling." Harmony smiled back and Sullivan pushed his way through the crowd to the men's room.

Cockran had an idea of what Sullivan had in mind, signal or no signal. He stood up and held a hand out to Harmony as the band struck up a soft dancing tune. "Care to dance?"

Harmony smiled and rose. "Aren't you full of surprises? I thought you'd never ask."

"I'm not that good," Cockran said.

"Don't worry," she said as he led her onto the floor and wrapped his other arm around her waist. "I'll show you what goes where." He felt her body, soft and warm, press against him as she deftly guided him in time with the music.

"We're leaving after this song"

Harmony looked confused. "Leaving? Why?" she said. "What about Bobby?"

"Never mind about Bobby," Cockran said. "We're being watched."

"We— "

"Don't look around!" he said, stopping her before she could turn her head.

She leaned in closer, resting her head on his shoulder. "How can you be so sure?"

"There's a gentleman in the back who is paying too much attention to us," he said. "When the song ends, take my hand and drag me to the bar to buy you another *Hefeweizen*."

The song lasted for another minute while they danced cheek to cheek, the scent of her hair doing nothing to distract him from the feel of her body against his. When it ended and the audience and dancers applauded, Harmony looked up to Cockran. "Now," he said under the noise of clapping. "And keep smiling." She took his hand and weaved through the crowd to reach the bar. The entrance lay off to the left of the bar; the narrow-faced man off on the right end of the bar. Cockran could see him turn his head in another direction, to avoid being spotted by Cockran and Harmony. They reached the bar but, before Harmony could signal the bartender, Cockran turned left and marched directly towards the entrance.

They pushed through the doors and out into the parking lot. A light rain had started since they had been inside. Their Audi R 19 rolled up and the driver's side door was flung open. Behind the wheel, Sullivan said, "Would you be up for a midnight drive, milady?"

Sullivan slid over to make room, a silent admission that Cockran's racing sports cars as a hobby meant he was the better man behind the wheel. Cockran ushered Harmony into the front seat and closed the door behind them, sandwiching her between him and Sullivan. He put the car in gear and pulled out—just as the narrow-faced man rushed out of the club, finally wising up to what was going on.

They were on a two lane road, heading back towards Munich and, aside from their headlights, they drove in darkness through the countryside. A few homes and shops sat close to each other along the way, but there were long stretches of country in-between. Traffic was light, but passing slower cars on a two lane road would be easy to spot. Cockran drove only as fast as traffic allowed, and kept his eyes on the mirror to see if they'd made a clean getaway.

Harmony was clearly nervous now. "Who was watching us in there?" she asked.

"Doesn't matter who," Cockran said. "My guess would be Nazis."

"How did they know we would be there?" she asked.

"Muller," Sullivan said.

"Oskar?" Harmony said. "That's impossible. He's trying to help us."

Cockran didn't reply, squinting his eyes at the headlights of oncoming traffic passing by in the left lane. After their meetings with Munich officials that morning, he certainly had his doubts about Muller. Most of the sincerity—and fear—from the officials were directed at Muller. But translators weren't supposed to instill fear in anyone.

Sullivan's voice was hard. "The only help he's offering is to place us in a plot of ground six feet under."

Headlights splayed shadows upon the dashboard as a long black Horch behind them pulled into the left lane to pass. "Stay calm," Cockran said as he let the car pass them on the left and pull back into the right lane, in front of them. Harmony snaked her arm through Sullivan's, taking hold of it.

The road bent to the left on a moderate rise and the lights of Munich were becoming visible in the distance when another pair of headlights cast shadows on the dash of their motorcar. Cockran glanced up, watching a second motorcar, an Opel, begin its passing maneuver in his rearview mirror. The Opel pulled even on the left when something up ahead caught Cockran's attention. The Horch was braking and closing the ground between them fast.

"Bourke…" Sullivan started, as the Horch closed to within ten feet.

"Hang on!" Cockran barked and slammed on the breaks just as the Opel swerved into their lane. Harmony lurched forward, but held on tight to Sullivan who had braced himself with his legs. The tires squealed under braking, but the Opel managed to clip the front end of their Audi. Steel shrieked at the impact and sent them fishtailing to the right.

Cockran wrestled the wheel and jerked the car back into a straight path as they reached the crest of the short rising hill. He stepped on the gas and swerved their car back into the left lane, passing the slower Opel on their right. They gathered speed downhill in the left lane where no on-coming traffic was yet visible.

Cockran saw the Horch ahead on their right and knew they weren't out of it yet. He down-shifted and accelerated. "Hang on tight!" he shouted. As they began to pass the Horch, it suddenly swerved into the left lane. Cockran pumped the brakes again, falling just behind the Horch as it screeched in front of them. He swerved back into the right lane, shifted gears and hit the gas, the Audi hurtling past the Horch before its driver could react.

Just then, their roadster was jolted from behind as the Opel crunched into their bumper. Damn! Cockran thought, its engine must be modified. A standard Opel shouldn't have been able to keep up with an R 19. Suddenly, the noise of the road fell away and the Audi felt as if it were floating, gliding up the moderate slope of the road. The wheels re-gripped violently, jerking Cockran's arms as he fought for control of the wheel. The roadster had spun into the left lane, veering dangerously close to the edge of the road and a short hill that fell away from it. The tires cut into the gravel and the little pellets rattled against the wheel well, but Cockran kept the car on the road, nearing the peak of the little hill.

Bright lights suddenly blinded their sight as a car cleared the hill moving in the other direction and bore right down upon them. Its horns blared and Cockran wrenched the wheel back to the right, avoiding a head-on collision. But he had overcompensated and swung them off the road on the right side, past the gravel and onto a short grassy slope that fell away from the road's edge. The weight of the car kept pulling them to the right, while Cockran fought to pull them back on the road. But he couldn't do it and he felt the entire left side of the car lift off the ground. The noise seemed to leave them for a moment—and Cockran could hear Sullivan cursing in Irish—until it all came back in an explosion of sound. Glass shattered in the passenger side door as the car rocked and jolted, skidding to a stop on its side in the short grass.

Everything was still. Cockran opened his eyes and was grateful to have achieved that much. He pushed the door open, pulled his Webley from its holster and stuck his head out, bracing his legs against the seat. He saw four or five shadowy figures approaching with guns drawn and fired two quick shots, taking down the lead shooter. Then he sensed, rather than saw the dark silhouette of Bobby Sullivan beside him, also standing through the open door, legs braced against the steering wheel. A .45 automatic in each hand, he was firing in rapid, controlled bursts. The light flashed around his frame as the withering fire from his two .45s halted their opponents' advance and forced a retreat, dragging their wounded comrade with them.

"Make sure they don't come back." Cockran said and turned his attention to Harmony, who lay limp inside the car, slumped against the passenger door. He put a hand to her face. "Harmony," he said. She didn't move. "Harmony," he repeated, his voice louder.

"Is she hurt?" Bobby's voice said from above as Harmony began to groan.

"I don't know. Are they gone?" Cockran asked.

Sullivan looked down into the car. "Those bozos knew better than to press their luck."

Cockran turned back to Harmony, but the only injury he could find in the darkness was a small bump on her forehead. She continued to groan, her eyes still closed. "Harmony," Cockran said again, stroking her face. Her eyelids flickered, then she opened her eyes, dazed and unfocused. Her eyes wavered between the two of them.

"Am I dead?"

"No, you're fine, the danger is past." Cockran replied

"Lass, you're as alive as a clear blue Irish morning in County Donegal." Harmony gave a quiet laugh. "All you've got is a little bump on your pretty forehead, right about here," Sullivan said, touching her with the tip of his index finger.

Harmony smiled up at him. "And you don't have a scratch."

"And isn't that the worst injustice? This ugly mug o' mine wouldn't even notice another scratch or two." Harmony laughed again as he turned to Cockran. "Bourke, can you take her back to the hotel? I need to visit the factory. If they hit us, they may have also hit our boys their first night on the job. After we get this car right side up, you can drop me off."

Cockran nodded. "We'll move to the smaller hotel two blocks down, remember it?" Sullivan did. "I'll take a suite there and register as Mr. & Mrs. William Donovan. We don't want to call attention to Harmony by checking her in as a single woman."

"Mr. & Mrs.?" Sullivan said with a raise of his eyebrows as he pulled himself out of the motorcar, stopped and looked down at Harmony. "Enjoy your honeymoon, lass, and cheer up." he said and jerked a thumb at Cockran. "At least we don't look as bad as he does."

Cockran put a hand to his face and felt the warm sticky texture of blood that he hadn't even noticed before. Harmony gasped, as if seeing his appearance for the first time. "Bourke, we've got to get you to hospital quickly!"

31.

Death in Egypt

Alexandria
Friday, 5 June 1931

WEBER proved to be more difficult than Sturm had predicted. During cocktails—surprisingly dry and icy martinis—he insisted upon telling them the modern history of Alexandria and its attraction to expatriates from all over Europe. A far more sophisticated city than Cairo, he explained. Each of the European nationalities—the French, the English, the Italians and the Germans—had its own enclave, its own churches, its own schools.

Unbidden, one of the servant girls brought in another icy pitcher of martinis. Mattie, following Kurt's lead, accepted a second drink, recalling that he had barely taken a sip of a first before surreptitiously depositing the contents of the glass inside a potted fern. Weber wanted to keep talking about the history of Alexandria but Sturm changed the subject. Soon, Weber was talking just as volubly about the artifacts prominently displayed on marble pedestals and walnut bookcases throughout the villa. Swords, shields, lances, pottery, busts and jewelry all dated back to the First, Second and Third Crusades. Weber was familiar with the provenance of each, telling his guests where in the Holy Land each object was discovered and to whom it had belonged.

Notwithstanding the four martinis Weber had consumed, talking about his artifacts finally reminded him that his visitors had more artifacts to sell. "I understood from Professor Campbell's cable and our conversation during lunch that you have brought photographs of the artifacts he has recently discovered in Mesoptamia. May I see them now, please?"

Sturm pulled from his briefcase a folder containing the artifact photos and opened it on the long, low carved wooden table in front of them. But before Weber could reach out to pick them up for inspection, Sturm unrolled three maps of Alpine terrain which covered the photos. Weber pouted at being momentarily deprived of seeing the prized photos but said nothing.

"As you agreed at lunch," Sturm said, "we'd like you to help the professor on his next expedition to locate ancient Roman objects hidden in a stronghold in the Austrian Alps. Somewhere on these three maps. You were an officer in Austria's Alpine troops in the war, no?"

Weber appeared surprised at this. "Yes, I did serve in that capacity but, as you can see," he said, gesturing to his considerable bulk, "that was a long time ago. I would like to help but I very much doubt I can. My memory is not what it once was." Weber replied, glancing nervously at the maps, sweat appearing on his forehead even though the early evening air was cool, aided by swirling fans above while floor-length cotton curtains fluttered in open doorways.

"Perhaps so, but at least look at the maps," Sturm continued. "If you can help, I'm sure Professor Campbell will offer you even more artifacts to purchase than previously agreed."

Weber reluctantly acquiesced and looked at the three maps as Sturm spoke again. "We believe the Roman artifacts were found by the Templars during one of the crusades and then moved to a castle of theirs in the Austrian Alps. We believe the three castles on these maps may be Templar castles. Are you familiar with any of them from your time in the military?"

Weber gave each map a cursory inspection. "Only the first one, the northernmost castle at the head of this valley" he said, pointing to the first map, "is a Templar castle. The other two are not. The third, in fact, is not even a true castle, more of a monastery. If your Roman artifacts were taken by the Templars and hidden in our Alps, as you say, then this would be the place. Personally, I doubt if you will find any artifacts, if indeed any were taken there to begin with."

"Why do you say that?" Sturm asked. "Have you been to any of these castles?"

"No, no, of course not." Weber replied. "But I've seen aerial photos of all three taken by Austrian army aviators."

"Well, take a last look at all three,"Sturm said and then you and the professor can review the photographs and bargain over a price while Mattie and I finish our martinis before dinner."

Weber did and both Sturm and Mattie watched the man's eyes closely. She wasn't certain but Weber seemed to spend less time on the third map, the so-called monastery, than he had on the others. When Weber shook his head and said he was sorry, it was the castle on the first map or nothing and he feared it was the latter, she began to speak. "*Herr* Weber…" but Sturm placed a restraining hand on hers.

"We are most grateful for your assistance *Herr* Weber and we appreciate your hospitality. Mattie and I will leave you two alone now to haggle over the Mesopotamian artifacts. I wish you luck. Professor Campbell drives a hard bargain." Sturm said, as he picked up his martini and joined Mattie on the other side of the room.

Once across the room, Mattie whispered "Why didn't you let me question him? He knows something about that third map he's not telling us."

Sturm took a sip of his martini and smiled. "Ah, the gin is much diluted. Perhaps we can finish these since we watered his plants with the others" he said as he clinked his stemmed glass against hers in a toast. "I saw the same thing you did. We have the answer we came for. The third map is the one. No more questions are needed. Go find Anwar. Have him transfer our bags to the motorcar. We will leave for the Hotel Cecil as soon as we finish dinner."

Dinner was even more luxurious than lunch and Weber continued his prodigious consumption of wine while Mattie and Sturm continued to sip. Weber was once more in an expansive mood as the hard-bargaining Professor Campbell had agreed upon a price for all ten artifacts in the photos as well as the financial protocols to effectuate their delivery. Mattie smiled inwardly at Campbell's wicked sense of humor. She wished she could see Weber's face when he found out the Swiss bank account number Campbell gave him turned out to be bogus.

Weber soon returned to his history of modern Alexandria which eventually degenerated into gossip about sexual affairs and scandals of the last ten years. Mattie was bored to tears but Campbell would interject a question each time Weber seemed to be slowing down. Suitably revived, he would resume his monologue. Weber's great body eventually gave way after his third cognac and he collapsed, falling face forward into a plate of dates and sweet cakes.

Mattie looked at Sturm and rolled her eyes as Weber began to snore loudly. She threw her napkin down and stood up. "It's about time. I thought the evening would never end. Can we go now?"

Before Sturm could respond, four men burst into the room through the billowing drapes, each dressed in black and holding a submachine pistol with a sound suppressor.

"No one move!" a tall man with a dueling scar shouted in French, then in English. Mattie immediately recognized him. The man in her compartment on the Orient Express!

Two of the servant girls screamed and turned to flee, but they had not taken more than three steps when two of the silenced weapons opened fire, striking each girl solidly in the back, their slender bodies jerking at the impact and falling to the floor. Red blood spread from their ruined backs, providing a vivid contrast to the thick white cotton of their long garments.

All four weapons now turned toward Mattie, Sturm and Campbell, the only one who had remained seated during the slaughter of the servants. The man with the scar spoke in German to the other three armed men. "Guard the Europeans. I will interrogate them later. First we must deal with the traitor in our midst. The man who has betrayed the Brotherhood."

The man shook his head slowly from side to side as he stared down at the unconscious Weber. He motioned to the other two men. "Round up all the servants. The two at the front gate will already be dead. Find and kill the other women who have been living in debauchery with this excuse for a man who was once our brother."

Mattie watched as the man with the scar slung his machine pistol over his shoulder, held there by a sturdy leather strap. The man walked over to the table, picked up Weber's head from the plate of dates and pulled him up by his hair, a date briefly sticking to his cheek before it fell to the table. He picked up a carafe of water and threw it directly into Weber's face. Weber sputtered and slowly regained consciousness. He was pulled to his feet and his hands were tied behind his back. Sounds of shrill screams and cries could be heard from deep inside the villa, followed by an ominous stillness.

"Come, old friend," the man with the scar said, as he pushed the stumbling Weber away from the table back into the salon where cocktails had been served. The man guarding Sturm, Campbell and Mattie motioned with his weapon for them to follow Weber. They walked behind him and the man with the scar to the far end of the salon where four marble steps led to a small landing and from there to bedrooms. The man with the scar pushed Weber up to the landing while their guard brought Mattie and the others to a halt just below.

Another man returned, smoke still curling from the ugly snout of the machine pistol.

"You have disposed of the servants?" the man with the scar asked.

He nodded as a fourth man emerged with a sword and scabbard nearly four feet long.

"The two guards were dispatched?" the man with the scar asked, raising his eyebrows.

"Yes. We cut their throats and hid their bodies in the guard shack."

"What of the driver for the Europeans' motorcar?"

"I saw no one," the fourth man replied.

The man with the scar frowned. "Did you find their driver?"

The third man shook his head. "No, only women."

The man with the scar frowned again. "When the ritual is complete, search the house thoroughly again while I interrogate the Europeans."

The man then withdrew the sword from its scabbard, the three-foot-long blade polished and reflecting the light from the chandelier above. Both edges looked razor sharp to Mattie.

"Down," the man with the scar said, as he forced Weber to his knees.

Weber had fully regained consciousness by now and began babbling. "Josef, it's me! Hans! I did not tell them anything. I swear it. Ask them! I have not betrayed the Brotherhood!"

"I am afraid, old friend, that you did," the man with the scar replied softly. "One of the maps you were shown," he said gesturing to the maps on the low table beyond him, "holds the location of Castle Lanz. Your eyes alone have already betrayed us." He said, gesturing in the direction of Mattie and Sturm. "They know. I heard them. You were exiled by the Brotherhood many years ago because your judgment was unreliable. An innocent man, a Christian, died by your hand on a mountain road in Scotland. You may have repented but betraying the location of the Holy Lance is of a different order. Our Lord may forgive you but we shall not."

The man with the scar made the Sign of the Cross and then held the sword in a two-fisted grip. Mattie watched, mesmerized, as one of the men grabbed Weber's stringy black hair and yanked it back, exposing his fleshy throat while the fat man continued to babble. Tears streamed down Weber's face as the man with the scar pulled the sword back as if it were a cricket bat and then swung it forward in a powerful backhand arc, Weber's sobs stopping abruptly when the polished steel sunk into his neck, just below his adam's apple. The sword seemed to meet no resistance as it continued in its arc, droplets of blood flying off the sword's edge after it had severed Weber's head.

Mattie screamed as Weber's head was held high by its hair, a wide-eyed look of horror frozen on Weber's face while blood spurted in a veritable geyser from the stump of his neck, nearly reaching Mattie, almost 20 feet away. Weber's large body fell slowly forward until its twitching neck rested on the top step and a cataract of red flowed down to stain the white marble steps. The force of the flow diminished as Weber's heart finally realized it was no longer receiving instructions from his brain and ceased beating. The stream of blood continued to flow out of the neck and down the steps, now only a phenomenon of gravity.

"Oh my god!" Campbell exclaimed, his voice high and unnatural.

Weber's head was dripping blood, and his eyelids and lips opened and closed in irregular rhythmic contractions for a good ten seconds until the spasmodic movements ceased, the face relaxed and the eyelids closed half-way.

"Hans!" the man with the scar shouted and Mattie watched in horror as the eyelids slowly lifted up, and Weber's eyes fixed on the man who had shouted, his pupils focusing as he did so. "You betrayed our Savior and the Sacred Lance!"

Several more seconds passed and Weber's eyelids closed again, his face relaxed.

"Hans!" the voice shouted and once more, the eyelids of Weber's head slowly lifted and the eyes again focused even more intently on the man with the scar.

"You will burn in hell, Hans!" the man shouted. Shortly after that, Weber's eyelids drooped but less than before and the eyeballs rolled up into his head, taking on the glazed look Mattie had seen in battlefield corpses. The entire exchange, Mattie realized, from the severing of Weber's head until his eyes rolled up, had taken nearly sixty long, horrifying seconds.

Stunned, Mattie took a moment to register the sound of gunshots as someone's arm knocked her to the floor. She looked up to see that two men already lay dead, their guard with two small red holes over his heart and the other missing the right side of his head.

Sturm!

So quickly did it happen that the two men on the landing had no chance to react. The man with the scar had immediately dropped his sword and attempted to bring his machine pistol around to a firing position. The man holding Weber's head dropped it and attempted to do the same, as the head hit on the first step and tumbled down, rolling to a stop as it hit Mattie's foot.

Sturm's next shot was off target and smashed into the machine pistol held by the man with the scar, and ricocheted off it to the man's right arm. He cried out and dropped to his knee. Mattie had jumped back when Weber's head touched her foot, but she recovered her wits and reached for her Walther from where it had been nestled in the small of her back inside the waistband of her trousers. She aimed at the man who had dropped Weber's head as he struggled to recover his machine pistol from behind his back.

"Hands away from the weapon!" Mattie shouted in German.

Sturm hesitated, then followed Mattie's lead and held his fire. "Do it now," he added "Slowly place the weapon at your feet. Do the same with your friend's weapon."

After the man did so, Sturm spoke over his shoulder to Campbell, "Professor". But Campbell didn't reply as he huddled on the floor, shaking, his hands over his head. "Professor!" Sturm shouted and Campbell looked up at him. "Please find Anwar and have him bring the automobile around. If they have killed him, you will find a spare set of keys in the glove compartment."

Just then, a small frightened voice came from the top of the landing. "*Monsieur* Sturm. It is me. Anwar," he said, speaking in French. "It is safe for me now?"

"Yes, Anwar. Bring our car to the main entrance. We shall depart in a few moments."

The small, wiry Egyptian's head appeared out from behind the corner and paused as he took in the carnage and the headless body in front of him. He tiptoed carefully down the right side of the marble steps as they contained the least blood. "You can count on me, *Monsieur*."

"Go with him, Professor," Sturm said. "You, too, Mattie."

Mattie stiffened "Why? What are you going to do?"

Sturm replied without taking his eyes off the two now unarmed men. "I am going to find out who these men are and what they want."

"But the one you wounded—with the scar—he's the one who shot at me on the train."

"I assumed as much. Another man with a scar in less than a week is too much of a coincidence. I don't believe in coincidence."

"You can't kill them in cold blood."

"Mattie. This is not the time to discuss matters of this kind."

"Kurt, please. Don't kill them."

"Then go to the kitchen. See if you can find some rope."

"**I WILL** kill you both," Sturm said, "before the woman returns, unless you tell me what I want to know." With that, he slapped the handle of his Luger down hard on the wounded man's arm, causing him to cry out sharply. But both men simply stared at him and said nothing, their lips moving silently as if in prayer.

Sturm briefly contemplated who was the weakest and, therefore, the one to shoot last. Neither man had flinched during the beheading, not the one holding the sword, nor the one holding the head. Sturm's hesitation saved their lives because just then Mattie returned and began binding the two men, showing no mercy even when the man with the scar winced in pain as she bound his two hands tightly together behind him.

Pleasing a woman should not influence his decision, Sturm thought, but he said nothing. The woman was a curious mixture of strength and softness. He weighed the odds and decided he could live with them. He spared the two men. Killing was something he did when he had no choice. It was not something he enjoyed.

"Mattie, we must move quickly. More of them may be waiting for us."

32.

A Cute Birthmark

BLOOD still streaked Cockran's face when he and Harmony walked—or in his case limped—into the Hotel *Leinfelder* shortly before midnight. It was nearly two hours after their motorcar had crashed off the road to Munich. He had persuaded her he didn't need a hospital. The cuts on his face had stopped bleeding and looked a whole lot worse than it felt. His hip, however, hurt like hell.

The lobby at the *Leinfelder* was a smaller, quieter affair than the *Bayerische Hof*, which supplied its own nightlife at its bar, restaurant and cabaret. Cockran only saw two men and a woman lounging just outside the *Leinfelder* bar. Both men stared openly at Cockran—not something you do if you're tailing someone—so he felt reasonably sure they weren't SS.

The hotel's desk clerk was a young man, thin with thickset dark wavy hair. He spoke decent English, as many hotel clerks in   Germany did, and became most sympathetic to their tale of being caught in the middle of a political street fight once "Mr. Donovan" handed him twice the amount of German marks necessary for the hotel room. He also understood words like "iodine" and "bandages," which "Mrs. Donovan" asked for.

Cockran regretted the necessity for leaving their hotel and checking into a new one under an assumed name but he had no choice. His client's safety came first. Now he and Mattie were in the same boat. He still had no idea where she was and, if she ever tried to contact him at the *Bayerische Hof,* she would find he had checked out with no forwarding address. Neither knew where the other was. What had started out as concern on his part was rapidly turning to anger. Damn it, after two years together, did he mean so little to her that she would simply cut off communications between them because of their arguments? He deserved better. But what other conclusion could he draw? Venice was *not* looking promising.

Once in their room—separate beds, not bedrooms, no suite being available—Harmony pulled Cockran into the bathroom to clean his face properly. Her damp blonde hair was curling and hung in a curtain over her face as she bent over the sink to start the water. With a flip of her head, she flung the curls out of her eyes and looked at him. "Why don't you find some place to sit down?" she said.

Cockran sat on the edge of the bathtub as she turned to him, her powder blue blouse sticking tightly to her skin. She placed a hand on his knee to push it aside and knelt between his thighs. One of the upper buttons of her dress had come undone. Stop that, he told himself. Get your mind off her chest and back in the game.

She reached out to his face with a soft cloth, soaked with warm water, and ran it over his face, the excess water running onto his already damp shirt. Her touch was firm and purposeful as she washed his wounds, the pressure when she applied the cloth to his cuts no different from that applied to the rest of his face. The cuts weren't deep and had stopped bleeding. There were clean cuts on his cheek and forehead that accounted for most of the blood on his face. Harmony reached to place a bandage on his forehead, but Cockran took her hand. "No bandages," he said. "Not on the face. Not yet."

"But you might start bleeding again." she said.

"I still have work to do. White bandages on my face are too conspicuous."

"So is blood running down your face," she said, like a good mother chastising her son.

He grinned. "Then give me one to stick in my pocket," he said. "I'll wipe it away if it starts to bleed." Harmony made an impatient face. "Blood is hard to see in the dark. Trust me,"

Harmony sighed, conceding. "Then at least let me wipe the iodine off your face." Cockran said yes and she leaned in close, dabbing the cloth at his face carefully. Her face rested inches from his, her breath floating over his lips. "There," she said, her face still close. She leaned her head to one side and gave him a kiss on the cheek. "That was for protecting me in the car. For saving my life." She leaned back. "Now take off your shirt and pants."

Cockran balked. "Can't you—"

"I am *not* cleaning the wound on your hip through your pants, and you're bleeding through your shirt," she said firmly. "Take them off. You're not the first man I've seen in his underwear. I'm only your client, remember? Your virtue is still safe. Relax."

Easy for you to say, Cockran thought. He unbuckled his belt, felt a burning twinge in his wounded hip, and dropped his pants on the floor. He watched Harmony's face for a reaction, but if she had one, he missed it. She was already going to work, pulling his boxer shorts modestly down on the side to expose the wound, then washing the deeper cut on his hip. Her hand rested on his leg as she worked, her thin arms tensing with the effort, the sweat beading on her breastbone and rolling beneath the open neck of her dress. Only the sting of the iodine kept his body from embarrassing him with her soft hands so close.

Harmony shot him a glance of concern when she heard his sharp intake of breath. Cockran stared straight ahead. "This cut is much worse," she said, looking up from his hip and pulling her hand away from his leg. "The wound won't close easily. You'll need stitches."

"I'll get them tomorrow," he said.

"May I at least bandage this one, Mr. Tough Guy?" she said, her hand back on his waist.

"You may," he said, as she began placing gauze and tape over his hip.

"Where did you get this?" she asked as she pulled his boxer shorts down lower and put a cool hand on a two-inch long purple crescent on his right hip beside the wound. "A tattoo?"

"From my parents. It's a birthmark." Cockran tensed. If she didn't take her hands off him, one way of showing his attraction to her was soon going to be impossible to hide.

"I think it's cute."

Cockran laughed. "It's never been called that before."

"Now for this last cut on your arm." She placed a hand on his bare thigh to steady herself and reached past him for the gauze on the sink. He didn't move as she strained to reach the supplies. Her damp hair rested against his face and Cockran could smell sweat mingled with perfume behind her ear. She leaned back to look at him, the gauze in her hand almost forgotten. Her face hung above him, her lips parted, waiting to be kissed, and he did. She kissed him back and her cool hand on his leg moved higher, inside his boxer shorts, curling around his unmistakable erection.

Cockran reacted instinctively and took her in his arms, pushing her back and up onto the marble shelf containing the wash basin. He slipped a hand inside her dress, beneath her bra, feeling her breasts. She gasped, pulled up the hem of her dress and guided his free hand along the inside of her bare leg. She slid her filmy step-ins aside and pulled him closer with her hand firmly grasping his hip. Cockran winced at the pain in his hip and tried to pull back but she held him firmly in place, kissing him and guiding his hand higher along her leg. He freed his hand and tried to back out of her embrace but both her hands were on his hips now pulling him forward. With a great effort, he leaned back from her arms, broke free and pinned them to her sides. Harmony shot him a look of surprise but her protest died in her throat when she saw his face. He released her arms and turned away, awkwardly pulling his trousers up. He didn't trust himself to speak so he silently reached for his shirt, breathing heavily.

"Where are you going?" she asked, gasping for air, the hem of her dress still well above her waist.

"Back to the *Bayerische Hof*," he said. "We need to steer them off our trail."

"Won't they be waiting for you?"

"Probably," he said, sticking the other arm through.

"What about the cut on your arm? I haven't bandaged it."

"Let it bleed," he said and left without looking back.

A LIGHT rain had begun to fall and it was a welcome sensation as he limped the two blocks back to the *Bayerische*. He took his time, gathering his thoughts, trying to pinpoint where exactly he had lost his head. What the hell had he been thinking? Harmony was an attractive woman, intelligent too. His kind of woman. But he didn't think much of lawyers who slept with their clients, especially vulnerable clients as Harmony most certainly was. Yet he almost had done just that. He was attracted to her in a way he did not expect. She was not an adventure-seeker like Mattie. He would not have to worry about her rushing headlong into danger at every turn. Like Cockran, she wanted a quiet life. With children? Cockran didn't know her that well yet. But he wanted children. Did Mattie? He didn't know that either. In fact, given her failure to contact him, he didn't even know whether Mattie wanted him anymore. He'd find out in Venice.

As for tonight, he passed it off to an old truism from his old CO and current boss, Bill Donovan. "When a man's little head gets hard, his big one goes soft." Cockran shook his head. If that wasn't the truth, nothing was. His father had told him the same thing but had used different and certainly more diplomatic words. He   just couldn't remember them.

Right before reaching the *Bayerische,* he turned left, searching for an unmarked doorway at the base of a short stairwell. Before leaving, Cockran had tipped the *Leinfelder* concierge—Rolf—one mark to find out whether the *Bayerische* had a service entrance where he could slip in without notice. Rolf knew of such an entrance but recommended a much smaller bribe than one mark to the laundry workers employed there. "Most of the staff there work two jobs. Many are Nazis," he had said "They have to pay for their own uniforms. They bribe easily."

"And you don't?" Cockran had asked.

"No, only tips for good service." He had smiled and then said. "The *Leinfelder* furnishes my uniform at no cost."

Cockran found the stairwell and waited. The dull pain throbbed in his hip and he could feel blood seeping through Harmony's bandage. It took ten minutes before a laundry worker emerged with a bag. A couple of twenty *pfenning* coins was all it took to gain access. Inside, he limped up the employee stairwell to their suite on the third floor. Spotting no signs of surveillance, he entered the suite and grabbed a change of clothes for both of them and stuffed it all into Harmony's hard leather suitcase. He worked his way down to the lobby. He knew he should leave the same way he entered. That was the safest thing to do. But he couldn't. Gathering a change of clothes wasn't the only reason he had come.

Someone was waiting for him. A tall man with close-cropped sandy hair holding a glass of beer, trying his best to remain inconspicuous in the bustling night traffic of the hotel lobby's bar. Cockran stood just out of sight in a hallway watching the man.. He scanned the lobby but no one else was so focused on the hotel's front doors. With the lookout's attention focused on the entrance, he was able to cross the lobby to the check-out desk without drawing any attention. With any luck, the SS lookout would be so busy waiting for Cockran to enter the hotel that he would not notice him leaving it. "Checking out, please," Cockran said. "Room eight-oh-four."

"Of course, sir," the clerk replied in English before bending down to rummage for the paperwork. He was an elderly man with white hair and big, expressive eyebrows. "Ah, here we are," he said as he rose back up. Squinting his eyes, he saw the name on the form and turned his glance to Cockran. He raised his voice: "Leaving so soon, *Herr* Cockran?"

Cockran did not respond. He did not need to turn around to know he'd been burned by the old man. "We're driving to France." he said. The clerk smiled thinly and nodded his head, letting his eyes drift from Cockran's and over his shoulder before returning to the paper work. Cockran kept still, as if nothing had happened, hoping at least to keep the appearance of ignorance, rather than alert his tail that he knew he was being watched.

"Have there been any messages for me?" This was the real reason he risked going back to the *Bayerische*. It was hotel policy not to give messages over the telephone.

"Messages?" The concierge looked up. "*Nein*. None that I can recall. Let me check."

He quietly hoped Mattie had left a message but he wasn't optimistic. He feared they wouldn't be in touch until she showed up in Venice. Or, he corrected himself, *if* she showed up in Venice.

"It was as I said," the clerk announced, his search completed. "No messages."

Cockran picked up Harmony's case and turned to leave. Out of the corner of his eye, he could see the tall man place down his glass and step away from the girl he'd been talking to. Cockran pressed on to the street, pushing open the glass door and into the rain. The sounds of the lobby died as the doors closed behind him. He put his hat on and turned left, walking briskly away from the *Leinfelder,* his hip throbbing with every step. The sounds of the lobby briefly came back to life as the glass door opened and closed a second time. He strained his ears to hear footsteps following him but the sound of the rain drowned everything out.

Cockran reached the end of the block and rounded the corner to his left. After five steps, he stopped and moved back to the edge of the building. He listened again for footsteps, Harmony's luggage gripped firmly in his left hand, his right hand pulling the Webley from its holster. Hearing footsteps, he lunged around the corner. The tall man reared back, startled, and stared stupidly at Cockran as he closed ground swiftly. He swung Harmony's suit case deep into the man's gut, doubling him over. Cockran came down hard on the back of his skull with the butt of his Webley and the man splayed out on the sidewalk.

Cockran bent over the prone figure and searched his pockets for a billfold and some form of identification. He found the billfold in an inside jacket pocket. In it were a few paper *Reichsmarks,* photos of a woman and child, several retail store receipts, and a National Socialist Workers Party membership card. Then he checked the other inside pocket and found something else—a business envelope inside of which was a folded piece of paper with a list of Germanic names and addresses, none of which he recognized. Aside from the names, there was almost nothing else marked on it, no headline or title. Just three embossed letters in the upper left hand corner of the envelope: I.C.E. Cockran refolded the paper, stuffed it and the envelope in his pocket, and left the unconscious Nazi to enjoy his cold, late evening shower on the sidewalk.

COCKRAN was met by the muzzle of a .45 when he returned to his room at the *Leinfelder* and he saw the blue eyes of Bobby Sullivan peering over the smooth black barrel.

"Anyone follow you?"

"Yes," Cockran said. "For a block. Then I convinced him to stop."

Sullivan pulled his head back to look behind him, allowing Cockran a glimpse inside the room. A blade of light divided the room, but he could make out the covered figure of Harmony asleep in one of the room's two beds. Sullivan loosened the chain from the door, but instead of letting Cockran in, he opened the door enough to let himself out into the hallway.

"Best to talk out here," he said. "The lass is sleeping."

Cockran nodded. "What happened at the factory?"

"Full frontal assault, as many as twenty Nazi storm troopers," Sullivan said, matter-of-factly. "They killed three of our boys. Paul's Tommy plugged at least two of theirs. Then the rest lost their courage and fled before Paul could take down any more of 'em."

"How did they break through?" Cockran asked.

Sullivan cut Cockran off with a shake of his head. "I don't know any further details. My German's not that good. I had a feeling everyone there wanted to tell me something else," Bobby continued, "but I couldn't understand them."

"I've got it covered," Cockran said. He told Bobby about Rolf, the *Leinfelder* concierge who had agreed to be their new translator. "We'll take him with us to the factory tomorrow but we're going to need more than a translator. We're going to need more guns." Cockran grinned. "Consider your hands to be officially untied."

"St. Thomas and I thank you," Sullivan said with a smile that only those who knew him well would consider a smile. "I'll place a call to Donegal today. Isn't the Squad always up for a good fight? And don't we have several German-speakers among them to boot?"

Cockran nodded. "Place the call. Bring as many of the Apostles as you think we'll need. NBM will pay the fare. Tell them I'll wire the funds to charter an airplane.

33.

Mattie's Nightmare

MATTIE sat in the back of the Packard with Sturm while the Professor sat up front in the left-hand passenger seat of the right hand drive motorcar. "Don't stop at the gate, Anwar. It should be open." Sturm then turned to Mattie. "If we see intruders, shoot to kill."

Anwar accelerated the big Packard up the driveway through the gate, which was open as Sturm had predicted. Machine gun fire erupted as they sped through the white arch, shattering the rear windscreen. Mattie winced, feeling shards of glass rending her blouse's sleeve and cutting flesh while Professor Campbell cowered on the floor up front and Sturm shot back.

"Anwar!" Sturm shouted. "Don't take the same route back. Head for the coast road. Take us to the marine terminal. We'll spend the night on the *Graf.*"

Mattie surveyed the damage to her arm. Most were minor scratches, but one shard of glass left a bleeding wound behind, which Sturm bound with a white handkerchief.

Anwar reached the coast road and hung a right, keeping at the 50 kilometers an hour posted speed limit. There was a full moon, and Mattie could see the ocean off to her left. The road ran along a bluff overlooking the beach. In some places, the bluff was only five to ten feet high, but elsewhere it was a 40 foot drop. There was no guardrail between the road and the beach and Mattie was grateful that Anwar was keeping the big motorcar within the speed limit.

Mattie's breath was slowly returning to normal when, without warning, a bullet shattered their left front windscreen, the noise of the engine masking the sound of the weapon. Both Mattie and Sturm turned quickly to look behind them, as Professor Campbell dove for the floor once more with a high-pitched squeal. A large pair of headlights was rapidly covering the distance between them. Before Sturm could issue an order to increase the acceleration, Anwar had already done so and the Packard's twelve-cylinder supercharged engine was more than up to the task. The acceleration threw Sturm and Mattie back into the soft leather upholstery.

The pursuing motorcar had an equally powerful engine and had closed to within 30 yards before Anwar's acceleration enabled them to maintain that distance.

"Keep your head down, Mattie. You load. I'll shoot."

Kurt handed her a box of shells and braced both elbows on the back of the seat and snapped off five quick shots, blowing out each of the pursuing car's headlights. Sturm fired five more shots and handed the Luger to Mattie, who quickly put her Walther in his palm.

"The two from the villa are the ones shooting," Sturm muttered under his breath but not too low for Mattie to hear, "I should have killed them when I had the chance."

Mattie could see the lights of Alexandria ahead as the motorcar behind returned fire. Anwar cried out and Mattie saw that he had been hit in the shoulder and was struggling to keep the Packard under control. She shoved the last shell into the clip and gave the Luger to Sturm.

"Anwar needs help," she shouted. "I'm going to take the wheel."

Sturm ignored her and fired a last shot from the Walther, which shattered the driver's side windscreen of the pursing vehicle, causing it to swerve momentarily.

Mattie clambered into the front seat and took the wheel. "I've got it. Move beside me!"

The car slowed briefly as Anwar took his foot off the pedal and shifted to the left behind her. Mattie hit the accelerator and the Packard leaped forward. More shots rang out and she ducked, tightening her hold on the steering wheel. Anwar's hands reached for his throat and he slumped forward, blood gushing from a bullet wound in his neck. His body slid with a curve in the road and bumped against her, knocking her grip free of the wheel and the Packard lurched to the left toward the bluff and its 40 foot drop. Mattie regained the wheel and jerked the car back onto the road as Sturm, with a thump and a curse, lost his balance. The Packard slowed from Anwar's 140 kilometer per hour pace and Mattie fought for control. Then, Sturm stopped firing and climbed into the front seat beside Mattie, pushing Anwar's body out of the way. Through the rearview mirror, she could see that the pursuer's vehicle had gone off the road to the right, the only illumination a spotlight attached to the driver's side, but now shining straight up.

Meanwhile, the Packard's left wheels were on the gravel and were less than ten yards from the edge of the bluff when the big motorcar hit a depression, bouncing several feet in the air. The right front door flew open when the car hit the ground, skidded and spun 180 degrees as Mattie brought it to a stop. She craned her neck to look out the open door. All she could see was the beach 40 feet below and the ocean beyond. She gripped the steering wheel even tighter.

Sturm applied the emergency brake and reached out for Mattie. "Take my hand." Which she did, grateful to feel the same strong hand which had saved her on top of the *Graf Zeppelin*.

"Put Professor Campbell in the back seat," Sturm said.

Mattie did so after Campbell had timidly crawled out from his hiding place in the front seat passenger foot space. Once the front seat was clear, Sturm lifted the slight Egyptian's body and pushed it out the open driver's door. Mattie watched it tumble down the side of the bluff.

"What the hell did you do that for?" Mattie asked as she re-entered the motorcar..

Sturm reached over Mattie, pulled the passenger door closed, released the parking brake, and engaged the clutch, moving the motor car slowly back onto the coast road. His voice was cold. "Anwar is dead because you stopped me from killing those men. The *Graf* leaves tomorrow morning. I don't propose being in Alexandria for another month as a material witness to the slaughterhouse we left behind at Weber's villa. That is what would happen if we didn't dispose of Anwar's body now. We must leave Egypt quickly if we are to find the Spear."

On Board the Graf Zeppelin
Friday, 5 June 1931

THE giant airship was bathed in spotlights as Sturm wheeled the big Packard through the gates of the marine station and pulled to a halt just short of the zeppelin's nose. Mattie watched, shivering from the cool night air, as Sturm bounded up the steps to the gondola's entrance.

He returned a few moments later with a blanket. "There's only one officer and several crew members on board. He has agreed that we may spend the night in our cabins."

Mattie nodded and shivered once more, barely taking in what Sturm was telling her.

"He will place several armed crew members at the marine terminal's entrance," Sturm said as he opened the door and extended his hand to Mattie. "How are you feeling?"

Mattie shivered again and Sturm placed the blanket around her shoulders. Mattie felt lightheaded as she leaned on Sturm. "Kurt, I think I'm going…" and then she felt herself falling.

Mattie regained consciousness moments later, cradled in Sturm's strong arms, as he started up the steps to the airship's passenger compartments. Mattie's adrenaline level was still high but, for the first time since the gunmen had burst in on them at Weber's villa, she felt safe and she sat patiently on the divan in her cabin and allowed Sturm to check her body for any broken bones or additional wounds beyond the superficial cuts on her left forearm caused by the flying glass. His hands were warm and comforting, as they gently applied pressure to her arms and ribs before moving lower, starting with her ankles, then her calves and up to her thighs where she felt a tingle at his touch. Sturm then rolled up the sleeve of her blouse and she winced as he applied alcohol to the cuts and wrapped them in a gauze bandage.

Sturm stood up from a kneeling position. "Would you like the ship's medical officer to examine you? I can arrange for one of the crew to find his hotel and wake him."

"I'll be fine. I just need some sleep." Her tired smile reflected her emotional exhaustion.

Sturm leaned over close and placed his large hands on both her shoulders. "You're safe now. I'm in the next cabin. Call out if you need me."

As she watched Sturm exit her cabin, she found it difficult to believe that he was only the assistant to the president of a large steel company. Kurt was a skilled killer and she was alive because of it. Who he really was could wait for another day. So could playing it safe. Those men had tried twice and failed. She wasn't going to let them keep her from finding the Spear.

Mattie closed her eyes and tried to erase the image of the beheading and harrowing chase in the motorcar. The danger she sometimes faced in her assignments was real but incidental. It didn't happen nearly so often as Cockran imagined. But tonight was different. She hadn't had so much gunfire directed toward her since that sixty seconds of blazing hell in Munich in 1923 where, like tonight, her only injuries were from a motorcar's shattered windscreen.

Munich
Friday, 9 November 1923

MATTIE and Helmut had walked back to their hotel through a Munich that seemed alive to the possibility of revolution as the news of President Kahr's concession to Hitler spread like wildfire. Fortified by a stiff scotch and water, Mattie had hastily written out her notes, obtained a long-distance line to the copy desk in London, and dictated a detailed account of the evening's events at the *Burgerbraukeller*. History was being made and she was writing it. It felt great.

She awoke from a sound sleep by the jangling of the telephone. She threw off the eiderdown comforter. Feeling the cold morning air on her naked body as she picked up the phone, she heard the voice of Putzi Hanfstaengl. "It's all gone terribly wrong. Our troops were meeting resistance at one of the armories and Hitler left to take personal charge of the attack. Ludendorff stayed behind and let Kahr and the others leave. Then Kahr repudiated his support."

"So the *putsch* is over?" Mattie asked.

"Maybe. I don't know. I think so." Hanfstaengl replied. "But it's all very confusing. I've never seen Hitler so unsure of himself. Everyone has a different opinion. There's talk of a mass march on the state capital at noon. Göring is pushing the idea. He has Ludendorff convinced that if he and Hitler lead the march, the police will not obey any orders to fire on them. It's lunacy, I tell you, but I'm afraid Hitler might believe it. Who knows? It might even work."

Mattie hung up the phone and walked to the black and white tiled bathroom and turned on the shower. Waiting for the water to warm, she then walked over to the tall french windows and threw open the drapes. She stood there, hands on hips, looking out at the cold, gray dawn and the glistening streets below. They were deserted. It didn't look like a day for revolution. After her shower, she called Helmut. "Come quickly. We need the motorcar at once."

The day was still gray and cold as Mattie and Helmut sat in their open Mercedes motorcar on the inner city side of the Isar River bridge. The Isar River separates the section of Munich in which the *Burgerbraukeller* was situated from the city center where the government buildings were located. In the inner city, somewhat to the north of the *Feld Herrn Halle* was the headquarters of the *Reichswehr* which Ernst Rohm and the Nazis had seized and fortified with machine guns. Mattie was at the wheel and Helmut was in the back seat, three cameras at the ready. Mattie turned up the collar of her long wool navy blue coat and shivered at the gust of wind coming off the water. She could see the column of Storm Troopers approaching the bridge.

"Start now, Helmut," she ordered. "Take as many photos as you can."

The fools, Mattie thought, as she looked at the small squad of police on the far side of the bridge. "They should be on this side," she said. "They have only twenty men, but if they put a machine gun or two on this side, the Storm Troopers could cross the bridge with no more than ten men abreast. The police might eventually be overrun, but I can't believe the Storm Troopers are prepared to put up with the kind of casualties that would entail."

Helmut, busy taking photos, didn't reply and Mattie watched as the long column of armed Storm Troopers stopped when they met their first obstacle at the Isar River bridge. A group of armed police confronted them with weapons drawn. Hermann Göring stepped forward and ordered the police to stand down, threatening to kill hostages if the police fired on them.

Mattie watched incredulously as the police surrendered their carbines and stood there abjectly as the Storm Troopers passed by them, shouting obscenities and spitting on them.

Mattie mentally kicked herself for her stupidity at what happened next. She heard Göring bellow an order and suddenly five armed men sprinted across the bridge, their rifles at port arms, bayonets affixed to each. Before Mattie could start the ignition of the big Mercedes, the five Storm Troopers had surrounded the car, their bayonets pointed menacingly at Mattie and Helmut. Moments later, Hermann Göring was by her side, his steel helmet tucked under his arm.

"Miss McGary. A revolution is hardly the place for a lady of your refinement. The Hanfstaengls' drawing room is far more suited to your beauty and charm."

"Bugger off, Hermann. I'm just doing my job. You may be a war hero," she said, eyeing the blue-ribboned *Pour Le Merite*, the Blue Max, tied around his neck, "but I've seen more dead men up close than you. Now, if you'll excuse me, my photographer and I have to be off."

"I am so sorry, Miss McGary," Göring said smoothly, "but we have need of your fine motorcar. As you can see," he said, gesturing to the column passing over the bridge, "we only have two automobiles. That is unfortunate because we have three machine guns. And so, we need your Mercedes to mount the third machine gun. I apologize for the inconvenience."

Later, Mattie was to regret her impulsiveness. But at the time, all she could think of was getting the story. "Look, Hermann, all I want is to report what happens. I was there last night and my newspaper in London already has the story. I wrote it before Kahr went back on his word. Let Helmut and me stay with the car. One of your men can drive.

I won't shill for the Nazis, but I'll give you a square deal. I'll tell the truth."

Göring smiled. "You'll be fair, Miss McGary, but will your Jew photographer be?"

"Helmut's religion is irrelevant." she snapped. "He works for me. He does what I say."

Göring then directed one of his men to take the wheel and another to mount a machine gun. "It's not his religion that bothers me. It's his race. But I accept your vouching for him."

Mattie cringed but, behind her, Helmut was silent. Their motorcar added to the parade, Mattie started to make notes and told Helmut to take photographs of the three thousand Storm Troopers behind them. Dressed in gray tunics with peaked caps, the men were in high spirits as if they were marching to a picnic rather than an assault on the center of government in Bavaria.

Göring had placed Mattie's Mercedes at the head of the column, immediately behind the front row of Ludendorff, Hitler, Hess, Göring and three others. Fifteen minutes later, Mattie saw they were approaching the narrow street which led into the *Odeon Platz*, the second choke point she had identified and where she had intended to cover the story. As they entered the long, narrow street, houses looming up four stories on either side of them, she began to question her decision. If they had not stayed with the motorcar, she and Helmut would have had time to reach the choke point ahead of the march. It was moving that slowly because of Ludendorff's age. Now, with a sinking feeling, she knew she was on the wrong side of the choke point.

Fifty yards ahead, she could see that the Bavarian state police, arrayed in battle gear and steel helmets, had set up a barricade exactly where she had predicted. She stood up on the passenger seat to get a better view and quickly estimated there were at least a hundred police, massed shoulder to shoulder, three rows deep, their rifles seemingly pointed directly at her.

The march came to a halt, its leaders barely twenty yards away from the police. Ludendorff, his Luger already in his right hand, addressed the police officer in charge. "If you are a German patriot, you will let us pass. We hold no ill will toward the police or the army."

Mattie was surprised that Hitler did not speak. He had linked arms with the man beside him and it appeared as if Hitler were holding on to him for support. Hitler's face was very pale, his right hand holding a pistol at his side, his trench coat tightly belted. She recalled Hanfstaengl's phone call earlier that morning about Hitler's ambivalence.

Then it happened. A shot rang out. The narrow canyon of the street was a sound chamber and Mattie could not tell whether the shot came from behind or in front of them. Mattie was no stranger to weapons fire. But she was ill prepared for the hellish fury which erupted. In front, the police opened fire with the deafening sound of a hundred rifles, a sound soon eclipsed by the explosive noise of the machine gun mounted in the rear of her Mercedes.

Mattie had instinctively taken three quick photos and then dove for the floor and huddled there while the firing on both sides continued. It seemed like an eternity, but eyewitnesses she interviewed later told her that it was only sixty seconds. Sixty seconds of blazing hell.

When the gunfire ended, the silence that followed was quickly filled by the moans and cries of the wounded and dying. The windscreen of the Mercedes had been shattered by the gunfire but, miraculously, Ludendorff was still standing ramrod straight. The others in the front row were all on the ground, including Hitler, his arm still linked with the dead man beside him.

"Helmut! Are you all right?" Mattie said in a stage whisper.

"*Ja*," Helmut replied.

"You've got to see this. Use your camera."

"I can't. The gunfire shattered it. Quick! Give me your 35 millimeter."

Mattie rummaged in the bag at her feet and reached back to Helmut with her Leica. As Helmut began to shoot photos, Mattie watched. Hitler was the first to rise, freeing himself from the grasp of the dead man beside him whose blood was staining the pavement from a massive head wound. Hitler moved quickly, clutching his left arm, the pistol still in his right hand. As he passed the car and Helmut continued to operate his camera, Mattie saw the same thing the camera captured, a look of sheer terror on Hitler's white, ghost-like face as he sped past, heedless to the cries of the wounded Storm Troopers left in his wake. Mattie's last glimpse of Hitler and Helmut's last photograph was of Hitler's back as he climbed into a waiting motorcar.

On Board the Graf Zeppelin
Friday, 5 June 1931

MATTIE made her way to the washroom in her bare feet. She stripped off her bloody shirt and blood-stained trousers. She winced at what she saw in the mirror. Streaks of dried blood covered her face and neck. Anwar's blood had seeped through and stained her undergarments as well. Using a washcloth, she wiped the blood away. Almost presentable, she donned her green silk robe. Once back in her cabin, she saw that one of the crew had made up her bunk. She opened her suitcase, pulled out a bottle of Johnnie Walker Red, and poured two fingers into a crystal tumbler. She drained the tumbler, feeling the liquor burn in her throat and then the warm glow spreading throughout her body. She quickly poured two more fingers.

Mattie shook her head. She had seen battlefields before and men killed or horribly wounded, but nothing could have prepared her for the manner of Weber's death. So much blood gushing from his neck. It was like something out of the middle ages.

There was a soft knock on her cabin door. Mattie opened her eyes and rose to her feet. Her loosely knotted robe fell open and she said "Just a moment," as she paused to tighten the robe and then opened the cabin door to find Sturm holding two half-filled brandy snifters.

"May I come in? I wanted to check on my patient's progress."

"Sure. It's going to be hard to sleep tonight. Another night cap wouldn't hurt." She took the brandy, walked back and sat on the far end of the bunk, pulling her feet up under her.

Unlike Mattie, Sturm was not dressed for bed, but had changed to a plain pair of linen pants and a white cotton shirt, its sleeves rolled up above his elbows, revealing his strong forearms. His blond hair was uncombed, falling in a comma over his forehead in a boyish way which reminded her of Cockran, not the cold, efficient killing machine of only a few hours ago.

"How is your arm?" Sturm asked, nodding at the gauze beneath her gown's left sleeve.

"I'm feeling no pain now, thank you," Mattie replied but, as she felt the glow of the brandy seep through her body, her mind flashed to the last time they had been alone together and she reminded herself that airships, adrenaline and alcohol had lowered her resistance once before to the strikingly handsome man barely two feet away. She resisted an impulse to pull her robe more tightly around her, aware that it would only draw more attention to her nakedness beneath.

"Excuse me," Mattie said. "Would you repeat that, please?" as she realized Sturm had been talking to her while she had been subduing her baser instincts. Sturm smiled, and she couldn't help smiling back. No, he certainly didn't look like a killer now.

"What I said was, we do not know who our adversaries are. Professor Campbell thinks they may be the same Austrian troops who hid the Spear originally. Perhaps. Perhaps not. But we do know they are ruthless and, for whatever reason, they are determined to stop us. I intend to ask the Institute for more funds. It will no longer be sufficient to hire only an alpine guide, a cook and some local men to attend to our needs. We need skilled marksmen as well."

Mattie nodded in agreement.

"I also believe you should reconsider your own participation…."

Mattie cut him off in mid-sentence. "Don't even think of it," she said, her voice tight with emotion and memories of her father. "You have no idea what this means to me."

Sturm held up his hands in a gesture of surrender and rose to his feet. "I didn't expect you to agree, but I had to ask. I fear we must start sooner than we had planned. We have weakened our enemy tonight but we must move quickly before they can regroup. I thought you might find your holiday in Venice with *Herr* Cockran more enjoyable and certainly safer."

Mattie rose too, placed her hand on Sturm's forearm. She badly needed to be held close and comforted but she was relieved Sturm was leaving. The temptation might prove too great. "That's sweet of you, Kurt, and very thoughtful. But this is my job. That always comes first." She forced a laugh. "Besides, Bourke thinks the search for the Spear is safer than the stories I usually cover. It's sometimes a point of dispute between us but I won't change my mind," she said as she kissed him softly on the cheek. "You saved my life today. Twice. Thank you."

After Sturm left, Mattie dropped her robe in a pool beside the bed. She drained the last of the brandy and crawled beneath the sheets. But sleep was difficult. The severed head kept flashing through her mind as she relived the image of it rolling against her foot in the villa. The more she tried, the harder it became to erase from her mind the severed head and twitching stump of Weber's neck. She tried to change the image to something more pleasant and finally settled on making love with Cockran last Sunday night at Chartwell. It worked, after a fashion, but in that twilight before sleep came, her mind kept flashing back between Cockran and Sturm, refusing to settle on either man until it all became a blur in her mind and sleep overtook her.

Nightmares. Mattie is lying in a dark alley doubled over in pain while heavy boots thud into her side. Her ruined Graflex and Leica lie in her field of vision on the glistening cobblestones, wet from rain. Someone grabs her head by the hair and pulls it painfully up. She feels the cold steel of a pistol pressed against her temple. "We warned you once about hanging out with Jews. You should have listened." The pistol fires and Mattie screams.

Mattie is back at the villa. She is naked and the man with the scar forces her to her knees and then down until she is resting on her heels. The other man places Weber's head in her hands and grabs her head by its hair. He yanks it back, exposing her throat, while the man with the scar swings the sword once more and severs Mattie's head from her body. There is no pain and she is still alive. She feels her head bouncing down the four steps and coming to rest at the foot of the steps, looking back at her headless body, still kneeling there, Weber's head held in her hands, while her neck spouts blood, just as Weber's had. Her blood splashes on the marble in front of her head and covers her face. Mattie screams and screams.

Suddenly, a man whose face she cannot make out appears to save her. Her head is miraculously reattached to her body and the man, naked to the waist, is embracing her. "Hold me, please hold me," she says and they kiss eagerly, and she feels his hands on her breasts. She knows she is in a dream now and she gives into it. She gasps as she feels one finger and then his tongue move inside her. Her hands hold his head tightly as the pressure builds, her breath growing short until she screams once more, this time not from terror, but pleasure. Her breathing grows more regular and, relaxed by her orgasm, her eyes grow heavy. She looks for a moment at the man's face but it is obscured by shadows. It doesn't matter. She knows she is safe and there will be no more nightmares tonight.

34.

The Last Honest Man in Munich

Munich
Saturday, 6 June 1931

COCKRAN walked stiffly from the taxicab to the entrance of the NBM factory, the stitches in his hip freshly sewn in hospital that morning. Sullivan was beside him and greeted the armed worker standing outside with a firm handshake. The man's eyes were swollen with the strain of a night without sleep. The worker let them inside and called for the plant manager Steinmetz who emerged from his upstairs office and loudly bounded down the stairs.

Cockran wasn't sure what to expect from Steinmetz. They'd come to improve security at the factory and instead provoked a platoon-strength raid on the factory. But Steinmetz greeted them like old friends, shaking Sullivan's hand with vigor and speaking in an uninterrupted stream of German which Rolf translated.

"They came last night, you know. They murdered three of our best. But we sent two of the pigdogs to their own place in hell. It was you who made us ready for them. It was you who gave us strength to fight back. We thank you."

"Don't thank us," Sullivan said. "We gave you the guns. The strength is yours."

Steinmetz nodded. He finally turned to the rest of Sullivan's company. Rolf translated. "He's talking about your last translator. A lawyer?"

"Yes. Name of Muller. We think he may have double-crossed us," Cockran said.

"You thought right," Rolf said. "Steinmetz says he's a Nazi. One of the first things Muller said to him yesterday was to ask how his mother and grandparents were doing. Knew their addresses and where his mother worked. He got the message."

"Your workers were also trying to tell me something last night, but I couldn't understand them. Any idea what it was?" Sullivan asked Steinmetz who didn't seem to know. "They said something about the police," Sullivan prompted.

Steinmetz cocked his head, as if something had just registered. "They must have been trying to tell you to see a police captain named Jacob Weintraub. A Jew." Rolf translated. "They say he's the last honest man left in Munich. If anyone in this city can help you, it's him."

"I SAW you in here yesterday," Captain Jacob Weintraub said through Rolf as he closed the blinds in his office. "I saw what was happening. You thought you were the ones talking to police officials, when it was your interpreter, *Herr* Muller, who was threatening each of them."

The captain was short, stout and aging, his balding hair compensated by an ample mustache under a long Semitic nose. He made little unnecessary movements, his hands folded on the desk before him after he sat down. His eyes were intense and focused.

"How could Muller threaten your officers?" Cockran asked.

"He has party support."

"Nazis?" Cockran asked. "What can Nazis do to you? You're policemen."

"*Herr* Cockran, you do not understand Munich," Weintraub said, looking at his hands. "At least, not today's Munich. I am but an old man in policeman's clothing. Any power that the law confers on me can be blocked by the actions of V-men."

"'V-men?'" Cockran asked.

"Yes, V-men. *Vertrauensmänner. Trustworthy men.* Secret supporters of the Nazis hidden within various levels of local and regional government even the national government."

"These are the men who block our efforts, as well?"

"The same."

"And what if we removed a few of these fellows?" Sullivan asked, leaning forward.

Weintraub's eyes narrowed. "You would be subject to prosecution to the full extent of the law." Now Weintraub also leaned forward. "But if some of these men were to have a crisis of conscience and decided, of their own accord, to let us do our jobs, we might be able to help."

"Who are these lads?" Sullivan asked. "Maybe we can pay 'em a visit."

"I do not know," Weintraub said, shaking his head. "I have suspicions but no proof. Much of what they do is hidden in bureaucratic machinery. You work for NBM, correct?"

"I'm its lawyer." Cockran replied

"Have you not figured out who is behind the sabotage at your client's Munich plants?"

"Of course. The SS."

"But why?" Weintraub asked. "Why bother to harass an American company?"

"Because the extortion revenue directly pads the Party's coffers."

Weintraub chortled. "Those sums are piddling compared to the steady flow of income from other sources. Go back to the origin of that income. Go back to the beginning. Before the bastards cut your pretty face. Think plainly, without passion."

Cockran took a moment to glance at Rolf, who shrugged: "That's what he said, I swear."

"Personally, I never thought you were that pretty to begin with," Sullivan said.

"Who would profit by NBM's demise?" Weintraub pressed. "And pay the SS to do it?"

"A rival company," Cockran answered immediately. Of course. That would explain the attack on him in New York and the finders' fee bribe offers to Harmony. He had suspected it in New York but put the theory aside in Germany in the face of one bureaucratic obstacle after another. The Nazis were running more than a protection racket—they were hired thugs, using terror tactics on behalf of a company that could fund them more deeply than any amount of extortion. And Cockran knew who. A sterilizing human breeding fanatic with a beautiful wife.

"Wesley Waterman. I.C.E."

"Exactly--International Calculating Equipment." Weintraub said. "It is no secret I.C.E. is behind the SS terror campaign against NBM. You may be the only ones who don't know."

"We do now," Sullivan answered.

Cockran was struck by a thought. He reached into his jacket for the envelope he lifted from the Nazi who tailed him the night before. He glanced at the letters in the upper left hand corner. I.C.E. He pulled out the sheet and gave it to Weintraub who leaned forward again, intrigued enough by the paper to warrant the exertion. He glanced at it for a few moments.

"Where did you get this?" he said.

"I took it from a Nazi who was following me. Do you recognize any names?"

"Yes. Yes, of course I do!" Weintraub said, his voice rising. These men—with one exception—they are all government officials. Many of whom I've suspected for months."

"Who are they?" Cockran asked.

"V-men!" the captain shouted. "These are your V-men! At least the ones that matter to I.C.E. and NBM. Yes, here is Dieter Hassenbach, Deputy Bavarian Minister of Trade. You get these gentlemen off my back and I can toss every one of those SS thugs into prison cells!"

"Not so secret after all," Sullivan said.

Weintraub's face began to sober. His finger pointed to a name. "This man," he said. "I know this man. He is the only bona fide, card-carrying Nazi on this list. This man is no government official. He is no V-Man," the captain said, turning the paper around to face them. "This man has to be their ring leader. He works directly for Himmler himself in SS Intelligence." They all leaned in closer to read the name printed in crisp black strokes: "Reinhard Tristan Hoch."

35.

Traitors Within Geneva

Berlin
Saturday, 6 June 1931

THE atmosphere in the White Mouse cabaret at 1:00 a.m. was pure Berlin. Wesley Waterman loved it. Loud and smoke-filled; half-naked women dancing on the stage; a telephone on each table along with a small lamp topped by a red shade. It was like nothing at home.

"What was Himmler's reaction?" Waterman asked, as he lit another cigarette.

"When I told him where Sturm would start his search for the Spear?" Munich replied.

You idiot, he thought. What else have we been talking about? "Yes. What did he say?"

"When I told him where the Kaiser's expedition would begin, his entire demeanor changed. He is a humorless man but he couldn't stop talking. I gave him all you suggested, including the three locations Sturm believes are most probable. The man is such a crashing bore. I had to listen to a history of who possessed the Spear from Constantine to Frederick the Great. He thinks he's the reincarnation of Henry the Fowler. He's delusional. Worse than Göring."

Waterman smiled. "But useful. Make certain he is kept informed of Sturm's progress."

"He's already well-informed. He learned nearly two weeks ago of the Kaiser's quest and had Reinhard Hoch, one of his best men, assemble an SS team to shadow it. But with our new information, Hoch will sign up with Sturm's expedition himself. It will be easy for the SS now."

Perhaps the man was not as stupid as he sometimes seemed. "Excellent. Well done, Munich. Here," Waterman said, handing him a slip of paper, "is the name and hotel room of the American journalist I want you to see. He's a stringer for the Hearst papers. Don't contact him at his office. Make him work. Send a note to his hotel. It will appear all the more authentic."

"I am to tell him everything? Even the Hindenburg assassination plot?"

"Yes, my friend. That is how we do things in America. Your enemies must never see you coming and they must always think someone other than you is responsible."

Waterman picked up the telephone and dialed two numbers. "Now, please excuse me while I enjoy that famous Berlin nightlife."   As Munich left, he turned away and spoke into the telephone. "Ah yes, *Fraulein*," Waterman said, as he raised his hand and waved at table 27 where a bottle of champagne had just been brought by a waiter. "Will you join me at my table?"

The woman at number 27 smiled and waved back, her jet black hair, rouged cheeks and painted lips disguising a 19 year-old girl, the only support for her war-crippled father. Waterman named a price and the girl at table 27 rose and said goodbye to the two women sitting with her, her low cut dress nearly exposing her young breasts. The girl sat down beside him just as the lights were darkened, a small band began to play and a chorus line moved onto the stage—eight German blondes, natural or otherwise, naked to the waist and flanking a tall American negress, her hips encircled by a string of bananas which did nothing to hide her nakedness beneath. "*Welkomin*," said the short master of ceremonies, a leer in his voice, a grin on his face.

THE man three tables away from table 27 put down the telephone. It was not well known, but the White Mouse cabaret had tables which, for a price, allowed a patron to eavesdrop on another table via a transmitting device   hidden in the telephone's base and a receiving device at another table, all controlled by a central switchboard. Everything in Berlin had a price.

The man signaled for his check, the Celtic cross tattoo on his left wrist exposed for a moment as he did so. So Himmler will be looking for the Spear also, the man thought. The Prior would have to be told. It would complicate their mission, but God's will would be done.

36.

Speechless

MATTIE was unsettled as she sat in her cabin after breakfast with Sturm and the Professor. She looked out the window as the *Graf* reached the eastern shore of Lake Constance, barely 30 minutes from landing in Friedrichschafen. She vividly remembered her nightmares. Being shot in the alley was not new but losing her head at the villa was. So too was the erotic dream which followed. Her subconscious had never before picked an unknown man to make love to her, possibly a stranger. What the hell did it mean? She wasn't sure. Her erotic fantasies for the past few years had been of Cockran, all of them during their absences when she was in the field. But with a stranger? At a minimum, the dream was more proof that she badly needed Cockran back in her bed. She missed him and still regretted their arguments. It seemed important at the time but now it seemed trivial. Life was short. She wished she were in Venice.

But Mattie knew she couldn't do that. No matter how much she loved Cockran. No matter how much there was to work out between them. The Spear was too important, too close to her father, to walk away. Sturm and Professor Campbell were right. They had to move fast if they were going to stay ahead of those guys in Alexandria. Venice would always be there. She hoped Cockran would be too. But she was increasingly uncomfortable with his beautiful blonde client spending entirely too much time making herself at home in his hotel room.

Worse, Mattie would have to come up with a good cover story to explain to Cockran why she was blowing off Venice. She couldn't very well tell him what had happened to her in Alexandria. He had enough ammunition for their arguments. She didn't need to give him more.

Once the zeppelin landed and they returned to their small hotel in Friedrichschafen, Mattie placed the first of several phone calls to Cockran's hotel in Munich, the *Bayerische Hof*, leaving the same message each time. "I miss you. Please call me. Love, Mattie."

After arriving in Innsbruck in the afternoon, she called Cockran twice more but each time the ringing phone went unanswered. Mattie faced a dilemma. They would be spending only one more night in civilization where she would have access to a telephone. Once they left Innsbruck, there would be no opportunity to talk with Bourke. On the train to Innsbruck, she had begun to compose a letter which she completed after their arrival.

> *Dear Bourke,*
>
> *I hate when we fight. I love when we make up. The weather in the Alps, however, is conspiring to keep us apart. Things can change suddenly in the mountains, I am told, but an extended forecast from the Zeppelin Company's chief meteorologist suggests more favorable weather conditions where we are heading if we start now rather than if we wait to begin our trek in two weeks.*

Two pages later, she concluded:

> *So please leave a message at my hotel in Innsbruck as to where I can reach you if you are no longer in Venice once I return to civilization, hopefully no more than a week from now. While it would be delightful if we could still have Venice together, I really just want to be alone with you anywhere.*
>
> *All my love,*
> *Mattie*

Joey Thomas was easier to deal with. For one thing, he was there in his Berlin hotel room when she called. For another, he had no choice but to do exactly what she said.

"Look, Joey, I worked a long time to get him to agree to an interview. I wanted you to interview him first. He could unlock the door which would lead to all the others."

"I know, Mattie, I know," Joey said. "I did everything you told me, but he's never returned my calls. I phoned the number you gave me. I said the right words. But nothing."

Mattie sighed. This was not good. "Have you interviewed the others?" Mattie asked.

"All but two. I'm meeting one for lunch today and the other tomorrow. You know what else?" Joey said, an eager tone in his voice.

"No, I don't."

"I've got an interview tonight that I've lined up myself."

"Oh?"

"Yes. Out of the blue there was an envelope waiting on the desk in my hotel room this morning. I don't know where it came from. Whoever it is knew all the people on your list that I had talked to by that time. The note said that talking to them was a waste of time but if I came tonight to the Club *Kakadü*, I wouldn't be disappointed."

"They actually identified all the people you interviewed?" Mattie asked.

"Yeah, spooky, isn't it? It's almost as if someone were tailing me."

"Have you been followed?"

Joey laughed. "How would I know? I can't tell these things. I'm not a spy."

Mattie didn't like it. It smelled like a set-up to her. Should she call it off? Or would that make Joey less enthusiastic about her story if she promptly squelched his first initiative? Would he think that she was trying to deprive him of a byline? Everyone had to grow up some time. It was Joey's turn now. "Well, be careful tonight."

"Don't worry. I may not be a spy, but I'm a big boy. I can take care of myself."

Innsbruck
Saturday, 6 June 1931

THAT evening in Innsbruck, Mattie placed a last call to Cockran's hotel in Munich. If she didn't reach him now, she would post her letter in the morning. When she asked for Cockran's room, however, she was astonished to be told by the hotel operator that Cockran had checked out and left no forwarding address. She immediately thought of Venice and the possibility he had finished sooner than anticipated and had gone on to get a head start on their holiday. But a call to the Contessa at the *palazetto* in Venice turned up nothing. Next, she called the Hotel *Adlon* in Berlin to see if he had returned there but no luck there either. Finally, she called Churchill's suite at the *Adlon*, hoping he had not left as well because she had not made a notation of the hotel where he would be staying in Vienna. She was in luck.

"Mattie, my dear. How good to hear from you," the familiar voice said.

"Winston, I am so glad I found you. Where in heaven's name is Bourke? He told me he was staying at the *Bayerische Hof*, but I just telephoned there and they told me he checked out."

"Ah, well, yes, I have heard from him. Bourke ran into a spot of trouble. I talked with him yesterday. I'm uncertain as to exactly what has happened. Gangsters attempted to run him and Mr. Sullivan off the road near Munich the other night and he left word for me at the *Adlon* that because of the trouble, he was switching hotels to a smaller one, the Hotel *Leinfelder*. He and Harmony are registered there under the name of Mr. and Mrs. William Donovan.

Gangsters? What in hell had Cockran gotten himself into? He was a lawyer for God's sake! Then it hit her. "Husband and wife? Whatever the hell for? What's going on?"

"*Incognito.* Nothing to be concerned about. He has Mr. Sullivan there to protect him. I believe more of Mr. Sullivan's former colleagues have joined them also. All will be well."

Mattie was comforted to hear that the Apostles were now with Cockran and Sullivan. From her own experience, she knew they were in good hands. But Churchill the politician had avoided her question. In some ways, politicians were all alike. Her father had on occasion done the same thing, not to mention all the other politicians Mattie had ever interviewed.

"Look, Winston, my question wasn't about his safety, not with Bobby along. I'm pleased the Apostles are there but my question was why he registered with Harmony as man and wife?"

Churchill chuckled. "Oh, that. Don't worry. It's all part of a cover story to help him keep her incommunicado. To keep her safe and away from their enemies."

Mattie could think of many other ways to keep Harmony safe, other than sharing Cockran's hotel room registered as husband and wife. Like putting her on a train or airplane back to England. But she said nothing of this to Churchill.

"The Hotel *Leinfelder*, you say?" Mattie asked.

"That's the one," Churchill replied.

"Thanks very much, Winston. I appreciate your help."

After Mattie hung up, she placed a call to the *Leinfelder* and asked for William Donovan.

"Hello, Mrs. Donovan speaking,"

"Harmony! It's Mattie McGary. Is Bourke there?"

"I'm sorry, no. He and Bobby haven't come back yet."

"Where did they go?" Mattie asked.

"They didn't tell me."

"What the hell happened that caused you to change hotels?"

Mattie waited and thought she heard Harmony sigh before she spoke. "It was so terrifying," Harmony said. "We were on our way back from a nightclub and two big black motorcars ran us off the road. Bourke saved my life. He decided to move from our hotel and check in somewhere else under an assumed name. We are supposed to be on our honeymoon. "

"Well, you're not exactly on a honeymoon now," Mattie replied.

Harmony laughed sharply. "No, I suppose not, but with all the intrigue and danger, it's easy to be swept away by the romance of it all."

"Romance?" Mattie asked.

"Well..." Harmony began and then hesitated as if she were not sure what to say next. "The two just seem to go together, don't they?"

"Were either of you hurt?" Mattie asked.

"Just a few scratches, nothing serious. Bourke had a rougher time of it than I did, but I must say he has a great body. I'd love to do a sculpture of it some day. He's really much more muscular than he looks with his clothes on. But then, you're his girlfriend, you'd know all about that, wouldn't you?" Harmony said, as if she were inviting a womanly confidence from Mattie who remained silent.

Harmony giggled. "And don't you think he has the cutest little birthmark?"

Bitch, Mattie thought. "Excuse me. The connection must be bad. I didn't catch that."

"Oh, don't worry. It was all perfectly innocent. I was just patching up his wounds. You must know how it is to be in a life and death situation with someone. It really brings you closer. You form a bond."

"No, I don't know what you mean," Mattie said.

"Well, it's not important. I admit I find your boyfriend to be a very attractive man." Harmony said and paused. "And he is so wonderfully protective of women, don't you think? I love that in a man."

"So, you have no idea when he'll be back?" Mattie asked as she struggled to keep her composure and process what she was hearing.

"No, but I expect him any minute now and I really must take a bath before he returns and catches me standing here starkers. A girl has to look her best, after all," Harmony said.

Bitch, Mattie thought again, but her heart wasn't in it. Not when the other woman was standing naked in Cockran's hotel room. "Yes, well, please tell him we need to talk. I'm in Innsbruck. I'm leaving on a train tomorrow for the Alps. Please tell him I'll call before I leave."

"I'll tell him. You can count on me. I know you're his girlfriend and all, but it's nice that we can share him like this. If only for a little while."

Mattie was speechless. It was all she could do to hang up the telephone and sit down on the bed. It hit her with the force of a body blow, leaving her legs rubbery, the wind knocked out of her. Cockran had only one birthmark. Even Mattie had not noticed it until the third time they slept together. Cockran's unreturned phone calls were beginning to make sense. The signs were all there but she had been too caught up in herself and her quest for the Spear to see them. It was like a physical ache. She could feel the hollowness in her stomach. Not only was Harmony blonde and four years younger than Mattie but, unlike her, she seemed appreciative of Cockran's protectiveness. She walked over to the desk and picked up the letter. She would wait for it all to sink in before she wrote a new letter, one composed not in haste or in the emotion of the moment. But this one definitely wouldn't do, she thought. Definitely. Cockran could be an infuriating man but, whatever else he was, he wasn't a one night stand kind of guy. Serially monogamous, he assured her, offering their mutual New York friend Anne Darrow as a reference. But Anne had already told her as much earlier. If he was sleeping with Harmony, then he was serious about her even if she might not be about him.

Mattie carefully tore the letter in two and dropped it into the hotel wastebasket. She repressed a sob but then gave into it and began to cry, the tears streaming down her face and dropping onto the torn halves of the letter below. She was still crying as she slipped beneath the sheets. The same two nightmares came again that night but this time no one came to save her. No one came to make love to her.

37.

The Night Belonged to the Apostles

THE Apostles arrived late in the afternoon, sooner than Cockran had anticipated. One by one, they paid him and Sullivan a visit at their rooms in the Hotel *Leinfelder*. Counting Sullivan, there were only eight of them now, four short of their original strength of twelve during the heyday of the Anglo-Irish war. The lads that remained were no longer the boys they were when Michael Collins recruited them and brought the British Empire to its knees. The fledgling nation that had found its freedom through boys like them no longer needed their ruthless skills now that the Irish Free State's independence was secure from Britain and die-hard IRA types alike. But they were still on call if the Irish Free State or an old mate like Bobby Sullivan needed their services. There was O'Neal and McNamara, Donal and Aiden as well as Murphy, Dennis and Ronan. Cockran knew them all and had fought by their side to destroy an IRA arms shipment in California two years earlier. Now he and Bobby were once more organizing them for mayhem, Cockran having been trained by the US Army's MID and Sullivan learning at the Big Fella's feet. Each Apostle received an assignment and an NBM worker to accompany him. One by one they came and one by one they left, quiet and unnoticed.

They finished their preparations early in the evening. Homework done, their studies complete, the killers recruited and trained by Michael

Collins waited for nightfall. They assured Cockran that these Nazi thugs didn't stand a chance. The night belonged to the Apostles.

Cockran and Sullivan were the last to arrive at the NBM factory, with Harmony and Rolf in tow. The sun hung low on the western horizon, casting the factory floor in amber twilight. The last seven members of the Squad were lounging in chairs set up in the middle of the factory floor, the two German speakers among the Irish forging a bridge with the eight factory workers recruited by Sullivan. Collins had taken care to recruit a few lads who spoke German, the better to deal with the Kaiser's men supplying them with weapons after 1916's Easter Rising.

"Listen up, men!" Cockran said. Everyone turned their attention to him as he took them through their assignments one last time, Rolf translating for the Germans. The Apostles and the NBM workers broke up into units of three, each with at least one bilingual member, whether a Tommy-speaking German like Paul or a German-speaking Irishman like McNamara. Cockran and Sullivan's own team would have four members. Each unit was to carry out its action within a five-hour window, starting at 8:00 p.m. Harmony would return to the hotel with Hermann Steinmetz.

"We reconvene at one a.m. at our rendezvous spot down the block from Reinhard Hoch's apartment building. Hoch is the SS man in charge of the NBM sabotage," Cockran said, passing around a small photograph Captain Weintraub had given them. "His apartment will be the final assault. You must make it to the rendezvous point near Hoch's apartment building. No excuses."

Cockran glanced over at Harmony, who appeared uncomfortable as he talked the team through their assignments. Her face was drained of color, as if she understood the danger.

Cockran knew communication was key. Its failure was the bane of any offensive during the war. It was the first thing Bill Donovan had taught him. Michael Collins had reinforced it. Communication. Information. Intelligence. These were the elements that won or lost any battle.

"Everyone understands?" Cockran asked, receiving silent nods. "Let's get to work, lads." The SS were about to find out the hard way what it meant to cross swords with the Irish Republican Brotherhood.

ONE of the advantages to hitting your enemy hard on his own turf is that he rarely expects it. The expansive home of Gunther von Goltz, the president of I.C.E.'s German subsidiary, was lightly defended by three listless security guards—one at the front gate, and two others patrolling the grounds on foot. Rolf shifted uneasily between Cockran and Sullivan as they crouched in the shrubs on a hillside that overlooked the president's home. It was a little after ten o'clock. They had taken for themselves the most heavily-guarded target. Still, Cockran wasn't worried so much about their own chances of success here, but more about the other lads.

Cockran could not have imagined Rolf getting as deeply involved in their operations as he had, but he had volunteered to be Cockran and Sullivan's translator with no hesitation. Rolf was young, still in his early twenties, too young to have had any real military experience, but he didn't like the Nazis. His sister's boyfriend was a Socialist whom some SA thugs had put in the hospital while breaking up a political rally. Cockran was more than a little concerned how Rolf would handle himself, whether he would freeze up at the wrong moment once guns came into play.

On the street below, one of their own NBM workers, Otto, strolled up to the brightly lit front gate. The guard came out to meet him and Otto began to gesture as if he were lost. The guard turned his head to point down the street and Otto, a pistol his right hand, swung hard at the back of the guard's head. The guard pitched forward to his knees. Otto struck again, knocking him flat. Satisfied he was unconscious, Otto quickly dragged the man back into the guardhouse where he was supposed to swap clothes.

"Now," Sullivan said, and the three of them made their move, creeping down the hillside that led to a five-foot wrought iron fence. They crouched at the base of the fence behind a row of bushes and looked for the first roaming guard. The guards were not SS, or even Nazis for all they could tell. They were employed by the same lax security service that NBM had used before Cockran had fired them. He had decided they would not kill guards if they could avoid it. He was after the men responsible—the V men and the SS—not the hired help. The one at the front gate had been taken out because he was best positioned to spot their descent from the crest of the hill. Only if the two roaming guards were alerted to their presence was Otto to approach the guards in his security uniform and kill them both at close range with a silenced weapon.

The house was dark. Cockran saw nothing through the fence but a single glowing window which appeared to be the dining room. Strange to be having supper at this hour. They knew from reconnaissance that von Goltz's wife retired at ten o'clock every night, so she would be in bed. They sat tight for three minutes, hoping to spot the guard, but he never came by.

"Keep a sharp eye," Sullivan said. "I'm going over." He climbed up and vaulted himself over the largely ornamental pikes that rested on top of the fence.

"You next," Cockran whispered to Rolf, who nodded and reached for the fence just as Cockran saw a faint orange dot hovering near the side of the house, glowing bright red, then fading back to a dull orange. Cockran snatched at Rolf's shirt and tugged him back to the ground. Sullivan turned to ask what was wrong, but Cockran motioned him down also.

They all lay flat on the ground, Cockran's eye on the glowing embers of a cigarette in the lips of the guard who finally appeared. The light spilling out from the dining room window was making it more difficult to see in the darker areas and he had nearly missed spotting the guard. The man passed in front of the window and disappeared around the corner of the house.

"Okay, go. Go!" Cockran said to Rolf, and quickly climbed up after him, dropping down beside Sullivan. He felt the strain in his hip when he landed, hoping he didn't split any stitches. They rushed across the open space to the side of the house and edged back towards the garden, where they knew von Goltz routinely left the French doors unlocked to facilitate early morning entrances after a late night with his mistress. Bobby had lock picking tools just in case. It was darker on this side of the house and easier to spot the other guard rounding the far corner and disappearing from view. Sullivan opened the door and Cockran and Rolf followed him in.

Cockran distinctly heard two male voices echoing from the dining room. He removed his Webley from his shoulder holster and peered carefully through the archway and into the dining room where, at the end of a long polished dark oak table, Gunther von Goltz was enjoying cognac and cigars with a smiling Oskar Muller. Cockran thumbed back the hammer on his Webley with an audible click and stepped into the room. Their conversation halted and they turned, confused, to look at their uninvited guest. "Good evening, *Herr* Muller," Cockran said. "You remember Mr. Sullivan, don't you?"

Sullivan now stepped through the doorway, his Tommy gun gripped menacingly in his big hands. "Ah, what a happy surprise," he said, and his face broke into a rare smile. Sullivan's eyes were fixed on Muller. "I'm thinking you're familiar with Mr. Thompson here, aren't you now? Make any noise and won't I be putting you on more intimate terms with himself?"

Von Goltz and especially Muller looked on the verge of panic, their eyes wide.

"We bring a message." Cockran said.

"What...what is the message?" Muller asked hoarsely.

Cockran gestured to Rolf, who entered hesitantly, glanced at Muller and von Goltz, then back to Cockran who said. "Please translate."

Sullivan stepped forward and spoke to von Goltz. "You've had three good men killed and six others crippled." Then he turned to Muller. "You tried to have us killed as well. Lawyers in America don't do that but perhaps things are different in Germany. Here's how we do it in Ireland. Pay close attention. NBM is under the protection of the Irish Republican Brotherhood. That means protection against the SS and I.C.E. or anyone working with them."

Cockran holstered his Webley and Sullivan handed him the Thompson. From his sleeve, Sullivan let a lead pipe slide out and into his palm. Von Goltz's eyes widened with fear.

"W-What are you doing?" Muller demanded.

"Delivering a message," Sullivan said.

"But…but you've already given it!"

"No," Sullivan said calmly. "That message was for von Goltz. This one is for you."

Sullivan towered over Muller. "No! No!" the lawyer cried. "You don't understand!"

Sullivan grabbed Muller by the lapels, lifted him off the chair and slammed him on the floor, flat on his back. With his left hand, he covered Muller's mouth. Then the Irishman raised his right hand high and swung the pipe down sharply on Muller's right knee. The sound of bones breaking as the kneecap shattered under the impact was followed by Muller's muffled screams into Sullivan's hand.

Rolf turned his head and stared at the floor, averting his eyes from the violence. Cockran looked on impassively. He knew this was difficult for anyone to stomach but it was necessary. Fear had to be instilled in these gangsters and their followers. The police weren't doing it.

"Quiet down, boyo, or I'll take more than your knee," Sullivan said. Muller's cries softened to a moan, then a whimper, as he writhed in pain. Sullivan shifted his eyes to von Goltz. "And you. I'll be back for your knee if an SS man even drives by an NBM plant or if you report our little visit tonight to the authorities. We clear?"

Rolf's eyes were still on the floor. "Translate Rolf," Cockran said softly. "The worst is over." Rolf lifted his head and quietly translated for von Goltz who finally nodded, terrified.

Sullivan rose, took the Thompson back from Cockran and marched out of the dining room. Cockran and Rolf followed as they slipped back into the night.

CAPTAIN Jacob Weintraub had placed his request to work the night shift after the American and Irishman gave him the list of V-men. He gave an excuse about his wife spending the evening with an ill friend. In fact, he wanted to be on duty to monitor all reports and to be sure that only trusted men went out to investigate the trouble he believed was coming.

Weintraub sat alone in his office staring at the pool of light from his desk lamp, the sun having already set, when the first report was placed before him. It was a call from a woman who refused to identify herself.

Two foreigners had accosted her escort on the way to the opera. The men had shoved her into a set of bushes, taken hold of her escort's arms, and firmly marched him in the opposite direction and out of her sight. The escort apparently put up no resistance. When pressed, the woman finally revealed that he was a deputy prosecutor named Eric Schmidt.

Between ten and eleven that night, reports of two break-ins arrived, one after the other, nearly identical in detail. Both were from high-ranking police officials, one of them the superior officer to whom Weintraub directly reported. Both were V-men from Cockran's list. In each instance, three armed men, two of them foreigners, broke into the homes and held the family at gunpoint. The family was ushered into another room while one of the foreigners traded his gun for a crowbar. What the foreigners told the V-men the family did not hear . . . and the crippled V-men refused to say.

After those two reports, events quieted down for the next hour or so. Weintraub had to remind himself to stay calm and be patient. It did him no good to appear uncharacteristically nervous at a job that rarely required him to leave his desk. When the next report finally came in at half past midnight, Weintraub was totally unprepared for what had happened. The Irish were mad! What in God's name had he allowed to be set in motion?

Reports flooded in, all describing the same event, but the most vivid report came from a widowed German matron who had watched the entire episode from her second floor window. She had noticed a pair of suspicious youths, snooping around some automobiles on her block and picked up the phone in order to report them. She lost track of the youths before she could complete the call. Still wary, she sat by her window and saw four nice young boys in their crisp, black SS uniforms emerging from their regular coffee house. They were such nice boys, she kept saying in the report. Always well dressed, well mannered and helpful around the neighborhood.

The four SS men said goodbye to each other and split in pairs to head towards their automobiles. As the first pair got inside a late model Opel, a man casually walked from the shadows until he was alongside the motorcar and rolled an object underneath, then sprinted off down the street. The two men inside the Opel may have realized what was happening as they tried to get out of the motor car, but the small explosion which followed triggered a blast from the petrol tank that obliterated the Opel and engulfed it in flames. Even on the second floor, the woman was knocked to the floor by the force of the explosion.

When she got up off the floor and peered back out the window, she saw the culprit fleeing towards a waiting motorcar at the next intersection. The other SS men saw him and rushed to their Horch, hoping to give pursuit, but as they closed the doors to their own motorcar, another man stepped out of the shadows from across the street. Before the SS driver could engage the clutch, the man unleashed a furious barrage of submachine gun fire into the car, shattering glass, puncturing holes and tearing the Nazis inside to shreds. The noise was more terrifying than the explosion, the widow had said. She kept watching long enough to see the machine gunner run off and join the waiting motorcar down the street.

Captain Weintraub exhaled sharply as he pushed away from his desk. He hadn't realized what he'd gotten himself into when he'd thrown himself in with these bloodthirsty Irish. In many respects, they seemed more terrifying than the SS men they had just destroyed. But at least the Irish would soon be leaving the country. He wished the same could be said of the SS.

Finally, shortly after one in the morning, a report came in that the deputy prosecuting attorney, the night's first victim, had been found unconscious on a sidewalk near where he had been abducted, sporting a broken jaw, broken wrist and a broken nose. Pinned to his chest were photographs of men inflicted with the very same injuries, each attached to hospital bills.

Though he was later to hear rumors, including a few comments about *verdamnt Irishers,* neither Weintraub nor any other official ever received complaints from Muller, von Goltz or any V-man.

THE Apostles and their new German allies gathered several blocks from Reinhard Tristan Hoch's apartment. News was swift—success on all fronts. The SS men who had tried to drive Cockran, Sullivan and

Harmony off the road were all dead, their motorcars obliterated. The top V-men had understood and received the message loud and clear— NBM is off limits.

Cockran, Sullivan and Rolf carefully ascended the stairs that led up to the fifth floor of Hoch's apartment building. Sullivan was one flight ahead, his Thompson at his side, pressed against his leg. Cockran had his Webley drawn and cocked. Rolf was beside him, an axe in one hand. The color had returned to Rolf's face as time had distanced him from the earlier violence.

Rolf began to speak softly. "I hated the Nazis after what they'd done to Peter," he said. "I thought I wanted to hit them back, punish them. Make their women feel the way my sister felt when she didn't know whether Peter would live." They were still three flights away, so Cockran let him talk. "I wanted to see them bleed the way they had made Peter bleed. I wanted them to suffer."

Rolf stared down at the axe in his hand and hefted it once to observe it, feel its weight. "But I don't think I'm like that," he said. "I don't think I'm capable. I don't think any man should suffer like that, even evil men like that man…" he swallowed. "Like that man Muller who got what he had coming to him. I'm just not cut out for this."

They were rounding the second to last flight. "You did fine, Rolf," Cockran said. "The worst is over. I understand why you don't like it but sometimes it's necessary."

"*Herr* Sullivan seemed to enjoy it," Rolf said.

"Enjoy? Not really." Cockran said as they neared the final flight of stairs. "Bobby has a very black and white sense of what's right and wrong and he is more eager than most to punish those who have done wrong. And he needs less proof of that than you or me."

"I don't want you to think I can't handle this," Rolf said. "I can and I will. It is only that…that I cannot fight like this forever. As soon as this is over, I am moving my family out of Munich, out of Bavaria." He laughed under his breath. "Maybe out of Germany entirely."

"Your English is good, not a trace of a British accent—you'd do swell in Ireland, even the States," Cockran said, as they took the last flight of stairs. "Quiet now. We've got a job left to do."

It occurred to Cockran that much of the world was filled with good and honest men like Rolf. The kind of men who were not trained to stop thugs like the Nazis. Only ruthless men like Bobby—and, in fact, Cockran himself—could do that. Men who knew how and who would do whatever it took to stand up to gangsters and terrorists like the SS. The world would always need men like the Apostles. Which included him, the Big Fella's last Apostle.

In that moment, Cockran thought of Mattie. Did she need a man like him? Probably not. She was too independent. He had always been quick—too quick?—to lecture her about risk-taking yet here he was, smack in the middle of a night of mayhem in Munich he had organized just as he had when he was an MID agent. A double standard? Pots and kettles and name-calling came to mind. A double standard? Not exactly leading by example was he? He'd think about it later. If he made it through the night alive.

Cockran, Sullivan and Rolf walked down the hall that led to Hoch's apartment. The other members of the team were spread out in the surrounding block to make certain no trap was being sprung. All that was left was snatching Hoch and taking him for a little ride.

Rolf now carried the axe in both hands. When they reached the apartment door, Cockran stood to one side and knocked three times. No response. Sullivan raised his Thompson and leveled it at the door. Cockran knocked again. No response.

"Ready?" Cockran looked to Sullivan. Sullivan nodded. Cockran held his hand out and Rolf handed him the axe. Cockran put his Webley away and gripped the axe firmly. He drew the axe head back and heard the door being unlocked. He froze, then recovered enough to lower the axe head to the ground and watch as the door swung inward. Instead of the tall Nordic figure they expected, they were met by a brown haired, unremarkable woman in a robe and nightcap. She stood in the doorway, a sleepy, tow headed toddler held at her hip and stared dubiously at the men before her. She raised an eyebrow at Cockran's axe and said something in German.

"She asks if there is a fire in the building." Rolf said.

"Ask her if Hoch is home."

Hoch's wife answered before Rolf could translate the question. "She says that her husband isn't here. That he received a telephone call during dinner from a woman, a business colleague. He packed his bags and left right after that. He told her he would be gone for several weeks. But it wasn't the first time the woman had called him here."

Hoch's wife then looked at Sullivan and the machine gun at his side. She took a step back and began to close the door but Rolf stepped forward asking his own questions. In moments, Rolf's easy manner had her smiling as she answered his questions. Behind him, Cockran could sense Sullivan's growing impatience as the two continued their conversation, punctuated by an occasional bitter laugh from her. Finally, Rolf shook his head, said a few final more words and turned back to Cockran.

"She suspects he's having an affair with the woman who called. A month ago, she found lipstick on his collar and several long blonde hairs on his black SS uniform. She once steamed open a letter addressed to him in a feminine hand. It was a love letter in rudimentary German to her "Tristan" from his "Isolde". Hoch promised to call his wife once he reached his destination. She wants to know if you have a message you wish her to deliver?"

"No," Cockran said. He couldn't say why but he believed the woman was telling the truth. A husband with a young son shouldn't have blonde hairs on his uniform, let alone another woman's lipstick on his collar. "Tell her we're sorry to have bothered her. Tell her we've delivered enough messages tonight."

38.

Joey's Big Story

IT was pouring rain when Joey Thompson left the Hotel *Adlon* and caught a taxi to the Club *Kakadü*. As he had been instructed, Joey carried a week-old copy of the *New York American* which he carefully placed at a table beside him.

"We'll find you. Wear a dark suit with a red tie and put a New York newspaper on your table." Joey had dutifully done both things. Now he waited, sipping a gimlet. It was dark and smoky inside the *Kakadü*. Joey had draped his trench coat and umbrella over the back of the second chair at his small table, leaving the third chair vacant, again as instructed.

Joey was nervous. This would be his first big story. And tonight would be the first interview that he had arranged himself, not one that Mattie McGary had found for him. Joey took another sip of his gimlet and, as he was popping one of the two pearl onions in his mouth, a large bald-headed man sat down at the table's third chair. He wore a white turtleneck under a dark jacket. He's the one, Joey thought, but first they had to exchange code words. Like a spy.

"Is New York pleasant in summer?" the man asked. "I've never been."

"Greatest city in the world. But better in the spring. You should go." Joey replied, completing the exchange.

The man nodded and rose. "Wait two minutes then meet me outside."

Joey waited and then walked outside. The streets were glistening from the rain, but now only a light drizzle was falling. A long, dark sedan was sitting in front of the *Kakadü*, its engine idling, side curtains obscuring its interior. The rear door opened and the man from the bar motioned for Joey to get in. As he sank into the seat, he noticed curtains between the driver's compartment and the back seat. With the side curtains, it wasn't possible to see out.

The big car leaped forward with sudden acceleration and a soft cloth blindfold was placed over Joey's eyes. "What the hell is going on?" Joey asked. "Why the blindfold?"

"You ask too many questions, Mr. Newspaperman. Be silent. Soon you will know."

JOEY was alone with his thoughts three hours later after they had returned him to the Hotel *Adlon*. He was still in shock. Who would ever believe him? A mysterious mansion. Two figures hidden in shadows. A plot to assassinate Hindenberg! Mattie McGary in the hands of a man sworn to kill her! It was all too fantastic to be true. Except... he had it all in black and white in the large manila folder on the desk in front of him. He poured himself another glass of bourbon.

What should he do? What would Mattie do? From the few times she had deigned to talk with him before this story came along, he knew what she would say. "Get the bloody story first and worry about anything else later." But even so, Joey didn't believe that she would go after a story first and leave a colleague in peril.

He took another sip of bourbon and saw that it was 1:00 in the morning. He hadn't realized how much time had gone by. There was no way he could wake the Hearst European Bureau chief in London at one a.m. for this. Ted Hudson wasn't going to be sympathetic to Mattie's plight anyway. He would tell Joey to get on the story and he would look after Mattie. Except Joey didn't believe he would. He had been taken to Hudson's club in London once for dinner with two other Hearst stringers when the subject of Mattie had come up as the butt of a ribald joke Hudson told as they lingered over cigars and brandy, something about her vertical rise in the Hearst empire being achieved horizontally. It was obvious from his comments that he didn't think much of female journalists in general or Mattie in particular. Given the rumors that Hudson had once proposed to Mattie and been turned down, Joey didn't believe Theodore Stanhope Hudson IV would lift a single manicured finger to save her.

But if it was after midnight in London, Joey thought, it wasn't in New York, where it was 7 p.m., or California, where it was only 4 p.m. Yes, he thought, he'd go right to the top. It all depended on where Hearst was working that day. And he most assuredly would be working, putting his personal touch on whatever he and his major domo, Joe Willicombe, decided was the big story of the day. He would call Willicomb because Joe would always be at Hearst's side. And the first place to start was the *New York American*. That was the flagship and Joe's New York secretary always knew where to find him. Always.

It took only fifteen minutes for the Hotel *Adlon* switchboard to connect him to Joe Willicombe's secretary. "Miss Moore? Joey Thomas in Berlin. It's after midnight in London and I've got to talk to Mr. Willicomb. It's a matter of life and death. Honest."

It took only five more minutes after that for the ever-efficient Miss Moore to connect him directly with Joe Willicombe at Hearst's northern California estate, Wyntoon. Miss Moore told him Hearst had been there all week supervising the construction of an authentic Bavarian village on the banks of the McLeod River amid the towering trees in the shadow of Mount Shasta.

"Yes, Thomas, what's up?" Willicombe asked.

Joey quickly explained everything, from his originally taking over Mattie's interviews right up through the few hours he recently spent in a secluded Berlin mansion.

"Hold on a second, Thomas. I'm sure the Chief is going to want to hear this personally.

Joey was nervous. While he had received two handwritten notes from Hearst, he had never met or talked to the man himself. He only knew what Hearst looked like from photographs and newsreels. He was unprepared for the high voice which came from such a large, rambling hulk of a man. Joey told the same story to the Chief that he had told Willicombe, only Hearst stopped him more often to ask questions.

When Joey had finished, Hearst was all business. Joey felt better just hearing the determination in his voice.

"Find her friend Cockran. I know him from personal experience. He's tough and he's resourceful. Tell him he has a blank check from the Hearst organization to do whatever it takes and hire whatever men are necessary to ensure McGary's safety. If Mattie gave you his address in Venice, then that's where he's going to be. Go there. At once. I don't want you working on this story while you're in Germany anyway. After you find Cockran, he can take care of finding McGary and you can get back to your story. But McGary comes first. Got that?" the high voice said.

"Yes, sir. Understood. I'll catch the first train to Venice."

AS the Hotel *Adlon* switchboard operator broke the connection, a tall man with close-cropped light brown hair was hovering over her. Bruno Kordt took the earphones off his head and passed them back to her. "*Danke, Fraulein*. You have been most helpful," Kordt said as he slipped her a 100 *reichsmark* note. He shook his head. Someone in the Geneva Group had betrayed them to an American journalist, revealing not only the Hindenburg assassination plot but also von Sturm's search for the Holy Spear. Zurich would have to be told. Something would have to be done. And Kurt von Sturm would know exactly what that was.

39.

A New Recruit

Innsbruck, Austria
Sunday, 7 June 1931

REINHARD Hoch did not like the question. That much, Sturm could tell. They were having a late afternoon lunch of ham, dumplings and a local red wine on the terrace outside the *Breinnössl* restaurant in Innsbruck. The Alps rose majestically behind them in a high, blue sky.

Sturm was indifferent to Hoch's feelings. He had wanted eight armed men to accompany him into the Alps in the event the black-garbed strangers who had attacked them in Alexandria had another go. But Sturm had been frustrated by his telephone call to Zurich, who had refused his request. He told Sturm to draw on his own private contingency funds as Geneva's Executive Director, but no charge was to be made to the Kaiser project. That meant he could afford only four armed men and Sturm didn't think that would prove sufficient. But four good men would have to do. The fact that Willi Wirth was one of them gave him comfort. He was barely twenty-one but, in many ways, he reminded Kurt of himself at that age. Even now, he was almost as good as his best man, Bruno Kordt, who would lead the Hindenburg assassination team.

Hoch, however, presented intriguing possibilities. He was a genuine volunteer with impeccable credentials and looking for adventure. A fellow naval officer, recently retired, with a letter of introduction and recommendation from Admiral Canaris himself. How Hoch had learned of Sturm's expedition was also explained in the Canaris letter, saying he was writing at the request of his good friend, Fritz von Thyssen, known to Sturm and the rest of the Geneva Group as "Berlin" and whose United Steel Works employed Sturm as his executive secretary. Perhaps sending him Hoch was Geneva's way of apologizing for not authorizing more funds.

"Explain to me again why you left the German navy," Sturm directed "It is unusual for a naval board of inquiry to convene over such a minor matter as a broken engagement."

"I quite agree, *Herr* von Sturm, but the father of the young woman is one of the largest shipbuilders in Bremen and he has many important contacts high in the Navy. She tried to blame her pregnancy on a defective diaphragm but I discovered the slut had been sleeping with two other men. Two brother naval officers. I think the device was simply worn out from overuse," Hoch said and then laughed with a loud, honking sound from his long and narrow nose.

"Both men testified in my defense, and exposed her for the whore she was. The Board of Inquiry had no choice but to acquit. But Admiral Canaris told me that I would never receive another promotion. He found a new and better position for me and I resigned my commission."

"And your new position is?" Sturm asked.

"Admiral Canairis requested I keep that confidential." Hoch paused, took a sip of wine. "But I was raised a Catholic and helping you retrieve such a holy relic would be a high honor."

Sturm decided to take Hoch on. A new recruit and an extra weapon might come in handy. "I will be pleased to have you with me, *Herr* Hoch. We leave for Zell-Am-See tomorrow.

Monday

HIS breakfast coffee untouched beside him, Kurt von Sturm held the telephone to his ear and frowned as he listened to what Zurich was telling him, more than mildly surprised to learn that Mattie's lover might soon be on their trail if the American journalist made it to Venice.

"Yes, I agree, Zurich. That is a most unfortunate development. But it's nothing we can't handle. I agree. There is a traitor within Geneva.

No one else could have known the details of our plans but we can identify and eliminate him later. Our first priority should be the death of the American journalist, Mr. Thomas. My men will attend to that."

"What about this Cockran?" Zurich asked.

Sturm shrugged. "The critical target is the American journalist. He must be stopped. If this Cockran follows us into the Alps, I will deal with him. Go back to your breakfast, my old friend. Do not let this interfere with your digestion."

Sturm hung up the telephone receiver which immediately rang, a clanging of high-pitched bells. He picked it up.

"Kurt, it's Mattie. Professor Campbell and I are down in the lobby. We've been waiting ten minutes. If you don't come soon, we're going to miss the train to Zell-Am-See."

"I apologize. It was business from Berlin. An accident at the steel mill required my attention. Please be patient. It will take me one more phone call to clean things up. I'll be down in five minutes."

Sturm then had the switchboard operator place a call to Bruno Kordt in Berlin. He reconsidered what he had told Zurich about Cockran. His prey was vulnerable. He didn't know why but he had a sixth sense about these things when it came to women. If the man she loved could be taken out of the picture permanently, the hunter was certain he stood an even better chance of once more tasting the sweet lips of his prey sooner rather than later.

"Bruno? Sturm here. I spoke with Zurich. Excellent work last night. Take four good men and catch the same train to Venice as the American journalist, Joseph Thomas, whose call you intercepted. Follow him. Wait until he attempts to meet with the American named Cockran, then eliminate him. No, you need not worry about any others. The journalist is your primary target but collateral damage is acceptable. Clean things up, Bruno. Permanently."

Part V

Italy, Austria, and Germany

8 June – 18 June 1931

In remote, isolated castles, a new generation will grow up in whose presence the world will shudder. A bold, imperious, violent, cruel generation—this is what I want.

Adolf Hitler, 1931
Joachim Köhler, *Wagner's Hitler*

Wewelsburg castle became—in Himmler's eyes—what Camelot had been to King Arthur and the Knights of the Round Table, Monsalvat to Parsifal and the Knights of the Holy Grail, a mystical seat hidden from the gaze of the uninitiated, the towered sanctum of the higher members of SS chivalry.

Peter Padfield, *Himmler, Reichsführer—SS*

40.

Death in Venice

Venice
Monday, 8 June 1931

SO what's a martini?" Bobby Sullivan asked as Cockran placed an order with their waiter on the terrace in front of Harry's Bar on the Grand Canal. The Apostles had left Munich for Venice the morning after what the newspapers were calling "Communist Mayhem in Munich." Most had then headed for Ireland, while McNamara and Murphy went south to see Rome and maybe a glimpse of the Pope. Cockran had persuaded Sullivan to stay with him until Mattie arrived. There were plenty of rooms in the *palazetto* he had leased and Cockran had assured Bobby the fishing in Venice was excellent even though he had no idea where to find fish here except at a restaurant.

Cockran and Sulivan had come straight to Harry's Bar after dropping off their bags at the *palazetto*. Harmony travelled with them to Venice to ensure she made it safely out of Germany but, once they arrived, Cockran had assigned an Apostle—Donal—to escort her on the first train to England which left that morning. She had objected, shaken by the violence preceding their abrupt departure, but Cockran had turned her down. She didn't need a lawyer right now. And, after what almost had happened with her the other night, he didn't want Harmony as a distraction while he waited for the woman he loved to finish her quest and return to his arms.

Donal was with her as a precaution against a possible SS attempt to retaliate. He was to check in with them by telegraph at each major station. The first had been Verona where things were fine. The next was Milan. Until then, Cockran could relax. He and Bobby were on holiday.

"It's a sophisticated drink, nothing you would understand," Cockran replied.

"And it's the high hat you're wearing now?"

Cockran smiled. "Nope. But I'm a martini connoisseur and Harry's is the only place in Europe that makes a decent martini. Try one. Expand your palate. Learn to be a gentleman."

Sullivan grinned and, for a moment, the hardness that perpetually lined his face softened and the cold blue eyes sparkled. "Not likely. But I'll have a martini just the same." Sullivan said to the hovering waiter. "I noticed you had a letter waiting for you when we arrived at the house today. Who knew to find you here?" Bobby asked after the waiter had left.

Cockran smiled. "Mattie. I expected to hear from her sooner. I didn't know how to reach her when we moved from the *Bayerische* so I left word with Winston where she could find me.

"Why haven't you opened it?"

"I like to combine my pleasures," Cockran replied. "Sipping an ice-cold martini while reading a letter from Mattie is the next best thing to having her here sipping one beside me."

The martinis arrived in a chilled silver cocktail shaker which the waiter carefully poured into two short frosted glasses. Harry didn't believe in olives or stemmed martini glasses.

Cockran took a sip and sighed. "Perfect. The best I've had since New York."

Sullivan took a sip and coughed. "'Tis a weird definition of 'perfect' you'd be having," he said as he took the top off the martini shaker and poured it back in. "You can have my share," Sullivan said as he quickly motioned to the waiter and ordered a Jameson's.

Cockran laughed and opened the letter. As he read, he felt the color drain from his face.

Sullivan noticed. "Bad news?"

"You could say that," Cockran replied. He picked up the letter and read it again, slowly.

Dear Bourke,

I have tried so many times to reach you and left so many messages for you to return my calls. I needed to tell you the search for the Spear would keep me from joining you for at least the first week in Venice and I just wanted to hear your voice again. Since then, however, the thought has occurred to me more than once that you may be avoiding me. On the few occasions when I have gotten through to your room, Harmony has always answered the phone and in our last conversation she dropped many hints that the two of you were on intimate terms. She even described your birthmark for me and told me how muscular you were without your clothes on.

Darling, I'm a big girl and you don't have to avoid me. I love you but I worried sometimes that what we had together was too good to be true and couldn't last. I'm not the easiest person to live with and I've always known that, much as I love him, I could never be a good mother to Patrick, certainly not like someone who could be there for him every day when he comes home from school. So it's probably better for all concerned if you found someone who could be everything to both of you. Maybe it's Harmony. I only know it can't be me, however much I wish it could.

Harmony said something about how nice it was to be sharing you but I guess I'm just not that kind of girl. Your many flaws notwithstanding, I've never been happier than during my past two years with you but I prefer my men one at a time and I never share.

I want you to be happy and it may be a long shot but I'd like us to still be friends.

All my love,
Mattie

P.S. Winston told me you had run into trouble in Germany. Listen to the Big Fella's advice, Cockran, and keep your ass low to the ground.

M.

Wordlessly, Cockran handed the letter to Sullivan who read it also.

"Harmony? You didn't...."

"No, of course not!" Cockran snapped, surprised at the harshness of his voice.

"I didn't think so. No offense intended. But where exactly is that birthmark?"

Cockran shook his head. "Nowhere you've seen," he said. That birthmark business would make a saint suspicious as if an additional reason were needed after Harmony told Mattie the two women were "sharing" him. Cockran felt the guilt wash over him. That he hadn't actually slept with Harmony was cold comfort. In the event, he had pulled back from the brink and Mattie was the reason despite her failure to call him. Yet, Mattie's letter said she *had* called him. Many times. And Harmony had not passed on a single message. Why? Had she been choreographing his seduction all along? He replayed their encounters from the transparent swim suit to the Pullman compartment to that Friday night in Munich after the SS ambush. It sure looked that way now.

Sullivan said nothing as Cockran stared at the canal. What could he do besides wait for Mattie to arrive? He'd never liked waiting. He wasn't good at it. Then he heard his name called.

"Mr. Cockran! Mr. Cockran! I'm so glad I found you."

Cockran turned to see the Hearst stringer, Joey Thomas, approaching their table.

"Joey! What are you doing here in Venice?" Cockran asked, introducing him to Sullivan.

"I came to see you. Mr. Hearst said to find you. Mattie's in danger and he said you'd know what to do. He told me to tell you the Hearst organization would reimburse you but to spare no expense in finding her."

"Slow down, Joey, slow down," Cockran said. "Mattie's in danger?" Joey nodded breathlessly. "Start at the beginning. Here, have a drink," Cockran said and poured the residue of Sullivan's martini from the cocktail shaker into a glass. Joey took a big gulp and then began his story, from the last time he talked to Mattie until his conversation early Sunday with Hearst.

Cockran listened intently, his eyes never leaving Joey, alert to only one thing. Mattie was in peril and Hearst expected Cockran to save her. Apart from Paddy, no one was more important to him. He would do anything to keep her safe. It didn't matter if he might be losing her. It never occurred to him for a moment not to go after her. He wasn't surprised Hearst felt the same way. He knew first hand Hearst's reputation for fierce loyalty to his employees.

"Mattie's letter to me is postmarked the morning after she talked to Joey," Cockran said to Sullivan. "If she's in the Alps with these people and this von Sturm character, she's had a good one- or two-day head start. It's going to be tough to catch up to them."

Sullivan nodded.

Cockran turned back to Joey. "You're sure Hearst said spare no expense?"

"Yes, sir. He said you used to work for him and that you'd know his word was good."

"What about that dossier those men gave you in Berlin? Do you have it with you?'

"Not the original. I left that in the safe at the Hotel *Luna Baglioni*. Mr. Hearst told me to get out of Germany for my own safety so I'm going to stay here in Venice and write the article. But I had a photocopy made at the Hearst bureau in Berlin before I left. It was developed in our own darkroom," Joey said, as he shoved a thick manila envelope across the table. "Mr. Hearst said to give it to you so you would know what you're up against. There's a map in there too."

Cockran took the envelope and set it down beside his chair. Joey looked exhausted and was having a difficult time staying awake, his eyes occasionally closing. Just then, Cockran caught rapid movement out of the corner of his eye. A motorboat was coming quickly into his field of vision, far faster than the five kilometer per hour speed limit in effect on the Grand Canal. Cockran saw a man braced in the rear of the boat bringing to bear a submachine pistol.

"Bobby! Joey! Down!"

Sullivan hit the ground a moment before Cockran who, on his way down, reached out and grabbed Joey's coat sleeve to take the reporter with him but he just sat there, confused, and inexplicably stood up rather than slide off his chair to safety. Cockran's hand was still gripping his sleeve when gunfire ripped into his back and exploded out his chest, his body jerking with the impact and then falling onto the table. He slid down between Sullivan and Cockran who released his grip on Joey's lifeless arm and saw only frozen eyes staring out into space.

The terrace in front of Harry's Bar was in complete panic, women screaming, men shouting. More than one person had been hit by the automatic weapons fire. Cockran saw that the boat was not returning and instantly turned in the other direction towards *Piazza San Marco* to see if it were more than a hit and run attack. It was. Two more men were half way down the *calle* leading from *San Marco* to Harry's Bar. They carried submachine pistols held low.

Cockran winced at the pain in his hip as he drew his Webley while Sullivan drew both of his Colt .45 automatics. "Take the one on the left!" Cockran said as his first two shots hit the man on the right square in the chest and blew him off his feet before he could raise his pistol. Sullivan simultaneously shot the much larger man on the left, squeezing off four shots in less than two seconds. But the big man did not go down and had raised his weapon by the time Sullivan's last two shots hit home. The first shot hit higher in the chest and the second higher still, tearing into the man's throat. He staggered drunkenly, one hand reaching for his ravaged throat, while a finger on the other hand tightened on the trigger of his submachine pistol, sending a burst harmlessly into the ground.

The renewed automatic weapons fire startled those remaining on the terrace, tending to the wounded. There were no new casualties, Cockran could see, but everyone was scrambling to leave the terrace as quickly as possible. "Out that way," Cockran said, pointing to his right. It would take forever to explain this to the Italian police and time was a luxury they didn't have. "Through the garden. But slow. Like we've got all the time in the world."

Sullivan reholstered his weapons. Cockran picked up the manila envelope and both casually walked past the patrons still sprawled on Harry's terrace from the Canal-side attack, mindful of the Big Fella's rules on blending into a crowd after you shot your target. *Don't draw attention to yourself.* They hopped over a small brick wall and were soon inside the small park which fronted on the Grand Canal beside Harry's Bar, full of arching trees to conceal them. They turned away from the canal and walked inland, towards *San Marco*. Soon they heard the sounds of a police siren on a boat in the Canal and could see a squad of six *carabinieri* on *San Marco* marching double time towards the closed end of the square.

Cockran and Sullivan casually walked down the path leading out of the park. They placed their hats back on their heads, keeping the brims low. They walked over to the *San Marco vaporetto* stop where they waited patiently with the rest of crowd, who were gesturing and wondering in excited tones about the cause of the recent gun fire.

Sullivan started to get on the first *vaporetto* that pulled into the dock, but Cockran held him back. "That one will take us directly across the Grand Canal to our stop at *San Saluté*," Cockran whispered. "If there are any more who are tailing us, we won't be able to pick them out of the crowd and we could lead them right to our *palazetto*. Take the next one going in the other direction. It will make ten stops before it reaches to the same place. We'll get off one stop before ours, just to be safe. If anyone who gets on here is still with us, it won't be coincidence."

Twenty-five minutes later, the *vaporetto* had almost made the full circuit and they stepped off at *Academia*, one stop before their *palazetto* near *San Saluté*. No one had followed them. Their landlady, *Contessa* DaSchio, an Anglo-Italian whose father had been a British diplomat, greeted them as they walked up to their three-bedroom flat above the family's living quarters. Unaware of the gunfire, she readily agreed to have the cook prepare a cold supper.

Upstairs in their flat, Cockran laid out the maps Joey had given them and saw just what a two day head start meant in Alpine terrain. If they left Venice in the morning, they would still be three days behind even if they managed to find a mountain guide. Cockran didn't like the odds he and Sullivan had alone against the men who were with Mattie. There was no time to waste. The germ of an idea was beginning to form on how to make up for Mattie's head start.

"Should I be checking the train schedules to Innsbruck tonight?" Sullivan asked.

"We're not going to Innsbruck. I've got to call Winston first in Munich and let him know about the plot to assassinate Hindenburg. He can arrange to let Hearst know what happened to their reporter here. If I know Hearst, he'll have his Rome correspondent pick up the original of Joey's dossier from the hotel's safe. He won't be able to resist covering a story as big as an assassination conspiracy. He'll send every Hearst reporter he has in Europe to Germany to follow up on all the leads in the dossier. Then I'll make a second call to Milan. I think we'll find what we need there but I want to make sure."

"Milan? But shouldn't we be after finding Mattie? Just because she thinks you've been getting a leg over on Miss Harmony . . ."

"We're going after her but we need a quicker way. Wire Donal about the danger to Mattie, our new plans and the shoot-out today. Then see if you can find McNamara and Murphy in Rome and ask them if they'll join us tomorrow in Milan."

"Not to worry. They'll come. The Squad sticks together. Always."

"And have them bring their guns."

Sullivan looked at Cockran, rolled his eyes in mock disbelief and smiled. Someone who didn't know him would never have described it as a smile.

41.

There May Be Another Explanation

MATTIE was in the lead Mercedes truck of the three-vehicle caravan as it slowly moved across the Alpine valley floor through a meadow alive with color. Two of the vehicles, including Mattie's, were the canvas-topped G-2 model with full time 4-wheel drive, three differential lockers and an independent suspension. The third and largest vehicle was the six-wheeled G-1 which had four wheels in the rear and a larger truck bed for carrying their supplies. Seeing the Alps from a distance in Innsbruck and the small lakeside town of Zell-Am-See had not prepared her for the grandeur of seeing them this close, erupting from the earth on either side of her. It was barely noon, but she had already shot two rolls of film. She made a note to limit herself to one roll of scenery per day until they reached the castle. The castle, not the scenery, was the story.

The driver of her truck was their guide, a small, leathery-faced man, not given to small talk which was why she had shot two rolls that morning. It kept her mind from thinking about Bourke and Harmony. People could love each other like she and Bourke did and still not be right for each other. In her heart, she knew she had no one to blame but herself. She was the one who twice told Cockran that they should take a break in their relationship; that she might not be the girl he needed. How was she to know that before they could talk things out he would meet someone like Harmony who was younger, prettier and appreciated Bourke's protectiveness?

Sturm and their Austrian guide had shown her their intended route deep into the *Hohe Tauern* mountains. Each night they would make camp beside a source of fresh water, either a waterfall or high mountain lakes. While the area they would be travelling through was largely uninhabited except for isolated farms, Sturm said they would avoid any mountain inns or villages and thereby minimize any local gossip which might follow in their wake. They hoped to cover more than half the distance to where the castle ruins were located on the first day, using the G-1 and the G-2s. But at the end of the second day or the morning of the third, they would have to leave the vehicles behind, as the mountain passes at that point would be too steep for the sturdy trucks to navigate. They would switch to even sturdier Austrian pack horses, *Haflingers*, and make the rest of the way on foot. In total, a four or five day trek, depending on the weather and terrain.

Mattie tried without success to put Cockran and their break-up out of her thoughts. It would be nice to have a diversion. That was what she needed. To take her attention away, if only for a while, from her heartache. And an attractive man like Kurt von Sturm would be an ideal candidate. A diversion. She recalled their one kiss. The thought brought her comfort.

When they stopped for lunch beside a fast-running stream which bisected the valley floor, Mattie noticed the newcomer, Reinhard Hoch, ordering around the four Austrians—the guide, the cook and two porters—as if they were indentured servants. She didn't like Hoch and the more she saw of him, the less she understood why Sturm had virtually made him his number two in command. After lunch—grilled fresh fish caught by Gregor, one of the two Austrian porters in her Mercedes G-2 and a skilled fisherman—Mattie had sought out Sturm to accompany him in his G-1, hoping to learn more about the arrogant Mr. Hoch. But the warmth of the sun and several glasses of Italian Soave, chilled in the same stream where the fish were caught, soon had her nodding off as the G-2 moved along.

THE Prior turned to the man beside him who was studying the small caravan through a pair of field glasses from a hidden perch high on the valley wall.

"They are the ones from Alexandria?"

"Yes, Major, I am certain. The woman's red hair alone is enough to identify them."

"How long do you believe it will take them to reach the first pass?"

"Not today. Some time tomorrow morning. It depends where they camp for the night."

"And we will be ready for them at the pass?"

"The explosives to trigger the avalanche are already in place."

"Good work, my brother. Let us be off. If the weather holds, we will be in place by dawn. If the Lord is with us, our first group of enemies will be eliminated. There is a second group shadowing the first. The SS. There are more of them. Twenty. They are on horseback and heavily armed, but they have no guides."

"What if the landslide does not get all of the first group?" the younger man asked."

The Prior shrugged his shoulders. "After tomorrow, time is on our side. The first group will have to leave their vehicles behind before they reach the second pass. The second group must dismount and sleep. Once on foot, they will be at our mercy. I have been roaming these mountains since I was a child. None of them will leave here alive."

DINNER that evening was more substantial than lunch, a hearty Austrian mountain stew, rich with local vegetables and chunks of lamb and beef. It smelled delicious and tasted better with crusty bread and several bottles of Barbera to wash it down. The fisherman Gregor doubled as their waiter. In his mid-forties, he had curly brown hair, large brown eyes and was clearly captivated by Mattie, hovering nearby, refilling her wine glass far sooner than the others. Their dinner was segregated. Sturm, the Professor, Mattie and Hoch sat at a table apart from the Austrians and Sturm's men. Mattie's table had candles and crystal. The other didn't.

Thanks to Hoch, dinner turned out badly. It had started well when, to her immense surprise, the arrogant Hoch had pulled out a black leather violin case, opened it, and began to play Pachebel's Canon in D major. By the time food was served, she, Sturm and the Professor had polished off one of the bottles of Barbera listening to the music.

Hoch may be arrogant, she thought, but he plays beautifully. His table talk, however, was as ugly as his music was beautiful. "In the animal world, as in the plant world, there are creatures we call parasites," Hoch said. "Take mistletoe or orchids. They do not live from the soil but rather clamp their talons into the bark of a tree where there is a wound into which they can settle. They drive their suckers beneath the bark to divert to themselves the host tree's vital fluids so they can live as parasites with a special sense that allows them to detect where easier or better nourishment may be found. Among mankind, the Jews are just such a parasite."

"Not true," Mattie said. "Jews are among the most talented, productive people on earth."

Hoch smiled and continued with more than just a trace of condescension. "I do not deny that many Jews are talented and hard-working. But it is rare for a Jew to become a factory worker and even less an agricultural laborer. That is because he is not willing to earn his daily bread by the sweat of his brow. No, he goes into law or medicine or retail where he can attract people with advertising and with display windows. Or he lends money and demands interest—thus, once again, sharing in the vital fluids of the work others have produced and promoted."

"Did it ever occur to you that law, medicine, retail and banking were the only professions countries like yours allowed Jews to pursue?" Mattie asked with an acid tone.

Hoch paused long enough to fill his glass and then continued as though Mattie had never spoken. "Jews take root everywhere. When wholesome national sentiment resists, they infuse a degenerating poison, a fiendish poison, into the nation. They speak of individualism, of universal human rights, of loyalty and good faith, of democracy! In reality, these are only the corrosive drops of the same poison that is used by the vegetable parasites to paralyze their victims, to destroy their ability to resist, to infect their bodies with disease and rot."

Mattie was astonished. Anti-Semites she knew were either ignorant, ill-bred, or both. But here was an intelligent, talented German, a superb musician, setting forth an entire racial theory of anti-Semitism—the Jew as parasite, not a person. She shook her head in amazement as Hoch continued. "Nothing upsets Jews more than a gardener who is intent on keeping his garden neat and healthy. Nothing is more inimical to Jews than order. They need the smell of decay, the stench of cadavers, weakness, lack of resistance, submission of the personal self, illness, degeneracy! And whenever it takes root, it continues the process of decomposition! It must!"

"You really believe this crap?" Mattie asked. "You sound like Goebbels."

Hoch looked at her and smiled. "It is not for nothing that time and again the Jews have been driven out of countries where they settled— from Babylonia, from Egypt, from Rome, from England, from the Rhineland, and elsewhere. In each of these, a gardener was at work who was incorruptible and loved his people. But now in Germany, you can once again see an enormous acceleration in the proliferation, the taking root, the stripping of corpses. Truly, if something does not happen soon, it may be too late. The National Socialists are Germany's only hope."

Professor Campbell shifted in his seat, clearly uneasy with the topic of discussion. "And does your party's leader, *Herr* Hitler believe in these…theories?"

"I have not heard the Fuhrer speak personally, but *Herr* Himmler assures me it is so."

"I see," Campbell said.

Mattie turned to Sturm, who sat stoically, watching Hoch with an enigmatic expression. "You've been quiet, *Herr* von Sturm, what do you think? Most Germans I've met don't share *Herr* Hoch's views on Jews. I've interviewed Hitler and even he doesn't sound like *Herr* Hoch."

Hoch spoke before Sturm could reply. "You would be surprised, *Fraulein*, at how many Germans agree with us on the Jewish problem but are too polite to say so. Soon the National Socialists will take power and Germans will be free to speak their minds once more."

"In my experience, Germans and free speech don't belong in the same sentence."

Hoch paused and then smiled unpleasantly. "Yes, *Fraulein*, just as the phrase 'an honest Jew' is an oxymoron." Hoch drained his glass of wine and poured another. "True Germans have nothing but contempt for your Anglo-Saxon conceit of free speech. We Germans don't need it."

Mattie turned again to Sturm who took the barest sip of his wine, still on his first glass. "What do you think?" Mattie asked. "Is *Herr* Hoch correct? Are most Germans anti-Semitic bigots just waiting for the opportunity to speak their minds?"

"No. They are not. Central Europeans and the French as well have virulent strains of anti-Semitism which are unknown in Germany, but the point you raise about Goebbels and Hitler shows much insight. Goebbels is the true anti-Semite of the two. For Hitler, I believe it is a political ploy which he discarded long ago. Like you, I have talked privately with Hitler on several occasions and, as with you, he never uttered any anti-Semitic slurs in my presence."

Sturm paused and nodded his assent at one of the porters who offered him a snifter of brandy. Sturm accepted the snifter and exchanged it for his half-full glass of wine. "Our young friend, Reinhard Tristan, here," Sturm said, "has neither had the experience of being in combat nor of meeting *Herr* Hitler. But Hitler served beside many Jews in the trenches, most of them honorable and courageous, as were the ones who served with me in airships. I know from my older brother that Jews served honorably with him in the infantry also, the blood they shed for the Fatherland as red as any German's. Hitler has acknowledged as much on many occasions."

Sturm paused and took a sip of brandy before continuing. "People deserve to be judged by who they are and what they have done, not by the circumstances of their birth. Hitler has told me this himself. But there are bankers and financiers who profited from the war and, some say, caused it. Not all of them were Jews but many were and out of proportion to those who served in the trenches."

"So what? Christianity once forbade charging interest and that led to more Jews in banking." Mattie said. "I know a lot about arms dealers and those who fund them. Naturally, there are Jews among them, especially the financiers. But the Bolsheviks had their share of Jews. And there are more Nordic types with blood on their hands from the arms trade than Jews."

Sturm smiled. "You've proved my point, *Fraulein*. Some Jews are loyal Germans giving their lives for the Fatherland while others are financiers attempting to profit from our misery. But that makes them no different than other Germans—Christians—who do the same thing."

"Okay, I understand that's your point of view. But is it Hitler's? The Nazis?"

"Not *Herr* Goebbels, certainly. Nor Himmler as well. They are true anti-Semites, as are others in the movement, our Reinhard Tristan here being one such example. But they do not control the party. Hitler does. And Hitler is a politician. He says many things to secure the support of many people. I cannot imagine a man as intelligent as Adolf Hitler spurning the contributions which could be made for the future of Germany by Jewish scientists and engineers. I have heard him express his high regard for Albert Einstein, to name but one. Hitler claims we will need all of our loyal citizens, Jew and Christian alike, if Germany is to regain its place among the great nations of the world. But Germany needs Hitler also. Someone who doesn't have calluses on his knees from genuflecting before the Treaty of Versailles."

"I see we agree on one thing, Sturm," Hoch said, "even if you are too soft on the Jews."

Sturm paused for a long moment, staring directly through Hoch, until Mattie could sense Hoch becoming uncomfortable with the silence. Hoch gestured dismissively with one hand, his wine shifting uneasily in its glass. His voice intimated a note of impatience, as if he spoke to a child who was slow to understand. "I did not mean, *Herr* von Sturm...."

But Sturm cut him off. "Exactly, *Herr* Hoch. It is difficult to mean anything when you have few coherent thoughts to begin with. Perhaps it's time you retire for the night."

Hoch rose at the insult and looked down at Sturm through what Mattie could only describe as hate-filled eyes. "In the new Germany, I assure you there will be no more class distinctions. It will take more than a "von" as a prefix for you Prussians to warrant the deference you believe you deserve." Hoch lingered for a moment, attempting to return the stare he had received from Sturm, then turned abruptly to leave, taking his wine glass with him.

Professor Campbell had one more brandy with them and then he too retired for the night, leaving Mattie and Sturm alone in the chill mountain air. They moved their canvas chairs closer to the fire and sat side by side. In contrast to their time aboard the *Graf Zeppelin*, Mattie did most of the talking, prompted by Sturm's questions and flattered that he had made the effort to research and locate so many of her photographs. He asked her about her photographs, the circumstances under which they had been taken, and how she came to be there to take them.

Each photograph had a story and an adventure behind it. She realized as she talked that, more often than not, she had gotten the photograph by instinct, following Eisenstadt's advice. *If your photos aren't good enough, you aren't close enough.* Mattie was always close enough. Sturm would describe the photograph; Mattie would recognize it and begin her story; and Sturm would interject comments from time to time, on her bravery, her skill and her luck. Mattie realized as she talked that she could have taken many of the same photographs with far less risk. She hadn't needed to be that close. It occurred to her more than once that Cockran had a point.

Then Sturm asked her about the Munich *putsch*. Not the famous photograph of Hitler scurrying away from the battle which had, after all, been taken by Helmut, but rather about one she had taken herself at the precise moment when the Munich police opened fire.

"How did I know to shoot the photo at just that instant?" Mattie said. "I didn't. I was lucky. I was standing with my elbows on the Mercedes' windscreen when I heard the first shot fired. I clicked off three quick photos as the police opened fire and then I dove for the floor."

"It's a remarkable photograph. To catch a moment like that, to catch a man exactly when the bullet strikes. Especially at such peril to your own life."

Mattie laughed. "Come on, Kurt. I may take a lot of risks which, with hindsight, were unnecessary, even dumb, but I'm not crazy."

"Crazy?" Sturm asked, looking puzzled. "I'm not sure what...."

Mattie cut him off. "That's American English for insane. I guess I've been there too long. Anyway, I didn't think the police would train their weapons on my motorcar until after our machine gun opened fire. I knew the primary targets would be the marchers. I thought I'd get in a few quick photos before our machine gun opened up and drew attention to us."

Mattie paused and took a sip of brandy. "To this day, I don't know who fired the first shot, the Nazis or the police. I only know it wasn't the machine gun in our Mercedes because if it were, I wouldn't have taken that photo. I would have been flat on the floor."

"What about those photos you took two years ago in Los Angeles of that warehouse full of arms? Those explosions were huge and shrapnel must have been flying."

Mattie drained her snifter of brandy and reached out and touched his arm, her hand lingering for a moment. "You've got a point. That was one of the first arguments Cockran and I ever had about my taking risks. Perhaps if I had let him win that argument..." Mattie stopped in mid-sentence, mentally completing the thought *he wouldn't be sleeping with that English bitch right now.* Then she continued, "But no, I couldn't keep my mouth shut. Cockran had been inside the warehouse and helped set the explosive charges. He had a gunfight with the IRA men who were guarding the warehouse and got himself shot in the process. That was a hell of a lot more dangerous than anything I did that night. Unfortunately, that's what he brings up whenever Hearst publishes my combat photos."

"What is it he brings up?"

"That he's taken my advice to heart and has never fired a weapon or placed himself in a dangerous situation since then," Mattie said and laughed again. "He's right, of course. He leads a pretty quiet life. He's a law school professor, for goodness sake, and he writes books and magazine articles. What's dangerous about that? True, he races motorcars and took up flying last year, but both are still safer than what I do."

Mattie felt herself begin to tear up at the thought of Cockran and she turned her head away so Sturm couldn't see. But he reached out and, with a soft touch on her cheek, turned her face back toward him. "You mentioned earlier today with a laugh, that you thought your boyfriend might be sleeping with his new English client. I wasn't sure if you were serious but, if he is truly having an affair with the Englishwoman, then he is a very foolish man indeed."

Mattie broke down in tears. Slowly, haltingly, encouraged by his empathy, she told Sturm everything about her and Cockran, from their argument in New York the day before she left on the *Zeppelin* to its renewal at Chartwell as well as her telephone conversation with Harmony about Cockran's birthmark on his hip and how they were "sharing" him. It felt good to unburden herself to a sympathetic ear.

Sturm was silent and let her talk. Eventually her sobs subsided. When she finished, he took her hand in both of his. They were warm and dry. She wanted him to hold her.

"I understand your concern. But I would not draw too many conclusions on such limited information. There may be another explanation for all of this."

Mattie had composed herself by now. "That's a gentlemanly thing to say, Kurt, especially from someone who was doing his best to seduce me a week or so ago on the *Graf Zeppelin*."

Sturm looked embarassed. "Really, I wasn't. Like I said, I was simply carried away by the moment, your beauty and the extraordinary way your face catches the light. Nothing more."

Mattie laughed. "I bet you use that line on all the girls you try to seduce. The thing with me is" she said as she stood up, leaned over and kissed him softly on the cheek while she whispered in his ear, "you nearly succeeded."

Back in her tent, naked beneath her blanket, Mattie waited for Sturm to arrive.

42.

Autogiros

YOU expect me to fly *that?* What in hell is it?" Bobby Sullivan asked. Cockran chuckled. People usually had that reaction once they saw a Pitcairn-Cierva autogiro. In some ways, it was similar to any other two-cockpit monoplane with a large rotary engine powered propeller in front. The difference was a vertical shaft, a pyramid of three yard-long steel beams on the fuselage above the front passenger cockpit. On top of the shaft was a large, four-bladed rotor, poised as if it were on top of a child's beanie, each drooping blade longer than the aircraft's wings. In fact, they acted as the plane's "third wing," a rotary wing.

"It's an autogiro," Cockran said, "but most people call it a flying windmill. I bought one earlier this year, a PCA-2, to fly to auto races. The Pitcairn Company in Pittsburgh manufactures it in America, but it was designed by Juan De La Cierva of Spain. They only have one for hire in Milan, a new C-19, but the Cierva factory in Madrid promised that two more will be here today."

Sullivan raised an eyebrow.

"That's right. Two more." Cockran said, his voice serious. "Hearst said to spare no expense and I'm not."

"It's not the expense I'm questioning but where you plan to find three pilots."

"I can fly one. I'll teach you to fly today and Sergeant Rankin's train will be arriving from Vienna tomorrow. That makes three pilots."

"Rankin of Scotland Yard is joining us?"

Cockran nodded. "Winston is sending him. Says he doesn't need a second bodyguard."

"A good man for a copper," Sullivan said. "You say he can fly one of these things?"

"An autogiro?" Cockran said. "No. But he was a pilot during the war in a de Havilland bomber. It won't take long for him to get up to speed on one of these as a pilot.

"You still haven't convinced me to climb into that thing as a passenger."

"Look, this is the only way to make up Mattie's head-start. I learned to fly an autogiro in a day and you can too. Each cockpit has its own set of controls. I'll start out as the pilot and I can retake control if necessary. You'll enter as a passenger and leave as a pilot." He paused. "But I'll go without you if I have too. I'm not letting Mattie die up there in the Alps."

Sullivan settled wordlessly into the two-passenger cockpit in the front, while Cockran climbed into the pilot cockpit in back. The controls in the Spanish C-19 were the same as his PCA-2 back home. He walked Sullivan through a lesson so that he knew where everything was—the altimeter, accelerometers, horizons—as well as what they all meant. Then Cockran fired up the Wright Whirlwind 420 HP radial engine and spun the nose propeller into life. Slowly, the rotor blades above his head started rotating as a small amount of power from the engine gave the rotary wing a boost to get it going. Unlike the propeller attached to the engine, however, the large rotor blades on top were not powered by an engine once it was in the air. They auto-rotated as the aircraft moved forward, providing lift like wings. Unlike its propeller, the rotor blades on top of the autogiro were clearly visible to the naked eye once aloft.

Cockran opened the throttle and the propeller pulled them forward. "Look at the controls in front of you," Cockran shouted into the speaking tube running from the pilot's cockpit to the passenger compartment. "They're connected to my controls and they move when I make them move. Don't touch the stick in front of you, but watch what happens when I pull it back." The autogiro topped 15 miles per hour after about twenty-five feet when he pulled back on the stick and the aircraft began to rise. The autogiro continued to accelerate and gain altitude, climbing to 500 feet. "I'll bring the stick back to its neutral position and we'll fly level. You understand?"

"Yes," came Sullivan's shouted reply back through the speaking tube.

"Good. Now watch the left pedal as I press it in," which Cockran did and the plane turned in a gentle left bank. Then he did the same with the right rudder.

"See, even a thick-headed mick like you can see that pulling the stick back takes you up, pushing it forward takes you down, left pedal turns you left, right pedal turns you right. No sudden movements. Easy does it. Everything you do with this plane, you do it nice and slow. Now you try. Take the stick and put your feet on the pedals. After that, follow my instructions but keep us steady. Most importantly, keep us level."

"Okay," Sullivan shouted over the roar of the engine.

"The controls are yours," Cockran said.

For the next two hours Cockran put Sullivan through his paces. Climbs and turns. Left, right, up and down—and always returning straight and level. Autogiros were definitely easier and safer for novices to fly than a fixed-wing aircraft. The greatest danger in flying an autogiro was tipping the nose so far down that you began to flip end over end, losing all control.

Cockran was right. Sullivan's reflexes were remarkable. He worked the stick and the rudder pedals as deftly as the trigger and hammer of his beloved Colt .45 automatics. Some people were born natural athletes and Bobby Sullivan was one of them. He often wondered how Sullivan would have turned out if, as a teenager, he had gone to university like Cockran instead of being trained by Michael Collins to kill British agents on the streets of Dublin.

"Okay, I can fly the bloody thing," Sullivan's voice came back at him through the speaker. "I can probably even take off, but I'd like some practice landing in one piece."

Cockran banked the autogiro to the right as they headed back to Milan's aerodrome where he brought the autogiro's altitude down to 100 feet.

"Remember how I said a pilot's worst fear was a stall?"

"Yes," came the shouted reply.

"That's when the airplane's speed becomes so low that the wings no longer provide lift until the pilot pushes the stick forward to regain airspeed and produce lift."

"Yeah, I know. What's your point?"

"Well, if you lose the airplane's only engine, the stall comes quicker. Like now," Cockran said, as he cut the engine.

"Are you daft?" Sullivan shouted, his voice clear over the silence of the engine.

Cockran laughed. "Trust me."

The rotors atop the plane continued to rotate automatically as Cockran kept the controls in neutral and the autogiro gently floated to earth, their speed declining until their descent was almost vertical rather than horizontal. The aircraft was down to twenty miles per hour as they approached the ground and bounced once as the main wheels touched the earth. Cockran gently raised the nose until the tail hit the ground, the plane rolling to a stop in about 15 to 20 feet.

"Did you see what I did? How as soon as the wheels touched, I lifted the nose?"

"Aye."

"That's about as slow as you want to land this thing, 20 miles per hour. Generally, anywhere between 20 to 30 miles per hour is ideal for landing and taking off in small spaces. We could even land almost straight down in an emergency, but that's not good for the plane."

For the rest of the afternoon, Cockran had Sullivan practice take offs and landings until Michael Collins' most feared assassin became as skilled at those as he was flying the autogiro. Cockran started him off landing at a 30 miles per hour air speed because it slowed down the vertical descent for the pilot and made for softer landings. Thirty miles per hour was slow enough to keep rookie pilots calm and confident. In truth, the worst possible landing—nearly straight down in an emergency—had the plane descending at a rate of seven miles per hour and moving forward at less than 15 miles per hour. The only problem was that jolting the plane too sharply in a vertical landing could damage the rotors, so a pilot didn't want to make a habit of landing straight down. Eventually, Cockran forced Sullivan to glide in closer to 20 miles per hour until he would have felt comfortable landing the plane on a rooftop in Hell's Kitchen.

They finished their final landing, touching down on a stretch of ground no longer than 30 feet, just as the sky turned a fiery orange on the western horizon. A few moments later, Cockran saw the familiar silhouette of two more flying windmills approaching the aerodrome, outlined against the the setting sun. Two factory-fresh autogiros from the Cierva Works in Spain.

The two men walked into the pilot's lounge, Cockran limping slightly as his hip had stiffened up in flight, and were cheered by the familiar figure of Sergeant Robert Rankin of Scotland Yard, red hair, red beard and six foot five inches tall. They both greeted him warmly.

"And here I was thinking that, with Mussolini running things and keeping the trains on time, they were also keeping Scottish riff raff out of this country," Sullivan said.

The big Scot laughed. "Now, lads, we're all Celts here. Just us against the Krauts according to Mr. Churchill."

"You're early," Cockran said

"I took the night train. Winston said it was urgent and that our bonnie Mattie was in danger." Rankin allowed a smile to emerge from his coarse red beard. "Just like old times."

43.

Her Nightmares Stayed Away

MATTIE was disappointed that Kurt had not come to her tent the night before. She had needed to be held by someone who wanted her and would keep her nightmare away. Dancing in the clouds their first night together on the *Graf Zeppelin,* his kiss had proved that Kurt von Sturm most certainly had wanted her. Maybe he no longer did.

The sky today was again high and blue as they left the valley floor and proceeded slowly up the incline to the first mountain pass, the only one passable in their Mercedes trucks. The guide assured them that the pack horses he had hired would be waiting for them at the far end of the next valley and the second mountain pass.

Mattie was driving the second G-2 with Gregor, another porter and the cook, while Hoch, the guide, Professor Campbell and one of Sturm's men were in the first vehicle just ahead. Sturm was with three of his men in the six-wheeled G-1 behind her. The incline was steep. She had never been a fan of motorcars with their steering wheel on the left instead of the right where God and Great Britain had decided it should be. At least, she thought, it placed her further from the edge on the right of the road. The vehicles were creeping along when Mattie heard a sharp report. She looked up to their left and saw that a small landslide had started at the top of the ridge. Hoch's vehicle looked in the clear up ahead but not Mattie's truck. The jagged rocks and debris were gathering speed and mass, heading directly towards them. Mattie reacted instinctively and floored the pedal on the truck. To stay where they were was suicide and she thought their only chance was to outrun the landslide. Her G-2 bounced over the rocks as it picked up speed and the muscles on her forearms strained to maintain control of the vehicle. Beside her, Gregor was holding on tight to the door handle and mumbling prayers in German. Mattie kept her eyes fixed straight ahead, not wanting to think of the sharp drop-off to the right. She made it past the main thrust of the landslide but not all of it. Smaller rocks and clouds of dirt blew past, rattling against the side of her vehicle. A broken tree branch whipped past, leaves clawing at the windshield and then the noise of the landslide began to subside, echoing beyond the cliff edge to their right. She could once again hear the whine of the engine, grinding the truck forward up the hill, dragging them to safety.

Just then, something slammed into the left rear of the truck, wrenching the steering wheel from Mattie's grasp and knocking the vehicle into a sideways skid. The G-2 tilted to the right, its left side tires in the air and she heard the doors on the right side fling open as gravity pulled at them while Mattie tried in vain to bring the vehicle back on all four tires. The truck landed on its right side amid the crunch of steel and shattered glass and came to a halt.

In the silence which followed, Mattie was dazed but knew that at least they were still alive. She looked behind her and saw that the cook and porter in the back seat had been banged up also but were otherwise okay. She crawled back and helped them open the left rear door, now facing the open sky above. She helped each of them climb out and start to scramble back up the steep slope to the mountain road. She heard voices shouting down to them from the road. Her head was clearing as she started to climb out. Then, she stopped, remembering. Gregor! There had been four of them in the truck! She ducked back inside but her stomach sank when she saw no one. Then she remembered the passenger door flinging open and closed her eyes.

The shouts from outside grew in intensity and Mattie knew what it was about. The noise had returned. The landslide wasn't finished. She could feel the vibrations building rapidly, and she stuck her head out of the window. She barely had time to duck her head before several rocks hit the undercarriage of the Mercedes squarely and tipped it over completely, dumping Mattie on the underside of the canvas roof. When the truck stopped moving, she slid out from under the seats above her and crawled back to the window. She looked out and gasped. All she saw was air and space. The vehicle was perched directly over the edge of the cliff and, as she looked down, she could see what had to be Gregor's broken body lying on the rocks hundreds of feet below her. She moved carefully back from the window and felt the truck shift slightly as she did so. This was not good.

"Mattie!" Sturm shouted. "I'm throwing a rope down. Tie it to the steering column."

Mattie looked up through the other window. Sturm was a good fifteen feet above her and the rope was in reach of the driver's side opening. She crawled along the underside of the roof until she was just below the steering wheel. Then she grabbed the rope and tied it securely to the steering column as Sturm had instructed. Above her, she could see that the other end of the rope was looped around a sturdy tree and held by one of Sturm's men, Willi Wirth, the young receptionist who had greeted them in Geneva. Mattie eased herself out of the vehicle, moving hand over hand along the rope. Above her, Sturm was inching his way down to the stranded vehicle with a second rope tied around his waist. The Mercedes groaned as it tilted further over the edge and Mattie could feel the increasing tension in the rope between her hands. She looked up and saw the tree at the end of her rope was slowly being pulled up by its roots with the weight of the truck.

Sturm looked back and saw the same thing. He quickly covered the last few feet separating them until he was beside her. "Take my arm. Then release your grip on the rope."

Mattie reached out for his extended hand and he grasped her wrist tightly just as the tree finally broke free of its mooring in the mountain side. They flattened themselves against the side of the incline and the Mercedes disappeared over the edge, the high-pitched sound of rocks scraping metal followed quickly by the uprooted tree tearing past them, spraying clumps of hard mud and soil over their faces.

Sturm pulled Mattie up with both his hands now until she was on his back, her arms firmly secure around his neck. "Willi will drop a second rope down. Loop it under your arms."

The loop came down and Mattie did as instructed, holding tight to the rope, her feet occasionally touching the side of the mountain as Willi pulled her up the last ten feet. Two minutes later he had done the same for Sturm. Mattie held her breath while Willi pulled Sturm up. When he too was standing on solid ground, she rushed to Sturm, her adrenalin racing, and clung to him, holding him tightly until he embraced her as well and she could feel his heart beat as though it were her own. They stood locked in an embrace until her pulse returned to normal.

Mattie stepped back and grasped both of his hands and squeezed. "Thank you. You saved my life. Again." Then she kissed him softly on his lips before she turned to Willi Wirth and hugged him also, much to the younger man's embarrassment.

THEY made camp late that afternoon near a tall and slender mountain waterfall which emptied into a small lake. The remainder of their trek after the land slide had been uneventful if a trifle crowded in the remaining two Mercedes. It had taken awhile, but Sturm's six-wheeled vehicle had proved as agile as a mountain goat as it slowly climbed up and over the aftermath of the landslide left on the road. As they made camp, the group seemed more subdued although, to her surprise, the guide, the cook and the remaining Austrian porter proved more fatalistic than Mattie about Gregor's death.

"The mountains are dangerous," the guide explained. "And Gregor knew the risks. We all know the risks. Sometimes the mountains bite back."

That evening at dinner, Mattie could have sworn Hoch was flirting with her. He avoided all the repulsive subjects on which he had expressed his equally repulsive opinions the night before and focused only on music and the arts, solicitously asking her whether she wanted more of this dish or that and keeping her wine glass filled as if he were a waiter hoping for a good tip. Perhaps he was embarrassed by his behavior the evening before but she had her doubts.

Mattie was civil during dinner, but barely and, his charm offensive having failed, Hoch retired for the evening shortly after Professor Campbell. The third bottle of wine was still half full at that point and Sturm poured the last two glasses out for Mattie and him. They drank them in companionable silence beneath a clear Alpine sky brilliantly lit by countless points of light.

Sturm finished his glass and turned to Mattie. "Mattie, there is something we need to discuss. Privately. I know the others have retired but sound carries far in the mountains and I would prefer that we have canvas as a buffer."

The adrenalin from earlier in the day had not worn completely off and the alcohol had loosened her inhibitions enough to cause Mattie to wonder if Sturm was about to seduce her. She hoped so. She was still depressed by the thought of Cockran with another woman. A younger woman. She needed a diversion. Her body, tingling from the alcohol, seemed to agree.

A stern lecture was not how Mattie imagined her seduction would begin. After sitting her down on a canvas chair by a small campaign desk, Sturm poured her a brandy and then began his lecture, pacing in the small confines of his tent as he did so, avoiding her eyes.

"Mattie, what you did today was both foolish and impulsive and a man died because of it. If you had backed your vehicle up as I did, none of this would have happened and Gregor might still be alive. You are a brave and beautiful woman, Mattie, and fearless. But also reckless. You remember your photographs we talked about last night?"

Mattie silently nodded yes.

"They prove my point. Half of them, maybe more, should never have been taken because you should never have endangered yourself. None of those photographs were worth losing your life. Maybe your Mr. Cockran is hypocritical and selfish when he voices concerns over your safety but he is right and you are wrong. Any man who loves you would say what I am saying."

Mattie was stung by his words. Sturm had risked his life to save hers earlier that day but she never thought for a moment that she had caused Gregor's death. She had seen the land slide start and she had acted instinctively and, she thought, responsibly. She wasn't going to be a sitting duck. But Sturm might be correct. The landslide missed his truck and if she had backed hers up too, Gregor might not have died. But damn it, wasn't that just second-guessing?

"When I was an officer in the Navy, I was taught that seeing to the safety of my men was my paramount duty, save only for engaging the enemy. I've not said anything until now, but I could not forgive myself if any more men die on this expedition, let alone a woman so beautiful and worthy of love as you. It was agreed that I would be in charge. So from now until the end of the expedition, you will obey my orders. Like everyone else. You will not be driving one of the trucks again. Anything you want to do, you clear it with me first. Is that understood?"

"Just who the hell do you think you are?" Mattie said, heatedly. "Have you forgotten it's my organization who's paying for half of this expedition?"

Sturm moved closer to her, standing in front of her chair, saying nothing for several seconds as he looked down at her, his blue eyes locked on hers. "No," he said softly.

Mattie looked up at his tanned blond face and open-necked white shirt, sleeves rolled up over his bronzed forearms and saw in his eyes the same look she had seen on the zeppelin that night just before he kissed her. Wait, did he just say that he loved me? What was it? Something like 'no man could allow the woman he loves to take the risks that you have'. No, that wasn't it. Wait! It was 'Any man who loves you would say what I'm saying.'

Mattie was still angry but he was telling her he cared for her, he thought she was beautiful and he was going to keep her safe. Mattie was all too aware of her strong attraction to this man. She had tried once to rationalize their zeppelin kiss as gratitude on her part but she had always known it was more than that. More even than her undeniable physical attraction to him. She couldn't quite put her finger on it but it had been there. And now she knew. From the beginning, their first dinner together, this had been a man she could fall in love with. That she later learned he could coldly kill others in an instant to keep her safe didn't change that. In her younger days, she had not been so strict about who she let in her bed. Now, there had to be much more. She didn't have to be in love with a man to sleep with him but the promise had to be there.

Like it had been with Cockran. Like it was now with Sturm hovering above her.

Sturm bent down, took her face in both hands and gave her a long, deep kiss which Mattie found herself once more returning, rising from her chair, their bodies pressed together in an embrace. She offered no resistance when he unbuttoned her blouse, and she moaned softly when his hand moved up to caress her breasts. Mattie felt his other hand move down to her waist and the buckle of the belt on her trousers. Unlike the buttons on her blouse, he paused as if seeking permission. She drew her face back and kissed him in reply.

She felt him unbuckle her belt and slip it off and then the buttons of her trousers were as magically liberated from the fabric as their cousins on her blouse. She wriggled her hips and the trousers fell in a pool around her ankles. She sighed as she felt Sturm's hand slip inside her silk step-ins. Mattie looked up at Sturm's face, touching it softly. "We don't have to worry about what the servants will say now, do we?" she said, reaching up with parted lips to kiss him again.

As Mattie was soon to learn, Sturm made love the way he danced. He led and you followed. There was no hesitation or indecision on his part once he drew her to his cot. Mattie started out as she always did with a first time lover—on top—and briefly straddled his waist. But he grabbed her hips and effortlessly pulled her forward until his face was between her legs and an image of Cockran doing the same thing flashed through her mind as she felt his hands smoothly slide off her step-ins. She gasped when she felt his fingers inside her and then his tongue. For a moment, Mattie had a sense of *déjà vu* from her erotic dream on the *Graf*. But, as it was with Cockran, sensation drove all thought from Mattie's mind and her orgasm left her reeling. When Sturm moved from beneath her, she fell forward and lay face down on the cot.

"You are still too tense," Sturm said, and Mattie felt his knees on either side of her as he began to deeply knead and massage the tense muscles in her shoulders and neck with his strong fingers, the rhythmic pressure flowing through her body, caressing the remains of her orgasm. Then he did the same to her back, her hips and, finally, her legs. Mattie was completely relaxed. and moaned softly as she felt him roll her over. He loomed over her and stripped off his shirt, his chest covered with curls of blond hair, then unfastened his trousers.

In the flickering light of the lantern, she had the unbidden image of Cockran as he had knelt above her that afternoon in his New York townhouse and lowered himself between her legs in a space lit only by fire. Moments later, the image of Cockran was gone, replaced by the ruthless man above her who was taking her body and making it his own.

Later, laying face down on the cot with a spent Sturm sprawled on top, Mattie was exhausted, as played out after making love with Kurt as she invariably was with Cockran. As her breathing returned to normal she was suddenly sad, sad now that someone else had done that for her, someone besides Cockran. A single tear slipped down her cheek at the loss of something so precious which only the two of them once had shared but would no more. All Mattie wanted now was for Kurt to hold her and keep her nightmares away as she slept.

As sleep slowly began to overtake her, with Sturm's arms wrapped tightly around her, Mattie felt warm and secure and, if not loved, then wanted. Her nightmares stayed away.

44.

We Have a Problem

Milan
Tuesday, 9 June 1931

COCKRAN had been calculating the distances they would have to travel and the fuel they would consume as the three men drove in the early evening from the aerodrome back to their hotel, the *Principe e Savoia.* The problem with autogiros was that while the rotary blades provided lift and made the aircraft easier to handle at remarkably low speeds—an Olympic sprinter could actually outpace an autogiro at its lowest airborne speed of 15 miles per hour—the rotary blades didn't make it any easier to propel the aircraft forward. Autogiros had to work harder and burn more fuel than fixed wing aircraft just to maintain their modest cruising speed of 75 miles per hour. What that boiled down to was they had a maximum range of about 300 miles before they needed to refuel.

Cockran was still going through the figures in his head as he and Sullivan walked across the *Savoia's* lobby to check Rankin in and pick up their room keys when, to his surprise, he heard the familiar and now unwelcome voice of Harmony Hampton.

"Bourke! Bourke! Oh, I'm so glad I found you," she said, wrapping her arms around him. Cockran stiffened at her embrace and abruptly pushed her away. She frowned and looked confused.

"What happened? Why are you here? Where's Donal?" he asked.

"I don't know. It all happened so fast. We stopped in Lausanne and I went with Donal to the telegraph office just as we did in Verona and

Milan. The woman's loo was right there, so I figured I could slip in quickly and be right back."

"You left Donal?" Sullivan said, his voice rising. "He wasn't on guard outside the loo?"

"No, but he was right next to it! Anyway, I wasn't in there more than five minutes or so. When I came out, two blond haired men tried to grab me. I recognized them. They had been on our train. So I screamed and shouted for the police. There were lots of people around and they let me go. I ran back to the telegraph counter but Donal was gone! I didn't know what to do!"

"Why didn't you return to the train?" Cockran asked.

"I was afraid to go back to the train without Donal. I thought they might be waiting for me. I bought a ticket on the next train back to Milan."

"How'd you know to find us here?" Cockran asked.

"It was in the telegram Donal sent you from Turin. Donal told me about the shooting in *Piazza San Marco* yesterday and that you were going into the mountains to find Mattie. I could see from the address on the telegram that you and Bobby were at a hotel in Milan that looked like Savoy or something. So that's what I told the taxi driver and he brought me here. I didn't know what else to do! I knew you and Bobby would keep me safe."

Harmony's eyes were red and filled with tears and her hands were shaking as she talked. She certainly seemed to be a frightened and distraught young girl, deserving of sympathy. But Cockran stood there impassively, unable to give any. Mattie's letter and the pain this woman had caused her was too fresh. He knew he ought to say something to comfort her but words wouldn't come. She could damn well comfort herself.

As Harmony stood there, a sad and bereft figure, Sullivan did something which astonished Cockran. He stepped forward and wordlessly took Harmony in his arms and she returned his embrace, hugging him tightly, burying her head into his chest as she cried.

It was the only outward act of warmth Cockran had ever seen Bobby Sullivan display.

"Take her to our rooms" Cockran said, "while I check for messages."

At the desk, Cockran discovered that Donal hadn't sent any messages but someone had done so on his behalf—Dr. Eric Kuhn, a staff physician at the hospital in Lausanne.

Back in their suite, Rankin was in an arm chair beside a sofa where Harmony and Sullivan sat, his arm around her shoulders. All three had drinks in front of them, scotch from the look of it. Cockran directed his comments to Sullivan. "We have a problem," he said. "Donal's in hospital in Lausanne. He was knifed today at the train station. The treating physician says he's going to be okay but they're keeping him under observation for twenty four hours. He won't be able to make it back to Milan until late tomorrow evening. I plan to book two tickets for him and Harmony on the first flight from Milan to Paris on Thursday."

Harmony slammed her drink down on the low table in front of the sofa and stood up. "No! You can't send me back! Not after they attacked me and Donal. He couldn't even protect me when he was healthy let alone now that he's been wounded. I can't do it, I just can't. Please don't make me" she said and began again to cry. "I want to go with you to find Mattie.

"Harmony. I know you're scared, but where we're going will be even less safe. Stay here in our suite until Donal arrives tomorrow night. Be sure to stick with him this time and don't leave his side. I know you're concerned but Donal's tough. He'll keep you safe. You can't come with us. You'll only be in the way. We don't need you."

"But you do need me," Harmony said. "I will *not* be dead weight. Do any of you have any knowledge of basic medical care? How to properly treat and dress a gunshot wound? I do. Didn't I prove myself in Germany when I took care of your wounds?"

Cockran didn't have time for this. They had to leave tomorrow morning for Zell-Am-See. He needed to buy supplies and study topographic maps. He needed to brief Sullivan and Rankin. Adding Harmony's weight meant less room for petrol—and that would cut their range to 275 miles, tops.

"No, Harmony. You're going to England with Donal. That's final."

"But I can't stay here alone to wait for Donal. They probably followed me from Lausanne and are watching this hotel right now, just waiting for you to leave. You promised to keep me safe and I won't be safe if you leave me here alone. Please, Bourke, you promised!" Cockran shook his head. Harmony was right. He had promised to keep her safe and he could not in good conscience leave her alone even after what she'd done to Mattie. They had to leave as early tomorrow as possible and there was no way on earth he was waiting for Donal to arrive tomorrow evening. He no longer trusted Harmony but they were wasting precious time. "OK. We'll take you with us. Check into your room and then come back here. I'll be briefing Bobby and Sergeant Rankin on our route."

"Thank you! Oh, thank you!" Harmony said, a sense of relief in her voice. She moved to hug him but he turned to the maps before she could reach him.

Harmony returned to Cockran's suite a few minutes later as he was describing the route of their journey and looked over his shoulder at the maps spread out before him. Zell-Am-See was only 157 miles from Milan, which would give him a good idea how their fuel mileage would be affected by the extra weight of Harmony and the surplus fuel containers he would pack into their baggage compartments. The map indicated a small airfield on the outskirts of Zell-Am-See so, with any luck, they would be able to refuel without tapping any of their surplus fuel. Mattie's expedition would almost certainly not be traveling in a straight line. If they left two days ago by automobile, they would only now be reaching the foothills of the mountain range where the castle should be. That meant they had at least another two days by foot. With more luck, and if the castle were where Joey Thomas' dossier indicated it was, they might even arrive there before Mattie's expedition.

All four of them then pored over the remaining topographic maps, trying to find potential spots to land after Zell-Am-See. They couldn't fly longer than a four-hour stretch before they would run short on fuel, so that meant they needed to find several potential landing spots in the *Grössglockner* Alps at 150 mile intervals. His calculations were rough, but Cockran estimated that they would need to refuel about three times in order to make the roundtrip journey from Zell-Am-See without cutting it too close. That meant packing sufficient containers of extra fuel—something he was hoping wouldn't weigh the autogiros down too much.

Before the end of the night, they had a complete route planned with two stops the first day and several landing spots within a mile's hike of the castle early the next day. Harmony had been businesslike and helpful, determined to prove herself and gain acceptance as more than a passenger. When Cockran complained aloud that he would barely have time to wire Churchill and keep him abreast of their plans while he taught Rankin to fly the next morning, Harmony offered to take care of it. With luck, Cockran thought, they would be airborne as soon as Rankin had logged a few hours of flight time. Then, he fell asleep with Mattie on his mind.

45.

By Packhorse

THE sky was beginning to lighten with the dawn as Mattie awoke in Kurt's arms. She dressed and walked barefoot back to her tent through the chill alpine air and a camp still asleep, warmed by the memory of their lovemaking last night. A life without Cockran was not something she was looking forward to. It was going to take a long time because she did not fall in love lightly, but a few more memorable nights like that could soften the sting of losing the man she loved. When she reached her tent, she began to look forward to tonight. It wasn't the same as looking forward to growing old together with Cockran, but right now it was all she had.

Mattie had second thoughts before they stopped in mid-morning to leave their Mercedes trucks behind and switch to sturdy *Haflinger* pack horses. The afterglow from Kurt had faded. The Roaring Twenties were over and so were her days of sleeping with a source to get a story like she did that one—and only one—time with Putzi or an occasional shag while on assignment abroad. In fact, Putzi and others in between had been disappointing lovers, in one way or another, compared to Cockran. But, after last night, she sure couldn't say that about Kurt. She tried to tell herself it had only been physical but she knew Sturm was attracted to her more than physically, just as she was to him. Alone with her thoughts as they moved along through the alpine meadows between high peaks on either side, her mind kept wandering away from Kurt and back to Cockran. She blushed as she caught herself comparing how the two men made love. She had never done that before. Ever. And it's not as if she really had the occasion to do so, being able, as she was, to count her lovers on two hands…with a few fingers left over.

Many things about the two men in bed were the same and yet different. Both equally enjoyable, both skilled and unselfish. But Sturm was more demanding. He knew what he wanted and decided what she needed. There was no room for improvisation by his partner, no time for her to think about what she might want to do next. Yet her sated body was the result. The same blissful point also arrived with Cockran but with him, though the destination was the same, she had a role in determining what route to travel. She was an equal partner in the endeavor. Not so with Sturm. He was the virtuoso in a symphony where only he knew the score. With Cockran, making love was like a jazz duet where their improvisations fed off each other, each one linked to the last. Kurt had been a sweet and tender lover but she really missed the jazz.

Also, Mattie was disturbed by the feelings Sturm expressed for her. She wasn't looking to replace Cockran. She just wanted some help getting over him. A diversion. That a ruthless man like Kurt might be falling for her in the process was more than she wanted. Maybe he was a man she could grow to love but she was nowhere near ready to let herself do that again so soon after Cockran. She needed time to heal from the hurt of losing Cockran. Last night had certainly been a pleasant diversion but Mattie decided she would not sleep again with Kurt and keep her entire focus on her quest for the Spear. She hoped that would keep both Cockran and Sturm out of her mind.

Mattie found herself avoiding Kurt's gaze once they had resumed their trek after lunch. Mattie was annoyed. If she had trouble looking Sturm in the eye on a hike in broad daylight, she didn't like what that said about her chances of resisting him tonight on a cot in the darkness. But, she had made her decision and she would stick with it. She looked ahead at Sturm's figure carefully managing the rock-strewn riverbank until the glare of sunlight reflecting off the river caused her to blink. She lifted her head, but found little relief in the sky above. The bright afternoon sun was high, blinding her view.

Just then, automatic gunfire erupted from both sides of the river and Mattie dropped to the ground, spared from the glare of sun off the river. She could see the gunfire was coming from a little ways up the hill, and was trained primarily upon Sturm and his men. The attack had been well planned. Ground cover and trees on either side of the canyon walls hid the enemy until it was too late, and now a withering crossfire had them pinned down.

Sturm's four men reacted quickly—Willi Wirth and three other hardened *Freikorps* veterans who had served together in the latter days of the Great War in one of the Kaiser's storm battalions. All were battle-tested and they immediately split up, two men darting right towards their attackers, while Willi and another peeled off to counter the attackers from the left.

At Sturm's shouted directions, Mattie took Professor Campbell, the guide, the cook, the remaining porter, and their three pack horses into a group of nearby trees, affording them cover, if not protection, from the gunfire which was not aimed at them. Not yet at least. The loud rattle of automatic weapons fire echoed on either side of her. To the left, Hoch was making his way up to where Sturm's two men were returning fire at their attackers. Mattie also could see that, to her right, Sturm and his other two men were not faring as well. Sturm was moving up to help but one of his men was wounded and out of action and the other was returning fire only sporadically. Sturm was facing a tough slog getting into a position where he could return fire. She knew her Walther would not be effective at this range, so she took an assault rifle from one of the pack animals, loaded it with a full clip, and put several more clips in each of the pockets of her trousers and headed out to help Sturm.

Mattie drew fire immediately and threw herself flat on the ground under an outcropping of rock. She sure as hell was a target now, she thought, as she huddled beneath the meager protection afforded by the rock, unable to move further as she heard the shots ricochet off the stone above her. Mattie crawled forward on her stomach, using her elbows and knees. She peered around the corner of the rock, not raising her head, and saw Sturm and one of his men engaged in a classic flanking maneuver, using cover in an effort to reach a higher level on either side of the intruders so they could turn the tables and place them in a cross-fire. Facing this new threat, the attackers were no longer concentrating their fire on her. Mattie thought that if she could safely cross 20 yards of open space ahead of her to more substantial rock cover, she would be able to offer supporting fire for Sturm and the other flanker.

Mattie raised herself to a sprinter's crouch and burst from behind the rocks just as she had done in the 100 yard dash and the 120 yard hurdles at university. Five yards from safety, she was no longer on a smooth track, only a rocky field. Her foot landed on the side of a rock and she felt a sharp pain in her ankle as her foot turned. She fell heavily, tearing the left side of her blouse as she landed. She knew she was a sitting duck so she began to pull herself forward, using her elbows, but more slowly than before, dragging her useless right ankle. Another volley and Mattie winced as rock fragments flew from the boulder above, stinging her back. She looked back and saw blood seeping from her right calf, staining her khaki trousers. A bullet? She hoped not. That would be a distinct impediment for the mountain trek which lay ahead. Twenty yards away, she saw the tall blond figure of Willi Wirth, crouched low, running towards her.

Mattie carefully peeked over the boulder's top and raised her assault rifle into position. She sensed Wirth beside her now but she was focused on the upper torso of one of the attackers as he fired his weapon at Sturm's man. Then, he had wheeled back in a 180 degree turn to shoot at Sturm when Mattie caught him in her sights and slowly squeezed the trigger. Yes! she thought as she hit him high in the shoulder and saw the man lurch and the rifle fly from his hands.

Nice shot, McGary. You finally made a difference, she said to herself, and turned her face toward Willi Wirth. "Did you see that..." she began but the words died in her throat as she heard the crack of a rifle shot and, almost simultaneously, Willi's head exploded, showering her with blood and grey brain tissue. She stifled a scream and used her sleeve to wipe the blood from her eyes as she heard two more shots. As she lay there, she was struck by the sudden stillness. The gunfire was gone and she raised her head to see Kurt von Sturm standing over the man Mattie had wounded. He was attempting to crawl away when Sturm drew his Luger, aimed it at the back of the man's head and fired. The body jerked once and then lay still as Sturm knelt down and rolled it over. Moments later, he stood up and began walking down the hill directly to Mattie's position. He did not look happy.

Sturm's voice was cold as he stared down at her and Wirth's body. "Can you walk?"

"No, I turned my ankle. It's pretty weak."

"Your leg, it's bleeding. How bad is it?" Sturm asked.

"It hurts, but I don't think it's serious."

Sturm said no more as he reached down and pulled her to her feet and carried her back to the trees where Mattie had left Campbell and the three Austrians. Sturm's silence was more of a reproach than if he had delivered another lecture on her recklessness.

Finally, it was Mattie who broke the silence. "Who were those people?"

Sturm waited nearly 30 seconds before replying, his silence serving as a continuing rebuke. "More of the same men who attacked us in Alexandria. The Brotherhood, whatever that is, is how they referred to themselves at Weber's villa. There were four of them. I've only seen the bodies of the two that I killed but I recognized one of them. It was the man who held Weber's head up after the execution. Both bodies have a tattoo of a Celtic cross on the inner portion of their left wrist."

46.

Stick With the Plan

Milan
Wednesday, 10 June 1931

THE autogiro squadron was airborne by mid-morning. Cockran had spent an hour and a half training Rankin while they waited for McNamara and Murphy to arrive from Rome. They left word for Donal at his hospital that Harmony was with them. Cockran took the point and Rankin brought up the rear, bracketing Bobby between them. Each aircraft carried line-of-sight two-way radio transmitters and receivers so that they could communicate. They had packed each autogiro with two sleeping bags, water, provisions, tarpaulins, and rifles in the passenger compartment, as well as surplus fuel containers in the baggage section.

Cockran took Harmony in his aircraft. She had to fly with someone, notwithstanding her deception, and it might as well be him. He decided against asking Harmony to explain herself. It wouldn't change anything and he was content to leave it alone and move on. Nothing was going to change until he found Mattie.

Two hours later, the trio of aircraft gently floated to earth on the shores of the lake at Zell-Am-See, a short walk from the airfield. The wind here was stiffer and came across their stern, making it difficult to keep the aircraft steady as they approached. Cockran had no trouble, but Sullivan came in a little steep and landed more harshly. Cockran and Rankin inspected the delicate hinges on the rotary blades but they appeared fine.

Cockran sent McNamara and Murphy over to the airfield to purchase more aviation fuel. Then he pulled out a topographic map and spread it out on the autogiro's wing.

"Lost already?" Harmony asked.

Cockran didn't look up. "Nope. But I'm thinking we should choose another spot than those waterfalls. Someplace with more room for Bobby to land."

"You can't do that," Harmony said abruptly.

"Why not?"

"Here," she said, taking the map. "Our plan is to fly as far as we can today. Virgental Falls are at the limits of our range. If we don't land there, the alternative is here in this valley."

"So?" Cockran said.

"It's 20 miles east of the falls, 20 miles further from Mattie. Doing that could cost us nearly an hour. Stick with the plan. Bobby's landing wasn't great here but he did better this morning."

Cockran wasn't so sure but as he looked up, he saw McNamara and Murphy approaching, carrying four large aviation fuel containers between them. Harmony was right, Cockran decided. Sullivan had done fine yesterday. The extra hour was more important, the risk worth it.

They flew low, their altitude rarely exceeding 500 feet from the ground, except when they reached the first mountain pass, which took them up several thousand feet, flying between the mountain peaks, stripped bare of all but the shortest vegetation, the wind gusting and unpredictable. Cockran saw a narrow mountain road snaking up the pass and, as he passed the halfway point several hundred feet above the road, he could see the wreckage of a motor vehicle and what looked like a body beside it. He couldn't be certain, but the wind currents in the mountain pass were too tricky to risk descending lower. By early afternoon, they arrived at the first point on Cockran's map, a spectacular series of cascading mountain waterfalls at Virgental.

They circled past once, to be sure they had found the right spot on the map, and it wasn't promising. From what they could see, the small strip of flat grass land couldn't be more than 30 yards long. It was an awkward plateau carved out by the streams running away from the waterfalls and cut into a sharp slope on a low, tree covered hillside. The plateau was grass covered, but the topographic map didn't include the jagged, rock-strewn terrain which greeted them, making their landing strip more challenging. The only good thing to say about it was that the approach itself was bare of trees which allowed them to come in nice and low.

Cockran landed first and it wasn't easy, the underbrush catching his ship's wheels to help bring the aircraft to a stop. "I'm in," Cockran said through the radio. "Try to come in low, close to seventeen miles per hour, but keep your engine running till you're over the plateau."

"I thought you said twenty miles per hour was as slow as I should land."

"It's going to be tight, Bobby. Try and bring her in around seventeen."

Cockran restarted the motor on the propeller to turn the plane around and pull it from the underbrush and out of Sullivan's runway path. He cut the engine and stepped out to watch Sullivan's approach. He looked good at first, descending to the plateau's level slowly and evenly but his angle of descent was too steep. His aircraft dipped below the plateau's edge and out of sight and Cockran held his breath. Several long seconds later, the autogiro reappeared and cleared the edge seconds before he cut the engine, its wheels nearly touching the grass as he landed with almost impossible smoothness. As the aircraft slowed on the grass, Sullivan had the space to turn just short of Cockran.

Sullivan looked down at the strands of greenery that clung to the wheels of Cockran's autogiro and then up at Cockran without smiling, "Could you use a wee refresher course?"

Cockran laughed. "You ungrateful Mick! I clear your path and that's the thanks I get?"

After Rankin landed without problem, they quickly set about refueling from their spare tanks before settling down bedside a rushing stream for a hasty lunch of sandwiches and thermoses of coffee they had picked up in Zell-Am-See. Thick bushes lined the muddy banks of the stream and Rankin wandered from the group over to the waterfall on their left, looking carefully at the ground. Cockran watched him scale the rugged terrain, pleased at the good fortune of having him here.

The Austrian Alps weren't the Scottish Highlands where Rankin had grown up but having a man used to the mountains gave him comfort.

Cockran had stooped to gather their belongings when the first rifle shot rang out. McNamara cried in pain and clutched his shoulder as he fell. Cockran dropped to the ground. Sniper! he thought as he scanned the horizon and heard the crack of a second rifle shot, a cloud of dirt puffing up a few yards in front of him. "Move!" Cockran shouted. A five second reload, he thought. The shots had come from the tree-covered hills on their right but the shooter hadn't compensated for distance. Cockran did not intend to give him time to adjust.

"Drop down to the stream bed! Up against the bank!" Cockran shouted again as gunfire erupted from the pistols of Sullivan and Murphy, who were using an autogiro for cover. Not there, damn it!, he thought. That was the wrong place to be. If the autogiros were damaged, they'd never catch up in time to rescue Mattie.

Cockran seized McNamara by his right shoulder and helped Harmony scramble with them through the bushes and down the muddy slope of the river bank just as the third shot rang out without result. Another five second reload he noted. McNamara dropped to his knees as soon as he was clear of fire and fell over, his face twisted with pain. Cockran and Harmony crouched over him. Blood seeped between his fingers as he clutched his shoulder.

"Stop the bleeding!" Cockran said to Harmony.

Behind the muddy bank, they were shielded from the shooter who kept them pinned down, unable to move. It wouldn't be long before he turned his fire towards the autogiros and they had to get to the shooter before then. Cockran peered through the bushes on top of the bank. Directly ahead of him, Sullivan and Murphy still crouched behind an autogiro, their handgun fire ineffectual at that range.

Cockran looked to the left and saw that Rankin was almost back from the falls, keeping out of the shooter's line of sight. The Scot hadn't been seen. He was their best chance. When Rankin reached his own autogiro, he opened the baggage compartment and pulled out an Enfield rifle with a telescopic sight. Cockran realized he had to keep the shooter's attention on him and away from Rankin, Sullivan and the autogiros. He pulled himself up over the top of the river bank and raised his head above the bushes. A bullet tore through the foliage, inches from his body, the rifle crack echoing off the mountainside. He had the bastard's attention all right.

Cockran was counting on a five second reload for the sniper as he burst through the bushes, turned right and raced along the bank of the stream in an all out, straight-line sprint. Three seconds. With any luck, the sniper would focus on Cockran, thinking he was trying to outflank him. One second. Time to bail out, Cockran thought as he dove through the bushes and down the muddy bank. The crack of a rifle followed but the bullet didn't find him this time either. His hip was not happy from the sprint and the sharp pain let him know it. He peered back up through the bushes.

Rankin, rifle in hand, was making his way to higher ground under cover of the trees. Cockran could not see the shooter but Rankin seemed to have a line on him. The big Scot took a prone firing position and brought the Enfield's telescopic sight to his eye. Two shots rang out but they did not seem to come from Rankin and they did not sound like the sniper either. Rankin still had the telescopic sight up to his face when suddenly he stood up and motioned to the others to join him.

Cockran ran back along the bank of the stream until he reached Harmony, who was still trying to tear off pieces of McNamara's shirt. "How is he?"

"It's still bleeding," she said, frustrated with the tenacity of the cloth she tugged at ineffectually. "Went clean through."

"Leave his shirt alone," Cockran said. "Go over to the medical supplies in our autogiro and get the gauze and tape. The coast should be clear."

Rankin stayed at the same spot until Sullivan and Cockran had made their way up to them. He gave the Enfield to Cockran. "Take a look." he said. "Tell me what you see."

Cockran put his right eye on the scope and saw the body and its shattered skull. He looked up at Rankin.

"Now look down and to the left, maybe another ten feet," Rankin directed.

Cockran did so and quickly found another body, seemingly down with another head shot. But there was no rifle beside the second man as there had been with the first.

"Snipers usually work with a spotter," Rankin said. "Someone has done us a wee favor."

They made their way up the hill between moss covered trees. "Would you be looking at that?" Bobby Sullivan said. "I don't want whoever took this lad down to have his sights on me."

Cockran looked at the corpse which had an entry wound at the base of his neck.

"Let's see if our man has any identification." As they rolled the man over to look through his pockets, it was apparent that no identification was needed. The uniform was all black, with dual silver lightning bolts forming the letters "SS" on both sides of his collar.

"How in hell did the SS know to set an ambush for us here?" Cockran asked.

"I don't care." Sullivan replied. "Who did this to the SS is what I'm wanting to know."

They didn't wait around to find out. Once McNamara's wound was bandaged and his arm in a sling, the autogiro squadron took off and flew another two hours before landing to make camp for the night near their second stop at a small mountain farm. Outside the farmhouse, two Mercedes trucks were parked. From his time in a prisoner of war camp, the wounded Gavin McNamara spoke passable German. The pain in his shoulder had diminished and he was able to learn from the old couple who lived there that a group of eleven people had passed through this morning, left their two vehicles and headed out with sturdy pack animals for the mountain pass looming high above the couple's cozy mountain hut.

"There were ten men and one woman," McNamara said. "And the woman had red hair."

"That's Mattie." Cockran said. "If they left this morning, we'll reach them tomorrow."

"There's more," McNamara said. "Eighteen men came through late this afternoon. All on horseback, dressed in black and heavily armed, each of them carrying a rifle and a sidearm."

"The SS again. Why the hell are they following Mattie's expedition?" Murphy asked.

"They must be after the Spear of Destiny as well. It looks like the Kaiser is not the only Kraut who's superstitious," Cockran said. But who they were no longer mattered. Barring another ambush, they would overtake both groups some time tomorrow. Mattie then would be safe with him and he could make things right. Only one more night to go.

47.

The Aftermath

BACK among the trees, Sturm decided to go no further that day and directed the Austrians to set up camp. Once they did so, he assisted Mattie to her tent and began to dress her wounds. Closing the tent flap for privacy, he helped her remove her torn bloody trousers and her blouse. Mattie was nearly naked, clad only in her brassiere and panties and, despite her painful ankle, his warm hands felt soothing on her body, tending to her wounds. Keep your focus, she told herself. Sturm, however, worked wordlessly and efficiently, showing no tenderness or any other sign of their shared intimacy the night before.

The cuts on her back from the rock splinters were superficial. He cleaned them with alcohol and swabbed them with iodine so that her back took on a polka dot appearance. The cut on her left calf was deeper but at least it wasn't a gunshot wound. He wound it in gauze and then tape. He took care of her ankle last, wrapping it in adhesive tape, criss-crossing the tape around her arch and the back of her heel to give the ankle lateral support.

Dinner passed in complete silence between Sturm and Mattie and almost complete silence among the others as well, Sturm responding in monosyllables to comments by Campbell or Hoch if he responded at all. Mattie could take a hint and didn't linger at the table after dinner, excusing herself and returning to her tent where she lit her kerosene lantern and pulled a camp chair up to the side of the bed. Shedding her clothes and putting on her green silk robe, she sat down and elevated her leg on the edge of the cot as Sturm had ordered. An after-dinner scotch was on the campaign table beside her. She took a long sip and savored the flavor.

It was dark outside by the time Sturm came for her. He opened both flaps to her tent and pushed his way through the mosquito netting, leaving the tent flaps open.

"Oh! You startled me," Mattie said, but Sturm did not reply. His face grim, he walked over, wordlessly picked her up in his arms and placed her on the cot. He gently pushed her onto her back and moved onto the cot himself, his knees between hers, moving them apart.

Mattie tensed, remembering her decision that morning to avoid the temptation of this magnetic man's bed and instinctively crossing her arms over her breasts. Sturm immediately grasped both of her wrists, pulled them apart and pinned them at her sides. He was stronger and, when he released her wrists, she left them there while he undid the sash to her silk robe, exposing her breasts. She tried to recapture her earlier resolve but that was easier said than done as she felt her pulse quicken, her nipples growing erect in the cool night air.

Mattie remained silent as he pulled his shirt over her head, unbuckled his belt and began unbuttoning his trousers, the same unbidden image once more flashing in her mind of Cockran doing the same. Sturm pulled the rest of her robe away and lowered himself between her legs. She knew she had to say or do something if she wanted him to stop but by then she could feel the rest of her body betraying her and preparing for him. That fleeting thought was the only resistance she offered, more to salve her own conscience than to stop him. Which it didn't. A single surge and her remaining resolve vanished. But it wasn't like the night before. There was no tenderness, no affection as he took control over her body again.

He soon had her gasping, the familiar pressure rising in intensity. Then, before she could catch her breath, he roughly turned her over. Indifferent to her pleasure, she felt her silk robe slip down the curve of her back while Sturm pulled her to her knees and once more mounted her from behind. Except it hadn't been the same as last night. He didn't lean over her back to kiss her neck, to caress her breasts. None of that mattered to Mattie as she felt the wave wash over her again and again, barely noticing when he reached his release.

Afterwards, he did not linger as before. Instead, he abruptly tugged free and left her kneeling on the cot, her face on the canvas, gasping for breath. Through her tears, she could sense the anger which had fueled him and that hurt her more than anything. As Sturm rebuttoned his trousers, he spoke for the first time. Initially, his voice was cold and even, not at all reflective of the fierce intensity of their coupling. "I wanted to remember what it was like to be with you because this may be the last time. I know this and you should too. There are men out there trying to kill us and, if you continue to act as you have the last two days, you and others like Gregor and Willi Wirth will surely die before this expedition is over." Then his voice broke and emotion emerged. "I would regret that more than words can say," he said almost in a whisper as he turned and pushed through the mosquito netting. He did not close the flaps. Only ten minutes had elapsed since first he entered.

Mattie continued to kneel in the position where Sturm had left her, feeling the cold mountain air on her exposed body and the rough, damp surface of the cot against the side of her face as her tears streamed onto the canvas. She was unaware of the presence of Reinhard Hoch in the shadows outside her tent, a silent witness for the second night in a row of the romantic spectacle she and Sturm had provided. As she slowly lowered herself face down on the cot, tugging her robe back over her body, her charms no longer so explicitly on display, a disappointed Hoch slipped away, vowing that if he were ever again this near her naked body, he would make Sturm's woman his own.

Mattie was miserable, her tears no longer the product of pleasure. For that was all it ever had been or meant to Sturm. Pleasure, not love. And she wanted to be loved. But she had lost that because of who she was and what she had chosen for a career. Cockran was with another woman and Sturm was no longer a diversion. She had even lost the thin romantic illusion that Kurt harbored tender feelings for her. The past few minutes were proof of that.

Mattie knew she should stop feeling sorry for herself, shake it off and focus on why she had come here. Her job. Her quest. The castle and the ancient Spear kept there which, if she could find it, would make her father proud. But that could wait for tomorrow. Right now, it felt good to cry and she did, rising slowly from the cot to extinguish the lantern, pull her robe closed, fasten her tent flaps and wrap a warm woolen blanket around her body before collapsing back on the cot, sobbing until sleep claimed her and the nightmares returned. Her beheading at the villa came first this time followed by the one that had been her constant companion, off and on, for the past eight years as her best friend once more died in a dark Munich alley.

Munich
Friday, 9 November 1923

MATTIE and Helmut were only three blocks from their newspaper's office. The day was still cold and gray. A light drizzle was falling, occasionally punctuated by a gust of wind which caused her to shiver, her heavy wool turtleneck and coat notwithstanding. Most of the Storm Troopers had fled after the gunfire stopped, leaving behind fourteen dead and three times that number wounded. Miraculously, only one police officer had been killed by the Nazi machine guns. Mattie saw that Göring had been wounded in his left thigh and she watched him make his escape with all the others. General Ludendorff was the only prominent figure among the marchers to have been arrested, but the Bavarian state police captain she interviewed said that the police had a list of all the ring-leaders and their favored haunts. He guaranteed that they would be hunted down and brought to justice within a few days at most.

Mattie and Helmut had not escaped uninjured themselves. The flying glass from the Mercedes windscreen had left them both nicked, cut and bleeding, Helmut more than Mattie. After completing their interviews, they had gone to a small clinic run by a physician friend of Helmut's who treated their wounds. They had been heading back to their office so that Mattie could file her story and Helmut develop the photographs. A few of the plates he had taken with the Speed Graflex before the action were undamaged and they had high hopes for them. More importantly, they had the roll of thirty-five millimeter film showing a shaken Hitler scurrying from the scene, leaving his wounded Storm Troopers behind.

They had not eaten all day and stopped at a small café for bratwurst and beer after leaving the clinic. Fueled by adrenalin and warmed by the beer and the food, they talked excitedly of the day's events. "I've seen the aftermath of battles," Mattie said. "I've even had snipers shoot at me. But I never experienced anything like that. Have you?"

Helmut nodded but said little. He still looked shaken. "I was in the second battle of the Somme. I still have nightmares. Trust me, today was nothing compared to that."

Mattie tried to lighten the atmosphere, changing the subject to how they could use the photographs of the fleeing Hitler. Later, Mattie realized that she had been too unguarded in her conversation about the photographs. They never noticed the four Brown Shirts in the curtained booth beside them, nor the fact that they were followed when they left the café.

It was dark when they made their exit from the café and they had barely gone half a block when they were attacked and roughly pushed into a nearby alley. Mattie doubled over in pain when a meaty fist slammed deep into her stomach and she fell to the ground and curled into a fetal position, gasping for breath. She saw Helmut go down also, no more than five yards away, three of the men and their hob-nailed boots raining heavy kicks into his body while the fourth man did the same to Mattie.

Mattie watched as the three men pulled Helmut to his feet, two of them holding him up, smashing their fists into his now bloody face. "Your camera, Jew! Where is your camera?"

Helmut gestured weakly to the canvas bag laying at Mattie's feet. Mattie's assailant now turned his attention away from her and toward the bag. He dumped out the bag's contents onto the rain-slickened cobblestones. The man made quick work of the plates from the Graflex with the heels of his boots. He then turned his attention to the rolls of film in the bag, exposing and unrolling them as if they were spools of thread. He fumbled with the Leica and, when he couldn't open it, he used his boots to smash the camera open, exposing the film within.

"Have you given us everything, Jew? You're not hiding anything, are you?" Mattie's assailant said, throwing the camera back on the ground.

His face bloody and swollen, Helmut could barely croak out his reply. "No, that's everything."

Mattie watched in horror as a large man with close-cropped light blond hair calmly took a Luger from the pocket of his overcoat, pressed the barrel against Helmut's temple, and pulled the trigger. The sound of the shot reverberated through the narrow alley as the left side of Helmut's head disintegrated in a shower of blood, bone and gray matter which hit Mattie full in the face. Mattie winced when she felt someone clutch her hair and painfully pull her head up.

"You should keep better company, Fraulein. Hanging out with Jews can be bad for your health. The next time it might be you."

With that he returned both hands to her hair, gripping it tightly, and slammed Mattie's head down with frightening force. Her head bounced off the pavement but she did not lose consciousness. She felt the tears building up inside her but she stifled them and kept her eyes closed waiting until she could no longer hear the SA thugs and was certain they were gone. She tried to focus her thoughts away from Helmut's horrific death but it was impossible. His blood and tissue on her face were a wet and unwelcome reality. She tried to think of something, anything. The future. Something to look forward to. Then she remembered. The 35 mm roll with Helmut's last photos of the fleeing Hitler was securely inside her right coat pocket. Helmut had died because he took those photos. That was all that mattered now. If it was the last thing she did, she had to make sure that Helmut's last photos, the unflattering photos of the frightened *putsch* leader, the man who dreamed as a youth he had held the Spear of Destiny in an earlier era, would soon be on the front page of the *Daily Mirror* along with her exclusive, eyewitness story of the failed *putsch* and the cowardly murder of her best friend.

48.

Fear for Mattie

COCKRAN had been awake for some time when the farmer approached their campsite to wake him, a silhouette against the faint blue of sunrise. He felt drained. Part of it was due to absorbing the vibration of an 420 HP radial engine through his hands, arms and chest. But it was also like the war, when his body shook with the impact of shells, the mechanical shrieks of artillery so ubiquitous he could hear them in his sleep. His body was shaken from the attack in Venice and the ambush in the Alps. The stitches in his hip didn't help either.

But his mind had been shaken most by fear for Mattie's safety. Worse, Cockran couldn't get past the pain she would be feeling, thinking he had left her for another. What kind of man did she think he was? If only he had told her how hard it had been to love again after losing Nora; if only he had told her how very special she was to make that happen.

The farmer halted short of their campsite, surprised to see Cockran awake. Cockran waved to him and said, "*Danke.*" The farmer nodded and turned away. Cockran rose to his feet and stoked the dormant coals of their small fire from the night before.

Sullivan was first to wake to Cockran's quiet activity and tied up his sleeping bag. "Have you decided where we're heading?" Sullivan said, holding out an empty plate to receive the oatmeal Cockran was stirring in the pot. Others were up now, washing out their tin cups and plates from supper the night before. He gave Sullivan a helping, followed by hot coffee.

"We'll check the western approach first." Cockran said. "See if they went that way."

The light had spread more evenly in the sky but the sun still hid behind granite peaks in the east as the autogiros climbed swiftly above the hills and dipped in and out of the miniature valleys that lay between folds in the rounded hillsides. They saw no signs of any human activity, neither Mattie's expedition nor the ominous SS troop shadowing her.

They flew for nearly an hour like this, following the hills as they rose into the mountain, but they found nothing. "Bourke?" a voice crackled in his ear. It was Rankin's. "It's after nine. Want to try the eastern approaches? I don't think they took this route."

Cockran craned his head to look at the terrain below.

"There's no reason they would come this far," Rankin added.

"All right, let's turn it around," Cockran banked the autogiro in a circle until they were headed back towards the eastern side of the mountain range. They regained altitude so that they could open the throttle and get back to 75 miles per hour. Then his thoughts returned to Mattie.

Why the hell hadn't he asked Mattie to marry him? Concerned that, if he did, Paddy might lose another mother? Who was he kidding? Just as he had done in taking on the IRA in 1929 and avenging Nora's murder, he had deliberately placed his life on the line in Germany and Paddy had been far from his mind. He was trying to hold Mattie to a standard he wouldn't or couldn't keep himself. That was going to stop. He knew it wasn't Paddy he was really concerned about. It broke Cockran's heart, but he knew Paddy had no conscious memories of Nora, no heartache. If they lost Mattie, it would break Paddy's heart but it would be for the first time. No, it was Cockran who just could not endure the agony of losing a woman he loved a second time. Well, that was goddamn well going to stop too. It didn't matter if Mattie wanted to continue her dangerous career. If that was what she wanted, then he was going to be in her corner. But first, he had to find her. Nothing else mattered.

"The central stream should be coming up on our left," Rankin's voice came over the radio. "Just over this next ridge."

"Let's take it then," Cockran said and pressed on the left pedal to start a gentle bank. Their speed dropped back down to 45 miles per hour as they followed the rising pine trees up the ridge. As they topped the ridgeline, the ground dropped away steeply, revealing a quick running stream hundreds of feet below with flat, wide forest lands ranging on each of its banks. The hills rose slowly with a modest foothill on the other side of the stream. Cockran closed the throttle and banked left again, sailing upstream into the mountains ahead.

Gentle waterfalls poured down from occasional overhangs that developed in the steep hill dominating their left flank. The low hills on their right inched closer to the stream, rising more steeply, creating a more canyon like feel that made Cockran nervous. With less room to maneuver, any sudden winds winding down the mountain would prove more difficult to handle. They continued their pace until he heard a shout on his radio.

"A body!" Cockran heard someone say. "I'm telling you, I saw a body."

"Where?" Cockran asked.

"Down on that hillside to our right, there in a gap in the trees," the voice was saying. It was Murphy. "I saw a man lying there, I tell you!"

"Were there any more of them?" Rankin asked.

"There could have been," Murphy said. "I thought I saw one more, but I can't be sure."

"Let's find a place to land," Cockran said. "We've got to check this out." Was it Mattie?

God, let it not be her, he thought. Just let it not be her.

49.

To Fight for Cockran

MORNING brought Mattie clarity. She didn't know how it happened but she woke up knowing exactly what she was going to do. Bugger self-pity and her ankle. She would find the Spear and then she would go back to find Cockran. That's what her father would expect. That's what she wanted. To be with Cockran. To grow old with him. And to hell with Harmony!

Sturm had them break camp in the pre-dawn twilight. Yesterday's attack had given him a greater sense of urgency. The sooner they made it to the castle, the better. The sky grew pink behind them, the trail easier to see, as Mattie went over her new resolve and its rationale. She was going to fight for Cockran. And Paddy too. The truth had been there all along. If Harmony had seduced Cockran, it didn't mean that he loved her just as she didn't love Sturm. She wasn't giving up Cockran without a fight. She had to see him, touch him, talk to him. Doing that would make it easier to let go. But she wasn't going to let go easily. If she couldn't hold onto Cockran against someone like that English bitch, then maybe she didn't deserve to. Or, maybe it just wasn't meant to be. But it wouldn't be because she didn't fight for it. She was James McGary's daughter, the woman her father always meant her to be. She would never give in. Never.

Cockran had been right. Her big, beautiful Irish bastard had been right. So was Kurt. Her life *was* worth more than a spectacular photograph or a sensational story. And so were the lives of those around her like Helmut, Anwar, Gregor and Willi. Mattie sighed. She could see what she had to do and why. She would find the Spear of Destiny and she would win back Bourke Cockran. She wasn't familiar with failure. She wasn't going to start now.

50.

No Time to Waste

THE three autogiros landed softly on a grassy bank on the right side of the stream. Murphy hopped out of his passenger's seat and marched off to inspect the hillside as Sullivan followed. Cockran couldn't bear to go with them and began to top off the fuel tanks of each autogiro to keep busy while he waited for their return.

As Cockran topped off the last plane, his foot sunk into a soft hole in the grass and he stumbled to his knees. He lifted his shoe out of the hole with a curse and looked back at the grass where he fell. Slowly, he became aware of several small depressions in the earth trailing away from the spot where he had fallen. He followed them with his eyes and saw that they trailed away in a path towards the tree cover at the base of the hillside.

He put the fuel container down and got to his feet. "Rankin!" he shouted. "Get over here!" Cockran followed the trail towards the trees as Rankin came over from the stream's edge.

"What is it?"

"Take a look at these." Cockran said. "Tell me what you think they are."

Rankin walked up beside Cockran and followed his eyes. He dropped his giant frame close to the ground. "Animal tracks. A hoofed animal, like a horse. Smaller. Maybe a mule."

Cockran moved forward, following the tracks to the edge of the forest. He stepped between trees and into a small clearing beneath a canopy of leaves. Hoof prints were joined by boot prints on the forest floor, most of them clustered by a circle of stones. Rankin touched the black and gray ashes that remained from a dead fire. "Still warm," he said, letting his hands dip into the ashes. "Whoever was here left this morning. Either they're not mountain men, or they didn't have time to dismantle the campfire and spread the ashes."

"Could this have been the SS campsite?" Cockran asked.

Rankin slapped his hands together, wiping off the ashes. "No. The farmhand said the SS were on horseback. None of these tracks are large enough for mounted horses."

They searched the surrounding area and found the assorted debris left behind—broken stakes, emptied food provisions, discarded gun clips. Rankin emerged from behind another tree carrying a small khaki blouse and held it out for Cockran to see.

"Is this Mattie's?" he asked softly. Cockran knew that it was and nodded. Rankin turned the blouse around before handing it to Cockran, revealing blood stains surrounding a few tears along the back of the shirt. Cockran looked at them closely, fingering the torn threads of the cloth and counting the number of holes. "She's been hurt, then," Rankin said. "But I don't think she's been badly hurt unless that was...." Rankin stopped, unable to finish the sentence

Something stuck in Cockran's throat and he voiced the obvious. "Unless she's the one Murphy saw up on that ridge."

Cockran moved back out of the trees quickly in search of Sullivan, but only found Harmony waiting for them back at the autogiros, her face a mask of concern over their sudden disappearance into the woods. "What is it?" she asked.

"Sullivan. Murphy." Cockran said. "Have they come back yet?"

"No," she said in a small voice. "But Bobby's coming back. I can see him."

Cockran turned without a word and picked up his pace, running across the grass towards the hillside. Sullivan was walking along a wide, stone strewn bank of the stream. "Bobby!" he shouted, short on breath. "Bobby! Was she there?"

"What?" Sullivan said.

"Mattie!" Cockran shouted again. "Was that her up there? Tell me!"

Sullivan looked confused. "No," he said. "No, it wasn't."

Cockran closed his eyes and let his shoulders sag for a moment. She was alive. He let his breath catch up with him and looked at Sullivan. "We found her campsite," Cockran said. "She left her shirt behind. It was torn and bloody. I wanted to be sure she wasn't the body on that ridge." Sullivan nodded in understanding. "What did you find?"

"They weren't SS," Sullivan said. "There were two bodies. Dressed for hiking. Basic supplies and two sleeping sacks. One killed long range, the other shot just behind his left temple."

"An execution?" Cockran asked.

"Probably," Sullivan said. "But he'd been shot in the shoulder from a distance with a rifle. No powder burns on that wound. It wasn't fatal. The shot to the head was. The boyo had a funny tattoo on the inside of his wrist, like an old fashioned Gaelic cross. Though I'd bet the farm he wasn't Irish."

"What about the second body?" Cockran asked.

"Same tattoo," Sullivan replied. "Probably the other bodies too."

"There were other bodies?" Cockran asked.

Sullivan nodded. "In the trees on the other side. I sent Murphy over to check it out." They turned and saw Murphy a little further up stream, climbing back down between the trees.

Sullivan shouted to him, "Murph! Did you find them?"

"Yes, I found the buggers!" Murphy shouted back. "They're both dead!"

"Did they have tattoos?"

"Same!" Murphy replied. "They were wearing a different tunic and few more bullet holes, but both sportin' the same cross inside their left wrist!"

"An ambush by the SS?" Sullivan suggested.

"Certainly a firefight of some kind," Cockran said. "We don't have time to find out. Mattie may be alive, and we don't have any more time to waste."

Back in the air again, Cockran felt energized. Flying close to the ground, near the right bank of the stream, he kept an eye on the terrain for further signs of Mattie's trail. They had scanned the maps again, searching for the pass that would take them northwest and over the hills on their right. The stream itself wound deeper into the mountain range, but turned to the southwest, away from the castle. He figured there were at least four more peaks to cross.

They reached a gentle slope in the hills on their right that rose between two of the lesser peaks and began their ascent. The pass between the rising mountains climbed slowly north, making small bends back and forth as it wound its way higher into the sky. Up ahead, Cockran could see the top of the pass make a sharp bend towards the west before disappearing from sight beyond the horizon. Cockran pulled back on the stick to gain altitude, and glancing at his altimeter, he saw that they were over 7,000 feet and climbing. The air was discernably thinner and the horizon widened as he climbed so that he had a clear view beyond the ridge to the next pass, a mile in the distance and considerably higher.

Cockran tilted his head over the side to look below and saw a narrow clearing between the trees. His eyes followed it up the hill until—there was movement! One, two, three—a host of figures, moving up the path just as the pass reached its summit and turned west. "Down below!" Cockran said. "Ten o'clock!" He increased their altitude to stay above the rising terrain. He arched his neck to the left again and looked below. There were eighteen of them, on horseback, and they were all dressed in black. The SS! Cockran's autogiro drifted close enough to the pass that he could see several of the men on horseback strain their necks to look up at the aircraft as they soared overhead, passing over the ridge and dropping into the next valley below.

They cleared the second pass at just under 9,000 feet and glided back into the final valley before the ascent to the castle. The majestic granite peak loomed over the forested dale which rose gently to meet the steeper inclines of the summit. The castle should be somewhere around a bend on the western face of the mountain, off to their left. They were cruising closer to the ground at around 3,000 feet as they banked towards the western face, Cockran saw something like dust rising up above the tree level. He kept his eyes on the source of dust and saw a train of figures moving slowly on an exposed pass leading up the hillside. Mattie! It had to be her! There was no way, even on horseback, that more SS could have gotten this far.

Cockran alerted the others to Mattie's expedition and led the autogiro squadron in a rapid ascent, aiming for 10,000 feet. He had wanted to do the same when they had flown over the SS outfit, but they were so high in the pass at that time, nearly 8,000 feet, that Cockran wasn't going to risk the autogiro's rated 15,000 foot ceiling capacity, certainly not without oxygen. As a consequence, the SS men below had gotten a good look at the three flying windmills as they passed by. He wasn't about to give the Kaiser's man, Kurt von Sturm, the same advantage.

Thirty minutes later, with Mattie's expedition safely behind them, they returned to a lower altitude just under 4,000 feet—only a thousand feet above the rolling contours of the mountain meadow below. Small elevated lakes rested in a chain of plateaus along the hillside, rising up to the final pass that wound around the eastern face of the peak. Within minutes, Rankin's voice came over the radio. They were nearing the area Joey Thomas had identified on the rough map he had been given.

Shortly after, a rigid structure emerged from around the bend as though it grew out of the mountain itself. The forbidding battlements of a medieval castle glowing in the afternoon sun.

51.

Sturm's Apology

TO Mattie's surprise, Sturm apologized right after a lunch where silence had been the rule. Taking her away from the others, he looked into her eyes with the same expression she had seen that first time on the zeppelin as well as the first night they made love.

"My actions last night were inexcusable. I was concerned for your safety and angry about what could have happened to you. But that is no excuse. Forgive me. Please accept my apology."

Sturm was clearly embarrassed, ashamed even. Her immediate reaction was to coldly ignore him. After all, she could have stopped him last night had she really wanted to, but his apology made him all the more dangerous. She knew now she had been wrong about him last night. She could see it in his eyes. He cared for her. He was in love with her. Being alone again with this man would tempt fate, a triumph of hope over experience. Last night proved that. What she needed was to find Cockran, win him back and start over again. Away from Kurt von Sturm.

"Accepted," she said with no trace of emotion "How long will our trek be today?"

"That depends. How are your knee and ankle holding up?"

"They're still tender but if it becomes too painful, I'll hitch a ride on a pack horse."

"In that case, my best estimate is no more than four hours at a steady pace. We ought to be able to see the castle once we clear this next ridge."

They were on a winding path approximately half way up the ridge when Mattie saw movement from the corner of her eye and looked up. They were too high to hear, specks in the sky, but overhead she could make out three aircraft flying in a single-file formation. She pointed them out to Sturm who nodded. "Yes, I saw them too. Unusual to see aircraft in the Alps. But they must be over 10,000 feet. I can't make out what type of aircraft they are."

Mattie's knee was throbbing when they crested the top of the ridge in early afternoon. Sturm took out his field glasses. "It's there," he announced matter-of-factly. "For castle ruins, it looks remarkably intact." He handed the binoculars to Mattie. "Here, take a look."

Mattie looked through the field glasses in the direction Sturm pointed.

"Another two hours and we'll set up camp at that lake just below the castle," Sturm said.

The castle loomed large above them as the Austrians began to unpack the horses and set up camp beside the lake. As they finished setting up camp, Sturm continued to treat Mattie solicitously, explaining his actions, inviting her comments, still trying to make up for last night. Kurt being kind and thoughtful rather than brisk and efficient was a side of him rarely glimpsed.

"I considered setting up camp inside the castle wall itself," Sturm said, "but it is unlikely the water supply is still working."

Mattie nodded. "We have two or three hours of daylight. Do we begin a preliminary exploration of the castle now or wait and get a fresh start in the morning?"

"What is your preference?"

Mattie grinned. "Now."

Sturm instructed Hoch to take two men and establish a perimeter guard.

Sturm turned to Mattie. "We'll take my other man with us. I'll be on point. He'll bring up the rear. Would you prefer to be armed with something more than your automatic pistol?"

Mattie was momentarily taken aback. "Armed with what?"

"One of the assault rifles, like the one you had yesterday."

"You weren't too pleased with that, as I recall."

Sturm's anger of the day before did not show, his voice low and even. "I sent you with Professor Campbell and the Austrians to keep them safe, not to take you away from the action. You were the rear guard to protect them, our horses and supplies in the event we failed to contain the enemy. Instead, you left them defenseless and yourself exposed to danger, which is why I sent Willi to come to your aid." There was no hint of rebuke in his voice.

Mattie nodded. "I understand that now. I'm sorry."

"If you understand, no apology is necessary. All I expect once I give you a weapon is that you will do what I say when I say and trust me enough to believe I have a good reason for each of my orders. Units in combat can function no other way and those men who have tried to stop us from reaching this castle may well be waiting inside."

Mattie nodded again, her expression serious, her eyes scanning the terrain along with Sturm. She had been shot at before without result but only as a journalist, not as a soldier. Now she was a member of a unit, a combat team, and her life depended now as it had earlier on the skill of the unit's leader, a man she had taken for a lover. A man who loved her. A man she trusted implicitly with her life. She turned to look into his blue eyes. "You can count on me."

52.

Keep Mattie Safe

THE castle looked like a giant trapezoid from the air, rising out of the 3,000 foot high mountain ridge, the stone of the structure blending into the mountain below so that it was difficult to tell where one ended and the other began. The autogiros circled the castle and Cockran noted the sheer sides on the eastern and western walls and the massive nature of the northern wall. He saw that the castle could only be approached on foot from the south.

After circling the castle twice and noting no signs of its being inhabited, the autogiros flew on into the next valley upon which the western wall of the castle looked down. After landing, Cockran could see that someone standing high on the castle's western wall could easily spot the aircraft below. He helped Sullivan, Rankin and the other two Apostles drape all three planes with camouflage netting where they placed green leafy branches and wild flowers.

Cockran caught the eyes of Sullivan and Rankin and motioned them to join him. "We don't have much time. Mattie's group will set up camp at the small lake we flew over. We need to get up over the ridge and into position so that we can intercept anyone going from the camp to the castle. If there's a chance, we have to try to rescue her before they make it to the castle."

The ridge climb was rough, a steep and steady incline which took them more than two hours, 30 minutes more than Cockran had anticipated. His hip was still bothering him. Once they reached the top of the ridge, Cockran signaled them to keep low. Their silhouettes would be backlit by the late afternoon sun. He paused behind a tree and raised his field glasses to look at the small mountain lake below the castle's eastern wall. Mattie's group had arrived. There were six tents in all, four small and two large, roughly 20 yards apart. Good, Cockran thought. Too late to visit the castle but time to set up an ambush and rescue Mattie.

Cockran saw that two men, each with a side arm and an assault rifle, had set up a perimeter, patrolling on a regular basis. He watched three Austrians preparing for dinner, surprised at how lavish it was. Four canvas and wood camp chairs around a campaign table with two wine glasses and china at each setting on a white tablecloth with two large candles.

Cockran focused his field glasses on the castle. He spotted movement in the trees above the campsite. A small group of four people was making its way up from the campsite to the castle. Cockran's anger rose. He knew Sullivan had seen it too—Mattie's unmistakable red hair.

Moments later, Sullivan was by his side. "There's no way to intercept them, Bobby?"

Sullivan shook his head. "We'd have to cross open ground."

Cockran raised his binoculars, his heart aching as he saw Mattie's profile. The man on the point and the man at the rear had assault rifles. While he could not reach the castle undetected, he could circle below them and reach the campsite's perimeter without being seen

"You three wait here," Cockran said to Sullivan. "I'm going to head down the tree line and get as close as I can to the camp, hole up there and wait for dark." Cockran picked up his Enfield carbine with a telescopic sight and slung it over his shoulder. "Wait here until they come out. If Mattie and Campbell aren't with them, kill them both. Got that?"

"No problem," Sullivan said.

"But if Mattie is with them, hold your fire even if Campbell isn't. Keep your weapons trained on them all the way down. Keep her safe. Just keep Mattie safe."

"How long will you be?" Sullivan asked.

"As long as it takes. I've got to talk to Mattie. If I'm not here by midnight, you three head back to our camp. I'll join you before dawn."

53.

The Castle

THE castle is remarkable," Geoffrey Campbell said as they began the trek up the steep slope. "It obviously was built by the Hohenstaufens but it shows a clear Cistercian influence."

"Hohenstaufen?" Mattie asked.

"Famous castle-builders," Campbell replied. "Emperor Frederick I—Frederick Barbarossa—was a Hohenstaufen. He died en route to the third Crusade. He was the grandfather of Frederick the Great who was crowned in 1214. With all the military campaigns he conducted in Italy, he built quite a few castles there, as well as in Germany and Austria."

"And Cistercians?" Mattie asked.

"Monks. Italian builders. Some say they were the forerunners of the Templars. Their designs were more advanced than those of contemporary builders. The Cistercians were famous for building remote monasteries in the mountains in an austere yet ornate Gothic style."

"I don't understand its shape," Mattie said. "Why so narrow there at the end?"

"It has four sides," Campbell replied, "but the narrow end is dictated by the configuration of the mountain ridge. We can't see it from here but I'll wager the western side of the castle will have a sheer face with rusticated walls so that it appears to be rising out of the stone."

"Rusticated?" Mattie asked.

"Rough-hewn," Campbell replied. "It's a Hohenstaufen trademark."

It was not an arduous climb but both her knee and ankle hurt. Mattie was sweating and halfway up had wrapped a bandana around her neck to absorb the perspiration. She undid it now, mopped her brow and looked at the front gate with a sudden chill. On a spike extending up from the stone was a human skull, bleached white by fierce winter storms. It was an unexpected sign of human presence. Mattie flashed back to Egypt. A hostile presence.

They followed the Professor around the front corner of the castle and there, exactly where he said it would be, was a small wooden door which appeared to be of a far more recent vintage than the castle itself, as was the brass lock halfway down the door on the right-hand side.

"Look," Campbell said. "This castle has been here for centuries, yet clearly someone has lived here recently."

"How recently?" Mattie asked.

"Twenty years. Thirty years. It's difficult to determine."

"The door looks quite sturdy. How are we going to get in?"

"Like this," Sturm said, as he undid the flap on his holster, pulled his Luger out and fired three shots, splintering the door around the lock. Sturm reholstered the Luger, picked up his assault rifle and hammered it butt first at the door. The door gave way to a small dark antechamber, the fading sunlight from the open door the only illumination. Sturm turned on an electric torch which threw its light down the hall, motioning to one of his men to advance.

Sturm turned to Mattie. "You and the Professor follow me. Frederick will stay here to cover the entrance to make certain we aren't taken by surprise from behind."

Mattie's eyes followed the light as Sturm walked down the hallway. She gasped when she saw it. "There, put the light higher," she said, which Sturm did, revealing what Mattie had glimpsed. A transformer. The castle had been electrified! Below the transformer stacked in a circle against one another were ten Mannlicher rifles. They looked old and were covered in dust.

Sturm saw them too and approached the transformer, grasped the lever and pushed it up. Nothing happened. "Take those stairs," Sturm directed and Mattie went, pushing the door open so that the hall was dimly illuminated at both ends. Sturm followed Mattie up the stairs.

They emerged into the castle courtyard which looked enormous, easily spanning over 200 yards in length. Professor Campbell stood beside her, his eyes squinting as they adjusted to the light. "Ah, just as I expected, the chapel is over there in the southwest corner. The stables will be along the eastern wall closer to the southeast tower than the northeast. The Great Hall will be along the wall connecting the two northern towers. Let's inspect it first before the light fades."

"Not so fast, Professor Campbell," Sturm said. "We must first make certain the castle is secure and that none of the men who attacked us are lying in wait. Once we have done that, you can begin your search for the Spear."

"But that will take too long," Campbell protested. "All the good light will be gone."

Sturm shrugged, indifferent.

"Kurt is right, Professor," Mattie said. "There are dangerous men who wish us ill. We must proceed cautiously," she said, turning to Sturm. "How do you want us to handle this?"

"Clockwise," he said. "Search this tower first, then the chapel in the southwest corner. Leave the living quarters along the north wall for last."

The search took the rest of the afternoon and early evening, but the castle was deserted. Not all of it was electrified, but metal conduits ran from the gasoline-powered generator they had found in the southeast tower, along the eastern wall, to the living quarters along the north wall. The generator's tank was bone dry and looked as if it had not been operational for decades.

By the time they reached the Great Hall, the sun had dipped below the western wall, plunging the large, high-ceilinged room into gloom and shadows, making it impossible to work.

"It's time to return to camp," Sturm said. "We don't know where our enemies may be waiting and we don't want to meet them in the dark."

54.

Mattie Was So Close

Castle Lanz
Thursday, 11 June 1931

COCKRAN was hidden in the woods, barely 50 yards from the six tents of the Kaiser expedition's camp but he paid them no mind. His gaze and his field glasses looked up at the castle's southeast corner. On his way down, he had heard three gunshots, his heart lurching at the sound. If Sturm and the other man emerged and Mattie didn't, they were dead. And that would be just the beginning.

The sun had dropped below the castle walls when he noticed movement. One man carrying an assault rifle came around the corner first, followed by Professor Campbell, and then,…yes! The golden red glow of Mattie's hair. She was alive. Finally, a tall blond-haired man stepped out from the castle, also holding an assault rifle. Cockran recognized him at once from the zeppelin at Lakehurst. The Kaiser's man, Kurt Von Sturm! The man looked around carefully in all directions. Cockran wondered briefly if the weapon meant Mattie was a prisoner.

No, Mattie definitely wasn't a prisoner, he thought, as Sturm reholstered his weapon and he could see Mattie's smile and a laugh as she touched Sturm's arm. But what were those shots about? Cockran kept his binoculars on the group as they made their way down the slope to the base camp. Closer now, it was plain that Mattie did not believe herself to be in danger, talking animatedly with von Sturm and Campbell. No tension visible among the three of them.

Cockran was not prepared for what came next, astonished when the group of four reached the tents and a new figure emerged to greet them.

The blond hair, narrow face and long nose of Reinhard Tristan Hoch! Identical to the photograph Captain Weintraub had shown them. What in hell was going on? SS men mounted on horses. An attack by the SS when they landed that first day in the autogiros. And now, the man responsible for Harmony's kidnapping and the attacks on NBM's plants in Munich was here. Could this be the "business trip" Hoch's wife said had called him away so suddenly? In contrast to her easy manner with von Sturm, Mattie's body language with Hoch was entirely different. Stiff and reserved. Sturm was trusted. Hoch was not.

An hour later, Cockran watched the servants light the candles on the table and serve wine with the first course. During that time, Cockran had been equally astonished to find himself entertained by Hoch from whose violin had come two of the four Brandenburg concertos. At dinner, Mattie certainly seemed to be having a good time, chatting amiably with von Sturm and Campbell and not showing the same reserve she had earlier upon first encountering Hoch on their return from the castle. After a while, Hoch and Campbell rose from the table and returned to their tents, leaving Mattie and von Sturm alone. If Mattie were concerned for her safety with von Sturm, she still was not showing it, laughing, once more touching his hand for emphasis, and finally rising, slowly shaking her head, placing a hand briefly on von Sturm's shoulder. Nope, no fear there. In fact, it was clear to Cockran that she liked Sturm. He watched Mattie walk back to her tent. Then Sturm did the same, the light in his tent staying on, the others extinguished.

In the twilight, Cockran observed Hoch exit from his tent and circle behind the other tents. He made his way down into the valley, carrying something but, in the darkness, Cockran could not make out what it was. A servant cleared the table and blew out the remaining candles. The only illumination on the scene below came from the glow in von Sturm's tent. Cockran decided that, once darkness fell, he would be able to make it unseen to Mattie's tent. It was the last one on the right, facing the lake, next to Campbell's.

Cockran had a cold supper, washed down with half a thermos of water. He looked at his watch. Forty-five minutes more. Mattie was so close and time was moving so slowly.

55.

A Last Night Cap

DINNER had been pleasant for Mattie in sharp contrast to the long silences of the night before. Their Austrian chef had prepared a feast, freshly caught fish grilled over an open flame, accompanied by wild morel mushrooms and a sauce made with shallots and the rest of the morels, the wine a Chianti Classico. Hoch's music had been pleasing, as always, and he was still acting like he wanted a date with Mattie. Professor Campbell had talked eagerly about how he would prioritize their search of the castle; and where he expected to find the sacred lance.

After Campbell and Hoch excused themselves, Mattie had politely declined Sturm's invitation to join him for a night cap in his tent. That train had left the station, never to return.

Mattie walked back to her tent, undressed, slipped on her robe and headed down to the lake to wash up before retiring for the night. On her way back, Sturm's tent was the only one lit. She felt a twinge of guilt. She was not experienced at letting down gently men who loved her but whom she did not love or would not allow herself to love. More importantly, she had to prove something to herself. She stopped at Sturm's tent.

"Your night cap offer still open?" Mattie asked.

Sturm was on his cot, shirtless, staring up at the tent's canvas ceiling. He gave her a small smile and sat up, the gold curls on his chest reflected in the lantern's light. He poured two fingers of scotch in a glass and gave it to her. "You have forgiven me for last night?"

"No, I haven't," Mattie said in a level voice. "But I accepted your apology and I believe you when you say it was out of character for you. Let's leave it at that." She took a sip, then softened. "I also accept that you were concerned for my safety," Actually, Mattie thought, it was much more. He was in love with her and she wasn't able to reciprocate. How much control did she really have over her body after three glasses of wine? She was about to find out.

Sturm shook his head. "I'm not entirely certain why I did it." he said. "But I've never forced myself on a woman before in my life."

Mattie smiled. "You didn't. I'm a big girl and I know how to take care of myself. I know where men are, well…, *vulnerable,* and if I had wanted you to stop, believe me you would have been well and truly 'stopped'." Then she laughed and took another sip, savoring the warm glow it produced. "If you don't believe me, just ask Mussolini sometime how I convinced him making love on his desk was a bad idea. I will say your tenderness last night suffered in comparison to the night before. But if I hadn't wanted to make love, we wouldn't have."

"Thank you," Sturm replied. "I have been bothered all day by my inability last night to control my anger. I take pride in my self-control."

Mattie smiled again and sat down on the cot beside him, taking his hand in hers. She took pride in her self-control as well but it had failed her last night. That was why she was here now. "Look, you helped me understand I would have been responsible if any of the Austrians you left in my care had been harmed because I hadn't done what you asked. I also know we lost Willi because of me. I feel a lot worse about that than I do about last night. So, no hard feelings, okay?"

"Hard feelings? I'm not certain I understand," Sturm said.

"An American expression. Here, let me show you what I mean," Mattie said, as she put her hand on his chest, leaned over and kissed him softly on the lips. Sturm pulled her toward him and returned the kiss. He turned the lantern off. This was why she had come, she reminded herself, as she felt her body begin to react as strongly it had the last two nights. To test herself and take control of her body. But she knew it wouldn't be easy and she sighed when she felt one hand on her breast.

What is it with me and risk-taking, she thought, as she gently grabbed his other hand snaking deep beneath her robe and across her taut belly and stopped it before it could go further.

"See?" she said with a smile. "I could have done this last night if I had wanted to, but I didn't. Now, it's different. I've made up my mind. He can be so stubborn at times but then so can I. The thing is I love Cockran too much to give him up without a fight. You may be right, there even may be an innocent explanation for how that woman saw his birthmark. But I don't care if there isn't. Being seduced by that English bitch doesn't mean he loves her. You've helped me see that, but I wish I had seen it two days ago. I didn't mean to lead you on, and I'm sorry if I did. I don't regret the time we spent together. I see things more clearly now, thanks to you. You are a dear man and I would like us to remain friends."

Sturm smiled and for a moment, Mattie thought he was going to laugh. Instead, he shook his head. "Yes, I would like us to be friends, Mattie" and then he did laugh. "This is the first time a woman has ever said that to me. I'm the one who usually says those lines."

"I can well imagine why," Mattie said as she rose from his cot. "I love Cockran. I really do. You're both alike in some ways. In others, you're not. Maybe in another life we could have been together." She ran her hand softly over his face. "Just not in this one."

Mattie headed back to her tent, happy with her decision, whatever the outcome. Alone tonight, her nightmares might return, but she didn't care. She had always enjoyed an evening of jazz more than the symphony anyway.

56.

Screams in the Night

Castle Lanz
Thursday, 11 June 1931

COCKRAN could wait no longer. He had to see Mattie. The camp appeared deserted, the tables cleared and all tents dark, save for a lantern illuminating the interior of Sturm's tent. He saw a shadow move down towards the lake some 50 yards away from the tent, but he could not make out who it was in the darkness. A few minutes after that, he saw another shadowy figure enter Sturm's tent. Moments later, the lantern was extinguished and Cockran looked at his watch. He climbed down the incline to the ground cover. He decided that he would wait until the lone sentry guarding the western approach had passed.

Ten minutes later, Cockran was near their tents, crouched low, waiting for the sentry to pass. Then, Cockran moved forward, commando knife in his hand, to the rear of Mattie's tent.

"Mattie? Are you there?" There was no response. He tried again, to no effect.

Placing his knife along the corner seam of the tent, he sliced it open, pushed the flap in and entered the tent. He saw nothing but an empty cot. Where could she be? Had she been the one he saw walking down to the lake? Or entering Sturm's tent? He gave her another few minutes and then moved on to Professor Campbell's tent where he aroused Campbell from his slumber, the academic opening the rear flap of his tent for Cockran to slip through.

In hushed tones, Cockran told Campbell all he had learned from Joey Thomas, including the danger he and Mattie were in once von Sturm and his men had secured the Spear of Destiny.

"We have aircraft in the next valley to fly you to safety. You must talk to Mattie as soon as you can tomorrow and arrange to make it over the ridge. Your lives depend on it."

"Nay, laddie, I cannot do it. We're too close now. We've come too far!"

"But this man Hoch is a Nazi. A killer."

"Aye, he's no gentleman, that's for sure. But I'll take my chances. I've seen more bloodshed than I ever knew I could withstand." He paused, as if carefully considering his words. "I saw a man beheaded in Egypt, you know."

"What? What are you talking about?"

"I don't know about Nazis but there are other men trying to stop us from finding the Spear. Religious zealots, I think. They attacked both of us on the train to Geneva."

"You mean you and Mattie? On the Orient Express?"

"Exactly. Shot at her and missed on the train. Did the same at a villa in Egypt. Shot all the servants and then cut our host's head off with a sword in front of us. We narrowly escaped and made our way back to Alexandria. We slept that night on the zeppelin. That's when Mattie's screams started, her screams in the night. I expect we'll hear them tonight as well."

"Even more reason to get you both out of here. But she's not in her tent. Where is she?"

"I don't know. Last I saw her, she and von Sturm were talking at the table, finishing their wine. They always dine together. If the light's still on in his tent, she might be there. They're always the last ones to turn in for the night." Campbell paused. "I trust *Herr* von Sturm. He's an honorable man. He's kept me and Mattie safe from harm's way more than once."

"That's not what our information says," Cockran said. He talked for a while longer, but he couldn't persuade the older man. So be it. He owed Campbell nothing. But Mattie was a different story. He wasn't going to trust Sturm with the safety of the woman he loved.

Cockran decided there was nothing to do but return to Mattie's tent and wait.

57.

Mattie Explains

Castle Lanz
Thursday, 11 June 1931

MATTIE was surprised to see her tent flap closed. She was certain she had left it open when she left. As she approached the tent, she sensed the presence of someone else and froze for a moment, her only thought that it might be Hoch. The hell with it, she thought. She knew a scream would bring Sturm to her rescue. She stepped into the tent, stopped and stared in open-mouthed amazement. "Bourke! Why are you here? My god! What's happened to your face?"

Cockran put a hand to his face, touching the gash on his right cheekbone and smiled. "Whoa, slow down. Keep your voice low. First things first," Cockran said as he stepped forward and took her in his arms. "I got your letter. Let me explain about Harmony."

Mattie returned his embrace and held him tight, kissing his cheek. "Bourke, I don't care about you and Harmony. I love you so much. I'm not giving you up without a fight."

Cockran grinned and ducked his head, the light brown hair falling over his forehead in a familiar comma. "There's not going to be a fight. No matter what you may have thought, we're not breaking up. Not if I have anything to say about it. You're the one I love. I'm sorry if I hurt you. Nothing happened with Harmony. Honest. I can explain that birthmark business. Really."

"I don't care about your birthmark or what happened between you and Harmony." Mattie hugged him tighter. "I love you so very, very much," she said, tears welling in her eyes. She pulled back and touched her hand gently to his forehead and cheeks, running her hands over the now healing cuts. "What in hell happened ?"

"Right now, we've got more than that to worry about. Are you okay?"

"I'm fine," Mattie said, and then started to cry. "No, I'm not. It's been terrible. We were attacked on the train; then again in Egypt; even ambushed yesterday. Something called the Brotherhood. Every morning I wake up knowing someone is out there trying to kill me."

"Campbell mentioned them. I've been here twenty minutes. Where have you been?"

"I was walking down by the lake. I've been having a hard time sleeping. I've had nightmares almost every night. So when they wake me, I go for walks until I'm sleepy again and, hopefully, too tired to dream," Mattie said, surprised at how easily the half-lie came to her lips. She paused. "But how on earth did you find me? Why are you here?"

"To rescue you. You're in danger from people in your own party. This Spear of Destiny business is a lot bigger than you ever imagined. Besides, after I got your letter, I wasn't sure you'd still want to come to me in Venice. So I decided to come to you."

They talked quietly for at least half an hour, Mattie doing the listening, interjecting a question here and there. She couldn't believe it. Joey Thomas dead. A plot to kill Hindenburg. Kurt an agent of the Kaiser! Mattie was horrified. My god, what had she gotten herself into?

"It gets worse," Cockran said.

"What do you mean?" Mattie asked. "How could it possibly get worse?"

"Reinhard Hoch, that's what's worse," Cockran replied.

"That bastard? He's probably a Nazi."

"Worse. He's SS. He's the one who had Sir Archibald Hampton killed, Harmony kidnapped, and their plants sabotaged. All at the behest of our old friend, Wesley Waterman,"

"I can believe that about Hoch," Mattie said and then she paused. "But it can't be true about Kurt. He saved my life and risked his own. If he meant me harm, I wouldn't be here."

"Maybe. Perhaps Joey's intelligence is faulty, but Hoch is a different story. I don't know who those other men are who have been trying to keep your expedition from finding the Spear, but I know from recent experience what the SS are capable of. And there are eighteen well-armed SS men on horseback who will be here shortly. You've risked your life too many times for this story. You've got to leave with me now. Before the SS arrive."

Mattie smiled and reached out her hand to touch his cheek. "Cockran, I love you. I know you only want to keep me safe and I love you for that, too. But your face is living proof that you haven't been out there avoiding risk yourself. Look, Hoch by himself won't be a problem." she said. "Not after I tell Kurt about him. He can handle Hoch. But if you've got Rankin, Bobby and two more Apostles on the other side of the ridge, why can't you set up a defensive perimeter here in the camp to hold off the SS and the other ones after the Spear?"

"We probably could, but why wait? Why not just leave with me now?"

"Bourke," she said, "I can't. We're almost there. I have to do this. I have to find the spear. It's not only for the story. It's for my father. I owe it to him and his memory. You know what your father was to you. Mine was the same to me. The Spear of Longinus meant as much as the Holy Grail for him. I can't quit now. I just can't. Give me one more day. Please. Sturm has good men with him. We can't leave them and our Austrian porters to the tender mercies of the SS. It wouldn't be right. Please. With you and the Apostles watching our backs, we'll have enough time to see if the spear really is in this castle. If we find the spear, flying out of here will be the safest thing we can do. One more day is no bigger risk than what you told me you and Bobby were doing in Germany."

Cockran shook his head, smiled and held up his hands in surrender. "Okay. You win for now. As the Big Fella used to say, '*Always retreat in the face of a superior force.*'"

Mattie laughed. It felt good to laugh again with the man she loved.

"Here's the plan." Cockran said. We'll set up a new defensive perimeter. Let Sturm know what we're doing but don't let him know we've been tipped on the Kaiser. Only the SS. Got it?"

"Yes." Mattie hesitated. This might ruin things but it wasn't right to keep it from him. No more lies. There was never going to be a good time to tell him. "Wait, there's something you need to know," Mattie said. "About Kurt and me. When I thought you and Harmony ...."

Cockran put a finger to her lips. "Don't," he said. "It doesn't matter. I love you. He saved your life. You thought I had fallen for Harmony. Whatever happened after that we can sort out later if you really want to. Getting you safely out of here tomorrow is all that matters."

Mattie fought back tears. How she loved this man. "I'm so sorry I ever doubted you."

Relieved, she composed herself. It still wasn't going to be easy telling him about Kurt, but she allowed herself a ray of hope. Maybe it wouldn't ruin things after all.

"Okay," Mattie said. "We'll talk about it later. I'll talk to Sturm tonight. But only about the SS. I won't let on I know anything about the Kaiser. If we find the Spear, I have no doubt Campbell will go with us for safety's sake alone. There are only so many places the Spear can be, and if we don't find it tomorrow, then I don't believe it's here. The Professor is a big boy and I think we can persuade him to come with us. Either way, I'm going with you. If we don't find the Spear tomorrow, I'm going to need your autogiros to check out those other two castles. With or without Campbell and definitely without Kurt von Sturm. 'Better safe than sorry' is my new motto. Trust me."

Cockran laughed.

58.

Did You Find Mattie?

COCKRAN made his way in the darkness back over the ridge to the camouflaged autogiros, elated he had found Mattie safe, even more elated to learn that they still had a future. But inside, deep inside, his heart ached. Had she slept with Sturm? Was that what she had tried to tell him about "Kurt"? Was that why she was so positive he meant her no harm? He didn't want to think about it. He had to focus on getting them out of there. But it was hard.

It was his fault, Cockran thought, if she had been driven into the arms of another man. He knew Mattie had been with other men before him. But after tonight, he damn well intended to be the last and he was going to have to banish any thoughts of her having slept with Sturm. After all, it's not as if he were in any position to cast the first stone. He had been no saint when it came to Harmony. It easily could have gone a lot farther than it did.

Cockran was nearing the camp when, suddenly, a bright light was switched on, temporarily blinding him. He raised his hand to shield his eyes and felt strong arms reach from the darkness to grab him from both sides. Instinctively, he leg-tripped the man on his right and smashed his elbow back into the nose of the one on his left, drawing his Webley and placing it against the man's temple. Then the light swung away from him.

"Drop your weapon or the woman dies" a voice from the darkness said and the light focused on a man clad in black with a Luger pressed against Harmony's very white and frightened face. A bound and gagged Sullivan was seated on the ground beside her.

Cockran placed the Webley down and the two men did a quick and efficient search of his body and bound his hands. They forcefully prodded him forward with the tips of their assault rifles until they were under the camouflage netting. He could barely make out the dim forms of Rankin, Sullivan, Harmony and the other two Apostles seated on the ground beside an autogiro, their hands bound behind them. Two other black clad men with assault rifles stood guard. They shoved Cockran onto the ground beside Sullivan.

"What the hell happened?" Cockran asked.

"They were good," Sullivan said out of the side of his mouth. "Got McNamara while Harmony was changing his bandage. Blinded the rest of us with flashlights and took us down."

"SS?"

"The same," Sullivan replied.

"I'm surprised they didn't shoot first. Why did they take us alive?" Cockran asked.

"The autogiros. The SS are going to assault the castle tomorrow and we're their air force if they need reinforcements. Then, they expect us to fly them and the spear to Germany."

"But there's no one in the castle now," Cockran said.

"We know that. They don't. They need us alive to fly those things. No need to give them a reason to change their minds. Did you find Mattie?"

"Yes. She's safe now but she's not going to be if we can't get out of this."

"You have a plan?" Sullivan asked.

"Silence!" an SS guard shouted and kicked Sullivan hard in the ribs.

"Don't worry, I'll think of something." Cockran said after the guard walked away.

"Wake me when you do."

59.

The Spear

MATTIE, Sturm and Campbell, along with two of Sturm's men, returned to the castle after an early breakfast. Campbell made a bee line for the Great Hall with Sturm and Mattie close behind. Warned by Mattie about the SS, Sturm posted his men on the castle battlements.

"But why was a castle built here?" Mattie asked as she took another photograph.

"Precisely because the ridge dictated the trapezoid shape," Campbell replied. "The only way to approach the castle is from the small end of the trapezoid, the south. Any attacker would have to concentrate his force there. Yet the defender could array his archers halfway down the eastern and western walls, catching the attackers in a cross-fire. Meanwhile, those who made it through the arrows to the gate in the south wall would find rivers of boiling oil flowing down on them. The archers would then ignite the oil with flaming arrows."

Light from the morning sun flooded the Great Hall as Campbell went straight to the fireplace, which was large enough, over eight feet high, for several men to stand inside. He went inside the fireplace and began feeling the stones with expert fingers. Thirty minutes later, he had found nothing. Suddenly, one of the stones moved and Campbell eased it out. He did the same with a second stone, followed by a third and a fourth. Then he reached inside and pulled out a six-foot long, oblong shaped object covered in canvas and bound with aging leather straps.

"How did you know to look there?" Mattie asked as she took several more exposures.

"Most castles built by Frederick the Great had a hiding place for valuables. Usually it wasn't this close to the fireplace but I noticed yesterday the stone wasn't that thick elsewhere."

Mattie watched, camera working, as Campbell took the package over, placed it in the sunlight streaming in a tall window, undid the leather straps, unrolled the canvas and carefully lifted the lance. "The Spear of Destiny," he said, "At last. Yes, yes, this is the *Heilege* Lance. See the four rows of binding here at the tip. The Roman nail from the Cross at its base?"

Mattie wasn't so sure. "May I see it, please?" Mattie asked and the Professor handed it to her. She inspected the spearhead closely and without nearly the same reverence as Campbell before handing it back to him. She was right. It *had* been too easy.

"Keep looking, Prof. That one's a fake. Just like the one in Vienna."

"I'm quite sure you're wrong," Campbell began. "That is the *Heilege* Lance. I would stake my professional reputation on it."

"Before you do, Geoffrey," Mattie said. "Please look at the spearhead more closely."

Campbell looked carefully at the Spear once more, turning it over in his hands several times. At first, he said nothing, but the crestfallen look on his face spoke volumes. "The bindings. They're too evenly spaced on the spear tip. Above the sheath. On the true spear, the second and third row of bindings are closer to each other than they are to the top and bottom rows. On this one, the bottom three rows are equally separated. I don't know how I could have missed it. I saw what I wanted to see, which is fatal for a scientist. Thank you, Mattie. You saved my reputation. If you hadn't spotted that and I had gone back to civilization and published these results along with the photo...." He shook his head.

"Well," he said, putting the Spear down, "it's a nice souvenir but back to our labors. Let's finish the living quarters and then head back to the chapel."

"Why don't we split up?" Mattie said. "We can cover twice as much ground that way."

"Fine. That's a good idea," Campbell said. "I'll start on the living quarters and you head for the chapel."

60.

The Men in Hoods

THE light of dawn brought visual signals among the Apostles. The SS had separated them into three pairs after they caught Cockran and Sullivan quietly conversing. They had moved them away from the aircraft and bound their feet as well as their hands. Murphy was next to McNamara and Sullivan next to Harmony—each pair guarded by an SS man seated on the forest floor about ten feet away with a cocked Luger aimed in their general direction.

Cockran's back rested awkwardly against a narrow evergreen trunk as he sat beside Rankin, his hands hastily tied behind the back. The bonds around his ankles were loosely tied as well but Cockran had no way of slipping them without detection. He needed a diversion.

Sullivan silently signaled to Cockran with his eyes that his feet were free, but not his hands. No one else had made that kind of progress. Sullivan's feet still appeared to be tied together, but his boots had an awkward bulge a couple of inches above the heel. The bonds were intact, but Sullivan's feet appeared ready to slip out of his boots entirely. Cockran guessed Sullivan was waiting for a distraction—or simply for the moment he actually freed his hands.

Time was growing short. The fourth SS man was off somewhere in the trees. Sullivan sent the same signal again, a slow and deliberate movement of the eyes, accompanied by an audible exhale of breath—his hands were nearly free. Sullivan wouldn't waste time sending the same signal unless something had changed. He was close. There was a stirring in the trees behind him. Cockran could feel it. An otherwise innocuous sound that broke the monotonous tones of the forest. The kind of sound that only becomes recognizable after hours of immersion in an empty forest. Cockran's SS guard noticed it too. He rose to his feet, staring at the trees behind Cockran. He paused. Cockran could see the dilemma in his face, balancing the need to move against causing noise that would hamper his ability to hear that sound deeper in the forest.

Sullivan's guard, the squad leader, spoke up. "Friedrich?"

Friedrich, Cockran's guard, held up a hand to quiet the squad leader as he began walking toward the trees. Cockran looked at Sullivan. This was the opportunity he needed. The other guards kept their attention on Friedrich. Sullivan's legs squirmed as he worked on his bonds, his right palm making headway, sliding between loops.

McNamara's guard noticed and barked a few sharp words at Sullivan, but he ignored them. Cockran watched Friedrich, walk carefully into the trees. Friedrich turned his head back again, once more gesturing to his partners to keep quiet when the back of his skull exploded in a splatter of blood and his tall lean body wilted to the ground. The other SS scrambled to their feet as Sullivan slipped free from his boots and headed towards the SS squad leader just as automatic gunfire erupted from every direction, hitting the SS with a lethal storm of bullets.

Cockran freed his hands and feet and clawed his way around the tree for cover. The roar of gunfire ceased when he reached the tree. He saw Sullivan standing upright, the SS squad leader lifeless in his arms, his pistol now in Sullivan's hands. Three armed men emerged slowly from behind the trees, dressed simply in khakis and mountain gear flecked with twigs and greenery. Hoods concealed their faces in shadow. Automatic rifles held at the ready, they converged on the campsite in a circle. Sullivan swung to face them, still holding the dead SS squad leader under his armpits as an organic shield in front of him, backing up against a tree to keep the gunmen in front of him, the SS guard's Luger trained on the men in hoods.

61.

The Stables

MATTIE knew exactly where she wanted to look and it wasn't the chapel. While she initially had been disappointed when the Professor discovered a spear in the Great Hall, she wasn't surprised to find it was a fake. Whoever made the fake spear in the Hofburg—and it was very good—could easily have made more.

Mattie had been thinking about where to search as she fell asleep after Cockran left her the night before, her slumber blessedly free of nightmares. The Great Hall and the chapel were obvious hiding places. The living quarters were less obvious but if Campbell believed the chapel was a more likely hiding place, he would have gone there first. He didn't. He put all his eggs in the Hohenstaufen tradition of tucking hiding places into the castle's stonework—the Great Hall.

Mattie had concluded, after listening to them on the Orient Express as well as at Weber's villa in Egypt, that the men who were trying to keep her from the Spear were as deeply religious as they were bloodthirsty. Fanatics. So where would religious fanatics hide a sacred religious symbol? Mattie thought she knew. It came to her with the same chilling clarity that she had the morning before about Cockran. She walked through the courtyard, its ground choked with grass and weeds brushing against the tops of her boots, inspecting the low-lying structures along the eastern wall as far away as possible from both the living quarters and the chapel so the odors there would not join the other smells which assaulted the senses of the castle's inhabitants. The stables. Mattie was looking for the castle stables, a fitting location for a sacred relic of the Son of God whose life had commenced in just such a humble location.

Mattie found the stables more easily than she had anticipated. They were not what she expected. Instead of hugging the outer walls, the stables extended out from the walls a good 100 feet at a right angle, openings visible on both sides of its peaked roof to provide cross-ventilation for the stable odors to dissipate in the mountain air, rather than fester and concentrate in an enclosed structure. The wooden doors to the structure were open and severely storm damaged but inside, the sturdy wooden stalls were intact.

Mattie walked through the entire structure, her boots kicking up dust from the dirt floor, the sound of mice skittering away at her approach. There were twenty stalls in all, ten along each side of the structure, but her search revealed nothing. Mattie knew what she was looking for—an oblong canvas package bound with leather straps like the bogus one in the Great Hall.

When Mattie reached the end of the stables, she sat down on a rough wooden bench, opened her canteen and took a long drink of water. She stared back at the stable's entrance, and then she looked up. Two broad beams ran down the center of the structure. They looked considerably older than the beams which formed the peaked roof, and she wondered at their purpose. A flat roof, she thought. Yes, at some point in the long distant past, the stables had a flat roof and these were the two major supports on which the cross beams were placed. When the new roof had been put in, the cross beams had been taken off. But there had been no need, and it probably would have taken too much trouble, to remove the main beams themselves, which were massive, at least a foot and a half, maybe two feet, wide.

Mattie tucked the canteen onto the webbed belt around her waist, and began to slowly walk back through the stables toward the entrance, looking up this time and not to either side as she had earlier. She had just passed the midpoint when she saw something. Up in the rafters, flush against the triangle of stone above the stables' entrance was an object of some kind, barely visible against the stone surface. Mattie was five feet from the stable opening, craning her neck upward. Yes! There was something there! But how could she get up there? The beams were twelve feet high!

Mattie retraced her steps through the stables. Where the hell was a ladder when you needed one? The closest thing she found was a large, rough-hewn cabinet, doors hanging ajar, resting in a corner next to the bench where she had sat moments earlier. She could see shelves inside it. If she could make it to the top of that cabinet, then she could access the nearest main beam and walk down it to the front of the stable.

Okay, Mattie thought, it was a plan. But she also had a tale to tell. She started to plot how her photo story would play out. Boring photographs of the Spear alone wouldn't cut it for Hearst. The Chief wanted suspense, action and adventure. Mattie made a mental note of the earlier photos she had taken and began her usual practice of silently drafting their captions and organizing them into a photo essay narrative.

- *Shot one.* From the lake looking up at the castle: *"At dusk, the battlements of the castle loom high over our campsite."*

- *Shot two.* The castle courtyard from the small end: *"At daybreak, a return to the castle to seek out its secrets."*

- *Shot three.* The Great Hall: *"Sunlight streaming in the broken windows, the search begins."*

- *Shot four.* The fireplace: *"A secret hiding place discovered."*

- *Shots five and six.* The fake spear and spearhead: *"A disappointing discovery of another forgery."*

- *Shot seven.* The exterior of the stable: *"Will the stables hold the sacred spear?"*

Mattie stopped. The sun was streaming in the open windows on either side of the stable. She adjusted the exposure and took several photographs. *Shot eight: "The search continues."*

Mattie slung the leather camera case over her shoulder and tentatively put her good foot on the first shelf. It held as she put her full weight on it, reaching up with her hands, stepping up to the next shelf, and then the next, until at last her hands reached the broad top. She pulled herself up, wincing at the splinters she was acquiring in the process. Once on top of the cabinet, she sat there for a moment and picked the more obvious splinters from her palm and fingers.

Okay, she thought. That damn beam was about three feet away and a foot and a half above her head. She could barely reach it with her hands and hold on, but to get up there after she did so would mean she'd have to swing her right leg up and over. She knew she wouldn't have the upper body strength to pull herself up using her arms alone. If she couldn't do that, she was in for a nasty tumble to the floor below.

What the hell, she thought. Her right ankle and left knee were still sore, but she could feel the adrenalin start to flow. She wasn't going to stop now. She stood up on the top of the cabinet, took a few steps back and then bolted forward, leaping into the air where, to her surprise, the strength of her leap carried the top half of her body onto the beam, her chest on the front edge and her fingers firmly fastened onto the back edge of the beam. In this position, it was just a matter of swinging her right leg up onto the beam, which she did.

Mattie sat astride the foot and a half wide beam, legs spread on either side, and swung the Leica around, taking off the lens cover. She adjusted the aperture, took two more photographs and put the Leica away. *Shot nine.* *"Something sighted in the distance."*

Mattie got to her feet and began walking carefully down the center of the beam, keeping her eyes on the package at the end of the beam, not looking down. Halfway down the beam, she stopped again and took two more photographs. *Shot Ten.* *"Could it be what we are looking for?"* Ahead, there lay a canvas-covered package flush against the stone wall, its six-foot length spanning and supported by the two beams. She stopped, knelt down, opened the Leica's aperture as wide as it would go because there was virtually no light here at the end of the stable, and took two more photographs. *Shot Eleven.* *"Success? What lies inside?"*

Next, she had to lift one end of the six foot long package off of the other beam and bring it back to her beam. She sat there, legs down and over the side and hefted her end of the package. It didn't seem like much. Slowly, she eased the package toward her. It left the other beam and was on the verge of plunging down, but she leaned back with the weight of her body on her end of the package, and slowly pulled it toward her. Soon she had the package securely on her beam. Sliding down the beam toward the far end, she rolled the package away from the stone wall several feet and then moved back over it and sat with her back to the stone wall, catching her breath. After a moment, she stepped back up, then bent over and picked the package up, holding it across her arms. As she did so, a pain shot through her left knee and she felt herself lose her balance and begin to sway to the left. She recovered by using the package as a tightrope walker would to regain her balance.

The next part was tricky. Usually she didn't mess with time exposures or photographs of herself because she was a journalist and not the subject of the story. This time was different. She was certain she had found the Spear of Destiny and she was bloody well going to have a record that she did. James McGary and his only daughter were going to be the heroes of this story. She stepped over the Spear, walked ten feet down the beam, took out the Leica, pulled the strap over her head, snapped off its cover and folded the cover under the camera so that its angle was focused up. She looked through the viewfinder. She decided to set the timer for thirty seconds. That would give her just enough time. It would be a great upward angle shot from below, which would make her look taller. She fished inside her vest pocket for her seldom-used compact and took it out. The light was dim but she saw a smudge on her nose and wiped it off. She tousled her hair, licked her lips, set the timer and moved, walking purposely but carefully back to the package. She stepped over it, turned around and picked it up. She took two steps forward and stared confidently straight ahead, so that the photograph would capture the straight line of her jaw. She had been mentally counting as she walked and waited, three one-thousand, two one-thousand, one one-thousand. Pause. Click. *Shot twelve.* *"Walking back to safety."*

Getting herself and the Spear down from the beam to the top of the cabinet posed no difficulties. Sunlight was streaming in at oblique angles as she placed the package down in one of the streaks of light and opened it, unfastening the leather straps and taking several photographs of the Spear in its package. *Shot thirteen.* *"The Spear revealed."* She moved closer and focused directly on the spearhead and took two more photographs. *Shot fourteen.* *"A closer examination."*

Mattie picked up the Spear and examined it closely in the sunlight. As she did so, a trick of the light made the Spear tip almost seem to glow in her hands. She moved her fingers from the shaft to the spearhead and found it surprisingly warm to the touch, even though it had been in the sunlight for only a few moments. She turned it over and found exactly what she had hoped. The second and third rows of bindings on the Spear tip were close together and equally far apart from the top and bottom rows, looking just as they did in the Hofburg photographs of the original Lance taken by her father. Mattie had no doubt. This was the Spear of Destiny. She fought back tears as she thought *"Papa, this is for you..."*

Mattie quickly rewrapped the Spear and rebound it with the straps. She took it outside into the courtyard, looking around for the most dramatic shot. If she propped it up against the south wall of the stables, she would be able to almost frame it between the northeast and the northwest towers. She would leave the canvas behind it, because it was lighter than the dark stone of the stable wall and would provide a better contrast.

Mattie quickly arranged the canvas and the Spear and experimented with several aperture settings before selecting the one she wanted. Then Mattie waited. The Spear was in shadow now but the sun would soon move across its face and she intended to take a series of photos as the sun struck, first one side of the blade of the spearhead, the full Spear and then the other side, before moving on. A triptych. *Shots fifteen, sixteen and seventeen.. "The afternoon sun illuminates the sacred Spear which mercifully ended the Savior's ordeal on the cross and enabled Him to fulfill His destiny."*

"Thank you very much, *Fraulein*, for going to all this trouble." Mattie was startled to hear Reinhard Hoch's voice as she felt a pistol shoved hard into her right side as he whispered "On behalf of *Reichsfuhrer* SS Heinrich Himmler and my fellow Teutonic Knights, please accept our everlasting appreciation for securing the Spear of Destiny for our *Fuhrer*. As your reward, you will have the high honor to accompany me to our mountain fortress in Wewelsburg where you will be accorded the privilege of participating in our sacred ceremony of consecration."

62.

The New Templars

Castle Lanz
Friday, 12 June 1931

ONE of the gunmen stepped forward, lowered his rifle and pulled the hood back from his head. Dusty gray hair topped his sharp, angular face, a prominent scar below his left eye. "Lower your weapon," the man said. "You would be dead now if that is what we wished."

Sullivan kept his Luger aimed where it was as he let the dead SS man drop to the ground.

"My name is Josef Lanz. I serve with the Lord's grace as Prior of the *Ordi Novi Templi*, the Order of the New Templars." Lanz then shifted his head to one side and lowered his gaze to Harmony. "We are not here to harm you, my dear," he said. "You are safe."

Harmony, relatively calm until now, had clearly been unnerved by the automatic rifle fire. Her eyes held the expression of a trapped animal. She shrank back.

Lanz nodded to his men and they flared out to each of the prisoners, cutting loose their bonds and raising them to their feet. Sullivan kept the Luger pistol firmly in his right hand as his loose bonds were severed, not yet ready to trust these new gunmen.

"Weren't the Templars disbanded and destroyed after the Crusades?" Cockran asked.

Lanz looked at Cockran. "Our enemies thought so. But that was long ago. It was easier to disappear into the shadows than remain an open target. Some leaders were more receptive to our presence than others. Emperor Franz Joseph and his predecessors were among them, and he formally recognized our new order early in this century. The Holy Lance which these Nazi scum and the Kaiser's men seek within the ancient walls of this castle was entrusted to us by the emperor many years ago to keep it from the hands of one who would use it for evil purposes."

"Who was that?" Cockran asked to keep the man talking until he put his pistol away.

"Kaiser Wilhelm. He schemed to acquire the Spear of Destiny before the Great War but we prevented that. Now he seeks to secure it for his son. We will prevent that as well."

"Your castle, I presume?"

"My family's," Lanz answered. "Castle Lanz has served many purposes over the years, most recently as the hiding place of the Holy Spear, but some within the brotherhood have lost their way and failed our Lord." Lanz appeared slightly sad at the words. "We must find a new place to keep it safe as I did before the Great War. The Hohenzollerns are not worthy, but the danger they pose is nothing compared to what my ancestors faced and what we may again face."

"What's that?" Cockran asked, noting the Luger was still pointed at them.

"Bonaparte. Fear of Napoleon is what brought the Spear to Vienna, to the Hofburg where it was placed under Templar protection. My great-grandfather had that honor. But these new men who seek the Spear, these SS who have sworn their allegiance to Hitler, a common Austrian? They may prove the gravest threat of all. They serve the next Bonaparte. I met Hitler before the war. With the Spear, that godless man will start a revolution for a new world order."

"I don't care about the Spear," Cockran said flatly. Hitler's interest in the Spear explained the SS presence here in the mountains and Hoch's infiltration of the expedition, but that didn't concern Cockran. Only one thing mattered. "A woman named Martha McGary and Professor Geoffrey Campbell are a part of that expedition. Before last night, they were completely unaware of the plot to deliver the Spear to the Kaiser. I seek only to rescue them."

"Our interests coincide. We can help you." Lanz said. "The woman has suffered at our hands and we have much to atone for. Campbell is a god-fearing man and a distant brother, a York Rite Mason. He never knew that the Kaiser was behind their search for the Spear." Cockran relaxed as Lanz reholstered his Luger and continued. "Campbell had no way of knowing his special knowledge of the Spear was being perverted to evil ends. Without his knowledge, however, the Spear would not be in such peril from these new barbarians."

"That's your problem, not mine," Cockran replied. "All I want is to rescue the woman. Campbell too, if possible, but the woman comes first. What do you need from us?"

"Your aircraft and your weapons. I have lost many men in the past few days. We are down to our last five and I cannot wait for reinforcements," Lanz said, nodding toward the crimson-streaked, black-garbed bodies, "With these four dead and the two we killed at the Virgental Falls that leaves fifteen SS in control of the castle, including their leader, Hoch. They have killed everyone else, all the Austrians and the other armed Germans. Campbell, the woman and von Sturm were alive an hour ago but we have little time to waste. The woman found the Spear. Now the SS have it and may leave with the Spear at any moment."

"How do you know all this?" Cockran asked.

"This castle has been in my family for generations," Lanz said. "I know the public areas and the secret passageways like the back of my hand." His smile faded. "Two of my men are there now watching. We are in two-way radio contact and your friends were safe when last we checked. Before all this," he said, gesturing toward the dead bodies.

"Please, check again. Now." Cockran asked.

A field telephone was brought forward for Lanz and he picked up the receiver and whispered quietly into it. Then he turned to Cockran. "The woman is being held in the Great Hall with the other two. The SS leader, Reinhard Hoch, and two of his men are there as well. The other twelve SS are in the courtyard or on the ramparts. Based on what we've overheard, they plan to pull out within the hour, some in your aircraft, the others on horseback. They intend to kill your friends before they leave. So, what's it to be? Will you help?"

Cockran retrieved his Webley and nodded. "Let's saddle up."

63.

Heed My Words

"YOU bastard!" Mattie said, spitting out the words. "I'm not going anywhere with you or your Nazi thugs." Mattie shivered as Hoch slowly stroked his Luger down the side of her face.

"Why not? You enjoy being fucked by Nazis. I saw Sturm take you twice. I guarantee that the more Nazis who fuck you, the happier you'll be."

"Kurt's not a Nazi!", Mattie said, repulsed by the thought Hoch had seen her with Kurt.

"Oh, but I assure you he is. One of our 'old fighters' who joined in 1923 before the Munich *putsch*. I'm told he's even a Hitler favorite. But he won't be after I report the kindly feelings he expressed toward the parasite Jews on this expedition. Not that it will matter much to Hitler when he learns that an old fighter perished in a tragic climbing accident in the Alps."

Mattie heard the crackle of automatic weapons in the distance.

"Don't you love the sound of Schmeizers?" Hoch asked. "There are my men now, cleaning up loose ends. They should be here shortly."

Hoch motioned with the Luger toward the Spear. "Wrap it well, my dear."

Mattie knelt down to do so, wincing at the pain in her knee and ankle. Moments later, four men clad in black darted around the corner of the stable from the southeast corner. All four stopped in front of Hoch, snapped to attention and saluted. Hoch casually returned their salutes.

"Report."

"All three Austrians are dead. So is *Herr* von Sturm's man who was left at the camp. The other two we killed in the castle only moments ago."

"Excellent," Hoch said. "But I heard no gunfire earlier."

The leader of the four-man unit grinned. "*Nein*. It was unnecessary," he said, as he removed a large-bladed knife from a sheath strapped onto his leg and held it up for inspection, flecks of blood evident on its polished surface. We cut all their throats like cattle."

"Fine work," Hoch said. "Send the signal for air transport. We will be leaving soon."

Hoch prodded Mattie in the back with his pistol. "Move, *Fraulein* McGary. My men will have captured Professor Campbell and *Herr* von Sturm by now and I want you to watch them die. If you do not wish to share their fate, you should reconsider my invitation to Wewelsburg Castle," he said. "Based on your tryst the other night, I know you like it rough. So do I." he said, and loudly smacked her bum with the flat of his big hand.

Mattie winced at the blow but said nothing, vowing to get even. Reaching the Great Hall, her spirits sank deeper when she saw that Sturm was a captive, his hands bound behind him.

"I told Himmler," Hoch said to Sturm, "that you old fighters were no match for our SS."

Sturm looked at him through cool appraising eyes. "In some things, perhaps," he said and paused for two beats before continuing. "Such as killing chickens and dressing them."

Mattie saw Hoch's face turn red with anger at Sturm's reference to Himmler's former occupation. "Your Jew-loving whore will soon discover I am your better in bed as well as battle." Hoch smiled. "After that, a night servicing the SS is something she won't soon forget."

Sturm's eyes narrowed, his voice low. "Touch her at all, SS man, and your life is forfeit."

Mattie could see Sturm's hands bound behind him as Hoch took two steps forward and slapped Sturm on the side of his face with his open palm, the crack echoing off the stone walls. "You old fighters need to be taught some discipline and manners. You arrogant heirs of

Prussian families look down your noses at other Aryans who are not so high-born. You won't be feeling that way when you witness your whore writhing beneath me."

Sturm's expression did not change. Mattie saw in his face the same ruthless killer she witnessed in Egypt. His voice was still low and cold. "You may heed my words and profit from them. Or ignore them and lose your life. The choice is entirely up to you."

"You are correct, *Herr* von Sturm," Hoch said and then laughed, a loud honking noise. "The choice is entirely mine. But it is not *whether* to have your woman. It's *when* to have her; *where* to have her; and *how* to have her." Hoch then launched a vicious kick at Mattie's left knee and she cried out at the pain, collapsing to the floor. He looked at Sturm. "That ought to make the British bitch easier to mount," he said with a grin.

Mattie writhed in pain but she had been watching closely as Hoch and Sturm exchanged their threats, looking for an opening but not finding one. The two SS idiots beside her were looking at their boss, not her. They had searched her for weapons but not with care, focused more on her chest than the small of her back where she kept her Walther PPK in a holster in her waist band. She knew she could retrieve her Walther and snap off several shots before the others knew what was happening. But she hesitated. Kurt's Luger lay several feet away. Would he be able to rearm himself in the diversion caused by Mattie blasting away? Knowing Kurt, the answer was probably yes. He might well free his hands and reach his weapon. He was that resourceful. But they both might well end up dead, as well, fulfilling Kurt's prophecy of the other night. It wasn't worth it. The odds were not in her favor right now. Cockran and the Apostles were nearby. She would bide her time until Bourke and Bobby came for her.

Mattie didn't realize it until later but, at that moment, she had started to turn the switch in her life back on. One step at a time. She had decided to be patient, not impulsive. She still intended to shoot that bloody bastard Hoch herself but only when the odds turned in her favor. She made a mental note to tell Cockran how she was living up to her new "Better safe than sorry" motto. Assuming, of course, she was still alive to do so when next they met.

64.

Assault on Castle Lanz

BOBBY Sullivan pulled back on the controls and crested the ridge, banking left to begin his approach to Castle Lanz while Cockran and Rankin's two autogiros followed directly behind. Murphy and Lanz sat in the passenger seats in front of Sullivan, chaffing against their ill-fitting, torn and bloodied black SS tunics. Along the southern parapet facing the approach, two black-clad figures could be seen pacing. As they neared, Rankin and Cockran increased speed and drifted in along Sullivan's flanks, headed for the eastern and western walls. On the southern parapet, Sullivan saw one of the SS guards lower his rifle and raise a hand to wave his greeting. Sullivan slowed the autogiro down to about twenty miles per hour, drifting close enough to make out the big smile on the Nazi's face. Bobby Sullivan raised his hand and waved back.

Murphy and Lanz lifted their assault rifles out of the passenger cockpit and leveled them at the two SS guards. Sullivan watched the Nazis' smiling expressions soften to one of confusion. One Nazi raised his Schmeizer machine pistol, but Murphy planted two quick rounds into the SS man's chest, pitching him back off the parapet and into the courtyard below. Beside him, Lanz made quick work of the other guard.

Sullivan watched the Templars seated in Cockran's and Rankin's autogiros strafe the parapets with rapid rifle fire. A lone SS guard squeezed off a few shots before the crossfire cut him down. Cockran and Rankin's autogiros made the wide turn to approach the courtyard. Sullivan lowered his speed to twenty miles per hour and dropped directly into the courtyard. He landed in the center, his momentum carrying him past the stables on his right and towards the Great Hall. He turned the autogiro left as it slowed to a stop just beyond the stables on the eastern wall. Lanz leaped out of the passenger cockpit and raced across the courtyard towards the western wall while Murphy made his way towards the Great Hall. Sullivan arched his neck towards the sky and saw the other two autogiros complete their turn and begin their approach. He needed to keep the courtyard clear of enemy fire so that they could land safely.

Sullivan pulled back the arming slide on his Thompson and edged around the corner of the stable. A man in black emerged form the Great Hall, his Schmeizer at the ready. Sullivan lowered the Thompson and released three controlled bursts of fire, watching the Nazi twist in the air and collapse in a heap.

Sullivan turned back and saw the other two autogiros were over the courtyard, no more than ten seconds from landing. Back towards the southern wall, he spotted another man in black peering through an open doorway into the courtyard. In his current position, the autogiros would land and block his line of fire on the SS man. He raised the Thompson and fired off a couple bursts, hoping to get lucky and catch at least a piece of the Nazi but he didn't.

The bullets cracked loudly off the stone wall surrounding the doorway, forcing the Nazi to lean back out of the doorway. Good enough. Sullivan left the cover of the stables and raced for a wooden wheelbarrow a little further south along the eastern wall. He was about halfway to the wheelbarrow, when the Nazi stepped out of the doorway and lowered his machine pistol. Sullivan dove headfirst over the last few steps to the wheelbarrow and felt a heavy punch in his right arm along with the roar of automatic weapons, twisting him back in the air. He landed on his left side, the Thompson still firmly gripped in his left, his right arm feeling warm and wet. He raised himself to his knees, staying low and remembering exactly where the Nazi had been when he fired. He could hear the Nazi take quick footsteps trying to close the ground and finish him off. Sullivan opened and closed his right hand fiercely, testing what strength remained—it would be enough. Using his left arm to steady the gun, he took the trigger handle back in his right hand again and popped from his crouch, firing immediately. The Thompson barked in his ears as six rounds punched through the Nazi's chest in rapid fashion, lifting him off his feet and landing him flat on his back.

Sullivan dropped to a knee, his right arm growing weaker as the two autogiros landed.

COCKRAN'S autogiro touched down in the courtyard and he steered it towards the Chapel on the western wall, keeping it apart from the other two aircraft. Murphy emerged from behind the cover of a stone well to help Harmony out of the passenger compartment before turning to help the wounded McNamara exit as well. They were dead weight in the assault but they needed to be near if a quick escape was called for. He looked at Cockran. "If the Templars are right, we should have taken care of most of the SS. Lanz says the rest are in the Great Hall. They'll hunt down any stragglers while we take the Great Hall."

"Where's Bobby?" Cockran asked, removing his Webley from its holster. Murphy pointed across the courtyard and Cockran spotted Sullivan sitting with his back against a wheelbarrow, tearing off his shirt-sleeve with a long knife. "You and Rankin get in position to move at the Templar's signal. We'll converge on the Great Hall from both sides."

Cockran turned to Harmony, her face still pale with fear. "Stay here with McNamara by the aircraft. Don't leave him."

McNamara smiled, chambered a round in his weapon, and gripped it firmly in his good hand. He nodded to Cockran and ushered the unresisting Harmony into cover beside the courtyard wall. Cockran sprinted across the courtyard towards Sullivan, who was balling up the cuff of his shirt to stop up the bleeding from a flesh wound in his right arm. Cockran picked up the long fabric of Sullivan's sleeve and wrapped it tightly around the wound. "Is it bad?"

"I've had worse," Sullivan said calmly.

"They got your right arm," Cockran observed.

"The left is just as good." Sullivan said. "Except I can't use the Thompson. Want a try?"

I wouldn't know what to do with it," Cockran said truthfully, and pulled on the shirt threads, tying the knot. "The Big Fella never taught me how to use one."

"We never had enough of them. Mick himself only fired a Thompson one time in training," Sullivan said. Using his patched-up arm, he removed a .45 automatic from his shoulder holster and reached for its twin in the other. "And it's a damned shame, too."

Cockran glanced at Sullivan's right hand, gripping its familiar .45. "Your right hand can't fire a Thompson, but it can handle a .45?"

"It's for back-up. It'll look the part but the left will be doing most of the work."

Sullivan smiled. It meant more Nazis were going to die. Cockran rose to his feet with Sullivan, holding the Thompson. "I'll give Murphy an early birthday present. See you inside."

Cockran rushed off to join Murphy at the northeastern corner of the courtyard, giving him Sullivan's submachine gun. He crouched outside the doorway leading into the castle's interior. Across the courtyard, Sullivan was beside Rankin, ready with his twin .45s. A panicked shout escaping the castle walls preceded the unmistakable sounds of automatic gunfire as the Templars began their grisly work. Cockran ran through the open doorway, Murphy following.

Inside, Cockran saw Sullivan and Rankin poised at the westernmost entrance to the Great Hall. He and Murphy peeled off and ran towards the easternmost. Trailing his left hand along the stone walls of the castle's interior, Cockran led with his revolver through an archway and into the Great Hall, followed by Murphy, who opened up with the Thompson. The noise was incredible, the air clouded with flying debris, but Cockran saw one SS man quite clearly. He stood firing behind an overturned wooden table at Lanz and another Templar who had improbably poured out of a concealed opening on the northern wall. The SS man suddenly swung his head towards Cockran, his Bergmann SMG slow to follow. Cockran fired once, twice—each bullet punching through his chest and knocking him back into the table legs.

Sullivan fired rapidly across the hall with the .45 in his left hand, the pistol in his right hand held low at his hip. The automatic gunfire faded suddenly, normal sound returning as Sullivan swung to one side, leading

with the pistol to his left. His gun was trained on the crouched figure of
Reinhard Hoch, hiding behind another upturned table at the southern
wall. The gunfire had been silenced and even Sullivan was not firing,
though he had Hoch easily within his sights.

Then Cockran saw why. Across the room, against the northern wall,
a man held a gun to Mattie's head, shouting in German. The hooded
Lanz was the only man whose weapon was trained on the Nazi. Sturm
and Campbell, their hands bound, were on the floor beside them.

Sturm's voice cut sharply through the SS man's shouts. "He's
ordering you to drop your weapons or Mattie dies."

The Nazi's eyes swung wildly, his voice raising in volume, exhorting
each man in the room to drop their weapons. Mattie did not look
panicked. In fact, she looked angry. The Nazi shoved the pistol against
her temple, shouting louder, as Mattie winced.

Cockran quickly glanced at Sullivan who gave him a barely
perceptible nod. The Irishman was assuring him that the situation was
under control. "Do it," Cockran said. "Do as he says." Cockran knelt to
the ground, lowered his weapon and saw Murphy and Rankin doing the
same. The other Templar looked confused and turned to Lanz for
instruction, but Lanz's weapon remained trained on Mattie and her
captor.

"Lanz!" Cockran shouted. "You gave me your word!" That damn
zealot was going to get Mattie killed. "Lower your weapon or he'll kill
the woman!"

Lanz did not take his eyes off the Nazi holding Mattie and the other
Templar did not lower his weapon. "The Spear is paramount, *Herr*
Cockran. It must not fall into their hands!"

"Lanz!!" he shouted again, as the stand-off smoldered. In the corner
of his eye, Cockran saw Sullivan kneeling to the ground and lowering
one gun with his wounded right arm but keeping the gun in his left hand
level. Cockran saw in his eyes what the earlier nod had conveyed.
Sullivan was not going to be disarmed. Someone was going to die and it
better not be Mattie or Lanz would be a dead man too.

Cockran shouted again to keep the Nazi's attention off Sullivan and
stall the two Templars. "Lanz! You gave your word! Your word as a
man of God!" Lanz took a sharp intake of breath, the automatic rifle

easing into his shoulder. The Nazi's eyes were riveted on Lanz. Then a single shot rang out and blood from the Nazi's head splattered the castle wall behind him. A thick red hole rested just above his eyes. A wisp of smoke escaped from the barrel of the .45 in the still-kneeling Sullivan's left-hand, which he slowly turned until it was pointing directly at Reinhard Hoch.

Hoch had already dropped his weapon, his hands held high in the air. He spoke German and English interchangeably, but the English was crystal clear. "Please! Please! Don't shoot me! Allow me to explain, please!"

Cockran watched Lanz and the other Templars quietly leave the Great Hall while Sullivan rose his feet and closed the short distance from Hoch, his trusted .45s held firmly in both hands.

"Please! I beg of you! Allow me to explain!" Hoch shouted again.

"Explain it to the river man," Sullivan said. "On your way to hell."

65.

The Great Hall

MATTIE caught her breath. It had happened so quickly. One minute she was a captive and barely able to put any weight on her knee thanks to Hoch; the next, her captor was laying at her feet, eyes wide, staring straight up, with a bullet hole in his forehead. Sullivan was every bit as deadly as Sturm. While Sullivan freed Sturm and Campbell's bonds, Cockran cut the ropes which bound Mattie's wrists.

Mattie embraced him and held tight. "Thank you," she whispered. "I love you." Just then, she heard automatic weapons fire outside. "Who is that? I thought all of you were here."

"Our new and temporary allies, sworn to safeguard the Spear," Cockran replied, as the gunfire abruptly ceased. "They were outnumbered by the SS and needed our autogiros as a distraction. They're the same ones who attacked you two days ago and earlier in Egypt."

Cockran paused and spoke to Sullivan. "Keep Hoch over there in the corner by the fireplace, his face to the wall. Lanz's men had the same success against the SS as we did."

"*Josef* Lanz?" Mattie asked. "That's who you were shouting at? I couldn't see his features because of the hood. That man tried to kill me on the Orient Express. He beheaded a man in Egypt. A European, someone he knew well. It was horrible."

Cockran looked around but Lanz and the other Templar had not returned. "I'm afraid so," Cockran replied. "After Lanz rescued us from the SS, it's not as if we had much choice."

"But who *are* they?" Mattie asked as she held onto Cockran for support.

"Templars. According to Lanz, the Order of the New Templars was formally recognized in Austria in 1905 by Emperor Franz Joseph, but they trace their lineage back to the Crusades. The Austrian branch of the Templars took the Templar gold from France in the fourteenth century, moved it to this remote location and literally built this castle around the gold."

"You mean there's gold hidden in the castle as well as the Spear?" Mattie asked.

Cockran laughed. "I asked Lanz the same thing. He said the gold had long since been moved to a bank in Switzerland controlled by the New Templars."

"What's going to happen to the Spear now?" Mattie asked.

"Neither the Kaiser nor Hitler are going to have it. Lanz made it clear that much is certain," Cockran replied.

"You mean there's still a chance…." Mattie began, but was suddenly cut off by Professor Campbell's cry of horror.

"Oh, my god! This is terrible! Not again. Oh, my god!"

Mattie turned to a terrified Professor Campbell, standing by a window overlooking the courtyard. They all moved over there to join him, Hoch prodded forward by Sullivan, Mattie limping along.

Mattie looked through the stained glass windows of the Great Hall. Many of the windows were already broken from the harsh alpine winters, more now from the recent gunfire. The carnage below was almost indescribable. Three SS men were sprawled around the courtyard, their black-uniformed bodies carrying the marks of multiple bullet wounds. But that wasn't what had caused Campbell to cry out in horror. Four men, some wounded but still alive, were on their knees, their heads held back by two of the warrior monks, exposing their necks, while Lanz stood in front of them, his sword held in two hands. Harmony and McNamara were nowhere to be seen.

Mattie turned away from the window and buried her head in Cockran's chest. "I can't watch this again, Bourke. It's so grotesque. Like something out of the middle ages." Moments later, she looked again and saw the two templars hold the four heads high, one in each hand as Lanz shouted "You will all burn in hell, you Godless vermin!" but only the fourth SS man's eyes were still open, blinking once at Lanz's words before his eyes also rolled up in his head. Moments later, all four heads were casually thrown to the ground in a haphazard fashion while Lanz wiped clean the blade of his sword on the uniform of his first victim before returning it to its scabbard.

Mattie lifted her head from Cockran's chest. Everyone else's eyes were still focused on the bloody scene in the courtyard below. Campbell had a horrified look on his face while Cockran and Sturm betrayed no emotion. Neither did Sullivan whose twin Colt .45s were trained on Sturm and Hoch, the latter looking as if he had seen a ghost. His face was white, his eyes were wide and the smell of urine told Mattie he had wet himself in fear.

Sullivan was the first to speak, turning towards Cockran. "Shouldn't I be taking these two down there before Brother Lanz puts away his sword?"

Mattie was chilled. "You can't let them do that, Bourke! Kurt saved my life and Lanz is a merciless man who tried to kill me on the Orient Express."

Cockran's eyes narrowed at this but he remained silent. She knew exactly how bad it looked to be pleading for the life of her most recent lover with the man she really loved. But she couldn't bear to have Kurt's blood on her hands. "Whatever happened was my fault. You can't let them kill him."

Cockran looked at her. "I won't. He saved your life. That's good enough for me." His voice betrayed no emotion.

"Have no concern on my account, *Fraulein* McGary," Sturm said. "If you allow me to retrieve my pistol," he said, looking at Cockran, "I will take my chances with these Templars."

Mattie turned back towards Cockran to see his reaction to Sturm's statement.

"Mattie tells me you were a German naval officer. Is that correct?" Cockran asked.

Sturm nodded. "I was once a naval officer."

"If I return your weapon, do I have your word as an officer that you will convey this scum here," he said, nodding at Hoch "to the appropriate authorities in Munich for trial?"

"If that is what you wish. But I offer no guarantee as to what the authorities in Munich may do with him. The SS have many friends in high places."

Cockran nodded. "I appreciate your candor. But I have in mind a specific person into whose custody I wish Hoch to be delivered. Captain Jacob Weintraub of the Munich Police."

Sturm nodded. "I've heard of this *Käpitan* Weintraub. A Jew. The 'last honest man in Munich' by reputation."

"You know him?" Cockran asked.

"*Nein.* I know of him and his reputation. Yes, you have my word as a German officer that I will deliver *Herr* Hoch to *Käpitan* Weintraub."

"Fine," Cockran said. "Bobby, keep your eye on Hoch while *Herr* von Sturm retrieves his weapon."

Mattie tugged at Cockran's sleeve. "Bourke, can we talk?" pulling him away.

"What is it?"

"Well…. I feel disloyal because Kurt did save my life and, since he gave you his word, I believe he'll keep it. But there's something you should know about him."

"Go on." Cockran said, his voice still cold.

"I think he's a Nazi. One of the old fighters who was a member before the Beer Hall *putsch* in 1923. I mean, he's nothing like Hoch but he's a party member. I'm sure of it."

"But you do trust him to keep his word?" Cockran asked.

"I do."

"Good, because we don't have many options anyway. You and Professor Campbell are flying out of here with us. Come on," Cockran said, pulling her by the arm, "let's go ask him. Our only alternative is to let Sullivan or Lanz execute Hoch."

Sturm admitted he was a Nazi but once more gave his word. Mattie could see that Cockran believed him. Still, she was not surprised when he asked "Would you mind if I had Brother Lanz have two of his monks accompany you? Even if you bind him, several nights alone with Hoch are not optimum conditions."

Sturm nodded. "So long as I have my weapons, I have no objection."

Sullivan tied Hoch's hands firmly behind him as Lanz returned from the blood-soaked courtyard and its four headless SS corpses. Mattie watched as Professor Campbell made straight for Lanz and, drawing him aside, engaged him in a spirited conversation with many gestures as he talked earnestly to him for a good five minutes. When he was finished, both Lanz and Campbell approached her.

Lanz bowed to Mattie. "I apologize, *Fraulein* McGary, for my un-Christian behavior that night on the Orient Express. I knew that Professor Campbell was a believer and that he was a member of a brother order in Scotland. But he did not know he was being used as a cats-paw for the Kaiser and I could not take the risk that this time the Kaiser might be successful in claiming the Spear for the Hohenzollerns. Professor Campbell has persuaded me that removing the sacred symbol of Our Savior's ultimate sacrifice from the European continent would be in the best interests of everyone. That such evil men as the SS have attempted to take the Spear from us is proof that it will be safer in England than it is here in Austria. That Gaius Cassius Longinus is also buried in Great Britain makes it all the more fitting that the Spear of Destiny should at last be reunited with its original owner."

Lanz turned away and then hesitated before turning back to Mattie. "There is something else I need to tell you. Over ten years ago, one of our own committed a grave injustice against your family. The Templars did not order it nor did we condone it. But your father died because one of our brothers feared he was too close to discovering the secret of the Spear. Please accept my deepest regret. Your father was a brave and holy man, a true scholar of biblical times. Hans Weber, the man responsible for his death, was expelled from our Order for his sin. It was fitting that you saw him die at my hands in Alexandria. Delivering the Spear of

Destiny to your father's homeland cannot excuse his murder but I ask you to accept it in his memory."

Mattie's mind was numb at revelation of her father's death as Lanz knelt, picked up the Spear in both hands and, staying on his knees, offered it to Mattie who accepted it wordlessly, still reeling from shock. Oh my God, she thought, recalling Professor Campbell's story about her father writing the Hofburg for recent photographs of the Spear after he first heard Campbell's theory. My father lost his life because he tried to find the truth about the Spear!

Mattie blinked back tears as she once more saw her father's smiling face, his gray hair and the twinkle in his eye whenever he called Mattie his little princess, his little Highland Princess. The father she would never see again. And then, she could blink back her tears no longer. They streamed down her face as she felt Cockran's strong arms embrace her and she continued to cry thinking only of all the years she had missed with her father and all the years she hoped she would have ahead with the man holding her.

66.

Tristan

Munich
Monday, 15 June 1931

WINSTON Churchill hosted a celebration two days later in Munich in a private dining room at the Hotel *Vier Jahreszeiten* where his party was staying. The chandeliers were crystal; the champagne Pol Roger and the food superb. Caviar to start, followed by Dover sole, and roast duckling. A new wine with each course. Mattie smiled as she recalled hearing what one of Churchill's friends had said. "Winston's tastes are simple. He is easily satisfied with the best."

It had taken nearly two days of flying to bring Mattie and Cockran to a private aerodrome near Munich, where Churchill and Paddy eagerly awaited news of their adventure. Paddy had hugged them both and then sat with his eyes wide as Mattie told the story of her quest for the Spear, carefully editing for his young ears all the blood, violence and romance. Mattie's number one fan hung on her every word. With Paddy tucked in bed by nine, Cockran and Mattie joined Churchill and Rankin for dinner.

At Mattie's request, Harmony had not been invited. Which was just as well since she had more or less kept to herself since their return to Munich. Mattie had been surprised to see Harmony with Cockran and the Apostles on their rescue mission. Tagging along to a firefight in the Alps did not fit with Mattie's image of an art historian. But it clearly had not been her cup of tea and Mattie took grim satisfaction in Harmony's shell-shocked appearance on their journey back to Munich. She told

Cockran all that Harmony had said to persuade her the two of them were lovers and he had agreed with her plea not to confront her over it. "I don't want the bitch to have the satisfaction of knowing that she put one over on me."

Churchill stood and raised his champagne flute. "To a most successful fortnight," Churchill paused, a small smile on his cherubic face. "All went according to plan."

"Plan? Winston, to whose plan are you referring?" Cockran asked.

Churchill smiled. "Mine, of course. Thanks to you, the late Sir Archibald's company has been made safe from the Nazis and, thanks to Mattie and her employer Mr. Hearst, the Spear of Destiny will soon be resting securely in the British Museum. Those were my hopes for which I made plans. And they have been fulfilled. Foiling the assassination of Hindenburg by depriving the Kaiser and his son of the Spear was an unexpected bonus. Using violence to achieve political goals is incompatible in any liberal democracy, including the Weimar Republic. So, let us be of good cheer."

Cockran laughed. "I'll drink to that."

At evening's end, Mattie was torn. Her knee was stiff and swollen from Hoch's kick and all she wanted to do was take two aspirin and go to bed. She was still trying to process and come to grips with her father having been murdered over the Spear. She really wasn't up to talking with Cockran about Kurt even though this was their first night back in civilization. It had been hard enough telling him what Harmony had said. She would have forgiven him for sleeping with Harmony because she had done the same with Kurt. Now there was no reciprocity, only her guilt. She had not been able to work out how and when she would tell him. She had tried twice in the Alps but he put her off. She would have to try again, soon. Their future—if they still had a future—depended on it.

She had asked Winston for his advice earlier in the day. He was the closest thing to a father figure left in her life and she needed—badly needed—someone to talk to. So she had told him everything. Her fights with Cockran. Jumping to the wrong conclusion about Harmony. And, most humiliating of all, her brief affair with Kurt. "I've tried to discuss with Bourke what went on between me and Kurt and what I was feeling. I wanted to have it out in the open."

Churchill pursed his lips but said nothing.

"But Bourke won't let me tell him. He just takes me in his arms, kisses me, and says we should leave the past in the past and focus on our future."

"Wise advice, I would think, my dear," Winston said.

"But I feel so *guilty*."

"It seems to me he's forgiven you for any, ah, *indiscretions*, you may have committed."

Mattie sighed. "I guess so. Maybe. No, not really. He says there's nothing to forgive. An innocent misunderstanding he calls it." Mattie let out a short laugh. "But there was nothing innocent about it. Maybe I'm asking too much. But I wish he would talk about his feelings."

"His feelings for you? Or his feelings about you and *Herr* von Sturm?" Winston asked.

"Both. But really the latter. He's very open about the other, how much he loves me."

"Well then, my advice is to leave well enough alone. You two seem to have survived what in the long run you may look back on as merely a small bump in the road of your romance. These things may happen. Take them as they come. Dread naught. All will be well."

Easy enough for Churchill to say. Would he be so calm if Clemmie had cheated on him? She didn't think so. But Mattie still had no viable plan to bring everything out in the open. She was relieved, therefore, when Cockran begged off their being together that night. He was limping pretty badly with his banged-up hip and its new stitches put in that day and they had each promised the other a rain check when they healed, maybe even by tomorrow night, Cockran had said with a wink. Mattie hoped she could come up with a new approach by then.

HARMONY awaited her lover's arrival. They had been separated for over two weeks and every moment spent apart had been agony. But always, she had done what she had been told and gone where she had been directed. She had even saved his life during that horrible night of terror in Munich. Soon he would be here and she would have her reward. She heard a knock on the door and opened it to see her lover, Reinhard Tristan Hoch, in all his black-booted SS glory.

"Hurry," she said, "before anyone sees you," as she pulled him inside and closed the door behind him. I knew you would come, just as you promised," she said as she eagerly embraced him, pulling her hero, her Tristan, towards the bed. "Your Isolde is ready."

67.

All I Care About Is Mattie

Munich
Tuesday, 16 June 1931

RISING from bed felt like rising from the dead, Cockran thought, his body heavy with sleep, his hip hurting even more than the night before. Mattie had quickly agreed with his suggestion that they sleep in separate rooms to give their wounds time to heal. And for that he was grateful as he had meant it literally as well as figuratively. They had not had much chance to be alone together and he feared that once they were, she would attempt to complete the confession she had started in the Alps about Sturm. What was it with women anyway? The odds were great that she wanted to tell him she had an affair with Sturm after Harmony had duped her and she felt guilty. He could understand that. He felt guilty himself about how close he had come to the same thing with Harmony in Munich. But he sure as hell didn't want to talk about it. It was in the past and it couldn't be changed. As far as he was concerned, talking about it would *not* make things better. Leave the past behind and move on. That was what guys did. It hurt him that Mattie had fallen for another man in a moment of weakness but they still loved each other and all he wanted now was get her out of Germany and as far away from that blond Nazi bastard as possible.

Only the prospect of a breakfast date in his room with Mattie at 8:30 a.m. could lure him out of bed and into the shower. He called in the order for room service at eight. The food came late, at twenty to nine. Mattie did not come at all.

Cockran placed a call to her room at nine o'clock, but there was no answer. He began to be concerned at a quarter past nine when Mattie still hadn't arrived. By nine thirty, Cockran stood outside Mattie's room as the tall and wiry hotel manager unlocked the door and pushed it open. "Oh! *Mein Gott!!*" the manager shouted in a broken voice. Cockran charged into the room and shoved the man aside.

Blood. There was blood everywhere. Pooled in murky brown beneath the headless body of a hotel bellman sprawled on the sofa. Splotched in dark stains along the carpet. Moving through the sitting room to the bedroom, he saw the blood was sprayed against the white sheets of Mattie's bed. The bellman's severed head lay propped on a pillow.

"Call the police!" Cockran shouted. The hotel manager said nothing, leaning against the door frame where Cockran had shoved him earlier, his face drained of color. "Call the police!" Cockran shouted again, getting the manager's attention. The manager stared back, slowly processing Cockran's words. Cockran pointed towards the phone that rested on a small table next to a desk chair and spoke again. "Call the police. Ask for Captain Weintraub."

The manager nodded and moved to the phone. Cockran scanned the room quickly from right to left, from the leather club chairs and bloody sofa by the window over to the door leading to the bedroom. He went through the open door and then into the bathroom beyond and found nothing. Nothing. There were no signs of Mattie. Or the Spear.

Cockran left the bathroom and went back into the bedroom where he saw a sheet of paper lying next to the bellman's head in a spot he had not seen from the other side of the room.

Herr Cockran,

My apologies but the safety of the Holy Spear is paramount and anyone who places it in jeopardy—man or woman—will be dealt the ultimate justice of the Lord. This hotel employee who attempted to stand in our way should serve as vivid proof of the strength of our convictions.

The Spear must remain hidden and I have determined to do so. Your woman is safe and the other woman as well. Only you can place them in jeopardy now by making any attempt to find them. When the Spear is safely hidden again, they will be returned to you, unharmed. By the Word of God, I beseech you— do nothing and wait for their safe return.

Josef Lanz

Cockran let the note fall from his hands. Lanz! The Templars! Why hadn't he spent the night with Mattie? This never would have happened if he had been there.

"*Herr* Cockran!" The hotel manager said. He held the telephone receiver to his chest.

"Is that Weintraub?" Cockran said, crossing the room. "Give him to me."

"No, *Herr* Cockran," the manager said. "*Kapitan* Weintraub is dead."

"AND the Spear?" Professor Campbell asked, the tension in his voice clear.

They had all gathered in the sitting room of Churchill's suite. Churchill sat in a leather chair, chewing on his cigar, deep in thought. The red-bearded figure of Rankin stood next to him. Campbell shifted uneasily in his own chair, his eyes red and fixed upon Cockran who stood beside Sullivan. Harmony, they learned after a brief inspection of her room, was also missing, presumably kidnapped along with Mattie— the "other woman" Lanz referred to.

"Sod the Spear," Cockran said. "It's gone and good riddance. All I care about is Mattie."

Cockran's conversation with the Munich police had been brief. Captain Weintraub had apparently hung himself in his office yesterday evening; a suicide note spoke of overwhelming guilt about his own personal corruption. The suicide note tidily pinned most, if not all, of the Nazi V-men's obstructionist activity upon Weintraub. Supposedly, he also despised the fact that he was a Jew. For Cockran, that was proof enough that Weintraub had been murdered. It was confirmed moments later when Cockran inquired as to the whereabouts of one Reinhard Tristan Hoch. There was a long pause before he was told that Hoch had been released for lack of evidence shortly after Weintraub's death.

Professor Campbell held his head in his hands. "This couldn't be worse. I have lost the Spear and Professor McGary's daughter! It wasn't supposed to happen this way!"

"Nothing ever happens the way you expect it," Churchill said calmly from his chair. "To fret over such an obvious condition does nothing to alter it. Action this day, gentlemen. We must think of solutions and act. Where could she have been taken?" The rest of the room was silent. "Bourke, do you have any faith in what the Munich police have told you?"

Sullivan answered first. "I wouldn't trust them if they told me the Pope was Catholic."

Rankin's Scottish accent sounded out from behind Churchill. "A corrupt police force is an incompetent police force," Rankin said, with an authority that bespoke his Scotland Yard credentials. "They are good for little else than pocketing bribes. When it comes to real police work, they can't tell their elbows from their arseholes." He paused, lowering his head. "If you'll pardon my French. Lanz may be a fish the Nazis find worth catching, but the police won't be the ones who reel him in."

"Sergeant Rankin is correct," Churchill said. "We cannot rely on the police to find this Lanz or his Templars."

Professor Campbell looked up from his hands. "Do you think we can accept this Templar's word that he has taken them only to prevent us from following? That he will return the women unharmed? Could he be sincere?"

"Unlikely," Rankin said. "Why would he kidnap Miss Hampton, as well? If insurance was truly the only reason Mattie was kidnapped, then there would be no reason to kidnap Miss Hampton. Certainly, Miss Hampton is a lovely young lady, but who among us finds a stronger attachment to her than to Mattie?" No answer greeted him. "My point exactly. If his note is genuine, Lanz already has his insurance with Mattie. Why take Miss Hampton also?"

"Who cares?" Cockran said, agitated. "We must assume the worst. You've seen the rituals these men engage in. Can you find any logic behind it? They beheaded a bellhop in the name of the Lord's 'ultimate justice,' for Christ's sake!" he said, consciously emphasizing the common profanity.

Churchill raised a hand and shot Cockran a hard glance, much like the glances he received when they argued about Irish politics nearly a decade ago. Cockran knew Winston wasn't much of a believer either, but he knew when Churchill was telling him he had gone too far. His father—who was a believer—would have done the same thing. With the same glance.

"Excusing Bourke for his understandably strained emotions, the point, my dear Professor Campbell, is that it would be wrong to assume the Templars mean no harm to Mattie. We cannot leave her fate to the hands of men who have already betrayed us more than once." Churchill rose out of his chair and walked into the center of the room, drawing on his cigar, gathering his thoughts. "There is something else, another peculiarity surrounding these events that deserves our scrutiny. Sergeant Rankin? Tell us what you found in your inspections of the two rooms—more to the point, tell them what struck you as odd about the crime scenes."

Rankin took in a deep breath, expanding his barrel of a chest. "To start with, there were no signs of a break-in at Mattie's room. That means that her abductors were welcomed into the room by Mattie herself."

"And the other room?" Churchill prompted.

"Miss Hampton's room did show signs of a break-in. But, although there were also signs of a struggle within the room, most of that struggle was spent carefully knocking over tables and chairs, creating an artificial tableau."

"What do you mean?" Campbell asked.

"I mean that there was no struggle," Rankin said. "The room was carefully made to appear as if there had been, but Miss Hampton did not struggle *with* anybody. The crime scene was staged."

Cockran watched while Churchill smiled slowly, as though the pieces were starting to fall together. Professor Campbell, however, continued to look perplexed, as if he were trying to wrap his mind around Rankin's detective work.

Sullivan placed a soft hand on Cockran's shoulder. "Stay here, Bourke. I'll be back in a few hours."

Cockran turned to face Sullivan, whose face was hard and determined. Sullivan had a plan. "Where are you going?"

"Never you mind," Sullivan said. "Stay with Churchill. I've heard enough. I'm going to pay a visit to an old friend."

68.

The Hotel Belonged to Us

BOBBY Sullivan was impatient. Once he heard Rankin's analysis of Harmony's room, he thought he knew who was behind Mattie's kidnapping. Maybe he was getting the hang of this detective businesss after all.

Sullivan sat on a crowded bench in a noisy hallway not far from the primary booking area in the Munich police headquarters, reading a day-old copy of *The Times*. No one stopped to ask why he was there. Sullivan's spot was carefully chosen, two doors down from the offices of the Chief of Police, where Deputy Prosecutor Eric Schmidt was in conference. Schmidt was the young lawyer who had been discovered lying unconscious on the street a week back, with multiple wounds and peculiar photos and hospital bills attached to his clothing.

Sullivan had not told Cockran, but he had asked one member of the Apostles, Ronan, to stay in Munich and keep up surveillance on V-men like Schmidt after he and Cockran had left town. Sullivan had caught up with Ronan after they had returned to Munich. According to Ronan's notes, the young prosecutor had become a recluse in his stylish Munich apartment since his little mishap. His broken nose was still swollen and his right arm was in a sling. The beating his kidneys received had apparently weakened his bladder, forcing him to visit the loo a couple of times every hour. He had returned to work sparingly in the last several days, and on the occasions when he did leave the comforts of his home, he only went to two places—his law offices and police headquarters. Nowhere else. Tailing him had not been difficult.

Glancing inside the doorway, Sullivan knew it was only a matter of time before nature came to call on young Schmidt. Sullivan turned a page of the paper to keep up the act. There was no way he could have told Cockran what he planned to do. With Cockran there was always a risk he would insist on near certainty before agreeing to utilize Sullivan's preferred methods. And in this case, Cockran would have a point. Reasoning his way through it, there was no way to rule out the Templars and point the finger solely at the SS for Mattie's kidnapping. But there were too many unexplained coincidences. Weintraub murdered; Hoch released last night; and Mattie's very real kidnapping immediately followed by Harmony's staged "kidnapping".

Frankly, Sullivan had his doubts about Miss Harmony Hampton. He had warmed to her at first. She was a fine looking young woman who seemed genuinely frightened. But, with hindsight, there were too many question marks. The SS had known exactly where to ambush them in landing spots chosen in Harmony's presence. And, despite her earlier kidnapping by the SS, she was remarkably unconcerned when she was recaptured by them in the mountains.

The Chief of Police's office door opened and a young woman stepped out, holding the door as Schmidt followed slowly behind her, nodded his appreciation and turned down the hallway towards Sullivan. He waited until Schmidt had passed him, headed for the lavatory, then rose to follow him, leaving the paper behind.

Inside the lavatory, a middle-aged policeman was scrubbing his hands at a sink. Schmidt passed into the far stall, pushing the wooden door closed behind him. Sullivan walked slowly behind the policeman to wash up in the adjacent sink. Keeping his head down to obscure his face, Sullivan saw the policeman finish up and leave without tossing him so much as a glance. Sullivan picked up a mop from the corner and jammed its long pole through the lavatory door handle. Then he reached inside his coat with his right hand to remove a knife, feeling a mild twinge of pain. His right arm still worked, but not with the same strength as the left. With a strong kick, he broke the flimsy lock on the stall door, knocking the young lawyer against the back wall, his pants down around his ankles. With his right forearm, Sullivan pinned the man against the wall, pressing the flat of the blade firmly against his neck with his left hand.

"Good afternoon," he said. Schmidt began jabbering in German, but Sullivan cut him short. "Knock it off. I know you speak English, so I'll start by cutting this artery right here if I hear another word of German. Cries for help will only speed the process. Understand?"

Schmidt nodded carefully, fully conscious of the razor sharp blade on his neck.

"I know you had Weintraub killed. I know you arranged to spring Hoch out of jail. Tell me what happened to the girls in the Hotel *Vier Jahreszeiten.*"

Schmidt's eyes opened wide. "Girls? I … I don't know who you are referring to…."

Sullivan applied greater pressure on the blade, drawing a thin drop of blood where the blade edge broke the skin. "I won't ask again. Tell me about the kidnapped girls."

Schmidt's breathing became rapid and panicked. "*Ja!*" he said and quickly corrected himself. "Yes! Okay! Please relieve the pressure of your knife. I might cut myself if I speak."

"Isn't that a pity?" Sullivan said. "You'll talk the way you are. Start with last night."

"Yes, okay," Schmidt panted. "I secured *Herr* Hoch's release on the basis of a lack of evidence. Afterwards, I escorted him to a clandestine meeting of the SS in Munich." Schmidt paused. "I…I was asked to attend, though I must assure you I'm *not* a member of the SS."

Sullivan waited and lessened the pressure on his knife. Encouraged by this, Schmidt continued in a firmer voice. "The English woman was working with Hoch. She would help gain access to the Scottish woman's room where *Herr* Himmler's coveted Spear was being held. They… they intended to behead someone—it didn't matter who—so as to make the abduction appear to have been committed by others. But I took no part in these activities!"

"Where have they taken the women?"

"I don't know. I swear I don't know. They didn't tell me. I'm not SS."

"You were there for a reason." Sullivan said. "Give me the reason."

"All he asked was that we remove all police forces from the area of the hotel in which the women were lodged and that all hotel security people be given the night off."

"How did you do that?" Sullivan asked. "You don't own the hotel."

"The hotel belonged to us. Just as most of Munich belongs to us." Schmidt said, his confidence rising. "Now, the Spear of Destiny is ours and soon, all of *Deutschland* as well."

Sullivan pulled the blade back from Schmidt's neck and transferred it into his stronger left hand. "Us? You mean the Nazis? But didn't you say you weren't a Nazi?"

Schmidt rubbed his neck and continued to speak with confidence. "No, I didn't. I'm a party man and proud of it. I'm just not SS. They're lunatics. I'm a German patriot."

Sullivan smiled, a thin-lipped smile under cold blue eyes that no sane man ever wanted directed at him. "And by party, you mean the Nazi Party?"

Schmidt nodded and quickly added, "But not SS.".

Wrong answer. "'Tis a distinction lost on a boy from County Mayo," Sullivan said, reaching out with his right hand to cover Schmidt's mouth. Before Schmidt realized what was happening, the knife had sliced deep into the lawyer's throat, severing the carotid artery, Sullivan taking care that the spurting blood from the convulsing body was directed away from him.

Sullivan watched with disinterest as the lawyer died. It took less than thirty seconds for Schmidt's heart to fail and the life to fade from his eyes. Sullivan left him seated on the toilet, his pants still down around his ankles. Sullivan closed the stall door behind him and moved to the sink to rinse the blade and wipe the blood off his shoes. Without a backward glance, he pulled the mop from the door, left the bathroom and blended in with the people walking in the hallway. Bobby Sullivan really didn't like Nazis.

69.

And I Have the Key

KURT von Sturm's arrival at Churchill's suite of rooms was unexpected. The handsome, blond German stood composed and business-like facing the cool stares from the men there. "I am sorry to disturb you, gentlemen," Sturm said. "But I have urgent news concerning *Herr* Reinhard Hoch."

For Cockran, the presence of Mattie's likely lover was as unnecessary as it was unwelcome. He hoped he had seen the last of Sturm back in the Alps. Cockran waved his hand dismissively. "If you've come to tell us that Captain Weintraub has been murdered and Hoch released from jail, save your breath. We already know and we have more pressing matters."

"My apologies," Sturm said, his face revealing no reaction to Cockran's comment. "I had not realized the news had spread so fast. Permit me to ask what matter could possibly be more pressing than bringing *Herr* Hoch to justice?"

"Rescuing Mattie," Cockran said harshly. "She was kidnapped this morning."

Cockran watched the German's eyes narrow in response to the news as he explained what had happened—the blood, the note from Lanz, and their doubts concerning Harmony's abduction. As Cockran spoke, Sturm's genuine concern was obvious in his eyes. Mattie had been right. The Nazi bastard really cared for her and had never intended to kill her, despite indications to the contrary within the dossier Joey Thomas died delivering to Cockran.

"I am most sorry to hear this news," Sturm said slowly, as though straining to control his voice. "I feel responsible for Miss McGary's fate because I agreed to allow her on the expedition. These are merciless men who have taken her. You have my word that I will not rest until we have returned her to safety. Please, allow me to help."

Cockran considered this for a moment. He winced inwardly at Sturm's attempt to absorb responsibility for Mattie's fate. Cockran's own guilt was far greater. If only he had spent the night with Mattie, this wouldn't have happened. Cockran shook it off. Finding her came first. His feelings could wait their turn.

"Can you locate Josef Lanz?" Cockran asked, laying down the conditions for Sturm's involvement. "We have no faith in the Munich police."

"If he is in Germany," Sturm said, "I will find him. I have many resources at hand."

At that, Sturm was provisionally accepted into Churchill's circle as they began to develop a plan of action that could garner them the information they needed to find Josef Lanz. As they talked, Rankin removed himself from the discussions and walked towards the outer door of Churchill's suite, the one that lead into the hallway beyond. The men in the room stopped their conversation and watched Rankin approach the door.

"Sergeant Rankin?" Churchill asked.

Rankin held up his hand, asking for silence and removed his own revolver as he peered through the spy hole of the door. He pulled his head back in surprise and then holstered his weapon. He opened the door, but not wide enough for anyone in the room to see beyond him.

After a moment, an impatient Cockran had had enough. "Robert, who the hell is it?"

Rankin turned back quietly, an expression of concern on his face as though he had some uncomfortable news to pass on. Behind him, Bobby Sullivan appeared in the doorway and now became the one to block the view past the door way. "Bourke," Sullivan said simply.

"Someone is here who insists on speaking with you. He says he knows where Mattie has been taken."

"Well let him in, for God's sake!" Cockran snapped. "Let him in!"

Sullivan stood aside. The harsh, lined features of Josef Lanz were momentarily framed in the doorway before he entered the room. The debates of the past two hours, the careful considerations of whether Lanz's "note" were genuine or not, were gone in a flash. Something snapped at the back of Cockran's mind, like the coiled spring of a mattress breaking free from its mooring. He burst forward with an incomprehensible grunt and flung himself at Josef Lanz. Cockran's shoulder plowed into Lanz's belly, the impact sending Lanz flat on his back. Cockran seized his neck in his bare hands and began squeezing with all the strength he could muster. Lanz had no chance of stopping him, the older man's strength no match for Cockran's rage.

"Where is she?!" Cockran screamed into the man's face. He used his hands to shake Lanz's head, knocking it back against the hotel's carpeted floor. In his mind, he saw his wife Nora, dead at the hands of an IRA thug. He saw old friends like Michael Collins, gone and dead at the hands of the same sort of ruthless men. He saw them all, his worst fear being that Mattie might join them. He could not bear to lose Mattie too. "Where is she, Goddamn it! Tell me!"

Cockran felt his hands pulled away from Lanz's neck against the will of his own arms. He leaned forward, trying to keep his weight on Lanz, but the strong hands of every man in the room soon made themselves felt on his arms as they fought to pull him off the man beneath him. Cockran strained against the men holding him back, until Churchill's voice began to filter in.

"Bourke!" Churchill said. "Stop this madness! We must speak to this fellow! We need him to lead us to Mattie. Bourke! Listen to me!"

Cockran eased his arms and began to relax into the hands that held him, his breathing hard and heavy, but slowing. A few hands remained on him, softly, making sure his acquiescence was not simply feigned. Cockran put a hand over the one on his shoulder to reassure them. "I'm sorry. Let him speak."

Lanz roused himself from the floor slowly, rubbing his neck. He held a hand up to gesture that he was having difficulty speaking.

Sturm placed a hand on Cockran's shoulder. "I understand your emotions, *Herr* Cockran," he said softly. "But losing control does nothing to bring Mattie back."

Cockran looked coldly at the hand on his shoulder as if it were an unwanted insect. Sturm took the glance, removed his hand and backed away.

Lanz was now up in a sitting position on the floor, Sullivan kneeling beside him. Sullivan looked up at Cockran. "I met him down in the hotel lobby after I returned from the police station," he said. "Lanz told me that he knew where Mattie was being held and insisted that he be the one to tell you. In person. I tried to explain to him that it was a bad idea, but…" Sullivan held his hands up in a helpless gesture. "Well, he insisted."

Sullivan then explained to the group what he learned at Munich police headquarters as a result of his "little chat" with Deputy Prosecutor Eric Schmidt.

"What happened to Schmidt?" Cockran asked.

"I left him on the toilet."

"So Hoch is responsible?" Cockran said. "Hoch kidnapped Mattie?"

"With a little help from Harmony Hampton," Sullivan replied.

"And Hoch took the Spear?" Professor Campbell asked.

"Yes," Lanz croaked from his seat on the floor. "What *Herr* Sullivan says fits with everything we understand. I left a rear guard behind to keep an eye on the SS because we feared they would make a move to retake the Spear. My men followed the SS motorcar caravan. They said there were two women in one of the motorcars. One with blonde hair, one with red.

"Where did they take her?" Cockran said urgently.

"Both the Spear and the women are now in the SS fortress at Wewelsburg where, I am afraid, it will be impossible to rescue either of them. The walls are ten feet thick, thirty feet high. Unlike my own ancestral home, I don't know any secret ways inside or secret passages within."

"I do." The voice was Kurt von Sturm's. The entire room turned to face him.

"Membership has its privileges." Sturm said. "Last summer after the Nazis' unexpected election victory which left us the second largest party in Germany, Himmler tried to recruit me into the SS because I was in Hitler's favor and represented to him the Nordic ideal." Sturm paused. "Knowing that, Himmler tried to impress me with what was to him the highest honor he could bestow. An invitation to visit his holy SS sanctuary at Wewelsburg."

Sturm explained that Himmler was inordinately proud of Wewelsburg Castle and had taken him on a Cook's tour, pointing out secret passages like a 12 year old boy with his prized toys. One passage led to the sacred ritual room where, Himmler explained, his enemies claimed he beheaded those who opposed him. Some people will say anything, he told Sturm with a laugh, but he had assured him that the SS were a knightly order.

"The castle is a shrine to the Spear of Destiny," Sturm said. "Himmler has designed a separate room there for every German leader who possessed the holy lance from Charlemagne through Frederick the Great whose room is kept locked and reserved for Hitler himself, should he ever visit the SS fortress. Each room has genuine period pieces such as swords, shields, and jewels which belonged to the heroic figures who laid claim to the Lance of Longinus."

Sturm paused. "You understand, of course, that Himmler is quite mad. Ruthless, brilliant… and utterly mad. But this much I do know. Castle Wewelsburg is not impregnable if you have the key. And I have the key. Do you still have your autogiros, *Herr* Cockran?"

Cockran nodded. "They're at a private Munich aerodrome. Gassed up and ready to go."

70.

The Heart of the New Europe

Outside Munich
Tuesday, 16 June 1931

THEY had been driving for hours, heading northwest with Harmony and the driver in the front seat of the big Mercedes touring car while Hoch sat beside a bound Mattie in the back, the canvas covered Spear resting on his lap. She still couldn't believe Harmony and Hoch were lovers. What she did believe was Hoch's threat that "No one you know will ever see you again."

Mattie had feigned sleep for most of the journey but, with the afternoon sun shining in her eyes, it was no longer possible. She looked over at Hoch. "Where are you taking me?"

Hoch smiled, his eyes fixated on the Spear. "The sacred ritual at Wewelsburg for consecrating the Spear of Destiny requires the sacrifice of two victims, a sworn enemy and a true friend of the German *Volk*. One of each. You, Miss McGary, qualify as an enemy."

"That's not what I asked, you sick bastard. I asked you where are you taking me?"

Hoch looked at her and smiled. "To the new Europe, Miss McGary, the very heart of the new Europe."

Wewelsburg Castle
Westphalia, Germany
Wednesday, 17 June 1931

OTHER than being locked in a castle dungeon, Mattie had been treated with courtesy by her captors, as if they were following some code of chivalry, the food warm and decent, her privacy respected. Tonight was different. They gave her a flowing white gown and said it was to be her only garment. They waited outside as she dressed. Then, they returned and placed on her head a long blonde wig which made her feel like a refugee from a Wagnerian opera.

Mattie was frightened. It had been two hours since her captors had dressed her in this fashion and it was growing dark. She knew she was in a medieval castle. She knew they were outside the town of Paderhorn in a large fortress-like castle on the banks of a river. By now, Sullivan and Cockran were probably back in the Alps, fruitlessly trying to find Lanz and the Templars. Hoch was right. No one she knew would ever see her again. Mattie lay on the cot, her eyes closed. She had to find a way out but after she had attacked the first guard to bring her food, they subsequently came in pairs, both of them armed. She had even managed that first time to wrench the guard's Luger from his holster but her unfamiliarity with where the safety catch was located had been her undoing. She wanted a rematch.

Mattie heard the key turn in the lock and sat up. She had been waiting for this. She wasn't going meekly into the night. They had left her clothes including her shoes which were workmen's high top leather boots with steel reinforced toes. Her only weapon. Mattie stood behind the door as the first SS man entered, his Luger still in its gleaming black leather holster.

"*Fraulein?*" he called out.

Holding the boot with both hands, Mattie swung it toe first into the bridge of the man's nose, hearing the crunch of cartilage, blood spurting from his nose as he cried out and staggered back into his comrade, carrying them both to the floor. Mattie took the Luger from the first man's holster as the other man fumbled for his. Mattie was faster and this time she knew where the safety was. The sound of two weapons discharging inside the small cell was deafening. The SS man missed. Mattie didn't. Coldly, she fired at the man with the broken nose. She would not repeat her mistake at Alexandria with Lanz's Templars. The SS gave no quarter and neither would she. Mattie briefly contemplated dressing but she couldn't waste the time. She quickly laced up her boots and cautiously entered the hall, a Luger in one hand and the clip from the second Luger in the other, wishing she had Bobby Sullivan's ability to shoot with either hand. The corridor was lit only by fire and she moved cautiously, sensing she was below ground level She made it safely up to the next level but no farther. She never saw what or who hit her, a blinding pain followed by blackness.

MATTIE awoke with her head throbbing and her eyes blindfolded. She was on her back and felt cold stone beneath her, her wrists and ankles restrained by ropes, her boots removed. Mattie heard more sounds as others entered the room. One voice sounded muffled, as if the person were gagged. She heard movement and then she sensed someone else beside her.

Mattie heard footsteps receding and assumed they had been left alone when, suddenly, her blindfold was removed. She was astonished to see Harmony Hampton beside her, wrists and ankles bound as well. Both women were on an elevated round stone surface, several feet off the ground. Harmony's feet were opposite Mattie's head. She was blindfolded as Mattie had been, but she was still gagged and dressed like Mattie in a flowing white gown. Just then, Reinhard Hoch came into view from around behind her and removed Harmony's gag.

"What is going on? There must be some mistake!" Harmony shrieked. I demand to see Reinhard Hoch! Immediately! Who do you people think you are?"

Mattie raised her head as far as she could. Hoch stood there, a smile on his face as he ignored Harmony's pleas. Finally, he reached forward and removed Harmony's blindfold.

"Tristan! My Tristan! I knew you'd come! Please get me out of this. There's been some horrible mistake."

"No, my darling, there is no mistake. You played a vital role in delivering the Spear of Destiny to the only men worthy of possessing it, the Teutonic Knights of the new Germany. You kept us informed of *Herr* Cockran's every move and your warning in Munich very likely saved my life. You have my thanks and eternal gratitude."

"Yes, I did everything you asked." Harmony said. "I did it because I believe in the new Germany. And because I love you."

Mattie looked around the room. It was round, like the stone surface on which she and Harmony were bound. She looked up. At the center of the high ceiling was a shiny black swastika within a circle of gold leaf that glittered in the light of twelve flaming torches. The torches were lodged in sconces along the perimeter of the room and provided the only illumination. Ahead of her, she could see a raised stone platform ten feet beyond Harmony's head on which sat an elaborately carved wooden chair. A large, blood-red velvet curtain was hung on the wall behind the platform with a black swastika inside a white circle in the center of the curtain.

"Yes, my darling," Hoch replied. "You did everything I asked, even urging your trustees to sell your controlling interest in your step-father's company which they did this morning."

"Oh Tristan, that's wonderful news. Now we can be together once I have my £50,000 and you divorce your wife."

"None of that will happen, my darling. Your benefactor withdrew his offer of a finder's fee for you and used it instead to bribe your two trustees into accepting what he assured me was a very fair price. So I am afraid our being together is now quite out of the question."

"But you promised. You gave me your word."

"I did not know you had a Jewish great-grandmother when I made my promise. Your blood is tainted, my dear, and you are but a parasite. No promise to a Jew need ever be kept."

Hoch walked over to the raised platform and picked up a long black garment which looked to Mattie like something an Oxford don would wear, except for the silver trim and dual silver lightening flashes of the SS at its collar. He put on the gown and approached Harmony.

"As deep as my love once was for you, my darling, my loyalty to the SS and the new Germany is paramount. I have agreed to make the ultimate sacrifice by allowing you to play the key role in setting Germany firmly on the path to the greatness which is its birthright. The Spear of

Destiny must be dipped in the blood of both a friend of the German *volk* as well as an enemy before it can be bent to the will of the one who possesses it. That is the legend handed down from all great leaders of the past who have held high the Spear. Constantine, Charlemagne, Henry the Fowler, Barbarossa and, above all, Frederick the Great."

Hoch looked down at Harmony and stroked her cheek. "I will miss you, my dearest, but a knight must put his honor above personal considerations."

The words chilled Mattie as Harmony screamed. She heard the creaking of a door behind her and Harmony's screams faded to a whimper. She heard the clicking sound of heels on stone as twelve men walked into the room and mounted pedestals which stood against the wall beside the twelve torches in a circle around the stone altar on which she and Harmony lay. They were all tall and blond, clad in black, silver-trimmed SS uniforms with gleaming leather boots and armed with holstered Lugers and ceremonial daggers.

At Hoch's command, they all snapped to attention, eyes focused on the platform and the curtain behind it. A short pudgy man appeared from behind the wall hanging, the Spear of Destiny in his right hand. He was wearing a black gown similar to Hoch's except his was trimmed in both silver and red. He wore a thick-lensed pince-nez and his mustache was trimmed in a manner reminiscent of Hitler's. His head was shaved at the sides but that did little to camouflage a round moon face on top of which was perched short dark hair. Mattie had never met him, but she recognized him from photographs. *Reichsfuhrer* SS Heinrich Himmler.

Himmler took a seat on the platform and banged the base of the Spear once on the platform floor, calling the assembled Knights to order. "My fellow Knights, Reinhard Tristan Hoch is a perfect specimen of German knighthood. His loyalty is his honor. He was sent by me on behalf of our *Fuhrer* on a special quest. Many brave knights went with him and paid with their lives."

Himmler paused and bowed his head as if in silent prayer before raising up his head and continuing. "But Reinhard Tristan persevered as any great Knight would. Just as Parsifal did in the past. He has brought the Spear of Destiny back to our ancient home here at Wewelsburg. As a reward for his bravery, Reinhard Tristan has earned the honor of consecrating the Spear, first with the blood of a friend of the German *volk*. After the Spear has been consecrated in the blood of a friend, it will taste the blood of a sworn enemy. Come forward, Reinhard."

Hoch approached Himmler, who had removed the pince-nez and held his weak chin high. "The honor is yours, SS man," Himmler said, handing the Spear to Hoch who grasped it with both hands. Hoch turned and approached Harmony and held the Spear tip high over her heart.

Mercifully, Harmony fainted but Mattie couldn't look any longer. She closed her eyes as she heard Hoch say, "You now belong to the ages and your name will be praised in songs and fables for a thousand years". Mattie heard the spear rending flesh and bone followed by the sounds of Harmony's impaled body thrashing wildly beside her. After a few moments, the convulsions ceased and Mattie opened her eyes to see the front of Harmony's gown drenched in blood, her eyes wide in death, the Spear standing upright, lodged deep within her heart. Hoch stood there, hands clasped casually behind his back, the grim expression on his face slowly turning to a satisfied smile.

Hoch stepped forward and took hold of the Spear with both hands, yanked it free from Harmony's heart and walked around the stone altar toward Mattie, holding the Spear aloft, blood dripping freely from its tip. Hoch leaned over her and said in a whisper, "No one will remember your name, you Jew-loving whore. You'll be one of the nameless vermin whose bodies will pave the road to a new world order."

Mattie watched mesmerized as Hoch lifted the Spear high above her and Harmony's blood dripped from its tip onto her white gown. Yet the spear thrust did not come. The tip seemed to be glowing and the muscles on his forearms were in evidence as if he were straining to bring the Spear down against some unseen resisting force. Now the knots in his neck were straining as well, his face red from exertion. The last of Harmony's blood had dripped from the tip of the Spear onto her chest and over her heart. The Spear tip now was completely aglow, almost as if a globe of light were surrounding it

Staring up, Mattie could see the swastika symbol in the ceiling above her, partially obscured by Hoch's head as the circle of gold leaf surrounding the swastika formed a halo around his head. Hoch's face was creased with intensity and he seemed to redouble his efforts to plunge the spear into her heart. Then, to her horror, the Spear began to slowly move down under his exertions, inch by inch coming closer to Mattie's heart. She screamed.

71.

Himmler's Camelot

En Route to Westphalia, Germany
Wednesday, 17 June 1931

KURT Von Sturm had not flown in an open cockpit aircraft since the war, let alone an autogiro. The roar of the Wright Whirlwind engine made conversation with the other occupant next to him in the front cockpit all but impossible. Which was just as well with Sturm because what did he have in common with Winston Churchill? Only one thing he could think of. The rescue of Mattie McGary, Churchill's god-daughter and the woman Sturm loved.

Back in Churchill's hotel suite earlier in the day, Sturm had sketched a rough outline of Wewelsburg Castle, a triangular structure built on a hill overlooking the Alme Valley. "The castle's dominant feature is its north tower," he had said. "A large circular structure some five stories tall with a flat crenellated top. The east and west towers are smaller although equal in height and the castle's main entrance is between those two towers."

Sturm then began to sketch the large hill on which the castle sat and to shade in the trees and foliage around it, far more dense on the east side than the west side. He had just finished sketching in the dry moat on the castle's east side and the concealed entrance into the castle's basement beneath the east drawbridge when Churchill took over. Sturm could tell at once the man was a soldier, eager for adventure and expecting to be obeyed.

Taking his unlit Havana cigar from his mouth, Churchill had used it as a map pointer. "We'll make a silent landing with the three autogiros here." Churchill said pointing with his cigar at a spot on Sturms's sketch, a small clearing amid a copse of trees adjacent to the castle Sturm had drawn. "We'll divide our force into two teams of four and approach the entrance beneath the east drawbridge from either side under the cover of darkness. We'll leave one of our numbers behind to secure the aircraft and another at our entry point into the castle. That will ensure a clear line of retreat. Then, a seven man team will enter the castle, find Mattie and Harmony and effect their rescue."

"Winston, don't you think…" Cockran began but Churchill ignored him. "Bourke, Sergeant Rankin and Mr. Sullivan are the pilots. Two of Mr. Sullivan's comrades from Ireland will accompany him. *Herr* Lanz, you and one of your associates will accompany Sergeant Rankin while *Herr* von Sturm and I will ride with Bourke in his aircraft."

"Wait a minute, Winston." Cockran had protested. "You're *not* coming with us. This will be exceedingly dangerous. These SS are ruthless. You could be shot or killed."

Churchill frowned. "As could my goddaughter. I'm the one who persuaded her to participate in this perilous undertaking and I am most certainly going to be there to rescue her. Her father would expect no less. Remind me, Bourke. What was your rank during the Great War?"

"Captain."

Churchill smiled. "I was a Lieutenant Colonel. And in how many conflicts have you seen action?"

"One."

"Yes, one. While I, on the other hand, graduated Sandhurst, fought Pashtun warriors in India, the Mahdi's Dervishes in the Sudan and the Boers in South Africa. As well as the Huns in the Great War. Once we land at this castle, you'll have operational command of our little raiding party but, until then, I'm in charge. Understood?"

"Yes sir, Colonel Churchill. Perfectly." Cockran said as he came to attention and snapped off a crisp salute, a wide grin on his face.

Churchill nodded. "Let's assemble our kit and make haste to the Munich aerodrome. We should plan to arrive at Wewelsburg Castle shortly after dusk has fallen."

Castle Wewelsburg
Westphalia, Germany
Wednesday, 17 June 1931

COCKRAN accepted Sturm's suggestion and the three autogiros approached the castle from the west, silently landing in a forest clearing within a hundred yards from the road which passed beneath the castle's north tower. Two deserted homes lay between them and the road.

"All the houses surrounding the castle are to be demolished," Sturm said as they tied the three aircraft down. "Himmler showed me the architect's three dimensional model for Wewelsburg. The castle will be at its center and its triangular shape will form the tip of a spearhead. New walls will flow out from the base of the castle to form a complete spearhead and within the walls will be an academy and lodging for the training of future generations of SS."

Churchill approached them now, Mauser in his hand, and spoke to Cockran. "As I promised, you're now in operational command. Much as I'd like to join you, someone must stay behind and protect the aircraft. As I'm the oldest among us by some 20 years and," Churchill said, patting his ample belly, "perhaps the least fit, I am the logical candidate."

Cockran was relieved and quickly agreed. They set out for the castle where scaffolding stood along the east wing. The eight men approached in four man teams on either side of the arched bridge across the dry moat. They met at an ancient wooden door beneath the bridge. Sturm tried the handle but the door didn't budge. "It might just be stuck," Cockran said. "The door looks slightly ajar."

"Let's see if you're right." Sturm said as he lowered his shoulder and rammed into the door and moved it several inches.

"Need a hand?" Cockran asked. Sturm nodded. Together the men rammed the door once more and it moved further this time. One more shove and a two foot space had opened.

Cockran turned to Sullivan who had been hard on their heels. "Leave one of the Apostles to guard the exit. I still don't trust Lanz."

Sullivan nodded and Cockran turned back to Sturm. "Where to?"

"Down this corridor to the right. The crypt beneath the north tower is where the SS hold their ritual ceremonies. Cells for prisoners are this way also."

The men moved down the dank stone corridor, peering into four empty cells along the way. At the fifth cell they found what they were looking for. Cockran peered into the cell and immediately recognized Mattie's tan slacks, a white silk blouse, leather jacket, boots and silk briefs. "They're Mattie's clothes." Cockran said. "Where do you think they've taken her?"

"The sacrificial chamber. We must hurry." Sturm replied but Cockran had already burst from the cell into the corridor and was racing for the the north tower.

"*Herr* Cockran! Wait!" But Cockran paid no heed and Sturm sprinted after him. Ahead, Cockran heard the steady thump of hob-nailed boots on concrete. Sturm caught up with him right before a stone archway, clasped his shoulder hard and pulled him back into the shadows. Cockran swung his head back, a look of fury on his face, and began to push him away but stopped when Sturm put his finger to his lips. Cockran nodded briefly to signal he heard the footsteps also and they were growing nearer.

Retreating into the shadows, they both watched twelve tall blond men dressed in black trimmed in silver march past, long daggers drawn and gleaming in the torch light, Lugers in shiny black leather holsters on their belts. The men disappeared through an open iron gate into a chamber beyond. Sturm turned to Cockran and whispered. "The ceremony has not started. Mattie and Miss Hampton are still alive. But we cannot all enter through this main gate. Leave *Herr* Sullivan here with Sergeant Rankin, the other Irishman and the Templar. You and I and *Herr* Lanz will enter from the opposite side in precisely 60 seconds."

Cockran frowned. "The other side?"

"Yes." Sturm replied as he reached out his right hand to the stone wall beside them and pushed. There was an audible click and the wall swung away to reveal a narrow corridor curving around to the right. Cockran checked his watch, compared it with Sullivan's and told him to come through the main gate in sixty seconds with guns blazing.

Cockran turned back to Sturm. "Thanks for stopping me back there. I would have walked right into those guys if you hadn't." Sturm nodded and gestured for Cockran to enter the corridor first which he did.

Sturm was behind Cockran as they carefully made their way down the stone passage, lit ahead only by a single candle in a wall sconce. They stopped at the candle. "The passage continues around the exterior of the chamber," Sturm said. "In another twenty meters, there will be an entrance from the passage into the chamber right behind the seat held by Himmler."

With Lanz behind them, Sturm and Cockran continued down the corridor and stopped short when, ahead of them came a barely muffled scream. Cockran recognized it at once. Mattie! He looked at Sturm and, without a word, each man began to sprint down the corridor, pulling their Schmeisser machine pistols from their shoulders.

72.

Kill Them All

Castle Wewelsburg
Westphalia, Germany
Wednesday, 17 June, 1931

MATTIE thought the glow from the Spear must be an optical illusion brought on by her brain's inability to process the horror of Harmony's murder and her own imminent death. But moments after the Spear tip grew incandescent, Hoch's strength began to force it down and it was within inches of her heart when Cockran burst from behind the left-hand side of the curtain behind Himmler and Sturm from the right, opening up with automatic weapons at the black-garbed SS standing on the pedestals surrounding the altar. On the other side of the chamber, Bobby Sullivan had opened up with his twin Colt .45 automatics and was followed by Rankin and several hooded and equally well-armed men.

In the tumult which followed, Hoch released the Spear of Destiny and it fell harmlessly beside her on the stone altar. In an instant, Sullivan was at Mattie's side, cutting her bonds, casting the Spear aside with no concern for its sacred history. Sitting up on the stone altar, Mattie quickly rubbed circulation back into her wrists and ankles while Sullivan offered her one of his Colts which she gladly accepted. It wasn't her weapon of choice. Its kick was far stronger than her Walther but she had fired one before.

Mattie moved away from the altar, the Colt held in both hands, and she scanned the room with it, looking for targets wearing black. As she scanned, she saw Bourke and Kurt together, back to back, firing their machine pistols. Just then, she saw movement to her right, above Sturm and Cockran. An SS man had clambered onto the altar, his foot resting on Harmony's lifeless body, and was drawing a bead on both of Mattie's lovers. Not on my watch, she thought, and squeezed off two quick shots. The first shot hit the SS man in the chest, slamming him back, but the Colt's kick caused the second shot to go higher, hitting him squarely in his forehead and knocking him from the altar to the floor.

Nice shot, McGary, Mattie thought. She scanned the room and she saw Himmler disappear behind the curtain from which Cockran and Sturm had emerged with Hoch right behind.

"Bourke! Kurt! Over there! Hoch is getting away," Mattie shouted. Kill the bastard, she thought. Kill him!

Behind her, Mattie heard the crack of automatic weapons fire over the sound of Sullivan's Colt .45 automatic and SS cries of surrender. The Templars and Michael Collins' most feared assassin were taking no prisoners. Good, Mattie thought, surprising herself at the vehemence of her reaction until she looked once more at Harmony's lifeless body on the altar. Kill the bloody bastards! Kill them all!

73.

Death From Above

COCKRAN reached Mattie's side and touched the blood on her white gown. "Are you hurt?"

"I'm fine."

Cockran looked back to the altar at Harmony's lifeless body. "The bastards!"

"She betrayed us," Mattie said. "She'd been working with Hoch the whole time, but he killed her anyway. Go after him. Don't let him escape."

Cockran saw that Bobby Sullivan was wounded again, clutching his side, but Murphy was there beside him. Cockran caught Sullivan's eye and watched him motion with his eyes toward the curtain behind which Himmler and Hoch had disappeared.

"He went that way," Sullivan said. "And Sturm followed."

His submachine pistol empty, Cockran flung it aside, pulled out his Webley and stepped behind the curtain. Opposite from the direction he and Sturm had come from were steps leading down, the dim light from the room behind barely illuminating their stone surface. The steps weren't many, eight or nine before his feet hit the dirt floor of the passage. Ahead of him, he heard gunfire. It was pitch black now so, with his left hand touching the wall, the Webley in his right, he moved toward the sound of the guns.

The gunfire had stopped and Cockran kept moving in the same direction on the dirt floor up a small incline. Ahead of him, he could see light. In the silence he thought he heard footsteps over to the right. He hesitated. There was another tunnel branching off. Should he follow the footsteps? Just then, he heard another gunshot from up ahead. Making up his mind, he headed toward the faint light, the barrel of his Webley pointed straight up beside him. He ran up a short flight of steps and heard the roar of a motorcycle engine. He reached the top of the flight and emerged into the courtyard of Castle Wewelsburg in time to see Hoch speeding away towards the Castle entrance as Sturm snapped off several shots with his Luger, all of them missing the speeding target. Cockran sprinted towards Sturm who by now had slung the strap of his machine pistol over his shoulder, leaped onto a motorcycle, kick-started it and roared after Hoch.

There were three motorcycles still there when Cockran reached the nearest one, all of them identical BMW Model R39s. Cockran grabbed the nearest bike and headed off after Sturm. He bent low over the handlebars as he raced over the wooden drawbridge. Ahead of him, he could see Sturm gaining on Hoch, now barely 50 yards ahead. Hoch twisted his upper torso around and blindly fired a burst of automatic weapon fire at Sturm from his Schmeisser. The burst shredded the front tire of Sturm's bike and sent it into a skid on its side. Cockran braked to a halt in order to avoid hitting Sturm. He put the kickstand down and leaped off the BMW.

Sturm was pinned under the motorcycle which Cockran lifted off him. Sturm pulled himself to his feet and gave a stifled groan. The left arm of his jacket had been ripped and Cockran could see that beneath, his left side was bleeding from a gunshot wound.

"Are you badly hurt?" Cockran asked.

"I'm fine," Sturm replied. "Go after Hoch."

Cockran looked into the distance and saw the tail light of Hoch's motorcycle fading into the darkness, 200 yards away and rapidly increasing the distance between them.

"Hop on the bike," Cockran said to Sturm.

"No," Sturm said. "Too much weight. You'll never catch him with me on it."

"We're wasting time," Cockran said. "Hop on. We're not using the bike to catch him."

Moments later Cockran skidded to a halt in front of the three autogiros they had flown from Munich. "Winston! Harmony's been murdered. The man who did it just went by on that motorcycle," he shouted over his shoulder as he sprinted to the lead autogiro. "The cargo compartment on the middle plane. There's a spare submachine gun and tracer rounds, the ones with a blue band. Find them and give them to *Herr* Sturm."

To Sturm, he said. "Hop in the front cockpit. We're going to cut that bastard off if it's the last thing I do."

Churchill brought the Thompson and the round ammunition drums over to Sturm and called to Cockran. "Is Mattie safe?"

"Yes, she's fine. Bobby and the others will be here soon. Keep the aircraft secure until we're back."

Moments later, with Sturm on board, the autogiro rose into the air, its takeoff using less than 15 feet. Cockran quickly ascended to 500 feet, but neither of them could spot Hoch's motorcycle in the distance.

"I'm taking her higher," Cockran said. "Keep your eyes peeled for his tail light."

At a higher altitude of 1,000 feet, they both spotted the small red light in the distance, nearly a mile ahead of them, making its way along the twisting road. Cockran opened the throttle wide, taking the aircraft to its maximum airspeed of 118 miles per hour.

"We'll be even with him in a few more minutes," Cockran said into the speaking tube. "Once I pull ahead of him, start firing the tracer rounds."

Cockran kept the autogiro at 1,000 feet. "Get ready," Cockran said as he pushed the stick forward. "I'll let you know when I'm down to 100 feet. Then let him have it."

Cockran brought the autogiro down, slowing its speed, and Sturm opened up with submachine gun fire, the red tracers streaming through the night, seeking out Hoch's bike, which responded by accelerating, heading for forest cover in the rolling hills around the next curve. Below him, Cockran could see where the twisting road exited the forest. From where they were, Cockran saw it was another two miles before the road reached the top of the hill and began its downward descent. There were no side roads.

"I'm going to get ahead of him," Cockran said into the speaking tube, "and come about across the road. I'll take her down to the lowest air speed I can, 15 miles per hour, so you can hit him with a broadside and maximize our fire power. Okay?"

Sturm made no response and Cockran could see that Sturm had slumped over to his right, unmoving, the left side of his jacket almost completely crimson with his blood. Damn! Cockran weighed his options. His maneuver assumed maximum fire power brought to bear on the target. It wasn't quite the same if he could fire only single shots from his Webley with one hand, keeping the autogiro steady with the other. With Sturm out of action, he would have to stop Hoch without guns. He gauged the distance from Hoch's location on the road to the top of the hill. Vegetation grew more sparse the higher the road went. At the peak of the hill, there were no trees lining the serpentine road and Cockran assumed it would be the same on the other side. Forcing Hoch's bike off the side might well spell death on the switchback road which climbed one side of the hill and down the other. If Hoch lived through that, Cockran would land and finish him off with the submachine gun.

Cockran increased the autogiro's airspeed again as it climbed higher over the hill. He had to time it just right. He checked his altimeter and ground speed once again and then swung the aircraft around in a wide arc. Cockran wanted to have the autogiro dangerously close to the ground, no more than fifteen feet, hurtling directly toward Hoch at 75 miles per hour so that when he cleared the top of the hill and began his descent down the road on the other side, Hoch would be confronted with a flying windmill bearing straight at him. With luck, Hoch would panic and lose control, sending his bike, and hopefully Hoch with it, over the edge of the road.

Cockran completed the autogiro's wide arc at a slow speed and started back up the ridge. Ahead of him, he could see the BMW's single headlight stabbing into the sky. He increased his air speed as quickly as the plane's safety would allow. By the time Hoch's bike crested the hill and turned with the bend in the road, the autogiro was only 50 yards away and closing fast. As hoped, Hoch panicked, braking the big motorcycle and spraying gravel as Cockran flew harmlessly overhead. Damn it! He wasn't low enough.

Cockran came around for another pass, this time from behind, barely 10 feet off the ground now, his speed nearly 90 miles per hour, a mere gust of wind standing between him and a crash of the autogiro on the road below.

Hoch ducked, hunching lower on the handlebars as the autogiro swooped overhead.

Still not low enough.

Cockran circled around for another pass from behind. Cockran opened the throttle as quickly as he could, trying to close the distance between them. Closer, he had to get closer to the ground. He was within 20 yards of Hoch, barely five feet above the tarmac but the stretch of road ahead straightened and leveled out, allowing Hoch to increase his speed. Cockran cursed to himself—the autogiro couldn't accelerate at the same rate. He had been within ten yards, but Hoch was beginning to pull away and he knew it, briefly looking back over his shoulder.

Distracted, Hoch saw too late that debris from the hillside had spilled onto the middle of the road. Hoch swerved to avoid a large rock but then hit the thick branch of a tree with his front wheel, popping the front end of his bike into the air a good 10 feet. Hoch hung on and was able to maintain control of the bike but the autogiro swept past him just as he and the motorcycle went airborne. The wheels of the autogiro hit Hoch at the bike's apogee, jarring the aircraft and sending the bike crashing to the road.

The autogiro shuddered now. Something was loose. The rotary wing still gave the craft lift, but it didn't sound happy. Cockran circled the autogiro around and made a low pass over the straightaway, scanning closely, evaluating the possibility of a landing. The motorcycle was 20 yards down the road and Hoch's body was pinned beneath it. Up in the passenger cockpit, Sturm was unconscious. He had lost a lot of blood and he might well not make it if Cockran didn't take a look at him soon. Worse, if he didn't land and check the rotary wing now, they both might not make it.

Cockran circled around and floated the autogiro gently to earth, landing in front of the forest debris that had spelled Hoch's demise. Once at a stop, Cockran lifted himself out of the cockpit and turned his attention to Sturm. He climbed forward over the main body of the plane and pulled Sturm from the passenger cockpit. He eased the unconscious man down, laid him out on the ground, opened his shirt and held a gauze bandage tightly over the wound, stopping the blood flow. Holding a roll of tape in one hand, keeping the wound compressed with the other, he wrapped the tape tightly around Sturm's bare torso. He could do no less for the man who had saved Mattie's life. Whatever might have gone on between them paled by comparison and Cockran would have to live with his role in bringing that about. Halfway though the process, Sturm opened his eyes and gave him a silent acknowledgement of thanks and closed them again.

Cockran then took a wrench and climbed back on the fuselage. He sat on the edge, peering at the frozen rotor blades in the moonlight, probing with his fingers at the delicate and complicated hinges. He had no idea what to look for but he could tell something was wrong with them. One of the blades was somewhat loosened, but when he tightened the bolts, its hinges still seemed to work. That was the most important thing. At least, he hoped so.

Finally, Cockran walked over to examine Hoch's lifeless body. Had Harmony really been working with Hoch and the SS all along as Sullivan and Mattie suggested? He had to concede it was possible and it anwered a lot of questions. But even so, she hadn't deserved to die, the image of her lifeless body on the altar flashing through his mind.

Standing over the bike, Cockran saw a pool of blood beneath Hoch's head. He knelt down to check for a pulse and stopped short when he heard Hoch groan. But the man's eyes were closed and he appeared unconscious. He felt for a pulse on his neck. It was strong. Probably has a concussion, he thought, as he lifted the bike off Hoch.

Cockran wondered what to do with Hoch now that he was alive. Killing him was one option; leaving him to die here exposed to the elements was another. One thing he wasn't going to do, Cockran thought, was take him to a hospital and file murder charges with the local police for his killing Harmony. That was a mug's game. The Nazis were too plugged in. Jacob Weintraub's "suicide" and Hoch's release were proof of that. He turned his back on Hoch to lower the motorcycle's kickstand.

"Behind you!" Sturm shouted in a hoarse voice.

Cockran whirled around to see the figure of Hoch surging toward him, his right hand holding a long SS dagger. Cockran raised his left arm in defense and reached for his Webley but Hoch was on him too quickly. The blade ripped along the sleeve of his leather flight jacket but Cockran ducked under the charging Hoch and threw him over his shoulder. Hoch hit the ground hard but his SS dagger was still in his hand.

Hoch leaped to his feet and spun the knife from one hand to the other, alternating grips with speed and agility. Cockran could see the knife clearly now. Nearly a foot long and double-edged like the ones the SS had carried back at Wewelsburg Castle. Hoch advanced, slashing the air in front of him. Cockran hated knife fights, his worst class during MID training. Hand-to-hand was more his style but not when the other guy's hand held a god-damned ten inch blade! Hoch lunged again but Cockran swept the first strike away with his right forearm and the next with his left, followed by a right jab to Hoch's forehead.

Hoch staggered back out of Cockran's reach, shifted his grip to his other hand and lunged. Cockran parried with his left arm but the next strike was too fast as the blade sliced across Cockran's injured hip. He cried out, collapsing to one knee. Hoch was on him in a flash with a wide backhand swipe. Cockran leaned back to avoid the strike but lost his balance. He reached his left hand to the ground to steady himself but a kick from Hoch knocked him on his back. Hoch smiled as he straddled Cockran's waist and shifted the dagger to his right hand for the killing strike at Cockran's heart.

Cockran seized the Nazi's wrist with his right hand and rolled to his left. Hoch tried to jerk his hand free but he only gave Cockran more leverage, forcing him over onto his side. Then Cockran joined his left hand to Hoch's wrist and twisted him onto his back. Both men struggled for control of the knife but Cockran's weight slowly reversed the dagger until its point was aimed straight at Hoch's exposed throat.

In the moonlight, Cockran could clearly see the inscription on the dagger's blade. He didn't know much German but even he knew enough to read *My Honor is Loyalty.* Loyalty to what? Cockran thought, kidnapping innocent English girls and then killing them after you used them? He decided then that leaving Hoch to die of exposure in the mountains was no longer an option. Exerting more pressure, Cockran slowly pushed the blade up under Hoch's jaw and against his throat, hearing the man cry out as the sharp tip pierced his skin, drawing a thin trickle of blood.

The man's eyes were wide with fright, silently pleading for mercy. "Please don't kill me. Believe me. I was only following orders. I was only following orders."

Cockran's hazel eyes implacably locked on Hoch's clear blue ones. Hoch's grip was weakening and he felt no remorse as he firmly pushed the dagger up though the base of Hoch's throat. The Nazi's hands fell away, resistance gone and Cockran thrust the dagger deeper, piercing the back of his tongue on its inexorable journey into his brain. There was no scream. Once it had gone up Hoch's throat to its silver hilt, Cockran twisted the dagger inside the SS man's brain until his eyes rolled up lifelessly into his head. Standing up, he left the dagger where it was.

Cockran returned to the autogiro and saw that Sturm was still conscious. "Thanks for the heads-up. I appreciate it."

"I could do no less. It was a matter of honor."

Cockran acknowledged that with a nod and helped Sturm enter the passenger's cockpit. The two agreed that they had to quickly get Mattie and their team away from Castle Wewelsburg. In the east, the sky was beginning to glow with a pink tinge as Cockran lifted off and once more pushed the autogiro to its maximum airspeed of 118 miles per hour. Sturm needed medical care; Sullivan was wounded as well; and Cockran's hip was killing him. He wanted any such care for all of them to be rendered as far from Castle Wewelsburg as possible.

74.

Parsifal Represents a Model

Westphalia, Germany
Thursday, 18 June 1931

MATTIE held one of Sullivan's .45s in her right hand and the Spear of Destiny in the other, both pointed directly at Josef Lanz. Over his protests, Sergeant Rankin had bandaged Sullivan's right side and fashioned a sling around his neck for his arm. Sullivan was seated on the wing of his autogiro, the second of his .45 caliber automatics also aimed at Lanz.

Not knowing when Cockran and Sturm would return and also not knowing when or if any more SS would return to Wewelsburg, they had all repaired to the two remaining autogiros being guarded by Churchill. Mattie had pulled out Sullivan's loaned .45 immediately after Lanz told her that he had reconsidered his offer to Professor Campbell and decided that the Sacred Lance would be safer in Templar hands, hidden away, rather than displayed in the British Museum, however well guarded. It was when Lanz took a step toward Mattie and the Spear with outstretched hands that Sullivan pulled his second .45 and even Winston pulled his Mauser.

"Not so fast, *Herr* Lanz. I may have missed the first time I took a shot at you, but I assure you, this time I won't." Mattie had said. That had been over an hour ago and the standoff continued, Murphy having relieved the three Templars of their weapons. During that time, Lanz had explained his position to Winston and her over and over until she was tired of listening.

Mattie continued to keep her eyes and her weapon trained on Lanz and his men, superfluous as it was with the three Apostles doing the same, when she heard Sullivan groan.

"Murphy, I think you should be taking my weapon..." Sullivan began and then slumped to the ground unconscious, his fingers losing their grip on his .45 which fell to the ground.

"Bobby!" Mattie shouted as she saw Sullivan collapse, his shirt soaked in blood.

"Hold it right there!" Winston said as she saw movement out of the corner of her eye, Lanz starting to step forward as if to help, but freezing at the command. She stuck Sullivan's other .45 in her waistband and knelt down beside him. His skin was clammy, the right side of his shirt dark with blood. Shock, she thought, he's going into shock from loss of blood.

"Murphy! See if you can find a first aid kit," Mattie said. "Winston! Shoot Lanz first if anyone tries to move." While she said this, Mattie knelt beside Sullivan, the Spear in her left hand on the ground touching Sullivan's right side as she brushed his hair back and put her face up against Bobby's cold cheek. "Stay with me Bobby. Oh God, please, stay with me."

The sunrise was beginning to break through in the east. Suddenly, Mattie felt heat in her left hand and looked down. The tip of the Spear was almost glowing as it rested against Sullivan. A golden aura seemed to be surrounding it. A few seconds after Murphy reached her side and thrust the first aid kit at her, she felt warmth begin to rise in Sullivan's cheeks.

Sullivan's blue eyes opened slowly and he smiled. "And won't we be keeping this our little secret? Doesn't that man of yours have a powerful temper and a mean streak of jealousy to go with it? We wouldn't want him to be getting the wrong impression now, would we?"

Mattie laughed in spite of the tears streaming down her face as she stripped away Sullivan's shirt, removed the old bandage and began applying gauze and tape to a long nasty wound where the bleeding had stopped and scar tissue astonishingly appeared to be forming.

In the distance, Mattie heard the now-familiar sound made by an autogiro's rotor blades and, moments later, Cockran's autogiro dropped softly to the ground. "Robert," Mattie said to Rankin, handing him the Spear and wiping her tears with her sleeve, "please hold this for me." Mattie ran to the autogiro as Cockran was stepping down off the wing and leaped into his arms. Grabbing him around the neck, she kissed him over and over. Then Mattie released him, turned to Sturm and, to his discomfort, embraced him as he kept his arms stiffly at his side. Suddenly, Sturm collapsed in her arms and she noticed the blood-stained bandage on his torso.

"Oh my God! Kurt! You're hurt! How bad is it?"

"Better," Sturm said, grimacing as he opened his eyes. "I passed out from loss of blood earlier. I may not have made it but for *Herr* Cockran binding my wound."

"Bourke," Mattie said, her entire attention focused on Sturm and the makeshift bandage. "Ask Robert to bring me tape and gauze. Have Winston bring me the Spear. Please. Quickly."

"The Spear?"

"Yes. Do it now! I'll tell you why later," she said, impatience in her voice as she began to unwrap Sturm's bandages, applying pressure to the fresh wound to stop the flow of blood once the bandage was removed. It looked bad and she accepted the tape and gauze from Cockran without looking around or saying a word, focused only on re-bandaging the man who had saved her life so many times, oblivious to the man she loved looking silently on.

"Winston! Where's the bloody Spear?" Mattie shouted, still barking orders like a surgeon in an operating room, reaching back with her right hand to grasp the Spear near the top of the wooden shaft when Churchill handed it to her.

"Please, dear God," she prayed softly, audible to no one but her. "Let it work again. Prove my father was right and I was wrong." Unconscious again, Sturm's face was pale.

The spearhead began to glow again as she placed it next to Sturm's bandaged side. If she were seeing it for the first time, she might still have thought it an optical illusion but the heat from the spearhead and the golden aura once more surrounding it were unmistakable as the morning sunlight created a near-halo effect around Mattie's auburn hair.

In an intimate gesture, Mattie gently and tenderly brushed Sturm's hair away from his forehead knowing that Cockran was looking on, knowing that her concern for Kurt might be misconstrued, knowing that her future with Cockran might hang in the balance, knowing that she had no choice. Too many people had died because she was so impulsive. Her photographer Helmut was the first so long ago on that cold dark night in a Munich back alley. Others had followed. Kurt von Sturm, a man to whom she owed her life, was not going to be the next.

A long agonizing minute passed before the glow of the Spear faded and color rose in Kurt's face. Mattie stood up, handed the Spear to Churchill, and knelt back down beside Sturm.

"Bourke, please help me," she said. "I need to check the dressing."

"But you just now put it on," Cockran replied as he knelt beside her.

"I know. But I must check something. Place your hands here and keep the pressure on to stop any new bleeding," Mattie said as she unwrapped the tape and re-inspected the wound.

"Oh, my God..." Cockran said, his voice barely above a whisper.

"You got that right, Cockran," Mattie said as she stared down at a still fresh but newly healed wound, scar tissue clearly having formed just as it did with Bobby Sullivan.

Sturm opened his eyes at that moment. "*Danke, fraulein.* And you as well, *Herr* Cockran. I owe my life to you both now."

A tear slipped from Mattie's eye. "Thank *you*," she whispered as she leaned over and kissed him softly on the forehead she had so recently caressed.

Mattie stood up and took Cockran's hand warmly in hers. "Cockran, we've got to talk."

Cockran froze. "Ah, Mattie, are you sure this is the right time or place?"

"No, my dear sweet love. Not that." Mattie said, feeling her face flush in embarrassment. "That's for later. Never if you wish. This is more immediate. I need to make a decision. Now."

Mattie explained her dilemma to Cockran. Her father had been right. The Spear was so much more than a historical artifact. The legends were correct. It really had healing powers. But since it did, shouldn't the Spear be in holy hands and a holy place, not in a museum?

"The Templars' claim to the Spear dates back to the Crusades," Mattie continued, "and while their hands are covered in blood, they may possibly be holy hands as well. I don't know. That's for them to work out with their Creator, not with me."

"Why not give it to a church in England? Possibly the one where Longinus is buried?"

"That has a tempting symmetry," Mattie said, "but I'm not certain it's the safest place."

"Professor Campbell and Winston were the ones who originated this little adventure," Cockran said. "Shouldn't they concur on what to do?"

"No," Mattie said firmly. "I talked with Winston earlier while we were awaiting your return. He agrees with me that my father started it all, not them. And that I'm the one to finish it. I just need a little time to think about it. To figure out what my father would want me to do. It's my decision, Bourke. And no one else. My decision. And my father's."

Mattie turned her back on Cockran and watched the sun rise higher in the east. She had come all this way, sacrificed so much, risked her life many times, cost others' lives, maybe lost the man she loved, all for what? To find the Spear which had consumed her father's life and led to his death. Could she give it up now? Especially to people like these blood-thirsty Templars, one of whom had murdered her father?

Mattie closed her eyes and saw, in her mind's eye, the pale, doughy face of Heinrich Himmler, eyes squinting behind the pince-nez, handing the Spear to Hoch. She saw again the Spear poised above her, Harmony's blood dripping from its tip to form a red circle over her heart; the Spear tip glowing incandescently while Hoch tried in vain to pierce her body. And then she saw it as if it were right in front of her. The scribbled handwriting of the impoverished young Viennese artist churning out painting after painting, tourist scene after tourist scene, hoping against hope that his portfolio would finally qualify him for his life's ambition—the treasured admission to the Academy of Fine Arts. *I knew with immediacy that this was an important moment in my life when I first saw the Spear. I felt as though I myself had held it in my hand before in some earlier century of history—that I myself had once claimed it as my talisman of power, that I held the destiny of the world in my hands."*

The vision faded and soon melded into the hypnotic blue eyes of a mature Adolf Hitler, less than three weeks earlier. *"The idea of a state built on the principles of a medieval order is one that for years has struck me as thoroughly feasible. Parsifal represents a model of what I want to create in Germany. I intend to form my religion for Germany on Parsifal. The man who sees National Socialism as nothing but a political movement knows hardly the first thing about it. It is more even than a religion—it is the collective will of a new race of men."*

Mattie knew what she had to do. Mattie knew what her father would have wanted her to do. She walked with Cockran and a recovering Sturm back to the other autogiros where Sullivan and Churchill still held the Templars at gunpoint.

"*Herr* Lanz," Mattie said, "the Spear belongs in the hands of those who believe in the divinity of Christ and the healing powers of this Spear. Taking the Spear to a church in Britain or leaving it with you would fulfill that condition. But more importantly, the Spear must be kept out of the hands of people who would wield the powers of the Spear for evil purposes. It is best if men like that never know the Spear's location. In Britain, it would be too tempting a target for men who are sworn enemies of Christ." Mattie turned to Rankin and asked him for the Spear. Holding it in both hands, parallel to the ground, she extended it to Lanz, who knelt before her, took the Spear, bowed his head, his lips moving silently as if in prayer for a few moments, and then stood up.

Mattie watched Lanz and the other two Templars wrap the Spear in a long woolen cloak and prepare to leave. She walked over to Churchill and gave him a hug while she spoke softly in his ear. "Thank you, Winston, for your wise advice earlier about me and Bourke. I'm going to take it. I'm sure my father would have told me the same thing. I love you, dear Godfather." she said, kissing him on the cheek.

Churchill returned the hug, then held her at arms' length. "I have little experience as a matchmaker, my dear, but Clemmie assures me I have done well with you and Bourke."

"You have Winston, you most certainly have." Mattie said and hugged him again.

When she released him, Lanz approached, the hood of his coat leaving his forehead in shadow. "Thank you, my dear. You have done a service for our Lord for which he will be grateful." He then lifted his right hand and made the Sign of the Cross in the air.

"Go with God, Martha McGary. Go with God."

Mattie turned, linked her arm through Cockran's, put her lips to his ear and whispered. "Come on sailor, I'd rather go with you to Venice.

After donning a snug, white pilot's helmet, Mattie climbed into the autogiro's passenger compartment and turned around and looked at Cockran. "There are two things I especially wish to do while we're in Venice and I need to know whether you'll be up for them."

"Try me. What's the first?"

Mattie smiled. "How much trouble do you suppose we'd be in with Mussolini if we landed this flying windmill smack in the middle of *Piazza San Marco* and strolled over to have martinis on the terrace at Harry's Bar?"

Cockran nodded. "And the second?"

"Given your weakened condition, not to mention mine, will you still be able to shag me silly every single day we're in Venice?" Mattie asked with a grin.

"As to both, there's only one way to find out," Cockran said, grinning back, as he fired up the Wright Whirlwind engine. Mattie watched the rotor blades above her slowly begin to rotate, glistening in the morning sun, and imagined her lover beside her at Harry's Bar on the Grand Canal as she savored the first sip of what would surely be more than one icy martini.

KURT von Sturm stood below the autogiros as they leaped swiftly into the air. It might not be flattering, but Sturm thought he knew why he and Cockran had been so attracted to the McGary woman. Her lover, Cockran, may have been a lawyer just as Kurt thought of himself as a airshipman but, under the skin, they were brothers. Honorable—but deadly—brothers.

Having watched Cockran at Castle Lanz, at Wewelsburg castle, in the air over the twisting roads of Westphalia, and the final knife thrust up Hoch's throat, Sturm knew that, like him, Cockran was a man capable of killing when necessary without hesitation. An assassin. And, like him, a moth to Mattie's flame. Her will was as strong as she was passionate. A fierce and loyal lover. But for her imagined belief in Cockran's infidelity, she would have cut Sturm dead in the Alps as surely as she did in the air over the Atlantic. He and Cockran shared other traits as well. But for loving the same woman, they might have become friends.

His one hand on the handlebar of the BMW R39, his other shielding his eyes from the sun's early glow, Sturm watched the three aircrafts' rotor blades sharply outlined against the warm orange circle. Gradually, they faded into dark specks which soon disappeared altogether, carrying out of his life the beautiful woman whom he had loved and lost.

Historical Note

The Parsifal Pursuit is a work of fiction but there are certain historical elements which provide a foundation and framework for the story.

Winston Churchill. Churchill did not travel to Germany in 1931 to research his biography of his great ancestor, the first Duke of Marlborough, as depicted in the novel. He had written his American publisher Charles Scribner in May, 1931 of his plans to travel to Berlin and Vienna that year for this purpose but the controversy over self-rule for India caused a change in those plans. Churchill did travel to Germany for this purpose the following year where Hitler backed out of a dinner with Churchill arranged by Putzi Hanfstaengl and, as Churchill later wrote, "Thus Hitler lost his only chance of meeting me."

Those with only a casual knowledge of Winston Churchill may question his being cast as a key character in an historical thriller. They shouldn't. Saving the world tends to overshadow lesser accomplishments but Churchill was a first-class athlete in his youth, an all-public schools fencing champion, and a championship polo player, a sport he played into his 50s. His detractors — of which there were many before 1940 — dismissed him as an "adventurer" and a "half-breed American." He was both of those things and more. He fought Islamic warriors on the Afghan border and in the Sudan in the late 1890s, bloody no-quarter battles where he killed many men at close range. He escaped from a prison in South Africa during the Boer war in 1899 and made his way over hundreds of miles of enemy territory to freedom. He bagged a rare white rhino in Africa in 1908, drawing the admiration and envy of Theodore Roosevelt who tried to do the same but was not so fortunate. He became a seaplane pilot in the early 1910s after becoming, at age 38, the First Lord of the British Admiralty. In the First World War and temporarily out of office, he commanded a battalion in the trenches in the bloody Ypres salient where Corporal Adolf Hitler also served and where both men drew sketches in their spare time of the same bombed-out Belgian church.

Bourke Cockran *(1854-1923).* Winston Churchill's real life mentor and oratorical role model was the prominent turn-of-the century New York lawyer, statesman and Congressman   William Bourke Cockran whose fictional son's exploits (Cockran was childless) are depicted in *The Parsifal Pursuit.* Churchill's feelings and comments about his mentor in Chapter 4 are accurately portrayed. A Democrat, a close adviser to President Grover Cleveland in his second term, and contemporary of William Jennings Bryan, Cockran was acclaimed by members of both parties, including his friend Theodore Roosevelt, as America's greatest orator. Churchill was only 20 years old when the two men were brought together in 1895 by Churchill's mother, the American-born heiress Jennie Jerome, with whom Cockran had an affair in Paris in the spring of that year following the death of their respective spouses. Sixty years later, Churchill could still recite from memory the speeches of Bourke Cockran he had learned as a young man. "He was my model," Churchill said, "I learned from him how to hold thousands in thrall."

Those wishing to know more about the Churchill-Cockran relationship are referred to *Becoming Winston Churchill: the Untold Story of Young Winston and His American Mentor,* by Michael McMenamin and Curt Zoller, originally published in hardcover in the U.K. and the U.S. in 2007 by Greenwood World Publishing and in trade paperback in 2009 by Enigma Books.

The Kaiser. Plans to restore the Hohenzollerns, either the Kaiser himself or the Crown Prince, to the throne of Germany as part of a constitutional monarchy and as an antidote to Hitler's National Socialists were underway at various times during the late 1920s and early 1930s, especially after the Nazis became Germany's second largest party in August, 1930. Even Winston Churchill once suggested a constitutional monarchy in Germany during the 1920s as the best way to nurture democracy and the best antidote to a Bolshevik takeover.

The Spear of Destiny. A spear once thought to be the lance with which the Roman centurion Longinus pierced the side of Christ to end his agony on the cross is on display today in the Hofburg Museum in Vienna where it was located for most of the twentieth century. It is the same spear which in the past was possessed by Constantine, Charlemagne, Frederick Barbarossa, and Frederick the Great. Its possession had been unsuccessfully sought by other world-historic figures including Napoleon and Kaiser Wilhelm II. All of these men believed the sacred spear to be a talisman of power, the Spear of Destiny.

Adolf Hitler. Hitler's views on the Spear and the legend of Parsifal are accurately portrayed. Hitler took possession of the Spear of Longinus in March, 1938, after the Austrian *Anschluss*, and had it removed from the Hofburg and given a place of honor in the Hall of St. Katherine's Church in Nuremberg. The only objection was voiced by SS Reichsfuhrer Heinrich Himmler who had renovated Wewelsburg Castle (not actually purchased until 1933) specifically to serve as the true home of the SS as well as a shrine for the sacred relic of the Spear of Destiny, dedicating separate rooms within the Castle to each of the world leaders who had possessed the Spear. With the Spear in his hands less than six months, Hitler bloodlessly regained the German Sudetenland in Czechoslovakia and a year later invaded Poland. The Spear of Destiny remained in Nuremberg throughout the Second World War until 1945 when it was taken by the American armies of General George Patton who returned it to the Hofburg where it still resides.

Reinhard Tristan Hoch. Hoch is a fictional character whose background, appearance and characteristics mirror his real-life namesake, SS Intelligence Chief Reinhard Tristan Heydrich. Hoch's monologue on "the Jew as Parasite", however, is not derived from Heydrich — who undoubtedly shared those views. Instead, Hoch's words are reproduced almost verbatim from private conversations of Adolf Hitler in 1931 as recounted by a close confidant, Otto Wagener. Hitler was a skilled politician during the years 1930 to 1932 when he was on the cusp of power, tailoring his public and private comments to fit his audience. The fact that he did not utter anti-Semitic comments in private to people like Mattie and Kurt who did not share his racial views is accurately portrayed in the novel as was the absence of overt anti-Semitism in his speeches during this period when he led the second largest party in Germany and was on the cusp of power only 18 months away.

The Order of the New Templars. Adolf Josef Lanz, a former Cistercian monk who renounced his vows in 1899, founded *Ordi Novi*

Templi in 1905 and served as its Prior through the end of World War II. The Order of the New Templars reached its peak between 1925 and 1935 with seven priories and over 300 monks in Austria, Hungary and Germany. While the New Templars were indeed inspired by the medieval order whose name they bore, their blood-thirsty role in hiding and protecting the Holy Spear as depicted in the novel is entirely fictional.

Born in 1874, Lanz was one of the principal theorists of Ariosophy, an odd combination of pan-Germanic nationalism, racism and mysticism. In fact, the ideas of Ariosophy and National Socialism share many common tenets. One scholar has written that the "ultimate aim" of the New Templars was "world salvation through eugenic selection and the extermination of racial inferiors." While a young man in Vienna, Hitler met Lanz and was greatly influenced by his ideas. Hitler was an avid reader of the pan-Germanic periodical *Ostara*, a self-described "racial-economic" magazine published by Lanz and the New Templars. Nevertheless, after Hitler came to power in 1933, the New Templars were officially dissolved by Heinrich Himmler's Gestapo and Lanz was forbidden to publish.

Eugenics. The pseudo-science of eugenics flourished in America during the first thirty years of the twentieth century as nowhere else, frequently supported by prominent religious leaders, Protestant, Catholic and Jew alike. The Nazi eugenics laws passed early in 1933 after their ascension to power provided, among other things, for the involuntary sterilization of mental defectives. The Nazis based these laws almost exclusively on model state legislation drafted by American eugenics supporters who had persuaded over half the states to adopt comparable legislation. And an aging Oliver Wendell Holmes did write such a shameful passage in *Buck v. Bell*, the underlying facts of which are accurately portrayed in Chapter 5.

Nazi V-men. A source of fund raising for the National Socialists in Germany during the late 1920s and early 1930s was extortion from businesses paying protection money to the SA and SS, who would otherwise terrorize their owners and their property, crimes winked at by "V-men," [*Vertrauensmannen*] secret Nazi sympathizers in state and local governments.

Alfred Eisendstadt. The German- born photographer who served as Mattie McGary's photographic mentor emigrated to America in the mid-1930s and became one of Henry Luce's top photographers on *Life* magazine. He is most well-known for the iconic photograph of the unknown sailor and girl kissing on V-J Day in Times Square in New York. A less well-known Eisenstadt photograph perfectly illustrated his "not good enough...not close enough" motto and served as the inspiration for Mattie's misadventure on top of the *Graf Zeppelin*. In the photograph, three zeppelin crewmen are on top of the ship over the Atlantic, clutching ropes and lowering a fourth crewman down the side of the massive airship to repair damaged fabric. It is impossible to tell Eisenstadt's vanatage point from the photograph but it certainly appears as if he was outside on top of the zeppelin hanging on to a rope running along the airship's spine just like Mattie was.

The Graf Zeppelin. The famed German airship made an historic around-the-world voyage in 1929 sponsored by the media empire of William Randolph Hearst. In the spring of 1931, the *Graf Zeppelin* flew a round-trip voyage from its base in southern Germany to Alexandria, Egypt as depicted in the novel. From 1930 through the crash of the *Hindenburg* in 1937, it conducted regular passenger service between Germany and Brazil, safely flying well over a million miles. The *Graf Zeppelin*, however, was never used for regular passenger service between Germany and America as depicted in the novel.

Autogiros. The Juan de la Cierva-designed autogiro was the next big thing in aviation when it was commercially introduced in the early 1930s. *Fortune* magazine devoted two articles to it in its March, 1931 edition, describing it as "a complex if not revolutionary addition to the science of aerodynamics." It flew and handled like an airplane but could take off and land in short spaces at safe, slow speeds. Lift was provided solely by the blades of its huge hinged rotor, a common feature on today's helicopters.

Michael McMenamin
Patrick McMenamin
January, 2011

Acknowledgements

We owe a debt of gratitude to many people who helped bring this book, our second Winston Churchill Thriller, to light. **Katie McMenamin Sabo**, our daughter and sister and the first writing teacher either of us ever had. With an MFA in Creative Writing from NYU, she really is, as she often reminds us, Rose Wilder Lane to our Laura Ingalls. **Kelly McMenamin Wang**, our other daughter and sister who, with her MBA from Dartmouth, is a really good writer herself and the engine behind the sisters' website www.pixiesdidit.com which offers home and life organization advice based on Myers-Briggs personality types. Patrick's wife **Rebecca Perkins**, the head make-up artist on *Law and Order SVU* and Michael's wife and Patrick's mom, **Carol Breckenridge**, an artist and art therapist, both of whom read and offered critical advice on numerous iterations of the book. Mystery writer **Les Roberts**, our close friend and ever-patient writing mentor, from whom Patrick took a college screen-writing course when he was a junior in high school and who, like any good mentor, validated our dream while continuing to give us candid and insightful advice. **Robert Miller**, the editor and publisher of **Enigma Books** who published the first paperback edition of Michael's book *Becoming Winston Churchill* and who agreed with us that the world really needed a series of historical thrillers set in the 1930s featuring Winston Churchill. **Josh Beatman** and the other creative folks at **Brainchild Studios/NYC** who came up with another killer cover design. **Alexis Dragony**, Michael's former assistant who typed many iterations of the book; her successor **Bonnie Daanish** who did the same as did **Jo Ann Chapman**, none of whom were shy on offering helpful advice. And, finally, to all our good friends and relatives who read and offered thir comments on this book as well as our third Churchill Thriller, *The Gemini Agenda* [to be published in late 2011 by Enigma Books].

Coming in the Fall 2011

The Gemini Agenda
A Winston Churchill Thriller
By Michael McMenamin and Patrick McMenamin
ISBN 978-1-936274-37-6 / *e-book* ISBN 978-1-936274-38-3

In the Spring of 1932, **Winston Churchill** receives ominous intelligence from a confidential source in Germany. Naked bodies, drained of blood, eyeballs extracted, are left at ten remote locations scattered across the U.S. Serial killer? Or worse? Churchill's source believes answers are to be found in Germany.

The out-of-office British statesman passes on the information to his American publisher **William Randolph Hearst** who assigns **Mattie McGary**, his top photojournalist and Churchill's god-daughter, to investigate the strange deaths. Aided by her lover **Bourke Cockran, Jr.**, a former Army counterintelligence agent, they learn that all ten victims were twins. Five sets of fraternal twins. In doing so, they become the target of an international conspiracy reaching from the canyons of Wall Street to the marble corridors of the Barlow Palace in Munich, home to the fast-rising Nazi Party.

In a deadly encounter at laboratories on Long Island's fabled Gold Coast, Mattie and Cockran discover there are ten more missing twins—identical twins—on their way to Germany. They are still alive but for how long? With additional information from Churchill's private intelligence network, the two embark upon a rescue mission which leads them to a sinister clinic deep in the Bavarian National Forest near the small border town of Passau where Adolf Hitler lived as a child.

In their quest to rescue the twins, the risk-taking Mattie and the ruthless Cockran find their own often rocky relationship tested. And never more so than when they join forces with two of Mattie's former lovers. Together, the unlikely allies risk their lives to expose a secret project financed by leading U.S. industrialists and elements of the U.S. Army's Military Intelligence Division to enable Nazi scientists to kidnap and conduct lethal experiments upon American twins in hopes of unlocking the secret to creating a master race.

The Gemini Agenda, the third in the Winston Churchill Thriller series, explores the true horrors of the eugenics movement in the U.S.

where, by the 1930s, science in the service of politics had delivered the state-sanctioned sterilization of 50,000 American women and led directly to Dr. Josef Mengele's mutilation of twins in "scientific experiments" at Auschwitz.